THE BUG

Also by Ellen Ullman

CLOSE TO THE MACHINE

THE BUG

a novel

ELLEN ULLMAN

NAN A. TALESE/DOUBLEDAY

NEW YORK   LONDON   TORONTO
SYDNEY   AUCKLAND

PUBLISHED BY NAN. A. TALESE
an imprint of Doubleday
a division of Random House, Inc.

DOUBLEDAY is a registered trademark of Random House, Inc.

Playground Twist, by Kenneth Morris, John Gareth McKay, Steven Severin, Siouxsie Sioux. © Dreamhouse Music (ASCAP) All Rights o/b/o administered by Chappell & Co. All Rights Reserved. Used by Permission. Warner Bros. Publications U.S. Inc., Miami, FL 33014

Book design by Jennifer Daddio
ASCII art by John Inciarrano

Library of Congress Cataloging-in-Publication Data
Ullman, Ellen.
The bug : a novel / Ellen Ullman.— 1st ed.
p. cm.
1. Santa Clara Valley (Santa Clara County, Calif.)—Fiction. 2. Computer software developers—Fiction. 3. Computer programmers—Fiction. 4. Computer industry—Fiction. I. Title.

PS3621.L45 B8 2003
813'.6—dc21
2002073289

ISBN 0-385-50860-3

PRINTED IN THE UNITED STATES OF AMERICA

May 2003

3 5 7 9 10 8 6 4

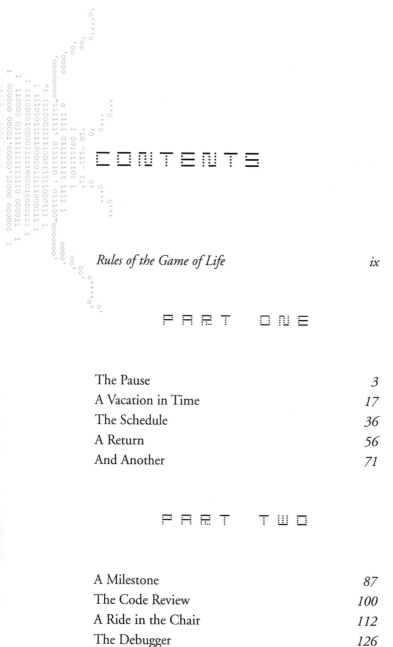

CONTENTS

PART THREE

PART FOUR

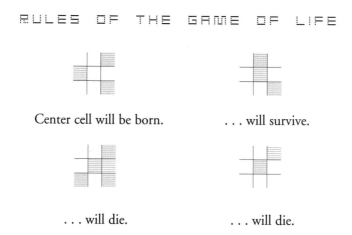

Center cell will be born.   . . . will survive.

. . . will die.   . . . will die.

"Life" as defined by the mathematician John Horton Conway is a digital universe consisting of two-dimensional squares, or "cells," laid out in a grid. Each cell has exactly eight neighbors: one on each of its four sides, and one at each of its four corners. On each pass, or iteration, over the grid, the program decides the fate of each cell by applying three simple rules:

A cell is born (grid-point turned "on") if it was previously "dead" (grid-point "off") and exactly three of its neighboring cells are alive.

The cell survives (remains as it is) if it has two or three live neighbors.

If the cell is crowded (has more than three live neighbors) or isolated (has less than two neighbors alive), it dies.

PART ONE

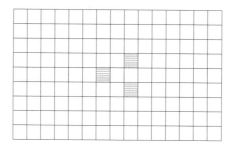

"It is remarkable," he said. "A man cannot make general observations to any extent, on any subject, without betraying himself, without introducing his entire individuality, and presenting, as in an allegory, the fundamental theme and problem of his own existence. This, Engineer, is what you have just done."

—SETTEMBRINI TO HANS CASTORP
THOMAS MANN, *THE MAGIC MOUNTAIN*

THE PAUSE

A computer can execute millions of instructions in a second. The human brain, in comparison, is painfully slow. The memories of a single year, for instance, took me a full thirty seconds to recall. Which is a long time if you think about it. Imagine a second-hand sweep going tick by tick halfway around the face of a clock. Or the digital readout of light-emitting diodes, with their blink, blink—thirty blinks—as they count off time.

"Passport, please."

The immigration agent at the San Francisco airport was a pleasant-faced young man, not at all threatening, the sort who does his job without particular fervor.

"Countries visited?"

It's right on the landing card, I wanted to say, but I'd learned not to be belligerent in circumstances like these. "One. The Dominican Republic."

He kept his face toward me, a certain blankness undoing his pleasant expression, as his hand disappeared under the counter of the little booth that stood between us. I knew he was putting my passport through a scanner. The first page of the United States passport has been machine-readable for years.

Then we waited.

"Nice trip, Miss, uh . . ."

"Ms. Walton. Yes."

"Roberta Walton."

"Yes."

The immigration agent looked down at his computer terminal, his hands still under the counter of the booth.

Then he said, "Good weather there this time of year?"

"Hot. Yes."

"Humid?"

"Yes. Not too bad."

Chitchat. Filler. His face trying to take on its pleasant expression again. Undone by his eyes flicking toward the screen half hidden under a shelf in the corner of the booth. He was waiting for an answer. Should I be allowed to pass, or should I be questioned? Was I what I seemed to be: an innocuous middle-aged woman who'd gone to get herself some sun in mid-November? Or was I a well-disguised drug runner, money launderer, sex slaver? He could do nothing until he heard from the system.

And so we waited. Tick-tock, blink-blink, thirty seconds stretched themselves out one by one, a hole in human experience. Waiting for the system: life today is full of such pauses. The soft clacking of computer keys, then the voice on the telephone telling you, "Just a moment, please." The credit-card reader instructing you "Remove card quickly!" then displaying "Processing. Please wait." The little hourglass icon on your computer screen reminding you how time is passing and there is nothing you can do about it. The diddler at the bottom of the browser screen going back and forth, back and forth like a caged crazed animal. All the hours the computer is supposedly saving us—I don't believe it, in the sum of things, I thought as I stood there leaning on my luggage cart. It has filled our lives with little wait states like this one, useless wait states, little slices of time in which you can't do anything at all but stand there, sit there, hold the phone—the sort of unoccupied little slices of time no decent computer operating system would tolerate for itself. A computer, waiting like this, would find something useful to do: check for other processes wanting attention, flush a file buffer, refresh a cache, at least.

Which is what I suppose my mind began doing with the pause at the immigration counter: some mysterious housekeeping process of the brain, some roaming through the backwaters of the synapses, trolling memory, cleaning lost connections . . .

It's the Telligentsia database! came the thought out of somewhere. Then came an understanding, step by step, like a syllogism: The system we're waiting for was made by Telligentsia. Telligentsia, where my technical life began. So it's my fault. This particular wait state is something I myself helped visit upon the world!

I looked behind the counter at the agent's terminal: Yes. That damned transaction interface. The Immigration Service was one of our first customers. In 1986, they were going to "revolutionize" international arrivals with our database. And here it still was after all these years, our software, its transaction interface, that sluggish component we testers had complained about to the programmers, too slow, too slow, who'll put up with this waiting? Ah, I saw how the immigration agent had learned to tolerate this waiting. A certain suspension of himself; an unattractive slackness in his body, his mouth; a gone-to-nowhere look in his already vague eyes. Odd how adaptable human beings are. The programmers had long accustomed themselves to waiting on machines, and then we, the software testers, soon adapted; and with every shipment of our software, out it spread like a virus to the world: human beings everywhere learning to suspend themselves, go elsewhere for little slits of time, not exactly talking or working or doing anything, since any moment—you never know which one—the system may come back, respond, give you the answer.

The long thirty seconds . . . Funny: It was the same pause we complained about. Strange how in all this time no one had tuned or fixed it. But of course it was still there. Who could have possibly worked on it? Soon after we went public, Telligentsia was sold off to another company, then that company was sold off as well, and our software disappeared further and further into the hands of people who'd never met us. Who would there be in all those changes to remember our problems, our arguments, the things we tried and abandoned? Funny to think of the code remaining there, unchanged, as it passed from hand to hand, newer and newer layers of code laid down over it like sediment. And inside—deep inside, in the places no one understood anymore so they just left them alone because that part of the code seemed to *work*—down in there the long pause still lived. The programmers and testers had moved on, changed, grown older, but here was the code, frozen, mindlessly running itself over and over: thoughtless robotic artifact of the lives that created it.

Ethan Levin.

Through the time tunnel of the long pause came his name. Ethan Levin, Telligentsia's senior engineer for client-side computing, inadvertent creator of the bug officially designated UI-1017. I tried to push him away. Standing there sweating by my luggage cart, I was not ready to remember what happened to him. UI-1017: the one thousand seventeenth bug in the user interface. One thousand and sixteen had come before it; thousands more would come after; and so what? Let it alone, I told myself. Don't dwell on this one ruined life. The world has moved on to other follies involving other programmers. Everyone seems so happy with the world we technical people have created. See here: even the immigration agent, after his little wait at his terminal, has gotten his answer, and now a real smile makes his empty, pleasant face almost remarkable as he taps data into his keyboard.

But Ethan Levin would not go away. That relentless bug of his I found, what happened to him while it came and went, what I might have done and didn't—all that was waiting for me in the long thirty-second pause. There was no way out now. There was no way to go home and forget all over again what had happened. I would have to remember the database as I first saw it, in the late fall of 1983. I would have to remember when I was a failed academic, a linguist with a Ph.D. during the Ph.D. glut of the 1980s, itinerant untenured instructor of Linguistics 101, desperate striver out of the lumpen professoriat. And how I became—through the recommendation of a friend, unbelievable to anyone who'd known me—a junior quality-assurance "engineer" at the start-up software company called Telligentsia. Where I was the primary tester of one Ethan Levin, a skinny, apparently confident man of thirty-six who'd been programming for twelve seemingly accomplished years when the bug designated UI-1017 first found him.

Time circled back on itself. Nineteen eighty-four. The IBM PC was three years old; the Apple Macintosh had just been released. I was seeing for the first time the famous Super Bowl ad that introduced the Mac to the world: The woman in running shorts breaking into the auditorium where men, dressed alike like prisoners, sat mute before a screen. On the screen that same huge head lit by a blue light—Big Brother, IBM, known as Big Blue for the color of the company's logo. And all over again, I knew what the woman must do.

And then she did it: she reeled and hurled a hammer at the screen, smashing it, breaking the prisoners' spell.

Rejoice! The age of the behemoth corporate computer was over. Individuals would now have computing power *in their own hands*. Somehow this would change everything. Oh, what a perfect advertising moment! The smashed specter of 1984. And done by a *woman*. Geraldine Ferraro was running for the vice presidency of the United States, the first-ever women's marathon would be run at the Olympics, so why shouldn't a woman in running shorts symbolize the end of technological tyranny?

"Welcome home, Ms. Walton."

The immigration agent, smiling pleasantly out of his pleasant face, offering me back my passport.

I only stared at it. I didn't want to touch that passport now. The whole story would open up out of its pages.

Tap, tap: the agent touching the passport to the counter.

"Thank you," I said, not meaning it.

Everything was in order. Page stamped, passport returned. The date and port of my arrival duly recorded by the system. The old database—traitor, time shifter—had not confused me with a terrorist. Later someone would enter the data from my landing card: where I'd been, for what purpose, how much I'd spent, on what. And later yet, some researcher might pore over the great masses of data accumulated in our marvelous Telligentsia database (maybe using the "data mining" software from the second start-up company I worked for). And he'd learn how frequently I traveled, never on business, always alone. And the researcher's report will conclude that I am rich—as I am, perpetual leisure traveler at the age of forty-eight. Nominal occupation: computer consultant. Home address: San Francisco.

I wheeled my cart toward customs and saw myself perfectly profiled through the computer's eyes: silicon mini-millionaire, stock-option retiree, lucky inheritor of the revolution proclaimed on television in 1984 by the woman in running shorts. In another mood, I might have been proud. The database, still working after all these years. The database, keeping an eye on us, watching over my comings and goings and those of my fellow citizens—my personal private contribution to the end of tyranny.

March 5, 1984, a day full of error. Erratic bugs were not supposed to show themselves; jealousy and suspicion were not supposed to ruin the day. My plan that day had been to find something wrong with recursion: queries within queries, questions inside questions. Select the customers whose last names started with S; from those select the ones with balances-due greater than $200; from those the ones who did not live in New York; from those the ones who were females; and so on, ad absurdum, to an arbitrary depth of fifty-three queries within queries. I was looking for a condition I could pinpoint. At a certain depth: crash. One level back: works fine. A model error, an exemplary bug, an on/off condition that came and went reliably, a relief from the confusions of the world.

Here is how the day was supposed to go: I was to drive my boyfriend James Havermeyer to the airport (he managed a traveling chamber orchestra; he was always coming or going somewhere), I was to go to work and run my excellent test (perfectly, predictably crashing the system at a specific recursive depth), and then I was to go home and work on the poem I was writing (poem-writing, a morbid habit I kept up the way I kept on smoking, imposing my exhalations upon others). Susanna Cantor, James's great unrequited love, should not have come up. Memories of my bad start with James—no. The stark, lost sensation that came over me as I drove into the Telligentsia parking lot—I didn't imagine the day would begin that way. A planned disaster was what I was looking for. A failure under my control. A perfect test.

The day began too early, 6 A.M., on the road to the airport for James's flight to New York, connecting there for Vienna, where the orchestra was performing. Even the weather was wrong that day, too hot for the season, the third of three days without fog, the sky going green at the edges like spoiled cheese. James was in a bad mood, rushed and harried and anxious. He was a small, compact man whose face could project a sweet boyishness, but more often than I cared to realize, he was the way he was that morning: distracted, unaware of me, lost in his own sense of being burdened.

"I'll park," I said as I signaled for the airport freeway exit. "I'll park in the garage, walk you to the gate, kiss you madly, then wave a little white hanky you can watch from the window of the plane." It's not a pleasant thing to remember, these attempts of mine to get his attention.

I was trying my baby chatterbox approach, my pose of happy abandon, soothing devotion.

What a fool.

"Oh, just leave me at the curb," he said. "I have to meet up with . . . someone."

Someone. The first of many errors on that day full of errors. In another person's life, I would have found it funny. *Someone.* Oh, yes, I suppose I now must remember all this: the situation I so stupidly put up with, the person I was then, a woman who was—what was I exactly? lonely? self-destructive? simply too lazy to look for something better? I'd rather not start the story here; I'd like nothing better than to forget about James, another unhappy note in a story that can't possibly have a happy ending. But with the bug must also come James, the two of them linked in my memory in an odd synchrony, as if James somehow brought on the bug or the bug, James.

So James must enter the story: James Havermeyer, thirty years old, two years my junior, my lover of over a year—and a man still pining away for a certain *someone.* I knew all about her: Susanna Cantor, graduate of Juilliard, Ph.D. from the Eastman School of Music, the orchestra's first violinist and concert mistress. A woman with long dark hair for whom James had felt the kind of insane unrequited love that no one past the age of twenty should ever feel. They were supposedly friends now, his passion for her over. But James still could not say her name to me in a normal tone of voice. Whatever existence they still shared—a conversation on the phone, a meal in a restaurant, seats together on the plane—he tried to keep secreted in a place that did not include me.

I should have known from the start; James was a man who liked his secrets. On a Sunday morning six weeks into our relationship, a mad woman came pounding on my door. James slept on, snoring. Through the peephole, I saw wild-flying blond hair, tearstained puffy eyes, a smeared-lipstick mouth, someone nearly tearing off the screen door. "I'm Sarah," screamed the woman I'd never seen before. "Sarah Postman. His girlfriend!" I opened the door. Her blouse was misbuttoned; her skirt hung askew. "Well," she sneered at me, "imagine my surprise to find I'm the *ex*-girlfriend. Where is he? Where is that lying bastard?"

I stared back at her. I had never even heard her name, had no idea she existed. His girlfriend. *Who?*

I sent her in to get James.

And there were others, I learned later, all musicians, all in his orchestra and still in his life in vague and suggestive ways. Before the wild woman pounding on my door there was Barbara, a cellist; and before her was Celine, a pianist. And directly before me, overlapping with the unhappy and duped Sarah Postman, was the unequaled Susanna. *Someone.* As I pulled up to the curb in front of United Airlines, I wondered: Had I once been a *someone* to the poor, wild-haired Sarah?

"Oh, really?" I said to James as I watched him take his bags out of the trunk. "Who's this someone you've got to meet up with?" It was cruel of me. I knew he would lie reflexively, floridly.

He fumbled with his suitcase. "Oh, just a contact from the tour operators. A guy. About the connections in New York." He went on: discounts, rebates, packages, faxes. The answer was too long, too detailed to be true.

"You're such a poor liar," I said to him, but almost tenderly, touching the back of his neck as he stood with his suitcases at his feet.

"I don't know what you mean," he said. He had a scared look on his face. He had lovely blue eyes, small but clear, and now they looked at me from behind a defensive squint.

"Good-bye," I said.

"See you in only six weeks," he said. He ran a hand down my back, kissed me briefly on the mouth.

"Good-bye," I said, slamming down the trunk.

Plans, rules, order—I should have known better. The relief I looked forward to at my desk, my perfect test—I should have realized even before I logged on to the system that morning that something else was going to happen. A linguist knows that following the rules is no assurance of anything. "Colorless green ideas sleep furiously," the linguist Noam Chomsky once famously said, his perfectly well-formed sentence: grammatically correct, signifying nothing.

Colorless, green ideas sleep, furiously.
Colorless green, ideas sleep furiously.
Colorless green ideas: Sleep! Furiously!

The parking lot at Telligentsia, the wasted feeling of having driven through traffic to arrive nowhere: a lake of asphalt in Fremont, California. The workstation in a cubicle. The morning begun not with hello but with a system prompt. Everyone's day begins like that now, but on that morning of March 5, 1984, only programmers and testers lived that way. From log-in to log-out, e-mail to e-mail, mouse click to mouse click—we were just then starting to make computers "friendly" for everyone, preparing the world for a programmer's life. In 1984, it was still possible to find it strange, and hate it: the monitor that showed me my face in its blank glass stare, the system that beeped at me when I mistyped my password, the machine whine that rose up from everywhere, like being sealed in a roomful of mosquitoes.

It took me half an hour to enter my test. Queries within queries, questions inside questions—point-click, point-click, a graphical query. A diagram with lines and boxes and arrows and field names that scrolled endlessly off to the right side of the screen. The first working part of the user interface, barely more than a demonstration module, full of errors, dead spots, bugs. I cursed at it it—clumsy mouse clicks and arcane control-commands, CONTROL SHIFT CLICK, all at the same time. Ethan Levin and his boss had designed the interface, stupidly, I thought. But what did any of us know about this business of graphical user interfaces? There was only the two-month-old Macintosh for a model, and the primitive graphics system on the SM workstation we were using. In those days, most computer monitors were monochrome character terminals. When you started up the system, there was nothing on the screen but a prompt. Until you entered a command, nothing happened. Windows, icons, buttons, menus—we were just then figuring out how all this should work. There might have been a hundred better ways to talk to a computer, but Ethan Levin had copied the Mac, which had copied the Xerox Star, which was later copied by Microsoft Windows. Who knew our mistakes would prove so durable?

I fought the interface and finished the query. Then I clicked on the menu RUN. It dropped open, and I moved the mouse toward the menu line CURRENT QUERY. I was about to click again, RUN CURRENT QUERY, but I was distracted and mistakenly moved the mouse outside the menu. I was about to move it back—when suddenly a long beep sounded, mad, like a stuck car horn. The display was a mess of lines, boxes, strange characters. The cursor stuck itself at the bottom of the screen. The keyboard was frozen. The mouse: dead.

A bug. One more in a cast of thousands. But not the one I was looking for. My query hadn't even made it to the database.

"Kill me, will you?"

I said this over the top of my cubicle to my neighboring tester, Mara Margolies. My workstation was dead. The only way to get it working was to kill the program from another terminal. Mara and I knew each other's passwords; we were used to cleaning up each other's rogue programs with the UNIX kill command. *"Meep!"* came the reply from Mara, a small, round person who had the extremely annoying habit of going around meeping like a robot.

And I thought that would be the end of it. I thought I'd report this unexpected bug, send it on to the responsible programmer—Ethan Levin—who would investigate it using the "core," a file full of hexadecimal numbers that showed the program's state at the moment it was killed, the contents of its "memory," what it was doing when it died. Then I'd go back to my test, my perfect test, the disaster I'd been waiting for.

But here was the next error on that error-prone day.

"Mara, where's the core?"

"Shit. I sent it a minus nine."

"Minus nine! How the hell could you send it a minus nine?"

The command `kill -9`, unconditional program death. A sure and certain way to kill any program. But one that did not produce a core file. No core. No record of the program's state at time of death. No postmortem by the programmer.

"I spaced out," Mara said.

"Spaced out! Shit, Mara. You're a tester!"

I didn't know then that this would be the bug's pattern—to escape without letting anyone capture its image in a core file. It would be some months before I understood that Mara, a new tester, would simply be the first of many novices who let this tease of a bug get away. At the time I blamed her for her stupidity, but there was nothing I could do. The program was dead; she didn't get a core; and now the body of the program had vanished without a trace.

But how had this bug come about? I still had to find the exact sequence of keys and commands that had led to the crash. Without notes to prove what I'd done, without a core file to show the result, I had to retrace my steps, reenter the entire query, go through the whole clumsy user interface over again. Which I did, impatient, irritable. Click open the menu, slide just past it . . . but nothing. No mess of windows. No stuck cursor. No beep. Everything fine.

"A flakey bug," my boss Wallis Markham pronounced it. "But a level-one."

Flakey: comes and goes. Level-one: crashes the system or freezes it. Needs investigation by the programmer even if it can't immediately be reproduced.

"Too bad about the core file, though," she said. "Oh, well. Just fill out a report and have a little chat with Ethan Levin."

"Oh, yes. A nice, friendly chat with Ethan Levin."

"Well, he can't exactly *kill* you."

"No, not exactly."

So I wrote up a report, and then didn't think much more about the bug. What was bothering me that morning as I filled in the particulars of the bug report (screen: VISUAL QUERY, menu: RUN) was something else, a jitter in the stomach that would not go away. The memory of Sarah Postman. The wild hair. The smeared-lipstick mouth of the betrayed. The ridiculous revenge scene as she tore the bedclothes from the naked James. Could that be me someday? Of course it could. One day I could learn that James had been with someone else for a month or two, that he'd finally won over Susanna, or moved on to a flutist—no, James hated the sound of the solo flute, perhaps to another pianist; yes, that'd be it, a pianist. And there I'd be with my clothes all askew on a Sunday morning, a wild, raging woman pounding at the door. Why not? I've learned there's a good chance you'll wind up like the person who came before you. People tend to repeat themselves in these sorts of things, is my experience. That's how it happens: they leave you the way they came to you.

"Put it over there," said Ethan Levin.

He was a tall man, lanky, sitting with his legs vining around the legs of his chair. A twitch of his long, poky neck indicated a pile of papers at the back of his desk.

And there I put it: the bug report, the first notice describing the bug that had just been officially designated UI-1017, its count of days open now set to zero and ticking. Ethan never even looked up. And I didn't bother to be annoyed. There were three programmers in that office: Ethan; Albert Herring, called "Fishy" by the testers; and Bradley Thorne, called, inevitably, "Badly Torn." I didn't like them, and they didn't much like each other. The quiet in that room was like lead crystal. If you broke it, you'd be cut by shards.

So I put the piece of paper on the pile and left. And that was it: a tester found a bug, a programmer ignored a tester, a bug report went to the top of a pile on a programmer's messy desk—nothing could have been more normal than what had just happened. Ethan went back to work. And I went back to work. And later I went home, to a desk and a yellow pad, to my twin nasty habits of poetry writing and smoking, breathing in and blowing out late into the night, jealous colorless green ideas not sleeping, unable to sleep, furiously. We could both be forgiven for not noticing that a turn of events had begun.

A VACATION IN TIME

He was running the compiler when the bug report came across his desk. The compiler, the program that translates a programmer's code into machine-readable bits—Ethan Levin had laid his code before its merciless gaze, and now he stared into his screen to see its verdict. Was he aware of the tester passing behind him? Did he take any notice of how carefully she slipped between his whiteboard and his chair, holding in her stomach so as not even to brush against him? No, of course not. Oh, all right: perhaps peripherally. Literally in his peripheral vision he might have seen her, and the thought "tester" might have formed in his brain, which would have led to the automatically accompanying idea that testers only bring news of trouble, and so why bother with whatever trouble she was bringing him now?

He was occupied by other troubles. Warning messages were scrolling up his screen, the compiler's responses, notices that this and that little thing in his code might not be legal, might not parse according to the rules, might prevent the compiler from turning his routine into an "object file," a little file full of ones and zeros, ready to be linked up with other object files to create the executable program. He wasn't getting fatal errors—no, not on this pass. There was nothing yet that caused the compiler to issue the awful message that began "Fatal error" and then, abruptly, stop. But such fatalities had already befallen him many times this morning, how many times, he'd lost track—twenty, fifty, a hundred? On each occasion, he had fixed whatever little thing wasn't legal, didn't parse, prevented his code from becoming machine-readable bits; and then he ran the compiler again.

Warning. Warning. Warning. Fatal error. Stop.

Fix the little thing in the code that wasn't legal. Run the compiler again.

Warning. Warning. Fatal error. Stop.

Fix the next little thing.

Warning. Warning.

"It'll compile this time" was the only thought Ethan Levin kept steadily in mind, over and over, on that morning of March 5, 1984. Even the phone had to go on ringing—once, twice, three times—until it reached him, three rings to get inside his window of attention so tuned to the nervous refresh rate of the screen: Warning. Warning.

"What! Are you still *there*?" said the voice on the phone. "You're supposed to be *here*!"

He sat confused for a moment. Yes, he knew the voice was Joanna's, but the words "there" and "here": What exactly did they mean? Then, all at once, his attention snapped into focus: It was Joanna, he was supposed to take her to the airport, and he was late.

"I'm leaving!" he said.

"I mean now. Are you leaving *now*?"

"I'm leaving, I'm leaving," he said again, but vacantly, automatically, because despite himself, his eyes had been drawn back to the screen, to the irregular pulse of the messages as they appeared: Warning. Warning.

"*Hello?* Are you there?"

"Yeah, yeah. I'm here," he said, just as the compiler suddenly displayed the message "Fatal error: MAXWINSIZE not defined," and came to a stop.

"Shit!" Ethan Levin muttered under his breath.

"Ethan! You're compiling! I know it!"

"Yeah, yeah, sorry," he said to Joanna McCarthy, who, as his girlfriend of four years, knew all too well the sort of exclamations he made when he was programming and compiling. "Sorry," he repeated, but again automatically, because—though he knew better than to do this now—his mind immediately began ranging over the places where MAXWINSIZE should have been defined. On one side of his attention was Joanna, the month-long trip to India she was taking with Paul Ostrick, husband of her best friend, Marsha Ostrick, and the promise Ethan had made to take them to the airport—and be on time! he swore! But on the other was this sudden and unexpected problem of MAXWINSIZE, this branching trail of questions that led off in many directions, curious and puzzling, down which his mind involuntarily started traveling. . . .

"It's an *airplane*, Ethan! It's not going to wait for a compile!"

"Shit! Yes! I'm leaving now."

"That's like *now* now, right? Not like a one-more-compile now?"

"*Now* now," he repeated, as much to himself as to Joanna. "*Now* now."

Still, even after he'd stood up and grabbed his jacket from the back of his chair, the face of the screen drew him back. He sat down again, reread the messages on the monitor, typed a command to the system that set it searching through the entire code library for all occurrences of MAXWINSIZE. Yes, much better now. The system would tell him where the problem was. Then, tomorrow, he'd fix it.

They rented a tract house on a street of tract houses. San Leandro, California, a "nowhere," as Joanna described it, its chief attraction being its location about half an hour from other places: from Ethan's office in Fremont to the south; from Joanna's job in downtown Berkeley to the north; from San Francisco, barely visible across the bay from their freeway exit at the top of the hill. The day was unseasonably hot and dry, just a degree or two cooler than yesterday, which had been the hottest March 4 on record. The overheated houses—uninsulated, in varying degrees of neglect—had sent the neighbors into the street. Horace, a black man of about thirty who lived next door, whose last name Ethan never knew, was tossing a football with his son, a spindly boy of about nine. A woman from across the street, whom Ethan thought of as "Carolyn-with-the-baby," was sitting on her porch with the baby. They eyed Ethan as he drove up but said nothing; it was Joanna who was neighborly.

Joanna glared at him from the front porch. "You're late!"

Ethan glanced at his watch. "Not very."

"Forty minutes! Or Marsha would have taken us!"

Immediately, the little grouping on the porch went into motion, Joanna dragging her heavy suitcase down the three porch steps, Marsha helping Paul haul his across the tiny patch of grass Joanna worked hard to keep tidy. Ethan got out of his car and found himself in a shower of white petals. The stunted old plum trees that lined the street had gotten themselves shocked into bloom by the heat, Ethan thought, as he watched the blossoms drifting down in the hot, still air. The trees were all that was left of the orchards that once climbed the hillsides before the subdivisions were built, according to Joanna, who knew things about trees and plants.

"Hey, Joanna!" said Ethan. "It's plum-blossom time again!"

"Goddamnit, Ethan! At least pop the fucking trunk!"

Ethan arranged the two bags while Paul Ostrick looked on. "Give you a hand?" Ostrick said finally. He was a wan-looking, skinny man with a kind of watery asceticism Ethan found extremely unappealing. Ethan himself was thin, but next to Ostrick he felt like Charles Atlas. "No, thanks," Ethan said. "I've got it."

"Oh! You two will have such a wonderful time!" cooed Marsha, as she took her husband around, hugged him to her, and engaged him in the kind of kiss that made Ethan turn away. Ethan and Joanna were supposed to go to India together, a vacation Joanna had started planning a year in advance. But then Ethan had started work at Telligentsia, eight months ago, where it had been made clear that no one would get a vacation for at least a year. "I can't go," he'd said to Joanna over her protests. "I can't go to India."

Ethan had tried to explain. "The other programmers can't start their work until I give them some working code. I'm a critical module!"

Joanna had given him a long look. "*I'll* say you are."

"I'm on the critical path!"

"Then stay there," Joanna had said. "And I'll go to India."

He never imagined she'd go without him. He was certain she'd understand about his job, wait, put aside the plans. When she came to him and announced that she and Paul Ostrick were thinking of going together, he was more startled than anything else. "I thought you forgot about the trip," he'd said. "Oh, no," she'd answered. "*You* forgot."

"We'll both be travel widows!" Marsha sang to Ethan after Paul's suitcase was in the trunk. She opened her arms to take Ethan in a hug. "Promise you'll have dinner with me!" Marsha Ostrick was a big woman, with bangle bracelets running up her arm to the elbow, all of them jingling as she implored Ethan to meet her for dinner. "Sure. Of course," he said noncommittally, ducking the hug. Marsha had wanted to make the trip, but she was a college teacher, committed to a semesterful of courses. And Ethan had committed himself to a relationship with his compiler. On the other hand, Paul Ostrick was a musician, hardly made any money at all, and was, in the odd logic of the poor, free. Joanna had already arranged her vacation with the environmental-action organization where she worked as an administrator, and it had all been decided over a long dinner at the Ostricks' house. Four courses, a decent red wine, a chocolate cake, a toast: "To India!" The two couples were such good friends, Paul and Marsha, Ethan and

Joanna. They agreed, they laughed, ha-ha. Of *course* Joanna and Paul should go away together.

"What's this?" Joanna asked, opening the passenger-side door and finding a ring binder on the seat.

"The window-system manual," Ethan answered.

"You mean you took a manual to see me off for a month?" She threw it onto the driver's seat.

"I thought I'd read it at the gate," Ethan said. He put the manual on the floor, got in, and started the engine.

"Bye-bye," Marsha called.

"Bye-bye," Paul and Joanna answered.

"Have a great time!" the neighbors said in chorus, waving at Joanna.

The wind suddenly picked up, and white plum-blossom petals floated down all around them, drifting across Ethan's slowly moving car and then over Marsha's, as she too got in her car and started off. Toot-toot, went Marsha's horn as both cars slowed down at the corner, toot-toot, under the shower of petals. "Bye-bye," she called and waved, bracelets bangling.

Ethan sat at the gate with the window-system manual open in his lap, but he couldn't concentrate. If they weren't changing planes in New York, he thought, they would have left from the international terminal, where only passengers were allowed at the gate, and he could have just dropped them off at the curb. He didn't like terminals and waiting rooms. He didn't mind travel once he got somewhere, but the preparations and the actual transportation from place to place always unsettled him. It was the time distortion travel produced: your life getting stopped up like a dam behind that single moment when your plane took off. As he sat there amid the annoying jitter of people coming and going, he admitted to himself he was relieved he couldn't go on this trip. He wouldn't have to deal with Joanna's need to get to airports and train stations two and a half hours in advance. A vacation, Ethan thought. Joanna can go off into her own conception of time—getting to the hotel before four in the afternoon, for instance, so as not to get the worst room in the place, as she was convinced would happen—and Ethan could go off into his, into his one-more-compile times, where the hours could simply bleed themselves out until he couldn't think anymore.

"We should be boarding now," said Joanna, looking down at her watch.

"Any minute," said Paul Ostrick, looking down at his.

"If this flight's late—"

"We'll miss our connection in New York," Ostrick said nervously.

Time compatible, Ethan thought. The two of them were certainly time compatible.

Otherwise, from their appearance, they were not so well matched, Ethan thought, as he looked across the row of seats at them, where they sat side by side clutching their carry-ons to board at a moment's notice. Joanna was robust and hearty-looking, with light brown hair that was cut in a way that required no maintenance, and sturdy arms and legs, tanned and freckled from her daily bike rides or runs. Paul Ostrick, on the other hand, was skinny and slack muscled and hollow chested, a vegetarian's body, thought Ethan, though Ostrick would eat fish and chicken, a "vegetarianism" Ethan considered silly if only for its inconsistency. Marsha and Paul had been Joanna's friends. Otherwise, Ethan thought, it was highly unlikely he would have ever known someone like Paul Ostrick, who played some Indonesian instrument called the gamelan, and who affected what Ethan thought were phony "Eastern" ways of thinking and acting.

Their flight was called.

Joanna and Ostrick jumped up, then Ethan.

Joanna took Ethan's hips in her hands, drew him toward her,

hipbone to hipbone, and looked into his eyes. "Give me a real farewell," she said.

Ethan knew he was supposed to feel something at moments like these. And when he tried to plumb himself, yes, he could just notice the beginnings of something that felt to him like anxiety. But what words could he possibly give to it? Could he say, I have this vague, uncomfortable feeling like something is stuck in my chest and I have to cough? He felt suddenly stupid to himself, an oaf, deficient in some kind of human graces other people seemed naturally to have.

He said what he was supposed to say. "I'll miss you."

"No, you won't."

"What do you mean?"

She withdrew her hands, backed up.

"No. You won't. Bye, Ethan."

Their row was called.

And immediately Joanna turned to go.

Ethan stood there, confused at the abruptness of the good-bye. To the end, he hoped Joanna would turn around and wave. But she set off with a jaunty, sturdy walk, swinging her carry-on, just missing Ostrick's shins as he trotted closely behind her. The rest of the travelers crowded in, Ethan had a momentary glimpse of Joanna's sensible, short new haircut, and then Joanna and Ostrick were suddenly gone, swallowed up by the long hall of the Jetway.

He opened all the windows when he got home, and he had the feeling that the air just whooshed out, heated to expansion. Then he could hear the clank of the neighbors' pots and pans, the sound of someone turning sink water on and off, a baby's cry, a dog barking from down the street. Without turning on the lights, he boiled water for pasta. It was his one staple meal: pasta and sauce from a jar with a shake of cheese on top.

While waiting for the water to boil, he stared out the window, listening to sounds of the neighborhood, for a while enjoying the spacey, empty feeling that water-heating always gave him. Then suddenly, despite the heat that had lingered into the twilight, a little shiver went through him. It was Joanna's face that came to him, the last look she gave him before she turned to go down the Jetway, something wrong there, something he couldn't quite put a name to. And he regretted all over again that he couldn't say the right thing when he needed to, his clumsiness in the crafts of love. But immediately he cut off the train of thought. Just anxious when she travels, he told himself, as always. Besides, it was getting late, he was hungry, and here was the water, spitting steam from the sides of the lid.

He took his little meal to the dining table, where he turned on the light and surrounded himself with books. The window-system manual, the UNIX operating system guide, a data sheet for the graphics workstation, specifications for the VT-200 character terminal—a circuit of technology ringing his plate. Then for the next hour, he read and ate with a childish absorption, like the pleasure of stuffing his mouth with buttered popcorn in the darkness of a movie theater. Joanna's being gone made it all the better: Time felt spacious, unbounded. All the little accommodations he normally made for her—not reading at the table, the how-was-your-day-dear conversation—were in suspension. He dove into his manuals the way he dove into his food. Soon spaghetti was stuck to the pages of the OS guide. Bread crumbs were folded into the workstation data sheet. Everything was dotted red with tomato sauce.

When all at once, as he reached for the one technical manual not yet in the circle—the database design document in its black leatherette binder—a panic came over him. It had a very specific representation, this panic, an image concrete and irrefutable: at his last job, only nine months ago, Ethan Levin had worked at an insurance company, coding input screens for claims clerks.

I don't know what I'm doing, came the inescapable thought into his head.

The heavy document in its black binder fell, closed, onto the table. And his next thought was of Harry Minor, his boss at Telligentsia, and how even he knew that Ethan had no particular qualifications for the job he was doing. "No one knows shit about front ends to databases," Harry had said at Ethan's second job interview. "At least no one who'll come work for us," he'd added with a big jolly laugh.

Ethan could still remember that laugh: the cynicism in it, the resignation. Was it supposed to reassure him, the fact that they couldn't find anyone better?

As it turned full night outside, and moths battered at the windows until they found their way inside to orbit the light, Ethan conjured up the interview, as he had many times before. And he slowly relived its most reassuring moment, Harry telling him that no one really knew what they were doing, that things were changing too quickly, and everyone was just making it up as they went along. "Look," said Harry, "you've worked on UNIX, with a database, doing business stuff. I can't find a single person in the world who has that combination. There are some of these academic guys I could get, but none of them has ever *built* anything that runs in the real world. They never had users. They don't know crap about business requirements. As for the rest of it, you're self-taught. You're motivated. You'll learn."

The rest of it, Ethan thought as he sat there behind his red-spattered books and cold, half-eaten dinner. He looked at the manuals surrounding him, thinking of everything in them he had to learn, and the memory suddenly lost its reassurance. *The rest of it.* Device drivers and system kernels. Processes and signals and memory segments. All the operating-system services that before were always just *there* for his programs to *use*. He'd spent twelve years as a corporate coder, writing programs for general ledgers, accounts payable, order processing—*insurance,* forgodsakes. Now he had to take the covers off, go deeper, where the machine was not some notion he had of it, but a layer of code that sat on top of another layer of code, on top of another one, very little of which he exactly understood.

But Harry Minor had offered him the job, Ethan reminded himself. The same Harry Minor who'd written part of the Internet Protocol, who was a legendary hacker from the days when "hacker" was an honorific for a brilliant programmer. "I'll help you," Harry said at the second interview. "I've already started designing it, coding it. There'll be you and me and six others. You won't be doing this alone." Harry had worked to convince him, and if Harry Minor, overweight bearded balding shaggy guy in a T-shirt who is the reason we have this stereotype of what a programmer should look like—if Harry thought he could do the job, Ethan said to himself, maybe it was true.

Then Ethan remembered what his group had to deliver: a newly designed user interface to a database. The front end and database running on separate machines, connected over an Ethernet network. A windowing system to support the UI. All of it in new code. Harry had dismissed the primitive windowing system that came with the workstation they were using. "Who knows if they'll keep supporting this kluge?" was how he put it. Aside from a few basic routines to interact with the mouse and graphical screen, the front-end group would write their own windowing system, built to run on multiple operating systems, with different types of screens, different kinds of input devices— a mouse, a joystick, who knew what else might come along in ten years? As Ethan recalled all this, he also had to remember that he'd never thought much about user interfaces. That he'd never written a program that used a mouse. That one of the operating systems his interface was supposed to run on he'd never even logged on to in his life.

"It helps to be scared," Harry Minor had said at the interview. "It keeps you focused."

Then Harry had laughed and laughed.

Ethan sat in his dining room and remembered the moment when his bluff and self-sell suddenly failed him, when he found himself muttering something about there being a "skills mismatch" between himself and the job. And then Harry leaning forward in his chair (with great difficulty, breathing heavily at the mere exertion of shifting his formidable weight), telling him not to worry about not having finished graduate school: "It's all mostly useless by now anyway," he said. "Look, Levin. Programming starts out like it's going to be architecture—all black lines on white paper, theoretical and abstract and spatial and up-in-the-head. Then, right around the time you have to get something fucking *working*, it has this nasty tendency to turn into *plumbing*.

"No, no. Lemme think," Harry interrupted himself. "It's more like you're hired as a plumber to work in an old house full of ancient, leaky pipes laid out by some long-gone plumbers who were even weirder that you are. Most of the time you spend scratching your head and thinking: Why the *fuck* did they do *that*?"

"Why the fuck did they?" Ethan said.

Which appeared to amuse Harry to no end. "Oh, you know," he went on, laughing hoarsely, "they didn't understand whatever the fuck had come before *them*, and *they* just had to get something working in some ridiculous time. Hey, software is just a shitload of pipe fitting you do to get something the hell *working*. Me," he said, holding up his chewed, nail-torn hands as if for evidence, "I'm just a plumber."

I can be a plumber, Ethan thought as he looked at those hands. I've always been a plumber. All I've ever done is crawl around trying to figure out what's going on.

Then Harry said: "Your users wanted stuff all the time, right?"

Users: claims clerks and adjusters and accountants. "Sure."

"And they didn't give a shit when you said something like, 'The system isn't designed to do that'—whatever it was they were asking for, right?"

"Right."

"And you had to make it do it anyway, right?"

"Right."

"So you know."

What did he know? Ethan felt like he knew nothing, had just wandered along from job to job, doing what he had to. What did he *know*?

As an undergraduate, Ethan hadn't taken a single course in computer science beyond what he needed to know to use the university system. He'd majored in organic chemistry, intending to become an epidemiologist. The thought of traveling around the world trying to figure out the cause of some strange disease seemed to him noble work, intellectually challenging, and (he had to admit, despite the fact that people would probably be dying) fun.

But just as he was about to graduate from college, in 1971, he read an article in *Scientific American* that changed his mind about his future. It was about a cybernetic universe called The Game of Life created by the mathematician John Horton Conway. The Game, at first look, seemed silly, simpleminded. There was a grid of cells, like a field of ticktacktoe games, and three rules that decided if an individual cell was to be turned "on" or "off" or remain in whatever state it was in. The rules themselves were ridiculously simple, based entirely on the state of the eight neighboring cells (if a cell had less than two "live," turned-on neighbors, for example, it was turned off, or died). But out of these simple prescriptions came surprising results. As the rules were applied over and over again, elaborate patterns sometimes emerged—stable arrangements of cells devotees called "life-forms"—all without design or intention. There came forms called blocks and beehives, boats and ships and loafs; the blinking shapes called oscillators; and the wonderful gliders and spaceships, moving forms that magically slid their way across the grid of the world.

Ethan found the implications of the Game tantalizing. He knew at once, with all the enthusiasm of an adolescent deciding to become an astronaut, that he had found his life's work. Conway's Game seemed to draw together everything he'd suspected while studying organic chemistry, feelings he couldn't articulate to himself at the time but that Conway now crystallized for him: the sense that if he could just work his way down and down into the heart of living molecules, he would find something simple and clean. Maybe life, the real thing, in all its variety and complexity, had the same source as the forms in Life the game: from the workings of a glorious machine.

"The miracle in the mechanism" is how Ethan thought of it.

He was not alone in his enthusiasm, he soon found. The author of the piece in the *Scientific American* received hundreds of letters from mathematicians and computer scientists; one researcher started a newsletter, "Lifeline," to which Ethan immediately subscribed. There he could follow the life histories of the forms as they were spawned from their cybernetic parents, the random starting-point arrangements named for their number of cells: the prodigious R-pentomino; heptominoes B and C; and heptomino D, which looked to Conway like the astronomical symbol for Uranus (h), whom he therefore named "Herschel."

The important thing about the Game, as Ethan understood it, was that nothing in the rules could possibly predict the existence and shape of the resulting life-forms, the way there is nothing in the chemistry of two adjacent water molecules that gives any notion of the shape of a cloud. Yet still the cloud exists, unique and unpredictable, not designed from on high but emerging, somehow, from the many mundane, small, "neighboring" interactions of water and air operating dumbly from below. When he considered it, yes, he was sure that Conway's Game was a way to understand the origin of life itself. How else to explain the emergence of organic life—living tissue, DNA, self-replicating—from a primordial soup of dead, inorganic chemicals? It was a mystery no science was able to explain: the leap from the predictable to the infinitely variable, from nonlife to life.

He absolutely had to be part of the Game.

He decided to abandon organic chemistry and epidemiology. The future of the study of life, he decided, was not at the lab bench but at the computer terminal. He became a seeker after the principles of artificial life. What makes humans any "realer" than some other form of self-replicating, self-directed life-form that might be created cybernetically? he thought. Why should we products of that inorganic primordial soup be more privileged in our "naturalness" than some other sort of creature that might emerge? His enthusiasm became boundless. He even decided that his study of the Game allowed him to believe in God again. His problem had been with God-the-Master-Planner, with the idea that all the change and complexity in the world was foreseen, designed from the outset. Yet now the audacious variety of the universe did not have to be worked out in advance. God was in the details, Ethan was sure. God, like Conway, had devised the basic, simple principles of life, the smallest rules for the most fundamental particles of matter. Then God sat back and waited to find out what would happen.

Ethan was accepted into a Ph.D. program in computer science at Berkeley. He began work on what he called a "simulated ecosystem"—a collection of digital creatures and habitats, and simple rules for their interaction. For six months, he worked in a fever, devising his rules, starting to program.

Then one day, when the code was barely started, he received word that his father had died, a sudden heart attack. There were bills, debts, anxious relatives who'd loaned him money. For the first time in his life, Ethan Levin, fatherless, had to face the terror of having no money. He had to pay back his uncle. He had to quit graduate school. He found a job: programming, general ledgers. Then another: accounts payable. Then the next: order processing. Then finally: insurance.

Harry Minor had been very interested in the simulated ecosystem. "Do you still work on it?" he'd asked near the end of the interview.

"Yes," Ethan had replied.

"How often?"

Ethan decided Harry already wanted him, so there was no point lying to him. Ethan had long ago lost the mathematics to work as a researcher. He had no time to read new books as they came out. His journal subscriptions, one by one, had lapsed years ago. Of a whole way of life he'd wanted, only the simulation remained. "I work on it whenever it seems that my life has just gone from thing to thing without my having much to say about it," he said, then paused. "Every six months or so."

Which caused Harry Minor to laugh and laugh. "You really should come work here," he said finally. "You'll be way too busy to worry where the hell your life is going."

The simulation was waiting for him, right where he'd left it eight months ago. He went up to his study, a small room in a kind of dormer on the second floor, sat down in front of the IBM PC the company had loaned him to induce him to work from home, and dialed in to the host at work. Then he sat listening to the screech of the modem. It was a sound he'd come to associate with his simulation, a sort of siren call, asking him to come back and work on it. He'd carried the program from machine to machine over the years, from minicomputer to minicomputer, and one failed attempt to rewrite it for a mainframe. Now,

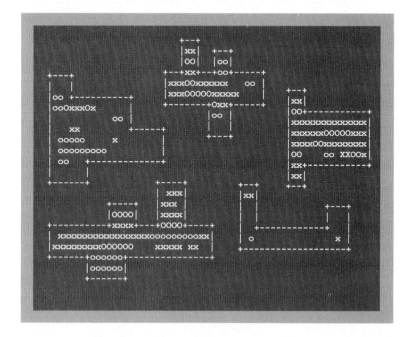

with Harry's encouragement, his simulated world lived on a UNIX server at Telligentsia, where it had been running all these months in the dark internals of the machine.

My little O-creatures, he thought with relief, as he tapped in a command and the simulation appeared on the screen. For a few minutes, he watched his creatures blink their way across their island habitats, stuttery in their motion over the 1,200-baud communication line.

Ethan was never sure what he'd find on the screen when he brought his simulation out of the invisible workings of the machine. Once, because of a bug, he'd found nothing but blank, empty space, as if some digital Armageddon had wiped his world out of existence when he wasn't looking. But this time, nothing significant had happened. The O-creatures—small o's if they were searching for food, capital O's if they were "feeding"—were still milling around looking for the X's that represented their food supply, reproducing if they were well fed, starving and dying if they weren't. The habitats still went blank and dark as the creatures consumed the food they found there; then, as the creatures died back and the habitats came under decreased population pressure, the islands replenished themselves, new X's appearing on the screen to show the growing store of food. Then the creatures slowly began to reproduce again, once more stripping the habitats of food stocks, and the islands again went dark.

Still stuck in alternating boom-bust cycles, Ethan thought, somewhat depressed.

He'd wanted to create something that would *evolve*. He'd hoped for a surprising pattern, an outcome not programmed, an unexpected turn of events, like the lovely life-forms that had emerged from Conway's world. Each time he brought the simulation back onto the screen, he'd have a moment of jittery anticipation. Maybe this time he'd see a leap. Maybe this would be the day when he'd bring the program out of the machine's internals to find a self-directing universe, a world that ran itself without the hand of the programmer. But except for the bug that once wiped the screen clean, it was always as it was now: a dull, repetitive place, a universe created by a not very imaginative God.

He sent the simulation back into the dark of the machine, opened a code file, and searched for the phrase "Here you are," his code marker, the words he always used to note the last place he'd been in the code. And below it, the message he always left himself when he was about to stop working on the simulation for a while.

```
/****************************************************************/
/*                                                              */
/* Here you are, Ethan.                                         */
/* To get out of endless cycles, introduce migration           */
/*                                                              */
/****************************************************************/
```

Over the years, he'd come to understand the message as a kind of rope line he was tossing to himself, a thought sent from the present day's Ethan to the Ethan of the future: to the Ethan Levin who would always return from whatever impossible job schedule he was afraid of now, whatever bills he had to pay, dinner he'd left half eaten, girlfriend he'd just lost or found or fought with. Here you are. He returned to the idea in progress, to the thought continued across time. The panic over his work at Telligentsia fell away. The argument with Joanna about the trip fell away. Her traveling with Ostrick, her face before she disappeared down the Jetway—none of that existed. There he was: back in the code. The code he'd started when he was twenty-three, still had a father, and knew what he wanted to do with his life. From message to message, "Here you are" to "Here you are," the moments Ethan spent working on his simulated world came together as they always did: sequential points along a solid line, the arc of a separate, private, parallel, unfinished life.

Time raced away from him. Children outside stopped playing in the street. Houses up and down the block turned off their lights. Cars stopped passing. Television sets went blank and silent. The long heat of the day cooled in the thickening dark. All around him, the people of one street in San Leandro, California, followed the natural course of the sun into evening and then night. Joanna's plane, where she sat sleeping next to Paul Ostrick, was already curving around the sphere of the earth toward morning. But Ethan Levin, the Ethan Levin who still believed in The Game of Life, remained at his keyboard, staring into the code of his simulated world.

THE SCHEDULE

Harry Minor sat down at the head of the conference table and sighed. A friendly fat-man sigh, Ethan thought fondly. There was something reassuring about the dome of Harry's belly rising like a giant bagel under his Mt. Xinu T-shirt.

Harry fingered the Xinu logo. "UNIX—"

"—spelled backwards," the front-end team replied, groaning. Harry was a man of habits.

"You know the order of the service, ladies and gentlemen," Harry said.

And they did; another of Harry's habits. It was the Tuesday-morning meeting of the user interface group, a weekly ritual with unvarying agenda, always beginning with confession: how far behind schedule they were.

"Three weeks," said Bill Werners.

"Two," said Dana Merankin, the next one seated around the table.

"Eight," said Larry Seidel.

"Six," reported Bradley Thorne.

"A month," said Tommy Park.

There was then a pause as they came to Albert Herring, officemate of Ethan Levin and Bradley Thorne, a slight, fussy man in a checked short-sleeved shirt who sat biting the edge of his mustache with his lower teeth.

"Herring?" asked Harry.

Herring bit, chewed, and twiddled, and finally said, "Three and a half months."

There was now another pause as everyone in the room stared at Albert Herring. It was a gaze of fascinated, guilty terror, the look wildebeest give the one of their herd just taken down by a lion: horror, warring with relief that it was someone else who got it in the neck. Bill Werners, in a black T-shirt and camouflage pants, suddenly slouched down in his chair, crossed a leg in front of him like a barrier, and edged his eyes over the top. Dana Merankin, whom Harry called a "girl nerd," happily shaggy and overweight like the guys she hung out with, found a certain compelling interest in a hank of her hair, then in Herring, then the hair again. Bradley Thorne, a small, intense, uncommunicative man, shook his leg compulsively under the table and kept sliding his eyes over to Herring like a cat wall-clock. Larry Seidel, a fat bearded fellow like Harry, only shorter, drummed his fingers on the shelf of his stomach and tried to look bored. Tommy Park, a pudgy Korean man with brown teeth who was still waiting for his green card, threw himself back in his chair and sat very still, barely blinking, as if his stillness would make him invisible. The last one around the table was Ethan Levin, who tried to do nothing, but suddenly craned his neck to look at Herring and found he'd propelled his rolling chair as far away from his miserable colleague as it could get.

"For fuck's sake, Herring," said Harry. "You said you could pound out some of the backlog. But you're in the same goddamn place. What the fuck happened this week?"

Silence. Herring breathing in and out, in and out, as if he'd just raced across a field. No one moving, just sliding their eyes back and forth between Harry and Herring, waiting to see what would happen.

"Oh, shit, Herring," Harry said finally. "Never mind now. We'll take this up off line, at our next—"

"I told you," Herring broke in with a whine. "It's the design of the device interface. I *told* you."

Harry sighed extravagantly. "We're not going there, Herring. I told *you*. It's definitely *not* the device interface."

Ethan felt everyone looking at him, waiting to see if he'd get into his usual argument with Albert Herring. The device interface: the library of routines designed to shield the programmers from the vagaries of the hardware. The front-end code created "windows" and "menus" and "buttons," and it was the job of Ethan's library to turn those abstractions into points of light and dark on a particular type and size of screen. It was the assignment Herring had wanted. But Ethan had been hired first, and by the time Albert Herring moved into what was already called "Levin's office" (forced to take the desk away from the window, since Ethan was already there), he'd found Ethan's completed design, which he never stopped criticizing. No one ever exactly rushed to Ethan's defense. They couldn't understand why Ethan Levin, known to have lightweight experience, had been given this most technical of the assignments. Harry never mentioned that he himself had done the foundation work, hacking out the first trial routines, establishing a model for how the device interfaces would work. He seemed content to let Ethan take the credit, or the blame. A corporate coder, is how Ethan's colleagues thought of him. From a *user shop*, not a software company. Worse, he had sat in on each of their interviews, apparently having a say about whether or not they'd be hired, and they never forgave him for it.

All of this had been communicated to Ethan in small, sly, cumulative ways. Technical questions they suspected he couldn't answer. References to "clueless corporate programmers." To which Ethan responded with an ever-tightening vigilance over his own work, a sense that his code had to be cleaner, more efficient, more complete than anyone else's in the group. It made him edgy; this constant standing on guard made him brittle when attacks came. Skirmishes between Herring and Ethan had become part of the weekly ritual, as common as the opening reports of schedule-slips. Ethan could see that his colleagues expected it, another argument, another round of sniping. Their faces had that look of amused detachment he'd come to recognize. Dana Merankin, especially, who already had that little curl at the corner of her mouth, which would stay there while she pretended not to enjoy the fight.

Ethan rolled his chair back up to the table. "I think it's my turn," he said.

Harry picked his head up from the cradle of his hands, where he'd been hiding his face after the interchange with Herring. "Go ahead, Levin."

"A week," Ethan said in an even voice. "I'm a week behind schedule." He paused. "No, not even that. Four days. Like four."

The response was silence. Ethan could feel his colleagues' annoyance but decided, too bad, it was their problem. Why should he apologize for knowing how to make a schedule and keep to it? His time as a *corporate coder* had at least taught him something.

"Goddamn!" Harry said with a laugh and a slap on the tabletop. "You're still on schedule! It's just like I said in the management meeting this morning. 'Go figure! Go figure that Ethan Levin is the only engineer in the company on schedule!' "

"I guess I padded my schedule well," Ethan said at once, to make a joke of it, to be collegial and not seem to be bragging.

"How else could you do it, Levin?" Dana Merankin responded, in what could have been another little collegial joke or perhaps a real jab at Ethan—who could tell?

So Ethan did the thing that was now required of him at this point in the interchange, which was laugh. As did everyone else. And with Harry laughing, and Ethan's colleagues laughing, and the occasional extra jab being tossed into the general merriment—"Levin's got enough stuffing for a mattress!" "Stuffed like the turkey he is!"—the meeting moved on.

The rest of the hour was taken up with grievances. Telligentsia was primarily a database company, Ethan knew. What had made venture capitalists hand over five million dollars was the prospect of a fast database, running on standard hardware, over a network—a revolutionary concept at the time. Before coming to Telligentsia, all the computers Ethan had ever worked on were like big islands, each a little isolated world unto itself. He knew about the Internet, but it was still a government and research network, with barely a thousand hosts. For commercial exchanges, getting information from one island to another was a clumsy business of mailing computer tapes or using the UNIX-to-UNIX copy facility, which worked over phone lines by handing files from machine to machine until they got where they were supposed to go. If he wanted to be sure that his mail or file got through, he had to know which machine was connected to which others, and mail addresses were full of routing information. To get to Ethan from SM Corp., for instance, the route was ucbpubhost!telligentspub!hubris!levin, with the exclamation point pronounced "bang."

The idea that small computers could be linked to one another, and that everyone on those linked computers could share the information in a single database—this was what had dazzled the investors, according to Harry, who said they were smacking their lips at the prospect of being first to market with a networked database. But the VC's forgot that all those people on the network would need some way to interact with the data, to formulate queries, to create reports, forms, displays. "We were an afterthought," said Harry with a laugh, referring to his "front-end" group of seven programmers. Meanwhile, the "back-end" database group had forty engineers, six managers, eight analysts, three product managers, and the vast bulk of the budget for hardware and support.

It was Harry's job to somehow convince his seven engineers, despite their shortage of programmers and hardware, that they were loved, brilliant, needed. He made promises: better cubicles, more hardware, better software tools, more frequent trips to conferences. He even hinted that they might get the okay for another hire. He'd do what he could, he said, because there was something they all should know beyond a doubt: that they were doing important, groundbreaking, *pioneering* work.

Ethan listened distantly to the complaints and promises. Something was bothering him about the first part of the meeting, something about Harry's response when Ethan announced that his work was on time. *Go figure,* Harry had said. *Go figure that Ethan Levin is the only engineer in the company on schedule.* Just what exactly had Harry meant by that "go figure"? As his colleagues peppered Harry with their aggrieved sense of being brilliant and hardworking and yet underappreciated, Ethan kept turning it over and over in his mind: Go figure *what?*

The meeting ended as it always did.

"Bug counts," Harry called.

Around the table they went again.

Bill Werners: "Sixteen level-ones and thirty-eight level-twos."

Sixteen bugs that crashed the system or froze it, thirty-eight that seriously interfered with its functioning.

Dana Merankin: "Twelve and eighteen."

Larry Seidel: "Nineteen and thirty-one."

Bradley Thorne: "Thirty-eight and fifty-one."

Harry raised an eyebrow.

"I write more lines of code than anybody," Thorne said morosely.

"And more bugs," said Albert Herring.

Harry sighed. "Park?"

"Nine and twenty-eight," said Tommy Park.

Albert Herring: "Twenty and thirty-two."

And finally Ethan Levin. "A slew of level-fours"—cosmetics, things that worked fine but looked bad to the user—"five level-twos. One new level-one. But the idiots didn't get me a core file on the level-one."

"No core?"

"No core."

"Then fuck it. Make them give you a core or you'll spin your wheels on nothing. Work on those level-fours. We have these demos coming up for the investors. We need to look pretty."

"I can do that," Ethan said.

"Ethan can be *very* pretty," said Dana. "It's his movie-star curly hair."

Ethan hated his hair, kinky rows of tight curls like a 1920s crooner. "Fuck you, Dana."

"You wish," she replied with a smile.

And another weekly meeting ended.

Chinglish, Ethan thought to himself with disgust as he read. Chinese barely translated into English. "When button down long time enough defined in SM_mouse->BUTTONTIME," said the e-mail from SM Corp.'s technical consultant, "signal is sent BUTTONDOWN value of SIGUSR1. Noted then in SM_mouse->button which button is LEFT MIDDLE or RIGHT else noted NULL."

Ethan was sitting on a splintery bench on the concrete back patio of his house. After coming home from work, he'd been restless, wandering around from room to stuffy room, finally taking the pages-long e-mail message outside to escape the heat that had accumulated in the shut-up house. He sat in a shower of white plum blossoms, which were still falling and piling up on the bench like snow. From behind him came a furious humming of bees, attracted to a row of lavender Joanna had planted. The tinny treble of a radio carried in from somewhere in the neighborhood. The humming bees, the tinny radio, the shushing rustle of the willow in the corner of the yard distracted him. His head felt full of buzzing.

He was afraid of the mouse. Among everything he had to learn, the mouse seemed the most impenetrable, and the more he read of the e-mail, the more afraid he became. He had never worked with a mouse before; neither had anyone else at Telligentsia, except for Harry, who had once *read* some code involving a mouse. There were perhaps a few hundred people in the world who knew anything about it, and most of them were working at Apple or at the two or three companies building mice. The documentation from SM Corp., the company that had built the systems Telligentsia was using, consisted of a few barely comprehensible pages, mostly C-code samples, which Ethan had puzzled over in growing alarm. He felt horribly stupid about this device that had suddenly become so central to the workings of the system. Everything in the graphical user interface was centered on it: Where was the mouse? Was a button pressed? Which one? Single- or double-click? It was an "event-driven" system, code that was constantly being interrupted by the user through the movement and clicking of the mouse, code that was *designed* to be interrupted by the user's intentions: here, now here, now here. The systems he was used to, in contrast, moved from instruction to instruction under the direction of the programmer's imagination—if this is true, go here; if not, go there. Now he had to rearrange his mind. He had to know how these interruptions were being generated, what happened to them as they percolated up from the mouse, through the mouse device-driver software, through SM's mouse routines, finally to reach his code. He had to understand the mouse.

And so he had written to the technical consultant at SM Corp., who wrote back in Chinglish. SM Corp., a company only a few years older than Telligentsia, was happy for Telligentsia's business and had assigned them a technical consultant for a few months to help them get started. After struggling on his own for months, afraid to admit to anyone how little sense the documented C-code samples made to him, Ethan had finally written to this consultant. A Chinese man, evidently. "If operator two time button press," Ethan read on, "and time is short time between defined in SM_mouse->BUTTONDOUBLE, signal is sent DOUBLECLICK and noted then DOUBLECLICK in SM_mouse->action. Important remember each press long time enough defined in SM_mouse->BUTTONTIME."

Soon, though, Ethan stopped noticing the plum blossoms, the bees in the lavender, the trebling radio, the rustle of the willow. Even the Chinglish began to take on a certain odd transparency. After the first mind-twisting page, the incomprehensible language disappeared, and he began to see into the design of the mouse: the rolling ball on the underside, whose motion indicated that the mouse was being moved. The device-driver software, a bit of low-level code from the mouse manufacturer, which read the state of the mouse buttons and sampled the movement of the mouse, taking snapshots, forty times per second, turning its continuous motion into a series of discrete moments—down one unit, up three, left two. Then software from SM Corp., which interpreted the mouse events to "place" the mouse on the surface of the graphical screen, turning the mouse's relative motion—up one unit—into a specific coordinate in pixels, screen picture elements. These were not the coarse-grained blocks of the alphanumeric characters Ethan was used to as screen coordinates, but tiny spots of light or dark, about a thousand of them strung across and down the face of the monitor. Finally, by the time Ethan's code knew where the mouse was and what button had been pressed, it had all been interleaved with input from the keyboard—key press, button click, mouse move—a series of human actions that had been so real and physical just a nanosecond ago, now turned into data structures, variables, concepts.

It all presented itself as a continuum: hardware at the bottom, with all its miniature mechanics and electronics, becoming at each step upward more abstract, becoming *software*. It produced in him a certain vertiginous pleasure—this glimpse into the slip-space between the hard and soft, the physical and mental worlds, layer upon layer of human thought turned into chips, circuit boards, programs. And it struck him, as it sometimes did these days, how briefly physical the computer was. All software on the top, then just a small layer where it was only dumb wire and plastic and silicon—beneath which everything immediately turned abstract again: the intelligence of the circuits, "logic gates" designed with software and etched into chips, through which moved the bits of stuff human beings had named "electrons."

The next time he looked up, he was surprised to see that a blue-white dusk had settled in. The plum blossoms, under the suddenly darkened sky, were almost luminescent, a pale cold white. Though the heat had lingered into the twilight, he suddenly felt cold. For a moment, he again thought of Joanna, the trip, Ostrick, Joanna's compact head disappearing in the crowded Jetway. Then he returned to where he was, in the yard, where everything around him was very still. The sky looked like a big reflecting lake. The house was dark. He went inside.

Three more meetings went by. Three more reports of schedule-slips and bug counts. And between meetings, the work: Ethan at his terminal for twelve hours a day, interrupted by a twenty-minute lunch taken in the basement cafeteria with Bill Steghman, lead programmer in the database group. They'd sit side by side on stools looking out into a dark corridor, eat a sandwich off a plastic tray, tell each other they were doing fine, then go back to their desks. For Steghman, company star, famous for a Ph.D. dissertation on memory management he'd written when he was twenty, that meant a private office, the only one afforded an engineer. For Ethan, it was the room he shared with Albert Herring and Bradley Thorne, six monitors, three tables heaped with manuals, and a sprawl of cables that groped their way across the floor. All of it under the cold stare of three banks of buzzing fluorescent lights, which Herring insisted they keep on.

The schedule haunted him. Ethan found no reassurance in being the only engineer in the company who was on time. Just the opposite. The closer he stayed to the committed dates, the worse the pressure felt, as if any fallback into normal lateness—into the average four-week lag time of his colleagues, into the unusual, intractable slip-zone in which all the programmers floated—would be a defeat, ignominious and unbearable. The schedule became something like a plane flight: a dam in time, a hard and unforgiving barrier, below which his sense of being alive was being reduced to a trickle.

Once each week, between the confessions and tensions of the group meetings, Ethan would go down the hall to Harry Minor's small office. There Harry would push aside the many office toys (a bright orange exercise ball, a set of water guns, a scooter, a bow and arrow, a wind-up dog, etc.), sit himself down cross-legged on the floor in his stocking feet (with great, huffing exertion), indicate that Ethan should do the same, then ask Ethan how his week had gone. Harry listened patiently to Ethan's accounts of arguments with Herring. He advised Ethan not to mind Bradley Thorne's silences. Above all, week by week, Harry said he hoped Ethan would learn to be more diplomatic in his dealings with his colleagues. "You're often right!" Harry once told him. "If only you didn't make everyone so mad, you'd even prevail sometimes!"

Evenings at home became orgies of reading, coding, debugging. With Joanna gone, the notion of dinner disappeared from his life. When he remembered to eat, it was pasta or eggs, and dishes left piling up in the sink. He stopped washing clothes; he quit shaving. He never turned on the stereo, not even to listen to the music he and Joanna had once enjoyed together, Schoenberg, Bartók, Shostakovich, Copland. Since starting at Telligentsia, he found that music bothered him, interfered with his thinking somehow, broke the chains of logic he had to work so hard to keep straight in his head. And now he was glad to have the house to himself, and have it quiet. Each night, he dialed in to the system at work then stayed at the keyboard until his back ached. Then he fell asleep surrounded by manuals and awoke in his rumpled clothes, the light still on, a book cradled in his arm, the stubble on his chin scratchy. He was at first surprised to find his beard coming in reddish but soon forgot about it. Twice, he called forth his simulated ecosystem out of the background of the machine, only to find again that nothing significant had happened. Despite his new code, his creatures weren't migrating to richer habitats; they remained in steady alternation with their current islands, creatures dying, habitats regrowing, creatures multiplying and dying again. Impatient, he sent them all into the background again, back into the innards of the machine, where he didn't have to think about them for a while.

Then the next morning he was back in the office: Bradley Thorne sitting silent with his back to the room, typing at a mad rate, his arms straight out like a race car driver's, prodigiously churning out code. Herring muttering, cursing at Ethan's design under his breath as he programmed. Overhead, the fluorescent lights buzzing. And the schedule—that dam—pressing against the rush of time.

Only once did he find some relief. Near the end of this three-week period, as Ethan was reaching across his desk to close the blinds, he knocked over the pile of things that tended to collect themselves in the right-hand corner of his desk. Files, reports, technical magazines, clippings, bits of cables—mystery things he wasn't sure what to do with—went sprawling onto the floor.

Ethan was about to bend over to pick up the fallen pile when something stopped him: a single sheet of paper still left on the corner of the desk, a drawing of a screen. Ethan remembered it instantly: it was the first one Harry had sketched for him, eight months ago, when he described to Ethan his ideas for the user interface. "*Bing!*" Harry had said, leaving marker points on the drawing, showing how the user could click here or here, on this icon or that menu. "Bing, bing, ka-ching!" he'd gone on happily, making the blue smudgy dots that still dimpled the paper.

Slowly, Ethan became aware that he should look over his left shoulder. And abruptly he turned, to the big eye of the graphics terminal. And there in its flickering gaze was the same screen, the one Harry had sketched eight months ago, the same icons and menus and places to go *bing*. Only now it was real. Paper lines turned into phosphor-glowing pixels. Ink dots become functioning icons and menus and buttons.

A light sweat spread across his chest, a rush of heat it took him a moment to recognize as pleasure. He looked from the screen to the paper, the paper back to the screen, and was aware of himself sitting in the middle, between them, the means whereby one had become the other. The press of the schedule eased. Herring's mutterings faded. The buzz of the lights silenced themselves. You are doing it, said a little voice in his head. You are building the system. *From nothing*, he thought. *From scratch.*

He printed an image of the screen, then pinned both sheets of paper—the original drawing, its completion in the screen image—over his desk where he would see them every day. To remind himself: that he was doing it, he was building the system. In only eight months, under his hand, it had already changed state, become actual, functioning, real. From Harry's head to Ethan's running code: thought that *worked*.

He stayed late that night, working without pressure or weariness, then stopped at what seemed a good place: something done, completed, checked off the list on the whiteboard behind him. Then a stretch. A walk through the empty office to his car at the lonely far end of the lot, the air visible in the searchlight intensity of the building's outdoor lighting. A drive home on mental autopilot. Then sorting through the mail in mindless mode. Junk, junk, bill, junk, bill, magazine, junk.

His first reaction was that some printing error had smeared yellow ink across the advertising circular he was about to throw away. He wouldn't have noticed it at all if not for that flash of garish yellow. Still, despite the intrusive color, his brain automatically interpreted it as something he should ignore: printing error, ink smear, toss it.

But before he got to the next piece of mail in the stack, there was this tiny *tick* as whatever it was hit the floor. And he turned to look at what was lying there. A postcard. Bright yellow. A picture of a temple with gold-ornamented spires.

It took a full thirty seconds for it all to resolve in his mind. Why was this picture of an Indian temple folded into an ad for television sets? It must be something intended for his neighbors around the corner. That cabdriver, that Indian fellow Joanna had gotten to know, and his wife who had been born a maharani, if Ethan believed it. He even pictured the supposed maharani's face: eyes outlined in dark chalky stuff, cheekbones like knife edges, slicky shiny hair drawn back into a braid down her back.

But slowly, sluggishly, another line of thought threaded its way through his consciousness: Gold. Temple. India. *Joanna.*

He stood up with a start. *Joanna!* It wasn't until that moment, the too-bright yellow still vibrating in his eyes, that he realized he hadn't thought about her since the day she left. He stood staring at the postcard on the floor, panic beginning to take hold in him. How long had it been since she left? It couldn't be that long, could it? Surely not long enough for this postcard to have found its way here from halfway around the globe! A few days, a week, he thought, two at most. He glanced over at the newspaper he'd picked up from the porch, the one he had no time to read these days: March 26, it said. He calculated: three weeks. Exactly three weeks.

He bent down and picked up the postcard. Inset into the photograph of the temple were what seemed to be pictures of the building's details. A pillar with a carving of a woman with a round, protruding belly and breasts like circles drawn with a compass. A statue of the many-armed god Shiva, fucking.

He turned it over. In Joanna's neat, printlike handwriting it said that she was writing this from a rooftop, where she and Ostrick were sleeping outside in the heat. Then, taking up a large space right above the greeting, was a sentence he read over and over, trying to make it resolve in his mind.

It said, "I hope you're also enjoying your time away from me."

I hope you're also . . . also enjoying . . . your time away from me.

Also. Also to *what*?

Also to her enjoying her time away from *him.*

His heart went a little skittery. He suddenly felt light-headed, as if someone had pumped helium into him. Something like embarrassment came over him; or was it shame? He should have missed her, he thought. He should have thought of her, wondered where she was, what she was doing. Maybe he should have sent a card to her, to one of the hotels on the itinerary she had so carefully prepared for him. Joanna had mentioned how to do it: "Hold for arrival," you're supposed to put on the envelope, she'd said. Maybe he should have done that, sent something to be held for her arrival.

He propped the postcard against the side of the counter. The fucking god looked back at him, the woman with breasts like compass circles. "She'll be home in a week," he found himself saying out loud. Just a week, repeated silently in his head.

Then he went upstairs to his study, where he dialed up and logged in to the office system. Just a week to get things done, he thought, a week to get a little ahead of schedule before she comes back. He worked until three in the morning. And he fell asleep as he had every night since Joanna's departure: in his clothes, with the light on, in the company of technical manuals.

The ringing phone woke him.

"You promised!" said the enthusiastic voice on the other end of the line.

"Hello?" Ethan mumbled into the phone.

"You promised! You promised you'd have dinner with me!"

"Who *is* this?" Ethan demanded, then recognized the voice. "Oh. Hi. Marsha." Marsha Ostrick. Shit. His head was mushy. His mouth felt like dried dough. "Jesus, Marsha. What time is it?"

"I'll make it for seven."

"You called me at seven in the morning?"

"No, no. I meant the reservation. I'll make it for seven tonight."

"I mean what the hell time is it *now*?"

"Ten."

"Ten! Shit. I have to go. I have a meeting."

"Go. Run. I'll see you at seven. The Chinese place on Grand."

And so, having no time to make up a story that would get him out of the dinner, he went.

Marsha was already in the restaurant when Ethan got there. "You're only half an hour late!" she thrilled. He gave her the obligatory hug, giving her his cheek to avoid the puckered mouth she always directed right at his lips. Then she sat down with a great bustle, arranging her big body in the skimpy chair, jingling her bangle bracelets, adjusting the yards of cloth she used to cover up her weight, as Joanna had once explained, but which only succeeded, as far as Ethan was concerned, in making her look like a walking tent. He'd tried to like Marsha. He could see that she was a warm and well-meaning person. But her constant fussing annoyed him, her jingling and bangling and shuffling. She talked too fast, he thought, and she filled in all the quiet spaces with chatter. So he resigned himself to an inconsequential evening, sitting silently through the meal, uhm-ing and nodding at appropriate intervals.

His strategy worked well through the pot stickers and hot-and-sour soup. And was still working fine when the moo shu arrived—ordered with pork this time because Paul wasn't there. It wasn't until they were on their second pancakes, both of them reaching at the same time for the plum sauce, when Marsha drew back her hand to let Ethan go first, and with her now free hand reached into the purse slung on the back of her chair.

"Oh! I meant to show you!" she said. "I finally heard from Paul."

Ethan could see the color coming at him before he took in anything else about the object Marsha was withdrawing from her purse. It was that same yellow. That same sense of smear and excess. He knew before Marsha even extended it toward him that it would be that postcard of the temple, the picture and the two inset photos, the woman and the fucking god, in the city where Joanna and Ostrick were sleeping outside on the roof. He felt himself go helium-headed again as he sat there, very still, his food a lump in his mouth he couldn't find his way to swallow.

"Shiva fucking, of course," Marsha was saying. "No one can resist Shiva fucking, can they?" And she laughed, too brightly, Ethan thought, but who could tell if the sense of alarm was coming from her or himself? Then she went prattling on. "Travel widows we are! Ha-ha. Too bad for us. Three weeks and only a postcard. Aren't you annoyed? I am. Oh, well. We wanted them to have a good time, didn't we? I don't suppose a month is a long time when you're that far away, now is it?"

And she kept going like that, posing questions to herself and answering them, brightly, brittlely, laughing a shrill little laugh every time she paused. Ethan knew he should stop her. He should tell her he'd gotten the same postcard and not to worry. But if he told Marsha about his card, it would somehow be too real: the scene of Joanna and Ostrick sitting side by side on the roof, about to sleep outside in the open air, each writing the same postcard home. It was all Ethan could do to stop himself from taking Marsha's card and turning it over to see if Ostrick had written, "I hope you're also enjoying your time away from me."

"They'll be back soon," Ethan said finally.

Marsha became still. "I miss Paul," she said in a quiet voice. Then there was a longer pause. After which she asked Ethan, "Do you miss Joanna?"

The question hung there. Then he answered: "Yes." Though he knew that, until the moment he'd read that postcard, it was a lie.

They got the bill, paid, walked outside to Marsha's car.

"Give me a hug," Marsha said, standing at the open door to her car, a dented old Volvo, holding her big arms open. Ethan looked at her, her yards of fabric now opened like the entrance to a tent, and he had a sudden horror of embracing her, as if a hug meant his entering into all the messy emotions folded up inside those yards of cloth and years of marriage. A truck came by. "Watch it!" he said, urging her into the car, closing the door on her.

"Thanks for calling!" he said through the door, backing away so she'd be sure to know he was leaving, she shouldn't lower her window for more chat, the night was over. *Toot, toot,* she answered with her horn, starting her engine and turning on her lights.

Ethan went to his own Honda Civic and sat there with the motor running, the windshield wipers going against the light drizzle that had started while they were having dinner. He suddenly didn't feel like going home. But he had no idea where people by themselves went at this hour of the night.

He went to work. Without exactly meaning to, he put himself on the freeway and kept driving past his house, continuing south to Fremont, parking his car in the vast lot in the middle of which floated Telligentsia's office building, hazy in the misty rain. He touched his badge to the door. The system flashed ENTER, ENTER on its red LED panel, then opened the door with a click.

It was dark inside but for a light in a back room, the night system administrator's office, he remembered, out of which came some kind of banging, clanking music. Ethan ignored it and went to his office, where a sudden odor of perfume met him at the door, rising out of the dark in a strong, sweetish wave. Odd, he thought, about the perfume, as he sat down behind his terminal, which showed the code he'd been working on, green letters on the black field of the screen.

```
/* Here you are, Ethan        */
/* Heuristics or mathematics? */
```

It was an algorithm he'd been working on, some way to speed up the workings of the user interface. He wanted to put some intelligence into it. When the user clicked or moved the mouse, the system told him its physical location, but he had to convert that into some logical thing on the screen—what window, button, icon, menu was the mouse on? He thought he might use heuristics, a few working rules of thumb, to help him guess where on the screen the user might be. Should he start looking in the top window, in the currently open menu, in the OK button? Or should he forget about what people were likely to do, and just stay with the mindless search he was already doing, top to bottom, left to right? It had all seemed so promising a few hours ago, but now the work looked stupid to him. And the green letters seemed to be swimming around in the dark—was his head full of MSG? That sound, what was it? Was the bass beat of the night administrator's music making its way all across the office? And the perfume smell—who'd come in here drenched in that too sweet, insistent smell?

He saved the file and closed it, then sat staring at the blank screen, the green prompt waiting, the cursor pulsing.

The bug report, he decided suddenly. He'd look at the bug report. He'd at least get one more thing done, something else accomplished, marked off a list. It was a level-one, wasn't it? He was obliged to examine it, fix it, even if Harry had advised him to wait until he had a core dump.

He picked up the report from the corner of his desk. "Slide mouse outside of open menu and freeze," said the summary. He started up the user interface, followed the directions on the report: He went to the screen, constructed the graphical query, clicked open the RUN menu, slid the mouse out of the menu. Now, he thought, the system should freeze up now. But nothing. Nothing happened. "Shit," he muttered, and did it all again: screen, query, click, slide, wait for the freeze-up.

Nothing. Everything working fine. "Asshole tester," he said. And then, annoyance rising, he did it all again. And again nothing.

A kind of rage moved through him. He picked up the first pen that came to hand—a thick red-orange marker—and scrawled "CANNOT REPRODUCE" in the programmer-response area of the bug report. Then in the line below he added, "Probable user error," underlining the word "user" in thick, angry strokes. The marker spread like fresh blood into the paper, which he found enormously satisfying. Fuck that tester. Why did she bring him this report when it was so clear there was nothing there? And he hated her boss, who shouldn't have even opened a number for it. UI-1017. Not a bug. They were idiots, all of them, incompetent.

He wasn't supposed to fill out the bug-status portion of the form. He was supposed to leave the whole bottom section blank. But—the music still pounding, the perfume smell insinuating itself into the room—he took hold of his marker and wrote "Bug should be closed!" in the status line, then watched as the letters bled themselves fat into the page.

A RETURN

If Ethan tried to return the bug report the next morning, he would not have found the person he called "that tester" at her desk. He would have been tired—1:10 A.M. was the hour listed on the bug report as the time of the programmer's response; yes, certainly he'd have been annoyed and tired. He would have wanted to hand the report to her personally, rub it in, wave the orange-bled paper in her face. But he would have been thwarted by the empty cubicle, the chair with memos piled on the seat, the yellow sticky on the monitor saying, "9:30–10:30. Back-end bug meeting. Wallis's office."

Where I would have been, surrounded by punning programmers. Trapped.

Eight programmers from the database group, six of us testers, my boss, Wallis Markham, all jammed into the cramped office out of which Wallis presided over the errors, faults, flaws, and disasters of Telligentsia's software universe. Her neat charts looked down on us from the walls—frequency of bugs per line of code, bug-counts by manager, number of bugs closed per month by programmer, programmer bug-count factored against severity level—clear and statistical evidence of programmer fallibility, despite their constant protestations that testers were technical idiots and they were always *right*. And outside the office, on a whiteboard for all passersby to see, a list in red marker of the most serious level-one bugs: a short description of each, the number of days it had been open, and in the middle column, in stand-out block letters, the name of the responsible programmer. "A little humility is a good thing in a programmer," Wallis was fond of saying.

Yet it did no good. Still they tortured us. *Punning.*

I would learn to be like Wallis, I decided, who sat there straight-backed in her desk chair wearing a superior, bemused, patient expression while she waited for this outbreak of programmer punning to subside. In her penny loafers, white button-down shirts, and the sort of slacks one could only call "trousers," Wallis exuded a kind of sturdiness and authority. She was in her midthirties, strongly built, wide and low to the ground, and in addition to her Ph.D. in anthropology from Harvard, she was known to have a black belt in kendo, the martial art where people wore medieval-looking padded cloaks and helmets and batted each other over the head with wooden swords.

It had all begun with an innocent remark—as it always does, of course. These punners prey on the innocent, the earnest, the one with serious intent. The meeting was almost over, we had nearly gotten through without a single pun-attack, and then came a simple question from Raisa Vastnov, Russian-Jewish émigré, a former professor of mathematics at a Kiev polytechnic institute, now a programmer working on indexing algorithms. She was a small, slim woman, and she'd asked her question in a small, slim voice, merely wanting to know the reaction of one Charles Glover, a programmer usually called Chuck, to several bugs originally ascribed to her but later reassigned to him.

"How much would Chuck admit to?" she innocently asked in her sweet voice.

But of course, as soon as "would" and "Chuck" were out, there was no escape.

"How much wood would a woodchuck chuck?" said Stan Morrow, senior engineer for file systems.

"If Chuck would chuck," from Chanjee Park, his colleague in data-file allocation.

"Oh, chuck it all," from Stan.

"I think that's 'fuck it all,' " from Chanjee.

"No, he ducks it all."

"Well, of course he ducks it. Chuck has no *steak* in it."

A groan from around the room.

"Chuck's steak was supposed to be well done but was—"

"Badly done."

"Hardly done. Hard to handle, that Chuck Glover, even with—"

"Kid *gloves!*"

"No *kid*ding."

Another groan.

"Even with gloves on, I wouldn't touch his code with a ten-foot piece of wood."

"Yeah, but would you touch his wood?"

"That's gross," said a voice behind me I couldn't place. "You're *pun*-ishing us!"

"*Meep!*" went Mara Margolies, cubicle neighbor of mine, who, though a tester, was a traitor in these matters of punning.

Say nothing, I commanded myself. If you show your annoyance, it will only inflame them. If you say, "Cut it out," they will simply find something in it, some sound of "cut it" or "it out"—my brain whirred to think where they would take this: shut it up? shoot it out? And then I had to command myself to stop having any thoughts whatsoever on the subject (an impossibility, of course), because in simply imagining their reaction, I was being drawn into it, this horrid, spinning mental game, this detestable, meaningless wordplay—parasite on the body of human communication.

My first reaction to programmer punning had been a certain curiosity. The reason for compulsive punning among computer people seemed interesting, ripe for study. Perhaps this would be my ticket to tenure, I thought. My time spent as a "quality-assurance engineer" would not be seen as falling away from academia but as . . . fieldwork! I would write papers. I would be invited to the next meeting of the Modern Language Association in San Francisco. There I would tell a learned but computer-illiterate audience how programmers had to work in the relentlessly literal language of code, where one slip of a letter reduced everything to incomprehensibility. The compiler, I would tell them, is a computer program that translates the programmer's code into a set of instructions that can be executed by the microprocessor, the chip at the heart of the machine. The compiler is the entity the programmer must talk to, the creature he or she must make understand the intentions embodied in the code. But this compiler-creature is error-intolerant to a fault; it demands a degree of exactness that is exhausting, painful for an intelligent human being. Leave out a comma, and the compiler halts, affronted at the slightest whiff of error. Fix the comma, run the compiler again, then it halts again, this time at a typo. Puns, I would say, represented a human being's pent-up need for ambiguity. That a word could signify two things at once! And these double meanings could be simultaneously understood! What a relief from the flat-line understanding of a programmer's conversation with the machine!

(People coming up to shake my hand. One of whom tells me about an opening at the University of X, for which I should apply immediately. I would be short-listed at once.)

But as my time at Telligentsia progressed, I began to see something more sinister in the programmers' penchant for puns. It wasn't an upwelling of humanistic impulses in the face of the mute machine; it wasn't a cry for the sweet confusion of being human. Quite the contrary, it was an act of disdain for the complicated interchange known as conversation: for its vagaries, lost and meandering trails, half-understandings, and mysterious clarities. For the meaning of a pun is clear, all too clear. It demands a leap in understanding, to the exact place the punner demands. It's the programming of a conversation. Like the GOTO instruction in code, it says, Go here, jump to this place, unconditionally. Forget about the person Chuck Glover, the desire to know something, Raisa Vastnov's hope for an answer to her question. Would. Chuck. How much wood. Duck. Fuck. A ricochet. A question goes out in a direction, to a listener, a potential answerer, then off it flies at some bizarre trajectory. To take a word at the level of sound, to feel absolutely free (and delighted!) to take that word anywhere language suggested, never mind the intention of the person talking to you—there is something fundamentally hostile in a pun.

"The answer to the question about Charles Glover," said Wallis Markham, her voice cutting into the punners' energy, "is that he has finally accepted all bug reports." She stared firmly at Stan and Chanjee, blinked several times, and said with an air of great satisfaction, "Charles Glover is well in hand."

"*Meep!*" went Mara again. And we all stood up, the meeting over.

As I made my way to my cubicle, I had one of the startled, queasy moments that sometimes came over me during my first years at Telligentsia. It was a feeling of displacement, the sense that I had landed in the middle of a newly forming planet where the laws of evolution were suddenly changed and unrecognizable. What was I doing surrounded by compulsive punners? By programmers who spent their time working in the cramped, stripped-down language of code? All around me, nothing but artificial languages: UNIX shell scripts and C programs and database queries asked in Structure Query Language—"impoverished languages" was the term I introduced to my students when I was a graduate teaching assistant. Artificial languages as poor human inventions stripped of history, usage, experience, connotation. All the dripping suggestiveness of language—gone. Around me an entirely new world was coming into being, and it was being made out of artificial, impoverished languages.

What a strange smiley-faced world we're building, I thought as I passed cubicle after cubicle, terminal after terminal, each screen covered with little pictograms, buttons and icons and symbols, a brand-new baby language the programmers were making up as they went along. It might have gone differently. A few poets at Xerox or Apple might have changed the state of the computing world. Even then, I kept hoping someone would come up with a better idea, some way to combine these little pictures with a simple command language, perhaps, alternative ways of telling the machine what you wanted it to do. Instead we were being flung into infancy, pointing like babies to get what we wanted. Were we going backward in time? Had human beings spent thousands of years of civilization getting to the wonderful, compact expressiveness of the alphabet—only to fly backward in an instant to the wild ambiguity of hieroglyphs?

"Will anyone know what this icon means?" Wallis Markham had asked one day. We were at a meeting, a demonstration of the new user interface, when she pointed to this symbol in the upper right-hand corner of the screen.

"Celtic cross?" Wallis said with a frown.

"Flag of the Knights Templar?" I hazarded with a grin.

But the responsible programmer—Ethan Levin—what did he know about Celtic Christians or the persecuted Crusader order of the Knights Templar?

"It's a navigation accelerator icon!" he protested. "Clear as day! If the user clicks the plus sign first, then an arrow, it takes them *farther* to the left, right, up or down."

"Eh heh," Wallis verbalized, showing her admirable talent at understatement.

"You're full of it," I stated, showing the complete lack of mine.

But what could we have to say about the matter? Wallis had a doctorate in anthropology from Harvard; I in linguistics from Yale. Why would anyone ask us about the way symbols acquired meaning? Why should we have had any influence on the design of the human-computer interface at Telligentsia, Inc.? We weren't *technical*, after all.

"The user focus group learned how to use it in a minute," Ethan Levin insisted.

"Oh, yes," Wallis answered in her sly, noncommittal way. "Human beings can get used to anything."

So there it was months later as I found my way back to my cubicle, on screen after screen: Celtic cross of the Knights Templar navigation accelerator icon, permanently settled into the upper right-hand corner of each and every window. Clear as day—hieroglyph of a new, confused, fascinating, but not quite authentic culture.

But if this world wasn't real, which one was? I thought as I sat down in my cubicle, two rows away from the nearest window. I thought about my friends, most of them still in academia in one way or another, all of them gone postmodern, giving up entirely on the notion of meaning. They had accepted the idea that any work was a mere collection of references to other works, and those to yet others, meaning ricocheting away like punners' intentions. Their research was about the cultural influences of sadomasochism, The Grateful Dead, and the Barbie doll—could those things possibly be more "real" than Ethan Levin's bizarre icon?

Oh, I should give it up, I knew. I was stuck in a nineteenth-century idea of the Real and the True, which I should confine to my journal writing and poetry scribbling. There I could indulge my tiresome need for the Essential and the Transcendent—for all those philosophical German words that began with capital letters—without bothering too many people about them. I'd been a student of James McCawley, the linguist who insisted on the study of meaning, not just syntax and structure. It had ruined my academic career, according to my dissertation advisor. "The future is in computational linguistics," he'd insisted, by which he'd meant the math of words, the formalism of language, the deduction of elemental parts of speech, like atom-splitting. When done well, the advisor insisted, computational linguistics would eventually eliminate the difference between natural and artificial language. You won't know if you're talking to a human being or a program, and you won't care. "You should go into computer speech-recognition research," the advisor had advised.

Yes, I should have, I thought as I stood up, feeling the need to get out of that warren of little cubicles. I should have seen that the future lay in functionality, in things *working* and *running*, in programs not in prose. I'd have gotten a grant, a position. I would not have gone from Yale to Berkeley to Hayward State, from there into a downward spiral of junior colleges, night schools, and adult ed, teaching Introduction to Linguistics again and again. Where I would have remained, vagabond scholar of the 1980s Ph.D. glut, if not for Wallis, academic who could outpun the punners, crossover artist who made a point of pulling others of our ilk across the line with her: we failed philosophers, cast-off classicists, sorrowing ex-sociologists, and poets manqués.

I sat back down. There was nowhere to go. A tiny, windowless break room that smelled like burned stale coffee. A hallway with a buzzing Coke machine.

Had Wallis really done me a favor by getting me hired? I remembered the day of my second interview, when she was walking me down the hall to meet the company president, William Harland. Harland had to meet all of Wallis's failed academics. "Bill's very skeptical about what he calls my 'little doctorates,' " Wallis explained as she led the way. "But don't worry," she went on, leaning close to my ear and whispering as if it were a dirty little secret, "Bill has one of those M.B.A.'s where they give you credit for *lifetime achievement.*"

He kept us waiting. A well-groomed man in a tastefully cut Glen-plaid suit, standing by the window as he talked on the phone. Slim but short, bland-faced. I wondered: What was there about this man that had inspired venture capitalists to hand him five million dollars?

After our five-minute wait at the doorway, he waved us inside to a group of armchairs around a little table. We chatted. He had a soothing, soft voice and the habit of nodding yes, no matter what he was saying. He asked where I grew up, went to college, graduate school. "Good school, Yale," said William Harland, nodding yes. "Yes," I said.

We discussed grades, honors, awards. "Phi Beta Kappa?" asked William Harland, nodding yes. "Yes," I said again.

Publications, syllabi, coursework. "Computational linguistics?" he asked.

"No," I said.

"Too bad."

"Yeah, that's what my dissertation advisor said."

A long silence. Then that excellently groomed man with a bland face leaned close to me and demonstrated exactly why people felt confident handing him money. "My concern," he said, his head going up and down in a short, compact stroke, "is that we'll train you, but you won't find this sort of work . . . satisfying."

He was right, of course. A little risk for him: that the company would invest time in me, teach me their impoverished, artificial languages, and then I'd leave. But I needed this job. My last hope for one last lectureship, one more round teaching Introduction to Linguistics, had just disappeared. It was this job or typing.

"I'm sure I'll find testing challenging," I lied.

William Harland eyed me slowly. Lifetime achievement, indeed; the man was no fool.

"I've always regretted not minoring in computer science," I lied yet more vividly.

Another silence. Finally he said: "Won't you miss your work in . . . ?" He looked down at my résumé.

"The linguistics of poetics," Wallis supplied.

"The linguistics of poetics," William Harland repeated. "Which is what? In a sentence or two."

In a sentence or two. Years of work in a couple of sentences. All right: I had to eat. "There is this idea that poetry somehow 'breaks' the rules of grammar. My work discussed the idea that the underlying language structures of poetics are the same as those used in so-called 'non-creative' prose."

The company president laughed. "You mean there's no difference between our user manuals and, say, William Butler Yeats?"

"Not at the level of deep structure, no. Language is an externalization of our thought processes. Any well-formed thought can find its expression in language, using the same grammar, the same rules."

"So what—"

"Meaning," I cut him off, anticipating the question. "The difference is meaning. Prosody. The emotional life expressed through the mental structures of language."

William Harland clasped his hands and looked down into his lap. Then he looked up and said: "You know, there won't be any use for all that once you start working here. Your job will be to test programs written by other people, period. At least for a year or two—that's it. Tell me," he said, beginning to nod again, "do you feel you've said all you need to say about the . . . what's it called . . . this linguistics of poetics? That you've decided you're done with it?"

I sat and gazed back at him as his yes-nods slowly came to a halt. Was that the purpose of those nods: to tell you how you must answer? For I saw there was no other reply I could make. I was supposed to say, Yes, I was done with it. That everything I'd cared about for the last ten years was a hopeless dead end. All those articles neatly listed on my résumé, all the talks at conferences, all the colloquia and symposia and everything else with Greek plural endings—over. The years I hung in there teaching the same course over and over, just to stay inside my profession somehow—why all that meant nothing, I was supposed to say, I was such a fool, what a waste. What was more, I was supposed to be grateful for the chance to leave it all behind, for a new start, even at the bottom.

"Yeah," I said. "I'm done. I suppose I've said everything I had to say on the subject anyway." Then I laughed without meaning to. "You know, the world hasn't exactly stopped in its tracks to listen to me."

William Harland studied me for a moment longer. He saw it: that I had no choice. And he came to his decision. "All right," he said, slapping his knees as he stood up. "Welcome aboard, Dr. Walton."

We smiled; we shook hands; Wallis and I left.

"Well," asked Wallis from across her desk back in her office. "What did you think?"

I didn't know Wallis very well then. I couldn't say how much I hated the company president's seeing how desperate I was. "It was . . . odd," I said.

"When you've come from academia, every single thing here seems odd," Wallis said. "Which particular type of 'odd' are you referring to?"

"How he wanted me to disown what I studied."

"Oh, yes," Wallis said. "The same thing happened to me at my first job. 'Did your fieldwork in Borneo? Not much computing there, dear!'"

I should have left it there. It might have been more pleasant for me. "Still," I said, "it was weird. I felt like he somehow wanted me to give up my Ph.D. To *renounce* it."

Wallis slid the job offer across the table.

I put my hand on the paper, still warm from the laser printer. Stock options, sick leave, vacation, more money in a year than I'd ever earned in four. At the bottom was Wallis's neat signature, and a blank line waiting for mine.

"Well," she said, extending a pen, a fat black fountain pen, its gold point shining in the light. "Isn't that rather what you're about to do?"

Ethan Levin was waiting for me in my cubicle.

"There's no bug here," he said.

I'd come back from a smoking break to find him there, rooting around on my desk. When he saw me, he dropped whatever he had hold of on the desk, reached into the back pocket of his jeans, and pulled out a wadded-up piece of paper—the bug report, which he slowly unfolded and passed in front of my eyes. "CANNOT REPRODUCE" was written in big orange-marker letters. And in the space for the programmer's action was written, "None. Bug should be closed!"

I went into the cubicle, sat at my desk, and gestured at the side chair, but he remained standing. "You mean UI-1017?" I asked, taking the report from him.

"Yeah," he said. "UI-1017. There's no bug."

"Well, I think there is. It may be that—"

"There's no bug. It can't be reproduced, so there's no bug."

"Have you even tried to reproduce it?"

"Yes. Tried. And no, cannot reproduce it."

"Well, I still think there's a serious bug there."

"Nope. No bug."

"I think—"

"Maybe you don't understand."

"I understand perfectly."

"You understand nothing. Until you can reproduce it, the presumption is it's your error. No bug. User error."

User error. Of course he'd say that. I put the report on my desk and smoothed it out several times as if I were petting it: that folded-up, rejected bug report.

Ethan Levin stood quietly for a moment. Then he put his hands in his pockets, wrinkled his nose, and said, "Have you been smoking?"

I didn't see as it was any of his business.

"No," I said.

"I can smell it. You've been *smoking.*"

The prig. "No," I repeated.

"I'm sure you have. I can—"

"Look," I cut him off. "Let's not argue. About this bug, what I think is, *Fugiunt suavia, molesta redeunt semper.*"

"What?"

"*Fugiunt suavia, molesta redeunt semper.*"

"Which means?"

"It's Latin."

"Which *means?*"

"Which *means* there's no sense worrying about it. Pleasure flees, trouble always returns. Which *means*, if there's a bug in there, don't worry, it'll come back."

It came back.

A week later, when I'd gone on to other fights with other programmers, the elusive freeze-up of the user interface returned.

It happened while I was in the middle of an argument with Bradley Thorne. I had come across a bug of his, some anomalous behavior in a window, nothing major, a level-three. "It's not my bug! Not my bug!" he was shouting. "It says right here it is!" I responded, holding up the printout of the code. "Created by Bradley Thorne," I read from the header. "Last mod Bradley Thorne." He squinted at the listing. Mara Margolies was his primary tester, and I had watched her go through this countless times with him: his terrifying forgetfulness, as if he had never before laid eyes upon this code. Thorne was famous for his "code production," lines of code written by the thousands, a prowess he had apparently achieved by not much bothering to remember what he'd typed. "This code can't possibly be responsible for that window!" he was shouting. "It says right on the header it is!" I was shouting back. When there came a "*Meep!*" then a hand holding a bug report rising over the top of the partition, after which came Mara Margolies's round, grinning face.

"You're going to love me," Mara said.

I read the report's summary. "Moved the mouse outside of an open menu, and the front end froze up."

"Oh, I do love you, Mara. I do." Thorne grabbed the listing and left.

Mara had been trying to reestablish a database connection. She'd clicked open the CONNECT menu, and then was about to select the last item down, RECONNECT, which was supposed to bring up a list of the most recent connections made under your user ID. A very stupid little screen. None of the convolutions of trying to represent my fifty-three nested queries inside queries with a graphical image endlessly scrolling off to the right. But otherwise, the resemblance could not just be coincidence. She'd clicked open the CONNECT menu, mistakenly slid past RECONNECT, and—characters strewn across the screen, endless beeping, keyboard nonresponsive, mouse dead.

Yes, here it was again: Ethan Levin's bug. There was something exhilarating in this bug's return. I'd been right; genius Smokey-the-Bear Levin had been wrong; and it would be utterly satisfying to point it out to him.

"Mind if this bug stays with me?" I asked.

"Not at all. You're his primary," said Mara, her face setting behind the partition.

"Where's the core?" I asked her over the wall.

"Shit. Didn't get one."

"What do you mean, you . . . ? Fuck. Levin will—"

"I panicked."

"How can you still panic! Haven't you seen enough . . . How . . . Fuck. Never mind."

UI-1017 had done it again, rushed out to scare the novice, then vanished. Mara's problem was like any beginner's, a deeply human response to this machine that presents itself as infallible: the quick, intimidated fear that whatever had gone wrong could only be the fault of the human being, whose nature is to err.

Wallis Markham raised an eyebrow at me. "Bad that there's no core yet."

I shrugged. "Mara."

"Mara," she echoed, imagining, as we all did, that we'd capture the core file next time. Then she reopened UI-1017, resuming its count of days open, and I walked the bug report down the hall to Ethan Levin.

"I told you, *Molesta redeunt semper*," I said. I held out the bug report. "It's back."

Ethan took the report, looked it over, and shrugged. So the bug was really there. So what. He'd fixed a nastier one yesterday, and there'd be another nasty one tomorrow. So this Latin-spouting tester was right—right, he hated to admit it—but still, her job was to find bugs, his job was to fix them, and everyone was only doing what they were supposed to do. "Okay. You've delivered it," he said. "So I have," she said. And there being nothing more for either of them to say, she left.

On his way out, Ethan saw Wallis Markham putting the bug on the level-one board outside her office. He still had no particular reason to take note of it; if he and the tester hadn't argued over the bug's existence, he probably would have had no recall of any of the events surrounding the bug's early appearances. But for some reason, Ethan stopped and watched as Wallis recorded it all in bright red letters. UI-1017. Slide mouse outside of open menu and freeze. Responsible programmer: LEVIN. Days open: 31.

AND ANOTHER

Debugging: what an odd word. As if "bugging" were the job of putting in bugs, and debugging the task of removing them. But no. The job of putting in bugs is called programming. A programmer writes some code and inevitably makes the mistakes that result in the malfunctions called bugs. Then, for some period of time, normally longer than the time it takes to design and write the code in the first place, the programmer tries to remove the mistakes. One by one: find a bug, fix it. Bug: supposedly named for an actual moth that found its way into an early computer, an insect invader attracted to the light of glowing vacuum tubes, a moth that flapped about in the circuitry and brought down a machine. But the term surely has an older, deeper origin. Fly in the ointment, shoo fly, bug-infested, bug-ridden, buggin' out, don't bug me—the whole human uneasiness with the vast, separate branch of evolution that produced the teeming creatures who outnumber us, plague us, and will likely survive our disappearance from the earth. Their mindless success humbles us. A parallel universe without reason. From the Welsh: a hobgoblin, a specter.

Ethan Levin had never encountered a bug that was anything like a specter. In his twelve years as a programmer, he had come to know debugging as nothing more than a normal part of his work. It began as soon as a piece of code got past the compiler—the program that translated his code into machine code, the instructions that could be understood by the microcircuitry of the chips. From the first easy bugs—the misplaced parentheses, missing brackets, counters not initialized to zero, ORs where there should be ANDs—to the deeper mistakes in design that meant a complete restructuring of the code, Ethan expected that the process of programming would be more or less equivalent to the process of debugging.

The first run of any program is laughable: a parody of the author's intentions, a slapstick mockery of logic. Objects solemnly appear on the screen only to disappear in a fritz. The cursor runs around like a clown. Every second mouse click or text entry is answered with nonsense. Characters run rampant across the screen; beeps sound without stopping. If the programmer is lucky, the program will crash at once rather than continuing on in that humiliating state of malfunction. Then, in the next round of coding, a few small bugs are fixed, and the program runs again, only a little less stupidly this time. And the entire process is repeated over and over again—a wild run, a crash, another round of bug fixing, then another barely improved run. Until, slowly, iteration by iteration, the true face of the program becomes visible. Programming is like sculpting: the image of the running program appears incrementally, chisel cut by chisel cut, a dumb block of wood imperceptibly carved into human designs.

So it was that Ethan knew that error was part of the process, inevitably. His problem was not to remove every error, but to remove the most serious errors he and the testers could find, knowing all the while that the process of finding errors was infinite. At some point the program would be declared "done"; it would be distributed to users around the world; but it would still be riddled with as-yet-undiscovered bugs. There was nothing to be done about it; this was just the way it was. The whole enterprise of computing—code embedded in the hardware, comprising the operating system, the network, the utility layers, the user interface, the final user-oriented application—was simply too complex for every last mistake to be found and fixed. The last bug would never come to light. There would only be reports of bug after bug after bug, appearing further and further apart in time in a limitless approach toward zero.

Then, just when it seemed that only the barest of bugs survived, there would be a new version of the software. And with that, a fresh opportunity for introducing bugs. And before those new bugs could be fixed, there would be another software version, then another, new bugs infecting the software like viruses picked up from a wet tissue. Meanwhile, the original programmers will have left, and their replacements—believing they understand the code—will make some truly spectacular errors, mistakes that will suddenly make everything completely stop working for a while. So that what had seemed to be a descending curve of bugs, a fall toward the ever-receding zero, will reveal itself as the shape of another equation altogether: a line relentlessly rising, bug-counts climbing in an endless battle against infinity.

For all these reasons, as Ethan Levin reached over for the bug report in the early afternoon of April 6, 1984, it was with a sense of utter normalcy: with the understanding that bugs were inevitable, everywhere, part of his job. And more: with the certainty that, while there would always be bugs in general, the cause of *this particular bug* would surely be found. For a bug always begins its life that way, as a creature of the programmer. It was a mistake, yes, a miscue, a slip of the mind; but *the programmer's* mistake, *his* slip, of *his* mind. If Ethan had taken any particular notice of what was going through his mind that day, he would have heard his usual internal conversation in which he told himself that this was merely the 1,017th bug in the user interface, 1,016 of which had already been fixed, with some untold number yet to come, each in turn to be fixed in good order.

He reached for the first bug report and reread the summary: "On screen VISUAL QUERY, click open menu RUN. Slide mouse outside of open menu and freeze." Then the second report: "On screen DATABASE, click open menu CONNECT. Slide mouse outside of open menu and freeze."

Immediately the underlying code came to him—the pyramid of routines, code calling code; Herring's that called Thorne's that called Ethan's; all finally resolving down to the operating system and the routines that managed the mouse, the disk, the peripherals, the network. If the bug appeared on two different screens, he reasoned, one programmed by Thorne and one by Herring, then the problem was not likely to be in any particular screen. No, it had to be in the code that supported all the screens—the routines responsible for the menus and the mouse, most of it Ethan's. Funny. That code had been out there for a long time, working. What was it about these particular steps that froze the system? Among all the possible pathways through the code, there was something in this one sequence of events that traveled a road no one had explored, a bad road evidently, one with program-death at the end.

How many paths were possible? Ethan tried to think his way through the permutations. The different operating systems the interface could run on; the variety of input devices; the types, sizes, and resolutions of the screens; then the particulars of the windows, their contents, icons, buttons, and the variations in the individual menus themselves—too many pathways to hold in his head. He'd designed it as a multidimensional matrix, and the cross-product of all the variables exploded. Three operating systems times four basic types of monitors, times two currently supported input devices, times twenty recognized screen resolutions, times thousands of individual variations in the appearance of icons and buttons and menus based on screen resolutions—hundreds of thousands of possible channels through the code, every run of the program potentially different from the one before, until each execution of the code approached a state of singularity. No, he couldn't possibly think his way through the many permutations. No human could. That's what machines were for.

Then, just as Ethan was about to start on the lengthy process of de-

bugging—that hunt for the one mistaken pathway through the code—
he was suddenly certain where to find the bug. All at once, he swept
away his hundreds of thousands of permutations (it was *his* code, after
all; naturally he could think his way to the heart of the matter, couldn't
he?) and he focused on a handful of routines responsible for the menus.
He watched the code roll through his mind like text scrolling on a
monitor. These routines were not complicated, he thought. They were
well structured. Working: they'd been working for months.

So what had changed? Code works for months and then suddenly
stops working: Something must have changed.

The answer came to him in a huge, head-clearing *Of course!* The
cause was simple, ridiculously simple. He'd been working on those routines in his attempts to speed up the workings of the user interface.
That night after the dinner with Marsha, the problem of heuristics or
mathematics—he'd closed up everything too quickly. He must have
put the wrong routine back into the code library. He could have con-
firmed this theory; he might have looked at the current version in the
source-code control system. But his certainty swept him away. The bug
had come back right then, on the very next day. Of course. All he had
to do now was rebuild the user-interface library. Then retest the two
screens. Which he did: Perfect. Working. Fixed.

Some part of Ethan's mind knew that not encountering the bug
right then was no assurance that the bug was indeed fixed. After all,
that tester couldn't reproduce it after she first found it, Ethan couldn't
reproduce it before, and he couldn't reproduce it now. And he also
knew that rebuilding a library was superstitious programmer behavior.
Everyone did it. Have a problem you can't find? Recompile and relink
the code, and hope the problem goes away. Like a ballplayer in a slump
who crosses himself before stepping into the batter's box, it was a ritu-
alized compulsion, a set of things you do over and over, things that may
not work, but you never know.

But he pushed these thoughts away. Ethan was still in the first
phase of debugging. He may have accepted the report of UI-1017,

since he'd had no choice, but deep inside him he was still convinced there was no bug. It was a user error, something wrong in the network, a glitch on the line, an out-of-date library, something else, but not a bug in his code. The stage every programmer with an unsolved bug clings to as long as possible: denial.

He picked up the bug reports. In the section for the programmer finding, he wrote, "UI library inconsistency." In the part for programmer action, he wrote, "Rebuilt library." And where it asked for programmer outcome, he wrote, "Fixed."

Of course he was late. Joanna's plane was supposed to arrive at five-fifteen, and here it was already five with Ethan still looking for a parking spot in the garage. What stupidity had made them pick a Friday-night arrival! The freeway was a mess, he'd inched along just to get a ticket to enter the short-term parking area, and now the garage lane markers infuriated him. Exit Only. Left Turn. One Way, One Way, Wrong Way. He was supposed to park in D-Area, but as he searched and turned and became enmeshed in the tangle of one-way lanes, he saw D-Area's red signs receding behind him in the rearview mirror. And soon he was in E-Area, with blue signs. Then in F, green. Then H, yellow. Compacts Only, said the sign, and a big minivan had stuffed itself in anyway, leaving only a sliver of a spot next to it. Cursing, nearly slicing off the van's sideview mirror, Ethan pulled in, locked the door, ran for the elevators.

Delayed. Now of course their flight would have to be delayed, he thought. He stood there sweating from his run across the airport, looking up at the monitor in the international arrivals terminal, thinking how much easier it would have been if they'd gone through customs in New York, as they had on their outbound leg. He could have just picked them up at the curb. No waiting around at customs. No need to park, race up to the terminal, worry. Only to find the flight late. Fifty minutes, the monitor indicated. What would he do with fifty minutes? In this jittery place, where people rushed around nervously, then waited?

Waiting: he sat staring into the giant fishbowl of international arrivals. From a mezzanine level, behind glass walls, he waited with everyone else, looking down into the luggage carousels and customs area on the floor below, into which moved great clumps of people as they arrived planeload by planeload. The people above, spotting their friends and family, jumped up and down, knocked on the glass, tried to get their attention, but Ethan could see it was useless: the arrivees were too tired, too jet-lagged and hassled, even to look up. They had the dazed look of people displaced in time. It was all they could do to find their baggage, load a cart, wheel it off toward the customs inspectors, who were just out of view from the mezzanine. Each time a cart rolled out of sight, a group of waiting people raced for the down escalator to meet their friends at the exit from the customs area. Then, between planeloads, long lulls, the hall below empty, the people above sparse, the ones still there bored, staring into space, waiting.

Ethan felt his annoyance growing. The benches lining the glass wall, the only places to sit, were tiled, hard, backless. He was bored and edgy, and he began cycling around assigning blame for his discomfort. It was Joanna's fault for coming in on a Friday. It was his own for not checking the actual arrival time before he left the office. It was Harry Minor's for talking him out of bringing a manual to read while he waited. "You're taking the terminfo guide to pick up your sweetie at the airport?" Harry had asked him, seeing the binder Ethan was about to tuck under his arm. "Sure," Ethan had shrugged, "what's wrong with that?" To which Harry had replied with a shake of his head. "Jeesh, Levin. Give it a rest." He wouldn't be bored now if he'd brought the manual, Ethan thought. He could look into that little problem with the function keys. Time would go by, not like this feeling of infinity that had begun to take hold of him. He looked at the clock: barely two minutes had passed. He got up and looked at the monitor: forty-eight minutes still to go.

When all at once, as he sat back down on his hard bench, a succession of images came to him. A manual, in a ring binder. Joanna, tossing it onto his car seat, that day he took her to the airport. Himself, sitting with an e-mail in the yard as the petals fell. Then Joanna's face as she disappeared down the Jetway. Then the postcard that came last week, the woman on it with the round breasts. Finally Marsha, her arms open, trying to take him into her big tent of a body. He stood up. Looked around. Sat down, relieved. He had a certain horror of running into Marsha here, he realized. He wanted to be alone when Joanna arrived. He did not want to be drawn into Marsha's anxiety, her fussing and worry. Everything was fine, he told himself. Fine. He looked at the clock: forty-seven minutes to go.

He reached into his shirt pocket, took out a pen and one of the index cards he always carried there. He'd think about the function-key problem, he decided. The only way to make time disappear was as he always did: by letting his thoughts expand into the open space. He began jotting tiny characters, pseudo-code jammed onto the card.

```
until (last character in string)
      keystring = keystring : current character.
search sorted terminfo database for keystring match.
if (no match)
      no op?? fallback to standard command set?? which??
```

He filled the card, then the back, then another. Meanwhile, as Ethan's hands became inky and his mind stepped character by character through the function-key strings, the hall below him filled and emptied, filled and emptied, filled and emptied again. Until the next thing Ethan knew, he looked up from his cards, and there, below him, were Joanna and Ostrick.

They look like hippies, is his first thought. Ostrick is in some sort of puffy shirt, Joanna is wearing a flowing skirt, and they seem to be trailing yards of cloth from everywhere. Her blouse is orange, hard bright orange, garish and blaring like the yellow on the postcard, and it flashes at Ethan like a searchlight. They seem to be confused, looking this way and that, carousel to carousel, trying to locate their bags. Then, before Ethan can start knocking on the glass (it's a stupid thing to do but irresistible, he now realizes, rising to his feet and already forming a fist), something happens. Ostrick's arm rises from his side, and his hand lightly touches the underside of Joanna's arm. It's naked, her arm, bare in the sleeveless orange blouse, soft and rounded and naked—and Ostrick just barely touches its underside with the tips of his fingers. And as he does, Joanna's entire body responds. Ostrick has seen their luggage, he's touched her lightly to direct her; and without a moment's resistance—she doesn't look over at him, doesn't say anything to him—her whole body turns and goes in the direction of that touch.

Ethan stands there looking at them through the glass. He simply stands there, watching them move together like two fish in a school, turning and turning with an unspoken agreement that's coming from somewhere deep in their bodies. The thought comes to him with uncanny clarity: they've slept together. As they continue to float together right there before his eyes, he knows it in a way he has never known anything else before: Joanna and Ostrick have been lovers.

He finds himself downstairs at the exit to the customs area. He doesn't know how he got there, has no recall of turning away from the glass, walking, taking the escalator, yet there he is, in the crush of people pressing forward each time the doors swing open and someone with a cart comes wheeling out. Then Joanna's blouse finds him, hits him in the eye with its color.

"Paul! Paulie! Paul!" shrieks a voice at his ear, and then Marsha Ostrick is in front of him, her big body cutting him off from Joanna. (Where has Marsha been? he wonders. Down here all the time?) "Paulie, Paulie!" she keeps shrieking, even though she now has Ostrick enclosed in a huge, enfolding embrace. (*Paulie?* Ethan thinks involuntarily. He can't imagine Paul Ostrick as *Paulie*.) Then Joanna is visible again: the soft brown eyes he knows so well, brown downy hair, scrubbed-skin face.

"Air!" she is saying. "I need some air!" she repeats, pointing to the exit behind him. "Let's get to the curb!"

And despite the press of people behind him, Ethan turns and starts parting the crowd to make way for their cart—they *shared* one, he thinks without wanting to; why didn't Joanna get her *own*?—and in the next moment the automatic doors fall open and all four of them are outside on the sidewalk.

"Do you still have my carry-on?" Ostrick asks Joanna.

"Here," says Joanna, reaching over and handing him a small green satchel.

Ethan still has not gotten close to Joanna, and he makes his way around the formidable presence of Marsha to approach her. "Oh, this air feels so good!" Joanna says before he can reach her. She's holding her face away from him, out and up to the sky, which is already dark and glowing reddish in the lights of the city. "Ethan," she says before he can get to her, "do you think you could get the car and bring it around to the curb so I can breathe some *real air* for a while?"

The air is foul, Ethan thinks, thick with car exhaust trapped in the small space between the terminal and the parking garage across the way. And then there's the matter of his car being so far away.

"I'll be a while," he says noncommitally.

"Oh, I don't mind," Joanna says, stopping there, her face still turned away from him.

"Sure," he says, not knowing what else to say.

As he turns to go, he sees that Paul Ostrick has what looks like a cigarette in his mouth, and that his hands are cupped around a match.

"You're *smoking*?" Ethan asks. "You went to India to take up *smoking*?"

Ostrick lights the match, then the cigarette, inhaling once, twice. He blows out a mouthful of smoke. "Oh, I'm not *smoking*," he says, his head still tilted upward in the direction of his smoke. "It's an Indian beedi, a clove cigarette. It's *natural*" is the last thing Ethan hears as he walks away.

THE BUG

Natural, Ethan thinks with disdain as he walks, walks, walks across the airport. *Natural*, he thinks as he finds his car, opens the door, eases out of the slot still crowded by the minivan. He finds the parking exit, pays, negotiates his way around the airport, all the while his heart full of hatred.

Marsha and Paul are gone by the time he gets back to the curb. Good, he thinks. He couldn't stand the sight of Paul Ostrick right now, in his hippie clothes, with his stinky beedi. He pops the trunk, and before he can get out of the car, Joanna has loaded her suitcase and jumped in. "Shit, I'm wiped out," she says as she settles into the passenger's seat.

And then they are on the freeway, heading home.

Silence. Ethan is afraid to break the silence. Joanna mumbles again that she is wiped, tired, desperate for air. She rolls down her window, all the way to the bottom, and then they sit there without talking: in the car filled with the roar of trucks, the buffeting of the wind.

At home, all Ethan can think is that they must make love. *Must.* It is the one way he knows how to reach her, tell her what he otherwise feels too stupid and bumbling to say. Sex: their one effortless, reliable connection. Joanna never just lying there like some women he'd known, waiting to be touched in some mysterious, particular right way, but somehow coming to him self-started, ready, responsible for her own arousal. And his response always as ready as hers: to those muscular bicyclist's legs with their soft fuzz of unshaved hair, to that sturdy body that smelled of camomile soap and Tom's of Maine's Natural Clay Deodorant and sweat.

But something is wrong. As he takes her around and waits for the dependable sensations to overtake them both, he is suddenly aware that everything is changed. It's her smell. Something is wrong with her smell. There's no scent of camomile, no spearmint, no familiar, pleasing mix of sweat. His nose nuzzled into her neck is picking up something acrid and dark, foreign. He struggles against it, tries not to notice, but against his will the smell clearly names itself to him.

"Cloves!" he says aloud without meaning to. "You smell like cloves!"

"No, no!" she protests at once. "No, I don't. I don't smell like cloves!"

It's her immediate denial that makes it so bad, the way she has tensed up, drawn back. If she'd only laughed or said, Isn't it awful? Or, It's Paul's damn beedis. But her denial—absurd, reflexive—makes it all too clear.

He rolls onto his back, crosses his arms over his chest. "You slept with him," he says.

Not a question. A statement. "Yes," she says without hesitation.

The quiet in the room grows huge. He can hear a car turn the corner, the hum of its engine slowly fade away. He can hear his own breath, as he lies there, watching his arms move up and down on his chest with his breathing. Just watching. Up and down. As if he had nothing to do with the part of him that was gasping for air.

"And what now?" he says finally.

Now silence.

The quiet grows huge and heavy again, like a dark heavy blanket that might smother him. "Look," he says, rushing in to do something, say something, make noise. "I know how these things can happen when you're traveling. I'm not a prude. It happened to me with Barbara before we met—remember? I told you? The stress. You're together. Close quarters and all. And the beggars, I know there were lots of beggars. And disease. And the heat." He knows he's rambling, but he can't stop himself. This is what he wants to hear. This is what he wants her to tell him: just travel, nothing in particular to do with him or Joanna or Ostrick, just bodies in motion, drawn to one another by forces as impersonal as the laws of physics.

More silence. "I think it was situational," she says at last.

"So it's over?"

"He's married, I'm with you, it's over."

He thinks he should probably look into her eyes. He should study her, read her face, see how exactly she means this. But no, he can't bring himself to. He decides, lying there with his eyes closed, to believe her.

Suddenly, improbably, he is hard. He can hardly believe what's happening to his body, but he has a sudden need to make love to her, penetrate her, fuck her. It's rote, hard lovemaking he's wanting, and to his surprise she wants the same. So they both drive at one another—eyes-closed, teeth-gritting sex—as if the heat of their intentions will somehow burn away what's happened. It's a decision, a determination of fact as they decide to know it: Whatever was broken, fixed. Just a trip, a situation, over.

PART TWO

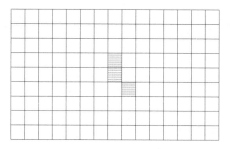

*Invention, it must be humbly admitted, does not consist in
creating out of the void, but out of chaos. . . .*

—MARY SHELLEY, AUTHOR'S INTRODUCTION TO
FRANKENSTEIN

A MILESTONE

"You knew it had to happen sometime," says the businessman on the leatherette sofa.

"Inevitable," says the one on the armchair drinking a scotch at 11 A.M.

A third sits next to me. "Nasdaq eventually down to 2,300 I think," he says.

They all laugh. The index is now at 3,500. Three weeks ago it was over 5,000. "So you're short in the market, right?" says the man with the scotch.

We are in the international business-class lounge at JFK, seated before a large-screen TV, CNN displaying the breathtaking fall of the United States stock markets. Today is April 14, 2000, and my money manager told me it would happen just like this: on a Friday, a drop with no hope of salvation on the way down, like 1920s financiers jumping out of windows. Down twenty, down fifty, down a hundred—we watch the indexes fall like the altimeters of crashing planes.

The three gentlemen in business-casual attire, cell phones clipped to their belts, are showing remarkable equanimity in the face of this unfolding calamity, as are the other inhabitants of the United Airlines business-class lounge. But of course nothing has changed yet; it's still possible to convince yourself it will all bounce back again, as it did ten days ago, when the Nasdaq sailed terrifyingly down through 574 points before coming back most of the way. Besides, everything still looks so normal: The sideboard with its heaping trays of bagels and pastries. The tea and coffee service kept assiduously clean by a roving staff of busmen and women. The neatly arranged piles of complimentary *Wall Street Journals* (still ignorant of what is happening before our eyes). It is a cool, gray space, reassuringly similar to business offices and lounges around the world, a Holiday Inn sort of motive: the same wherever you go. Along one wall, the fax machines hum industriously as they do everywhere. Rows of laptops still sing their little musical modem songs.

It's usually delightful to pass time in the business-class lounge. I love being greeted by the attractive, professional women at the reception desk—not too young, these women who mind the biz- and first-class lounges, late thirties, early forties. To gain admittance, you must first show your ticket, and they never flinch when your ticket betrays you (as mine does) as an upgrader, someone promoted to business class on miles, not the real, your-company-paid-hard-money business flyer. Or perhaps they do. Maybe they do subtly withhold favors—how would I know? Why should I care? I feel queenly as they tap my name and flight number into their special computers, so they can call my name just before the business-class passengers are about to board, no need to crowd the gate with all the economy flyers. "Have a good day, Ms. Walton," said one Diana Wilcovsky, handing me back my ticket after I presented myself this morning. "*Love* your blouse," I said to her as I took the folder in hand. "And I *love* your glasses," said she. Such exchanges of female compliments are required for the solitary woman traveler. Otherwise, these women who really control your life in the air, able to make it miserable or marvelous, will concentrate on the men, look through you, forget you. We smiled. She touched a hidden button. The frosted-glass door panels behind her, with a *shush* like the doors on the Starship *Enterprise,* slipped open to admit me.

It is perhaps only at the drinks counter that I can sense the change in atmosphere today. The tall woman posted there—wonderful haircut, I think as I look over at her, a remarkable shiny helmet of a bob— is being kept busy pouring free mimosas and bloody Marys and screwdrivers and the occasional scotch. "Watch my things?" I ask the businessmen as I go off for a vodka of my own.

"*Love* your hair." "And I *love* your necklace. Lisa Jenks?" "Mexican." "Beautiful!"

"Grey Goose?" she smiles, reaching down to a little cupboard with a hidden stash of premium vodka. "Ice? Olives?" "How nice." No, I'm not short in the market. I didn't take my manager's advice. I'm long, heavy into tech, betting (against all reason) that overvalued stocks will continue to go up.

"I can just hear the talking heads on *The Nightly Business Report* tonight," says scotch-drinker as I rejoin the business buddies by the TV screen.

"Yeah," says opposite-sofa. "Everyone will say they saw it coming."

"And did they advise everyone to sell all those Internet phantoms?" scotch-drinker says.

"No!" says the one next to me.

"No!" says scotch-drinker.

"No!" says opposite-sofa.

Then they all laugh, a too-large laugh, their eyes sliding over between "ha"s to get a look at the screen, which shows the Nasdaq down another ten, ten more, another fifty. The one next to me suddenly stands and finds his collar needs adjusting. Opposite-sofa runs his hands through his thinning hair. Scotch-man drains his glass. I'm guessing we're all in the same boat: still denying to ourselves this is really happening, watching our wealth disappear.

One time, in an instant two years ago, the thought crossed my mind that I could stop working, possibly forever. I was a consultant by then. I went around advising new companies on how to set up quality-assurance departments. That day I was visiting a new client, an Internet start-up. I met with the president and two of his managers—trim, clean-shaven men in their midthirties, all wearing khakis and polo shirts with the company logo (which looked to me like a spider) over the left nipple. We talked for about ten minutes, and then the president looked at his watch and said, "Why don't we finish negotiating your contract over lunch." I envisioned pink tablecloths and chardonnay, a waiter quietly stepping his way around us, the president and managers sending each other secret messages by radio frequency on their Palm Pilots.

We drove a short way from the company's offices in a suburban office park to a nearby strip mall. I followed them across the parking lot. The president, as it turned out, was taking us to Wendy's, where they all ate hamburgers, which were square, of course, not round, and drank Diet Cokes through straws in enormous paper cups. There was a heavy smell of grease. Their hamburgers oozed blood and ketchup. And then between bites the president asked me, "Will you trade hourly pay for stock? We'll give you ten options for every ten dollars per hour you knock off your price."

It was then that the thought of never working again crossed my mind. Through the grease smell and Coke-slurp, it came quite clearly: You don't really need any more dollars per hour. You can say no to everything. You can say no to everything for the rest of your life.

"Yes," I said, because I had made this deal as a consultant several times before, and it was the right thing to say. Take the stock. A reflex: "Stock options instead of dollars. Yes, of course."

I drove home in a state of strange light-headedness, as if I were hyperventilating. This would be my seventh start-up company: Telligentsia, then the company that did "data mining," then five more as a consultant. My seventh set of stock options, seventh bet on a company going public, maybe to be successful like three of them. But still: exactly how much money does a person need to give up working? I read once it would take ten million. *Ten million dollars.* Even if I could accumulate that enormous sum of money, what exactly did that cover? Illness, medical bills, stock market crashes—it's simply not possible that a life avoids misfortunes. What if I planned to live to eighty and kept on until ninety-five and ran out of money? How long would I live anyway? I looked at my hands on the steering wheel. Knobby knuckles. Thumbs already deforming. Mortality. That was the idea that killed the thought of not working. Like any normal person, at the mere whiff of mortality I immediately retreated into denial.

So I avoided thinking about stopping working. But the idea, even as I let it shiver through me and (I thought) out of me, established itself like some viral colony that hides out in obscure tissue and bides its time.

The symptoms of idleness revealed themselves slowly. As the end of the contract with the spider-logo company drew near, I did nothing to try to extend it. Then I did nothing to actively look for a new contract. When prospective clients called me, I quoted them ridiculously high rates, and was disappointed when they said yes. I stopped being obsequious at meetings, then I gave up politeness altogether, but this only served to make clients consider me more valuable, since my gruffness and impatience seemed to make them think I was some sort of genius.

The end came with two short contracts. At a meeting with Company One, I quarreled with the manager, then I said to her, "Do you want to build a piece of junk or do you want to work with me?" At Company Two, a start-up running software over the World Wide Web, the twenty-something president informed me that the notion of quality assurance "was so over" since Web users told them instantly about anything that was wrong and the programmers could fix it right away, anytime.

"You mean you don't stage the software?" I asked him. "You don't test it?"

"Why should we? Everything we do is live all the time, always new, minute by minute. This is the Web! Code it, post it, run it, change it, run it again."

"Don't you make any distinction between development and production code?"

"Production code!" He laughed at me. "What a mainframe idea. We don't have ancient ideas like software releases and versions, you know."

I stared at the young little president: cool eyewear, eyebrow pierced with a tiny silver ring, lock of hair stained blue. He imagined he had just invented the world, as the young are supposed to do. But usually we don't let them run things while they're still in that state.

"You're an idiot," I said.

I never actually made the decision to stop working. For a year after my meeting with the idiot, I told people I was "between contracts." Then, over the next year, the state of between-ness somehow became permanent. I did volunteer work for a group that helps nonprofits with computing problems, but gradually a sort of miasmatic depression took me over, a dreary kind of fog in which it became harder and harder to do anything at all. When you're working and hurrying to the laundry before it closes, it seems that having all the time in the world will be glorious. But then, suddenly without the structures of a job, why get up at any particular hour? Why get to sleep? It takes great internal discipline, I found, to make up each and every day for yourself. I began to tumble around in time. I went to movies in the morning. I drank in the afternoon. I began going out to dinner with friends every night. There are three or four very good restaurants in town that have come to consider me a regular. No longer having an office to go to, no place to offer the sort of formal friendliness business acquaintances give you, I found in these restaurants a substitute impersonal solace: the welcome at the reception stand, the satisfaction of being seated ahead of everyone with reservations, being treated as if I'd come home. It's possible that those places have indeed become what I can count on as home.

Whatever guilt I felt at my extended idleness (which was considerable; my mother worked until the last months of her life) was tempered by the admiration I received from the new paper millionaires the Internet boom was creating by the thousands all around me. Young people I met admired me—though they found me a bit slow, retired as I am at forty-eight, not thirty-three. It did no good to remind them that the companies I'd worked for had had to show a profit before they could even think of going public, two consecutive quarters in a row, actual revenues in excess of costs. It seemed so quaint to them, passé, the notion of having a product, paying customers, profits. They believed the public markets should finance their fantasies. "What is your business plan for revenues?" I asked a young man I met at a party who had founded a start-up. "Go IPO!" he said.

Still, absurd as it all was, it was almost possible to be a believer—for a slim moment to marvel at the sheer, frightening, muscular power of capitalism. Whenever I'd travel for a few weeks, I would come home to find whole corners demolished in the SOMA I live in, Internet central, every former factory now chockablock with offices for start-ups. The teetering building that held the very useful Mail Boxes Etc.—a pile of rubble, soon to be a hotel. The lighting wholesaler where I bought replacement halogen bulbs—a hole in the ground, preparations for an office tower. An old, leaning warehouse that sold discount shelving—torn down to make way for new live/work "lofts" of appalling construction. They'd been crummy buildings anyway, those just-demolished ones, thrown up after the 1906 quake even more hastily than the new ones going up now. Good riddance. A whole quadrant of town that had lain dormant, languishing, decaying—swept away in a great capitalist surge of creative destruction. An orgy of risk taking, construction lending, bridge financing, banking derring-do. Only a dream as compelling as the Internet could have propelled otherwise sane men and women to set their sights on real estate, that horribly trailing indicator, where it takes a generation to get your money back from a hole in the ground.

I can already tell I will miss the madness. The exhiliration of a full-employment economy, billboards on the highway advertising for laborers. The after-hours excavations to lay fiber-optic cable, the streets lit like stage sets long into the night, the crews vanished like phantoms by daylight in time for the morning commute. The companies named Yahoo! and Google, Red Gorilla and Gazoontite. In what world before or since will people believe they should invest millions in a concern named Gazoontite?

Of course everyone knew it couldn't last. The poor Internet, land of a thousand dreams, trampled in a stampede for quick money. Markets always go to extremes before reversing, my brilliant money manager told me. I knew, even as I looked up at the new office tower, the hotel, the shoddy lofts, that it was all just a great big piece of bubble gum blowing up and up. "Inevitable" that it would burst, as my friend the scotch-drinker in the business-class lounge put it. But such a beautiful, juicy pink bubble. Mesmerizing. Even its ferocious burst astounds us. As CNN reports the relentless downfall, the three businessmen and I sit transfixed before the screen, too fascinated even to speak.

Then the smooth, professional voice of Diana Wilcovsky comes on the intercom. "Mr. Falcon, Ms. Walton, Mr. Brand, Mr. Broudover. Your flight for Paris is now boarding."

"Good day, gentlemen," I say, pleased with myself, imagining this is what a well-bred man aboard the *Titanic* would say as he went out on deck to watch all hope sail away with the women and children.

But on the plane, waiting for takeoff, my bonhomie fails me. The display on the handle of the in-flight telephone keeps updating the market: down, no sign of a bounce. And a real fear takes hold of my stomach, which is sorry now for the generous double premium vodka the woman with the helmet-hair poured me at eleven in the morning. Maybe it won't come back this time. Maybe the whole world, simultaneously, is waking up from its two great mass delusions: the Internet and the idea of rushing in to buy on market dips. Should I sell now, into this downdraft? I'm afraid to calculate how much money I've lost.

It does no good at all to tell myself it's just paper wealth, money I never really had, because I was depending on that paper wealth to live out my days on earth. How far will this sell-off go? Where will the bottom be? There is no way of knowing if this will mean one less trip to Europe or a wipeout, dusting off my two-year-dormant résumé and trying to convince somebody I still know enough to give me a job. I can't even pity myself. A forty-eight-year-old coupon clipper going back to work: serves her right.

Just then a man of about my age takes the seat across the aisle. He is tall and lanky and frizzy-haired, and I find myself staring at him. Then with a jolt that frightens me almost as much as the falling markets, I realize he reminds me of Ethan Levin, or what Ethan Levin would look like if I were to see him now. He too stares into the handle of the in-flight phone, cupping it in his spidery hands to shield the display from the glare of the window.

That could have been Ethan Levin, I think, as I watch the man's nervous swipes at his hair and remember the whole story again, like it or not. Ethan had eight times the stock options I did. He wouldn't have had to work for the next six start-ups, wouldn't have had to do consulting. He'd be long retired by now, well into his own life of compensated idleness. He would have traveled the world, would have sat in business-class lounges everywhere, drinking a complimentary alcoholic beverage as he watched his fortune melt away. Money as transient as electrons. Wealth as weightless as data broadcast through the air, rising and falling in currents like weather, beyond anyone's control. Yes, that's how it should have happened: Ethan Levin was supposed to be rich like me.

DAYS OPEN: 60

James and the bug returned on the same day. As I said, *Molesta redeunt semper.*

The bug came first, in the afternoon, May 4, 1984. Of course I knew it would be back. An intermittent bug like UI-1017 couldn't be proved "fixed" by a programmer's single test run, but when it couldn't be reproduced during several runs by the testers, Wallis took it off the board outside her office and put it on a thirty-day watch. The bug stayed active, days-open count still incrementing, but if nothing happened in thirty days, it would be declared fixed, closed, and archived.

Then it reappeared. Just as its thirty-day watch period came to an end, and very publicly. What had been a small, private matter between tester and programmer—Ethan Levin and I in a covert, personal contest of will and intelligence—suddenly broke out to become a subject of general talk. A company joke, in fact.

It was a Friday (another Friday; all changes of fortune seem to happen on Fridays). The venture capitalists funding the company were visiting. Four partners from Revell Ventures—"revile vultures," we testers called it—arrived in their gorgeously expensive suits, paying us no attention when they were led around the quality-assurance area. The VCs then disappeared into the conference room, where they were in all-day meetings with Telligentsia company officers. Close to five in the afternoon, they emerged, ties loosened, for an all-hands meeting, where there was to be a demonstration of the system.

William Harland himself officiated. A monitor, keyboard, and mouse had been set up in the main room of the office. Partitions had been collapsed and cleared away, a wide-open expanse had been created for this all-important first show of Telligentsia's progress.

"Thank you all for coming to witness our first major milestone!" our company president declared.

Wine bottles were opened, glasses were filled, the four men in suits held their wineglasses up in salute.

And the demo began.

Harland added data, changed it, added more, changed more. It was all going swimmingly; Harland was smiling and nodding yes and showing how queries could be constructed graphically. Point, click. Point, click. I almost saw it happen in slow motion. A menu dropped open. The mouse slid toward a line in the menu. It kept sliding and . . . The screen was full of crap. A piercing beep sounded. The keyboard and mouse were dead.

"What's happening?" said poor William Harland, pounding on the useless keys, clicking and clicking the dead mouse.

"I'll kill it," said the product marketing manager, rushing into an office nearby.

The glasses of wine descended to the VCs' sides. The smiles fell from their faces.

"Ethan Levin's bug," Mara Margolies and I intoned together.

My boyfriend James came later, close to midnight. He always did that, took late-arriving flights, putting him into San Francisco in the middle of the night, European time. It was better that way. We both had the excuse of exhaustion.

I always envisioned bodice-ripper scenes. There I'd be, looking down from the glass windows of the mezzanine that overlooked the international arrivals floor. He'd look up and see me. Ecstatic waves. Blown kisses. And when he'd finally emerge from customs, we'd embrace, look into each other's eyes, kiss, but slowly, lightly, nicely.

His flight was early. I had to race downstairs to meet him.

"Shitty flight" was how he greeted me. "Where's the car?"

There are some disappointments you simply can't let yourself feel right at the moment. There were obstacles to negotiate, after all—the luggage cart to be gotten through elevators and onto ramps, the car to be found, the Bay Bridge to be crossed—and how could I have attended to them if I'd given in to the feeling that was pulling me? An actual sort of sickness is what it felt like, an invader in my chest, some rogue organism hurtling around in me. Then anger: a flash of bitter anger.

"Well, aren't you the romantic one?" I said. "Aren't I glad I drove out to get you in the middle of the night?"

He looked surprised. "You don't expect romance at . . ." He looked down and stared at his watch. "What the hell time is it? Does that mean morning or night?"

"Night. Yeah. Okay."

And we wheeled the cart, found the car, crossed the bridge.

His apartment looked as if it had exploded. The lampshades were askew, the standing lamps leaning perilously against chairs and walls. Fallen piles of newspapers covered the floor. In the kitchen, garbage and dirty dishes and crumbs from months-ago meals. Unopened mail on the counters, summonses to appear in traffic court, unpaid bills, junk mail. The dining table held the sediment of the past six months. A vase of dead flowers stood in the middle of it, stems decomposing in a breeding green soup.

Bee-deep came from his answering machine. *Bee-deep.* "Shit. Too many people knew when I was coming back," he said. "Just let me check my messages." And he went off to the answering machine in the bedroom.

I stood next to his baggage in the middle of the living room.

"I'll be out shortly," he called.

Bee-deep. A muffled voice. *Bee-deep.*

"No rush," I said.

And I meant it: no rush. I was in no hurry to examine the disappointment that was thuddering around in my chest. I was grateful for now to keep my expectations far away from this experience of standing next to his luggage in the middle of his exploded living room. This particular disappearance—James into the bedroom with his messages—was like all of James's disappearances: it gave my imagination space to grow. I could seed another anticipation, spawn another fantasy of communion. As I waited, I could look forward to our only dependable, trouble-free connection: sex.

Which, shortly, as soon as James had checked his messages, we had.

Hydraulics: I had long ago decided that sex with James was mostly a question of hydraulics. Pipes and tubules and liquid secretions—automated, operating according to the laws of physics and fluid dynamics. No matter what was or was not happening between us, the fluids flowed, the pipes filled, the laws of gravity were defied then ultimately obeyed. When we'd first gotten together, it used to bother me. It seemed wrong that James's interest in sex seemed to have no relation to anything we might be feeling. In the middle of an argument, in the doldrums of the evening news, after the drudgery of washing dishes and carrying out trash: James was ready. I'd been cynical about his mechanical apparatus, sad that it didn't necessarily signify closeness or devotion or love.

Now, though, I was grateful for it. I was relieved at its reliability. There was something fortunate in the way it drove out chatter, negotiation, doubt. Weeks gone, words unsaid, and still, here was this marvelously unpremeditated act of desire. And so I reached down and simply appreciated it: his excellent, hydraulic forgetfulness.

THE CODE REVIEW

"It's not working correctly," said Ethan Levin. He went up to the whiteboard and began drawing circles and lines and arrows. "This section in particular is completely wrong. The call should go from here to here. Here," he insisted, stabbing the marker point into one of the circles.

"You made your point," said Herring, whose code Ethan was reviewing and making short work of.

"Even if we accept your premises—and I don't, Herring. It's absurd to make the user verify all those steps. Even if we were to accept your premises, the whole interface as you've done it is implemented highly inefficiently."

"I said, you made your point."

Ethan watched Herring's eyes roam around the conference room hoping that Harry or one of the other team members would intervene. Herring's code was under review that day—a normal-enough experience for a programmer, an annoying but helpful exercise in which your programs are scrutinized by colleagues. Ethan's own review, three months ago, had been brutal. Thorne's, last week, had been even worse, dissolving into arguments over his teeming collection of bugs. So Herring had nothing to complain about, Ethan thought; he had to go through this like everyone else. But Ethan knew he was taking a certain pleasure in getting back at Herring. He hadn't slept—since Joanna's return, going to bed was an act Ethan avoided to the point of exhaustion—and his cranky mood made him more inclined than ever to give Herring a dose of the sniping he continually directed Ethan's way. Herring's code was implemented like shit anyway, Ethan thought, to excuse himself.

"This section here should be system-independent," Ethan went on. "System-independent: I'm assuming you know what that means, Herring?"

"Of course—"

"Of course *not*. Evidently *not*. To reiterate: Your code should reflect zero knowledge of the underlying operating system and input hardware. It should—"

"Point *made*, Levin," said Herring.

"And you should not, I repeat, *not*, be using these system-dependent routines. These are private to my libraries. I don't know what made you think—"

"What made me *think*? I did what you *told* me to do."

"Not possible. It's simply inconceivable that—"

"Oh, don't start on that 'inconceivable' shit—"

"Inconceivable! Thoroughly. If you had any understanding of how the front end was supposed to function, you'd—"

"What's inconceivable is your interface. It's not coherent. Not consistent. Not compact. A long list of things it's not."

"Not trivial. Not simpleminded. Not brain-dead."

"Not elegant. Not even intelligent. Not—"

"Okay, you two," Harry Minor said finally, "okay, okay." He turned, laughing, to the rest of his team, who were sitting slouched in their chairs in front of the whiteboard. Bill Werners and Tommy Park rolled their eyes and fell into deeper, yet-more-resigned slouches. Bradley Thorne simply looked angry, as he often did, and Larry Seidel appeared to be on the verge of sleep. After thirty minutes of listening to Ethan and Albert have at each other, only Dana Merankin, it seemed, had the energy to respond. "Now, Harry," she said. "Normally we all enjoy them enormously, as you know. Why, it's like watching two tiger cubs at play—so fun! But really, haven't we had enough for one day?"

"Hey! Don't cut us off," Ethan protested.

"Yeah! This is fundamental, a question of—"

"System coherence! Design principles!" Ethan turned to the whiteboard again and resumed stabbing the point of a marker pen into a circle representing a section of Herring's code. "He should not be *here*. As a fundamental principle, this section *here* should be completely system-independent. *Here* is completely wrong."

"You're killing the point," said Albert Herring, grinning, turning around to the room to see if everyone got it: the marker point, the programming point, the pun.

"It's not a joke, Herring. You should not be calling these routines. I've documented it thoroughly—"

"Who has time for fucking *documentation*?"

"You can *read*, can't you?"

"There's reading, and then there's programming."

"There's intelligence, and then there's—"

"Okay, you two," Harry broke in again. "Okay, okay. That's enough. Enough! Here's how it's going to be. Herring, you will change your code to stop calling those functions. And you will read the fucking documentation, all of it. Levin, you will change the names of all routines not legally callable outside of the device-interface libraries. Start them with 'Dv' for device."

"Extra work! The schedule!" Ethan protested.

"Screw the schedule. We only get one chance to do it right the first time. Just do it. That's it. Thank you very much, everyone. Meeting over."

No one said a word. They all picked up their yellow pads and filed out: Dana Merankin to her cubicle by a window; Tommy Park to his next to Dana's; Larry Seidel to his next in the row; Bill Werners, the last one hired, to his cubicle by a wall; Bradley Thorne, Albert Herring, and Ethan back to their shared office full of lead-glass silence. At the office doorway, Herring looked directly at Ethan and, knowing that Ethan liked to work in a darkened room, reached across him to turn on all the lights.

```
/* Here you are, Ethan        */
/* Heuristics or mathematics? */
```

Ethan sat down at his desk after the meeting, and staring at him from the monitor was this message he kept returning to, emissary from a region of thought he'd now have to abandon. For the note related to his efforts to speed up the user interface, the question he kept asking himself about the difference between a smart human and a smart machine. It was an *interesting* question, the kind of desirable problem engineers called *hard*. But now he had to put it aside again, and there was nothing but dog-work ahead of him. Rename his routines! Find all the cross-references, redo the makefiles, rebuild the libraries, rewrite the documentation—mindless details, mental junk! All the while the clock ticking way, Ethan slipping the schedule, each day falling a little further behind.

Herring and his damn lights! Why the hell did he always have to turn on the lights? Were they buzzing? Ethan had complained and gotten the bulbs changed only a few weeks ago, so why were they buzzing? He was tired, hadn't slept well for weeks. Since Joanna's return, a tense silence had come between them, an unspoken rule: they would pretend nothing had changed. They were not supposed to mention Paul or Marsha Ostrick, the trip to India, or anything remotely related to any of it. The one time Ethan dared to ask Joanna if she'd been in touch with Ostrick, she gave him a firm, one-word "No," and there everything had been left.

Except the nights had changed. The nights had become sexless. Each of them in pajamas clinging to a side of the bed.

Here you are, Ethan.

Here.

When Ethan looked up from his terminal, there was no way to avoid looking at the back of Herring's ugly ovoid head. Herring was shuffling papers, too loudly, probably Ethan's documentation he was throwing from pile to pile. To make matters worse, overnight someone had installed two server machines in the room. They sat near Bradley Thorne's desk, whining at a high pitch and blowing hot air into the room. If Thorne minded about the machines, there was no telling. He sat with his back to the room and beamed out a hostile, hunkered-down energy that was very effective: everyone stayed away.

Ethan slapped at his keyboard, opened one code file after another, closed it.

E-mail: he'd read his e-mail. He didn't feel like starting on the dull work ahead of him, so he did what he always did to avoid anything: read e-mail. Something about another stock meeting, the stock being split, everyone getting double their number of options at half the original value—oh hell, they're diluting the stock already, he thought. Bad enough, but do they need another *meeting*? Mail from Haber, head of the operating-systems group. Bad news: A key module was being redesigned; the database schedule was slipping. Schedules. Slipping. He had a spike of panic. Let it go, he thought, let it go.

No more e-mail. No more diversions.

Diversions. From what?

Renaming half his code.

At the thought of the task ahead of him, a red stain spread across his cheeks. He felt humiliated at the stupid mistake he'd made. Harry was right: he should have named the routines more clearly. He could have avoided trouble if the function names clearly told the other pro-grammers which routines they could use and which were private to his device-interface libraries. It was so simple, so ridiculously easy, but he'd missed it. To have made such a dumb mistake, and then have it pointed out, in the group, in a meeting, in front of Herring, above all—humil-iating! He felt caught out, found out, ashamed at having been discov-ered to be . . . what? He didn't know exactly, only that the thought of his mistake made him cringe, his face burn, his back sweat. And then it made him angry, at Harry, at that fat snide Dana Merankin, at that chicken-necked Albert Herring, at the hostile hunkered back of Bradley Thorne, whom Ethan was sure could smell his humiliation from across the room.

"Lunch?"

It was Bill Steghman, his stooped shoulders just inside the door-way. He was a short man, his spine slightly twisted as if he were per-petually turning to ask a question. His voice was so soft everyone bent down to hear him. "Lunch?" he asked again.

Ethan looked up. He checked his hunger by the system clock. Noon, it said.

"Okay."

They sat as they always did, side by side at the counter looking out into the empty hall. The same lunch: turkey on rye, no mayo, wrapped in paper on blue plastic trays.

"How're things?" asked Ethan.

Steghman's group was slipping its schedule; the key module being redesigned was his.

"Fine," Steghman said. "And with you?"

Ethan's girlfriend had slept with another man; he had to rename half his code. "Fine," he said.

They both stared out into the hallway.

"Network's been really slow," he said after a while.

"Uhm," said Steghman.

"Are they backing up the files in the daytime now?"

"Dunno," said Steghman.

So the two men—who, if they'd been women, would have discussed and dissected their current professional and personal terrors; would have relieved one another of the burden of shame with the tender blessings of personal confession; supported and sustained one another by simply letting themselves be seen and known; in short, *talked*—no, the two men could do nothing of the sort, and so sat quietly chewing.

"Finished?" asked Steghman.

Ethan looked down at his tray and was surprised to see balled-up paper where there'd been a sandwich.

"Finished," he said.

And the programmers made their way back upstairs. At the unmarked back door of the office, Ethan touched his badge to the security lock, which flashed ENTER, ENTER, ENTER on its LED screen, and released the lock with a click.

The humiliation was there waiting for him. It was as if it had settled itself into the office, along with Herring and Thorne, the whining machine fans, the relentless fluorescents, and now a beam of sun that had bounced its way across chrome and glass in the parking lot to send shoots of light directly at him. Ethan reached over and yanked the blinds closed.

He got started. He dragged his attention through resentment and irritation, forced himself to concentrate, calm down, be methodical. Make a list of the procedures to change. Get the code files out of the archive. Search for the name. One by one: Edit file. Search for the name to change. Substitute new name for old name. Save. Next file.

Should have written myself a program, he told himself suddenly. A program to scan the text of the code files and make the changes for me. Let the machine do the dog-work! But no: that would take even longer by the time he got it working and tested. And what was the use of writing a program if he was only going to go through all this once? Once only! He was never going to change these names again!

Edit. Search. Substitute. Save.

The hours went by. He scribbled notes on a yellow pad to keep track of the modules he'd searched, the ones still remaining. He was dimly aware of Herring and Thorne leaving, the sun fading behind the closed blind, the cleaning woman vacuuming around him then turning off the lights. He was vaguely aware that he should call Joanna. But the combination of exhaustion and repetition—edit, search, substitute, save—lulled him into a certain forgetfulness of everything. He felt his irritation rise and fall, memories of the meeting—Herring's stupid grinning face!—float up at him until he forced them away. Edit, search, substitute, save. Anger then boredom; boredom then anger again.

Enough! came to him at some point. I'm fried, tired, finished.

He deleted his temporary files, checked his yellow pad, left himself a note for the morning. He was about to turn back to his keyboard to log out, when he felt something staring at him from the monitor:

```
hubris: ~/src/temp> vi GetInp.c
hubris: ~/src/temp> rm *
```

It was the last two commands he'd given to "hubris," his workstation. The first to edit the code file GetInp.c. The next to remove all his temporary files. Between them should have been another command. How could that command not be there? Impossible that he'd forget it! But where was it? Where was the command putsccs, his script to put all the code files back into the source-code control system? *Where was it?*

The cursor sat blinking at him. Slowly, inevitably, his mind accepted the evidence of his eyes. He had not put his work back into the archive. He hadn't run putsccs. He'd taken the code files out of the archive, edited them one by one, then deleted them.

Gone. All the work he'd done that day was gone.

He glanced around as if he didn't want anyone to see his second incredibly stupid mistake of the day. No one was there. His office, the hall outside it, were dark. He sat there breathing in and out, too rapidly, unable to stop. He could hear his blood pulsing in his ears, squishy and insistent. He checked the contents of the directory. Empty. Looked at a neighboring directory where he'd done some work, to see if there were anything there he could salvage. Junk.

He sat without moving.

Then, over the pulsing in his head, he could make out what sounded like a hammer beating on metal, then something like gunshots, and some shouting that couldn't exactly be described as singing.

The night system administrator's music, he remembered. It must be after eleven. She'd be in that little office in the corner backing up the files.

"Were my files backed up during the day?" he yelled even before he was fully inside the office. He didn't greet her, barely noticed the back of the close-shorn head he was looking at. "My directories, slash user slash levin, were they backed up today?"

The figure sitting with its back to him didn't move. The loud, clanging music went on, a man's voice shouting lyrics he couldn't understand.

"What *is* that?" he said.

The administrator switched off her boom box and slowly swiveled her chair around.

"And you would be who? This person barging in and barking at me would be who?" asked a voice accented in something that might have been German.

He gave his name, but gruffly. It was an embarrassment: this need to tell the administrator you've deleted your own files.

"*Ley-veen,*" she pronounced it. "Herr Ethan Levin, how do you do? I am Ute. This human person you have just barked at is called Ute Weiss."

Oo-teh *VICE*, he thought, as she pronounced her name. That name he'd seen on e-mail, and assumed to be attached to some nice Jewish woman from Berkeley, had turned out to be this imperious, startling-looking woman with a foreign accent. Ooh-teh *VICE!*

She pointed at the boom box. "Einstürzende Neubauten."

"What?"

She laughed. "German group. But certainly every person knows them now."

He mumbled something.

He watched her as she stood up to arrange some tapes on a high shelf. She was tall, about five-eight or -nine, Ethan estimated, with broad shoulders and long arms. She was wearing jeans and a jeans jacket, and under it she had on what looked like a man's muscle undershirt, white, with no bra. She was slim but curvy, a little hippy, with big breasts. She wore her hair cut very short, shaved almost to the scalp, which showed off the shape of her head and her long neck. He noticed she had one little earring in one ear but six or so in the other, a row of tiny silver rings marching up the margin of a small ear. But it was her face that he found most startling of all: large green eyes heavily outlined with some dark smudge of makeup, high cheekbones dusted with color, pouty lips painted dark red. It was the effect of all that makeup next to the denim, muscle shirt, and shaved head. The face of a model on what had dressed itself up to be a boy biker.

"No, we did not back up your directories during today," she was saying over her shoulder at him. "Nor anyone else's. All you programmers were complaining how it slowed the system, it slowed the system! Ah, your precious compiles were taking too, too long. All your precious brainpower wasted waiting and waiting! So now what do you want from us to do?"

Zoh now vhat doo yoo vhant fwom us too doo. It sounded charming to him in her German accent, even if she was annoyed at him for being a member of that complaining race of programmers.

"Can you check the status of this directory?" he asked her, hoping for some miracle, writing on a scrap of paper "/usr/levin/src/temp."

She said nothing, simply took the slip of paper, sat down at her workstation, and started scrolling through the backup logs. He went over to stand behind her and look over her shoulder. Ethan became aware that the entire office had a spicy smell, insinuating but pleasant, a smell he knew from somewhere but couldn't place.

"Here it is," she said after a while.

"Where?" For he had been distracted. Yes: now he recognized it: the scent in his office that night after his dinner with Marsha. Perfume, hers. Now drifting toward him from the nape of her neck. Shaved head. Muscle shirt. Denim jacket. *Perfume.*

"There. Last night. It was last backed up last night."

"Last night," he repeated.

"If I restore you," she said, "you will be back to yesterday."

Restored. Back to yesterday. Which was to say, not restored at all. The reality of his lost work came back to him. And again his cheeks reddened, the back of his neck went hot. Then out of nowhere came a kind of fury. "Don't you have anything later?" he found himself yelling. "You must have something later. How the hell can we work if you don't back up more often! What the fuck do you sysops do if you're not keeping the goddamn backups up to date? What good are you! Why the fuck is the system so slow if you're not backing up—"

"Do not bark at me! No. I told you. You programmers complained and we complied. Last night. The latest was last night."

She stood up and took off her jacket. There were her breasts, clearly visible behind the thin white shirt. There was her long bare neck rising up to her shaved, sculpted head. There was the scent of her perfume rising and filling the air of the small office. She ran a hand slowly over the dome of her head, and it came to him she must know exactly what she's doing. She must know he hasn't slept for days. She must know he hasn't had sex for weeks. She must be intending to do this: cast this spell of desire over him.

Which she broke abruptly with a laugh. "What did you do—delete your own files? Oh, all you brilliant, brilliant minds! Running to big sister Admin to save you, as usual."

He stood staring at her breasts, round and full and low-hanging, and tried not to look at her red mouth laughing at him. She switched the boom box back on, loud, and did a little dance move as she took the two steps to her desk. Ethan could barely bring himself to leave the office, where Ute Weiss was now somehow mixed up with Joanna McCarthy, with his lost sense of comfort and safety, with broken trust and vanished pleasure, and all the other things that were suddenly lost and could not be restored.

A RIDE IN THE CHAIR

"I'm going to work," Ethan said.

It was a Saturday. Joanna usually minded his going to work on a Saturday, but since the trip to India, no, she seemed to prefer his being out of the house.

She was kneeling down at the cabinet under the sink, rearranging things. She reached behind her, put some scouring cleanser on the floor, then put her head inside the cabinet again.

"I said, I'm going into the office," Ethan said.

"I heard you."

She kept moving things around, her head swallowed up inside the dark hole of the undersink.

"You could say something," he said.

She sat back on her heels, swiveled her head to look at him over her shoulder. "Are you asking me to say, 'Wonderful! Have a great day at the office, dear!'?"

This was more like the old Joanna, annoyed that he was always working. So he too immediately fell into his old habits. "I have this bug," he said, finding his excuse.

She removed a smashed old box of aluminum foil from the undersink, a filthy rag, a rusted scouring pad, a dirty sponge. "Don't you always have bugs?"

"Yeah. But this one's . . . unusual."

She stopped what she was doing to look at him. Maybe she'd noticed something in his tone, he thought, something he hadn't intended. Right now he didn't particularly want anything from her. "A bad one?" she asked.

He gave a little laugh. "You could say that. It brought down the first demo for the investors."

She squinted her eyes a little, a gesture he recognized as concern. "What makes it so bad?" she asked. "Beyond who was there when it happened?"

"Comes and goes."

"Flakey."

There was a time when they used to talk about their work. He'd taught her about flakey bugs, and she'd told him about NGOs. How long ago was all that? "Right," he said. "Flakey bug."

She looked at the undersink detritus arrayed around her and idly picked up the dirty sponge. "Can't you do what you always do with those?" she asked, waving the sponge around. "You know, do the simplest case. What was it Carl Wolfson used to call it?" she asked, naming Ethan's boss at his former job. "*Reductio ad* something?

"*Reductio ad absurdum.*"

"Yeah. When you—"

"Yeah, you take out everything. Make a minimum case."

"That's it. I remember you talking about it. The bare minimum of whatever you're doing."

Ethan considered it: a single window, one menu button, a menu with one line. Take out the menu and see if the bug's still there. Why didn't he think of it before?

"Then you add stuff, one thing at a time," she said.

"Yeah, yeah. Until it breaks."

"Then you take it—"

"Right, right. Take it out, put it back, make the bug come and go. I know all this. You don't have to recite all this shit back to me."

She tightened her mouth. The squint went out of her eyes.

"It won't work for this bug," he said.

She stared at him for a moment then put her head back under the sink.

"It won't work. I can't make this bug come at all."

"Whatever you say."

"I'll see you later."

A laugh came from the undersink. "Later? I won't even ask how much later!"

"Until dinnertime."

"Whenever."

And he left.

Here you are, Ethan.

Here.

Heuristics or mathematics?

Much better, Ethan thought, settling into his chair in the empty office. Now he could relax and come back to this question that had kept floating off just beyond his reach, each time deferred by something pressing or annoying. He didn't feel like working on his bug; he wanted to think about this conundrum. The ventilators had been turned off, but it didn't matter. He somehow liked the peculiarly still and odorless air, a room without an atmosphere, it seemed, clean as a vacuum. The perfect environment to ponder the nature of the human user. The difference between human and algorithmic intelligence, if there was one.

He was ready to accept the idea that the computer and the human brain shared a structure, and that his code, therefore, should strive to "think" like a person. But each time he sat down to write his "smart" search for where the user had just clicked the mouse—applying expectations about what a person was likely to do—his routine got bogged down in if-clauses. If the user isn't in the top window, then find out which other window is most visible, and look in there. If it's not in there, then figure out which window was most recently used, and look there. If not in there, then if there's an EXIT button. . . . When he tested it against the "dumb" version—a compact loop of code that simply searched the screen systematically, top to bottom, left to right, without any nod to human expectations—the dumb one was faster every time. It depressed him. Maybe he had tried the wrong reasoning. Maybe machines weren't yet fast enough to match the speed of human thinking.

Then he began to wonder if he wasn't making a mistake in even trying to mimic human behavior in the code. Maybe the computer was simply better at being fast than at being smart. Maybe what we called "intelligence" in a computer was just the fact that it could do a bunch of dumb things at lightning speed. Then again (his mind going back and forth over this conundrum), maybe humans were no different, and underneath all the apparent complications of human thought there was nothing special, like his simulation: a big collection of dumb things.

In any case, he wanted to spend the day thinking about this question, fiddling with the code, just to see where it led. It was the first time since leaving graduate school that a programming job had offered up an interesting question, lifting him out of the mundane pressures of schedules and specs and bug lists. He felt released; his mind felt crackly with thoughts. A grand and glorious exercise it seemed as the hours wound themselves away, this musing on the nature of the human being, whose existence Ethan considered a design problem, which maybe one day he would solve.

"Hello?" Ethan called into the darkened house.

The phone was ringing. "Hello," he said into the handset.

There was no reply. "Hello?" he asked again.

There came a click. A hang-up.

"Shit," he muttered. Then: "Joanna?" he called, wandering from room to room.

Immediately the phone rang again. "Who is this!" Ethan demanded into the handset.

A pause. "I'm sorry," said a quiet voice. Another pause. "Sorry. Didn't mean to hang up on you."

"Yes, you did! You distinctly did mean to hang up on me! What the hell do you think—?" Then he knew who it was. "Marsha! Isn't this Marsha Ostrick?"

"Yes, it's me, Marsha. I thought . . . I was thinking . . ." She trailed off and stopped.

He said nothing, his annoyance simmering.

"Oh, I'm sorry, I'm sorry," she went on. "Please. I hung up on you. So rude. So rude of me."

She fell quiet. He could hear her heavy-woman's breathing, a storm in his ear, something imperative and nervous in it, some question Ethan knew—dreaded—was coming at him.

"Ethan. How *are* you?"

The question hung there. He didn't want to tell her anything. How much did she know anyway? "Fine," he said. "I'm fine."

There was another pause. She continued to breathe in and out into the phone, and Ethan realized they were both doing the same thing: hanging back, hoping neither of them would bust through the pretense that nothing had changed.

"Joanna's not here," he said, speaking rapidly, not giving her a chance to interrupt. "I came home from work and have no idea where she is. I'll take a message, okay? It's Joanna you want, right?" Why was he making it into a question? Marsha was Joanna's friend. Of course she was calling for Marsha. "I'll tell her to call you," he said, with what he hoped was definitive finality. "She's probably at a neighbor's. She'll call you soon. Okay? So long."

"Okay. Just—"

"So long, Marsha."

The moment he hung up the phone, he was aware of the deep quiet of the house. One instant there was Marsha in all her breathy, anxious energy, and the next: nothing, silence. He had an impulse, crazy, that he should call Marsha back. It would be so easy: the Ostricks were still on their speed-dial buttons: press 5 and get Marsha. He could ask her questions, find out more about what happened, see if it were really true that Joanna was not in contact with Ostrick—but no: no. He was not going to do it. The thought of gossiping on the phone with Marsha gave him a sudden feeling of revulsion. He wasn't going to call her, and what's more, he wasn't going to tell Joanna about the call. He'd forget to mention it, had forgotten already; he could always apologize if he needed to. Sorry, sorry, sorry, why didn't Joanna ever say she was sorry?

He'd barely dropped his briefcase in the study when the front door banged open.

"Joanna?" he called.

There was a high-pitched whooping, then a voice wailing, "Whee-ee-eee!"

"Joanna? Is that you? Hello? I'm up here."

"What?"

"I said, I'm up here."

"And I'm down here," she yelled, "with Carolyn and Betsy."

Carolyn and Betsy. The woman from across the street and her baby. That baby that screeched at the top of its lungs.

Ethan went downstairs to the kitchen, lifted the lids off the two pots on the stove. Empty.

"We ate at Carolyn's," said Joanna. She and Carolyn were standing near the kitchen table, Joanna holding the baby, which was wriggling and kicking fiercely.

"She's going to be a soccer player," said Carolyn. "Aren't you, my precious flower?" she said, squealing, leaning over the baby girl and making faces at her.

"That's okay," Ethan said.

The two women turned to look at him. "I mean about dinner," he went on. "Your having it without me. That's okay."

Carolyn and Joanna exchanged looks. He'd been talked about, he knew, and they'd judged him to be distinctly not okay. Their neighbor was a big, strapping woman who'd run a gardening business before she took time off for the baby. "Kind of butch" was how Joanna described her, admiringly, referring to Carolyn's physical strength and no-nonsense manner. Her husband—Ethan could never remember his name—raced and sold motorcycles, and Ethan often saw him in front of their house, stripped to his undershirt, fiddling with his collection of bikes. Husband-what's-his-name had a wiry, muscled body—washboard stomach, great quads, tight pecs—and Ethan, who was getting more slack-muscled by the year, had to console himself with the thought that Carolyn's husband probably wasn't very bright.

"Is there still any of that hot stuff?" Ethan asked, his head in the fridge.

"You mean the curry?"

"Yeah. The curry."

Joanna exhaled. "It's not my job to take refrigerator inventory, Ethan. You can probably see for yourself." She paused. "I thought you were going to be home for dinner."

"Right," he said, putting his head in the refrigerator then withdrawing it.

"Were you there?" Carolyn was asking Joanna. "Where those people were killed?"

"What's that?" Ethan asked. "What people getting killed?"

Joanna bounced the baby a little. "Sikhs," she said, giving Carolyn a look. "In the Punjab. They've been agitating for autonomy, and today the Indian army killed about twenty of them. Yeah, we were there."

We were there, Ethan thought.

Ethan and Joanna looked at each other for a moment. Then she turned to the baby in her arms. "Does your mama's precious flower want a ride in the round-and-round chair? Round-and-round? Round-and-round-and-round. Whee-eee-ee!"

Too bad Ostrick didn't stay in the Punjab, Ethan thought, so he could die along with the Sikhs. Then he put the thought out of his head as something more nasty than he should allow himself, turning his annoyance instead to Joanna, who kept squeaking nonsense at the baby. Ethan could never understand why people felt compelled to coo at kids in those squeally voices. Shouldn't children just learn how people really talked? He was relieved when the two women left him alone in the kitchen, and their piercing voices, now joined by the squeals of Mama's little precious flower, receded up the stairs. He made himself a sandwich and decided he'd work for a while in his study.

But as he made his way up the stairs, there came a screech. It was the baby, wailing, in what could have been extreme pain or pleasure, Ethan couldn't tell. Then came more screeching and squealing, and Joanna's voice suddenly shrilling "Whee-ee-ee!" It seemed to be coming from his study—no, that couldn't be right; why would the baby be in his study? But when he got to the doorway, he stood still, amazed at what he was seeing.

"What the hell are you doing?" he asked.

Joanna and Carolyn looked up at him, suddenly quieted. Even the baby shut up and turned its startled little face to look up at Ethan. Precious Flower was sitting in his chair. Joanna was sitting on a pile of his books, Carolyn on the stool he used to keep papers handy. The papers were now scattered across the floor, the piles of books all rearranged, even the stacks of stuff next to his monitor shoved aside. He'd never find anything again. All the things in piles and stacks had a place, an order, a spatial arrangement in three dimensions he kept in his head without thinking. And now everything was scrambled, chaotic, lost.

"She likes to ride in the chair," said Joanna.

Ethan stared at her, uncomprehending for a moment. "What the fuck do you mean, ride in the chair?"

"I turn her around and around, and she likes it."

The child still had her face turned up to him. Joanna's hand was on the arm of the chair—*his* chair, now holding a half-naked baby in rubber pants. The whole room stank of a dirty diaper. "This isn't some goddamn playroom!" he exploded. "Just what the hell do you think you're doing in here!"

The child, who'd been sitting there still and open-mouthed, gave off a terrifying wail. Its big face turned darker and darker red, then suddenly issued fluids of all sorts from nostrils, eyes, mouth.

"Poor precious flower," Carolyn cooed, reaching over for the girl and bouncing her up and down in her arms, while Precious Flower continued to produce great, thick wads of snot and tears and drool. "Poor, poor precious flower."

"I'll never find anything again!" he went on. "You've fucked up the whole arrangement. Everything. How the hell do you think—"

"What fucking arrangement?" said Joanna. "This shithole? This mess you disappear into and never come out? I don't give a damn. It'll be good for you to—"

"To what? *What?* Have my whole life messed up by you?"

Joanna suddenly stood up and said nothing. And Ethan said nothing. There was only the screaming of the baby and Carolyn's voice trying to soothe it, then Carolyn saying, "I think Betsy and I better go now." She edged past Ethan.

"Wait for me," said Joanna, as Carolyn got to the top of the stairs. "I'm coming too."

And then Joanna also edged past him, saying nothing, not looking at him. At the last moment, without his having deciding to, he grabbed her wrist.

"Marsha called," he said.

Joanna looked down at her wrist. "Let go."

"I said, Marsha called."

"I heard you. And I said, Let go of me."

He let go. "What do you think Marsha wanted?"

"How should I know? You're the one who talked to her."

He couldn't think of what he should say next. Should he get into this?

"Are you going to call her back?"

"I don't know. I just don't know anything. Who knows. Yes. No. Maybe." And at that she continued past him and started down the stairs.

He had to get everything back where it was. The files, the piles, the papers—an arrangement that had organized itself over time—how could he get it all back where it was? He gathered up a stack of fallen papers, carefully drawing it together like a deck of cards that had been spread out on a table. Was that the correct order? Yes, he had to trust it was. Then that stack of books and manuals: wasn't it over here, in this precise coordinate of the room? He moved it back and forth, this way and that, looking for the exact spatial arrangement that would let his hand, as before, find its object without his having to search for it. He sat down in his chair—his executive chair that probably smelled like baby shit now—relaxed his head against the headrest, and let come to mind the polar coordinate system that had surrounded him, each pile and object, book and paper, chart and memo, deposited one by one over the years. To re-create this world in all its particularity would be like trying to rewind and rerun evolution! Not possible, he thought, running his hands through his hair. No: nothing would ever be the same.

Still, he could approximate it. He could fiddle and adjust and come close enough so that the territory of his study might not be the foreign, invaded landscape it now was. He got up and moved a book down two layers in a stack. He rotated the stack: ten degrees south by southwest. No, too much, back two. No, too much again, over three. The stool that had sat within reaching distance—he slid it forward, back, forward again until, sitting in his chair, eyes closed, he found it without fail. His private world had to return to the map of it that lived inside his head: *had to*. He got down on his knees and nudged a pile again, a centimeter left, a few millimeters right. Then the next pile, then the next.

Midnight, said his system clock when he sat back down in his chair. He held out a hand to survey the papers, the stool, the pile of books: Yes, this would do. The house was quiet. His study hummed. Where was Joanna? Twelve-oh-two, said the clock when he looked next. She was never out this late. She was always in bed, reading, at this hour. He got up and looked out the dormer window that gave onto the street: Carolyn's house was dark. Maybe they're in the back, he thought, on that porch, where they have the TV. Twelve-oh-three.

He dialed in to the system at work.

"You have new mail," it said.

Three messages. One from the company president, William Harland, saying that representatives of Revell Ventures would be meeting with each senior member of the technical staff. The next from Harry Minor, forwarding Harland's message, adding: "Your meeting with the VCs is scheduled for 9am Monday. My office." The third, also from Harry: "And btw, better fix that bug that crashed the demo. Harland is acting like he never saw a bug before."

VCs. Monday. What did they want?

And the bug. The demo disaster. The bug he probably would have worked on today if Joanna hadn't started telling him what to do.

Twelve-fifteen. Where was she?

Of course he should have worked on the bug today. Even if he still didn't get a core dump—that idiot tester! How can someone be a tester if they don't know how to get a core!

The bug. Better fix that bug.

He sat back and tried to make his mind still. He knew that bugs could hide in your mind like motes in the corner of your vision. If you looked too hard, too directly at them, they had a way of becoming invisible, evaporating under the too-clear focus of what you thought you knew about the code. He tried to tell himself: It's a bug because you *don't* know what the program is doing. You have to look at the code like it's something you've never seen before, an artifact dropped to earth by an alien. But the effort seemed impossible just now. He kept looking at the clock. Twelve-twenty-five. Twelve-forty. Where was she?

His screen was soon filled with code. Eight files. Then ten. Windows of code papering the display with their tiny white letters on black. His mind shuttling from one to the next, following the flow of control from statement to statement, routine to routine. If this is true, then go here. Else if that, go there. Else if this, there. Else here.

One-ten. Where was she? It broke his concentration to have her gone.

And there was something else distracting him. A thumping. A low note somewhere near the bottom of his hearing limit. More like a sensation in his chest than a sound. But rhythmic, slow and regular and even, a low, steady beating that seemed to be coming from everywhere.

He stood up. Looked out front. Nothing. To the house on one side. Nothing. To the house on the other, the one with the wild, overgrown lawn. An unfamiliar pickup truck in the driveway. Rock music heaving from an opened window. There it was, the source of the thump. A visitor, he told himself. Someone who would leave, taking the bad loud music with him. Maybe it would stop soon. He waited. There was a pause but then a beat in another rhythm, faster this time, a deeper bass vibration, more like a boom than a thump. He went back to his study, but the more he tried to concentrate on the code, the more sensitized he became to the thumps and booms and crashes and smashes, the beat as it was relayed into his study in its varying frequencies and amplitudes, faster and slower, but always regular, pulsing. It interfered with his brain. It washed away logic. His slow, careful trails from `if` to `then` to `else if`—dissolved.

He gave up, closed the code files, logged off. Then, as he stood up to stretch, he saw a car stop in front of the house, engine idling. Then the car door opened, and he was surprised to see that the person getting out was Joanna.

"Where were you?" he asked Joanna as she came upstairs to the bedroom.

"Just out to talk," she said, taking her clothes off in the closet.

"With Carolyn?"

"Where else would I be?"

Her T-shirt flew to the floor. Her bra.

"Carolyn was in the car you got out of?"

"Yes. Carolyn."

"What about the baby?"

"She has a husband, you know. She's allowed to go out after dark."

Joanna emerged from the closet dressed in her cotton pajamas. She pulled back the covers and got into bed, Ethan following a few minutes later. Then they both kept to the edges of the bed, Joanna on her side, Ethan on his, each one breathing, pretending to be asleep, careful that not even a finger or a toe should touch.

Minutes later, something occurred to him.

"That car," he said into the dark, "it wasn't Carolyn's."

"No," came her muffled reply. "It wasn't Carolyn's."

"So whose was it?"

She turned over, sighed. "A friend."

"A friend of hers?"

"Yes. A friend."

He stared at her lying beside him, his eyes seeing popping lights in the dark. Did he really want to question her more? He lay back, not sleeping for hours. Off and on through the night, he thought he heard—softly, barely, under the steady sound of Joanna's slippery breathing—a low, dark, driving beat coming through the walls. It seemed to have traveled all the way across the house, through the guest room, the study, to come and drum at the bedroom door. He held his breath: Was it really there? No, he told himself. It's not there. It's your imagination, you're just tired, there's nothing.

THE DEBUGGER

The two venture capitalists were waiting for him.

"Am I late?" Ethan asked as he stepped into Harry Minor's office and closed the door behind him.

Both visitors looked down at their watches impatiently.

"Oh, no, no," said Ethan's boss, directing himself to the VCs as he stood up from behind his desk. "Meeting times at Telligentsia are always a little, uh, fluid. Ethan Levin, Marshall Toulsen and Tom Knightbridge. Marshall and Tom, Ethan."

The two men made no move to shake hands. "Well, just so we're clear that *schedules* aren't, uh, fluid at Telligentsia," said the one to Harry's right. (Was it *Marshall*, Ethan thought, like a *sheriff*?)

"Heh-heh," went Harry in his nervous little laugh.

Ethan wasn't sure what to do with himself. He was clearly late. Sunday night had been like Saturday: He'd lain awake for hours, eventually falling into a black, thick sleep that kept him unconscious through his alarm. Now he stood awkwardly leaning his back against the door. The VCs had taken the two chairs in front of Harry's desk, and there were only two other places people generally sat in Harry's office: on the floor, which Ethan instantly ruled out as inappropriate for this situation, and on the *ball*. The ball in question was a two-and-a-half-foot-high, bright orange exercise ball that Harry's wife had brought from an aerobics class, one of the many toys left around for amusement during meetings. There was the purple water gun. The red plastic scooter. The bow-and-arrow set with rubber-cup-tipped arrows. The mechanical dog that begged and barked when you wound it up (required if you got caught in a mistake). A miniature basketball and hoop. A harmonica. A ukelele. And the orange ball itself, upon which one squatted and skuttled, balancing with a peculiarly suggestive rolling motion of the pelvis.

Ethan hesitated then did what he had to: He sat on the ball.

"Oh, that's a standard seat here," Harry said to his visitors with a grin. "Keeps us *on the ball*, if you know what I mean."

The capitalists did not grin back. "I see," said one.

"Let's begin," said the other. And as the VC sat back comfortably—leg crossed ankle over knee, hands made into a steeple—Ethan realized he'd completely forgotten his name now. What did Harry say it was? And the other one—was he Night-something? Joanna had tried to teach him how to remember people's names. Repeat them right away when you're introduced, she'd said. Pick out an identifying characteristic and match it to the name as you're saying it. But how was he supposed to do that while he was wondering how it would look for him to be sitting on a bright orange exercise ball? He looked from one man to the other and tried to concentrate. Both in dark suits. Both in red ties with diagonal stripes. Cuff links—God, who wore cuff links anymore? Loafers, the kind with a fringe. Mid- to late thirties, no facial hair, not much to distinguish them in a crowd. One was handsomer, Ethan decided, the other one balding.

". . . and so we're talking to all the people identified as key personnel," Handsomer was saying, "and we were told you're one of them."

"Key to the front-end product," said Balding.

"Thank you," said Ethan. "I'm happy to—"

"Where'd you go to school, Levin?" Handsomer broke in.

"Berkeley," Ethan answered.

"Good man, good man!" Handsomer said heartily. "I'm a Cal man, too. Good school. Graduate work there, too?"

"I did some coursework toward a doctorate, but no degree."

"You didn't get a Ph.D. or just not there?"

"No. No degree."

"No master's?"

"No. No degree."

"I see. That's right. I remember now. Any particular reason why not?"

Ethan was about to answer when he felt the ball go wobbly under him. He rolled himself slightly forward to compensate, then found himself too close to the two VCs and skuttled back. "Unstable," he said, meaning the ball.

The two men stared at him.

"No degree, why not," Ethan muttered, steadying himself. "Well, I was offered a good job, then another one. It seemed that the opportunities outside school were too interesting to pass up."

The men smiled; a good answer, apparently. One was supposed to want opportunity, adventure, *ventures*.

But immediately Ethan was terrified: Was that what he'd told Harry? He thought back to his job interview: Didn't he tell Harry about his father dying and having to drop out of school? He wanted to turn around, look at Harry, see if anything registered on his face. But there was the problem of the *ball*. If he moved abruptly, he'd get the ball unbalanced, so he'd have to hedge, tell everything, cover his bases.

"*And*," Ethan hurried to add, "my father passed away." He put his head down, waved a hand vaguely. "There were . . . you know . . . re-sponsibilities. To the family. Things . . . You have to take care of things at times like that."

"Of course," said Handsomer.

"Very sorry," said Balding, though he looked not sorry at all.

Handsomer then reached into a briefcase he'd kept at his feet, rifled through some papers, and came up with what Ethan recognized as his résumé. Now what? thought Ethan. What would they make of his experience? Would they see a solid programmer with twelve years of delivering finished projects, or a corporate coder, a drone, someone unworthy of options to buy forty thousand shares of their stock? He braced his legs, determined that whatever happened, he would not lose his balance on the ball.

But something went odd immediately. Did Ethan know Tom Binerd at Unitek, Balding wanted to know, his old school buddy? No? Strange. Balding was sure Tom was there when Ethan was. How about John Simms, Balding's old frat brother? Not him either? Handsomer's uncle had worked at Insuracorp; did Ethan remember Charles Whiting? What about Wo Len Chan? No? Or Stuart Chalmers at Macy's? Also no? Really? But how could that be?

"I was just a programmer" was all Ethan could offer.

As they went on to question his projects—their scope, size of the team, his place in it, schedules, completion times—Ethan had the horrible sense that these men were trying to catch him in a lie. Would they see that he'd exaggerated about that job at Unitek? That period of "consulting"—would they see through that, too? Ethan had a sudden vision of himself through the eyes of these venture capitalists: A graduate-school dropout. A kid with an ordinary résumé. A programmer who didn't know any of the key people where he worked. Someone sitting on top of a *big orange ball*, forgodsakes.

"I'm very much involved with research into artificial life," Ethan supplied in his own defense.

Handsomer and Balding dropped their little steeples, sat back, blinked at him.

"Artificial life," Ethan went on. "Are you familiar with The Game of Life developed by the mathematician John Conway? No? Well, it's a universe of two-dimensional cellular automata. Imagine them as squares in a grid, or cells, each cell having eight neighbors, one at each of the four sides and one at each corner. Anyway, Conway devised three simple rules that decide if the cell gets born, survives, or dies, depending only on how many neighbors it has. For example, if a cell is either too crowded or too isolated, it dies. Anyway, what's interesting about all this is that from those simple rules came patterns of great complexity. Really amazing, actually, very complex. Which leads to the idea that maybe life—ha-ha, the real thing, small l—maybe life . . ."

He watched the eyes of the two venture capitalists grow wide with alarm. He knew he should stop himself, but since graduate school, he hadn't talked in detail about the Game to anyone, except to Joanna, who'd reacted with sarcasm—Don't think about her now! he ordered himself—and so here was his mouth running on without him—stop! he thought—but where?

". . . anyway, to the idea that maybe the complex patterns of life came from the same source. You know, in the operation of many, many small, simple rules. You see, there's a discontinuity between the domain of the rules and the actual resultant phenomena—you can't predict the phenomena from the rules—so maybe this means—"

"Look, Levin," Handsomer broke in finally, "let's just get down to it."

Ethan was aware of relief: they'd stopped him.

"We're talking to you because we're trying to gauge our confidence level for a Q2 85 FCS."

"Cue two eight five eff see ess," Ethan repeated without understanding what he was saying.

"First customer ship," supplied Balding. "By April eighty-five. June the latest."

Customers. Ship something to them. In a year from now, thought Ethan. *Soon.*

"How comfortable are you with that date?" asked Handsomer.

Ethan looked over to see Harry's reaction. But—oh no!—the sudden motion of his shoulders set the ball moving under him again, and Ethan had to roll his pelvis forward, then back, then forward again, to compensate. "Well, we've been right on schedule," he said, still rolling around, "or *I've* been on schedule, that is."

"Yeah," said Harry, "but you're the only one on time, and anyway, that schedule has us done about ten months later. March eighty-six. Or maybe April."

The two programmers looked at each other.

"So we're accelerating?" Ethan asked.

"Accelerating," Harry replied flatly.

No one spoke for a moment.

"And that bug we saw," Handsomer went on. "We're assuming that's a fluke?"

The bug at the demo. The system freezing up in front of everyone. The bug Harry said he'd better fix. "Just a bug," said Ethan, with a thrust forward of his pelvis.

"Not a problem," said Harry.

"I'll fix it," said Ethan in a confident voice.

But by then Ethan was skuttling left and right, back and forth, to keep himself from falling off the ball. For some reason, turning to look at Harry had set off not only a roll but some kind of bouncing motion, and now Ethan's every attempt to counter it was only adding energy to the ball. He felt himself start to sweat, as the simple problem of staying seated had become real exercise. "I'll fix it," Ethan repeated absently as he teetered around, left, right, left again. "Just a bug." When suddenly he lost it. The ball took a lurch, Ethan tried to counter it, and the big orange blob shot out from under him.

"Damn!" he said, jumping to his feet.

But luckily for Ethan, the venture capitalists also decided it was time to stand up. They never mentioned the ball. They simply stood there quietly as Ethan kicked it into a corner and Harry came out from behind his desk. They'd decided, evidently, that they'd learned what they had come to learn, and it was time for the meeting to be over.

They shook hands with Harry and Ethan, said they'd be hearing from them, and then they were gone, leaving the door open behind them.

"Close it," said Harry.

Ethan closed the door.

"Shit," Harry said.

They sat down in the chairs the VCs had occupied.

"Let's meet tomorrow and look at the schedule," Harry said.

"Yeah," said Ethan. "What'll we take out?"

"They don't want us to take anything out."

"You mean they want the same work in like half the time?"

"Yep."

"Shit," said Ethan.

Harry reached down to pick up the little mechanical dog, which had lodged itself under his desk. Slowly, breathing heavily from the effort of bending over, Harry wound its key. Then he released the dog to make its way across the floor. Until the spring wound down, Harry and Ethan stretched out their legs and watched it: its little mouth yapping silently, its furry plastic legs pawing at the air.

Ethan went to his desk and put the bug under the debugger. His idea was to fix UI-1017 by the end of the day, close it, start fresh at tomorrow's meeting with Harry. He'd put everything aside for now: Joanna, new work, the schedule. One less worry, he thought.

A cyborg experience: On one side of Ethan was the large graphics monitor that would run his program, a test version of the user interface, with its freeze-up waiting to happen. In front of him was another monitor, but this one a plain green-on-black character terminal, on which he would run the debugger, a monitor program, under whose observing eye the front end would run. The debugger and the graphics terminal could not share a screen; they lived in two different computing universes, one as old as teletype (the debugger) and one just coming into being (the bit-mapped graphics screen). And if all this hardware weren't enough, there were also two workstations involved: one to run the front end and the debugger, and another running the database, the back end, to which Ethan's front-end machine was connected by a long network cable that stretched down the hall. Ethan was therefore surrounded: two monitors, two keyboards, a mouse, manuals, cables, connectors, a tangle of cords.

He turned to the character terminal and typed:

```
dbx ui-levintest
```

In response, the system started the debugger, loaded his user-interface test program into memory, and replied:

```
dbx version 1.2
Type 'help' for help.
reading symbolic information . . .
(dbx)_
```

Where it stopped, the cursor blinking after the prompt (dbx), as the debugger waited for Ethan to issue his next command.

Ethan had his ideas where the bug might be hiding. All the certainties he'd considered and abandoned when he last decided that the bug was fixed—the lines of reasoning he'd been following before he swept them all away into the slop bucket of "library inconsistency"— all this came back to him. The freeze-up had occurred on two different screens, two different menus. It was probably not a factor, then, of a particular screen or menu. It would have to be the underlying code for any menu.

So at the waiting prompt, he entered:

```
(dbx) stop in CreateMenu
```

Which would cause the user interface to stop running when it entered the function named CreateMenu. He did the same for PutMenu and GetMenu, and he now had three "breakpoints," three places that would cause the user interface to pause, wait for further instructions, and let him look around.

Then on the debugger keyboard he typed:

```
(dbx) run
```

On the big graphics monitor at his side, the front-end program began running. The screen cleared, becoming an all-over middle-gray tone, in preparation for putting up the first window. Then it stopped.

On the debugger monitor, a line of code was displayed:

```
int CreateMenu(curr_window, curr_menu)
```

His first breakpoint. The front-end program, as it was running, had come to the first of Ethan's stopping places and, under the control of the debugger, had duly stopped. After which Ethan entered:

```
(dbx) step
```

Which told the user interface to go on and step its way through the code, one programming statement at a time. The program resumed execution—for a single code line—then stopped again:

```
if (curr_window == NULL)
                ui_err(CR_MENU, "null win pointer");
```

Ethan looked at the line of code—a standard check at the top of a function for a valid incoming value. Okay, fine. Nothing wrong here. And again he typed:

```
(dbx) step
```

And again the program ran for one more line of code, the debugger screen then showing:

```
if ((curr_menu =
            winalloc(curr_window->curr_menu_spec))
                                        == NULL)
                    ui_err(CR_MENU, "winalloc failed");
```

Again the code looked fine, and again he was ready to go on. Step, he wrote. Line of code, the debugger answered. Step, line of code; step, line of code. Step, step, step. Now and then he would check the values of some of the variables, this time the width of the newly created menu in pixels:

```
(dbx) print curr_menu->menu_region->width
125
```

Which looked right for the screen he was using, and again he stepped, and again he asked for some values, until he had gotten all the way through CreateMenu without seeing any problems. Now it was time to let the user interface continue running, and at the debugger keyboard he typed:

```
(dbx) cont
```

On the graphics terminal, as the program continued execution, the initial window of the user interface appeared. Ethan looked at it carefully, at all the text and icons and buttons the program had just painted on the screen. Okay, he decided. Everything fine. Then he took the mouse in hand, waved it around for a while, and clicked on a menu button. This would take the program to Ethan's next breakpoint, and instead of displaying the drop-down menu, the program paused as it was supposed to. Ethan turned back to the debugger screen, which showed:

```
int PutMenu(curr_menu)
```

The start of the function responsible for showing the menu. And again he stepped his way through the code. And again he checked the values of variables. And so on: step, look at a line of code, check some values, step again. On through all of PutMenu. Step, step, step. Into the functions called by PutMenu—step, step, step—and then into the functions *they* called. Down and down into the layers of code calling code. Step. Check some values. Looks okay. Step. Ethan went walking through the code one statement at a time, watching his program run not in the nanosecond world of the machine but at the paltry, moment-by-moment speed of human attention. The debugger showing him not the program as he had imagined it while coding—when his mind had been ablaze with details and procedures, and he'd been struggling to get it down, line by line—but the actual program, its operation, its functioning, its effects in the "real" world of chips and hard drives and main memory.

Step. Check some values. Looks all right. Step.

And so began his most sustained (and strained) relationship with the debugger. His daily, repetitive, compulsive—almost addictive—conversation with this electronic guide through the minefield of bugs. His digital companion, algorithmic pal, one of the two programmatic assistants with whom a programmer comes to pass more time than with a friend, or a parent, or a lover, or a spouse.

First comes the compiler. Between the programmer speaking code, and the chip speaking zeroes and ones, stands the compiler, translator of code into chip-speak. The chip's humorless factotum, who verifies that everything written by the programmer—every comma, every dot—is syntactically legal; who checks that if one is supposed to be speaking C or Pascal or COBOL or BASIC, one is indeed speaking proper C or Pascal or COBOL or BASIC. But merely proper. The compiler doesn't know if your instructions will actually do the job you want done, only that they are expressed correctly. It is a United Nations translator under a headphone, a passive processor, mindlessly turning French into English, with no power or inclination to stand up, rip off the headphones, and shout, *Mais monsieur! C'est complètement stupide!*

Which brings up the next difficulty: Once your instructions to the chip are expressed in a language it understands, it will do your bidding, mindlessly. But perhaps your instructions make no sense in relation to the task at hand? Yes, that is precisely what had happened to Ethan Levin. His program had made it through the compiler. He had a file full of legal instructions ready to run. But when they ran, the program went inexplicably wrong.

And so to the debugger. To see the results of his instructions. The actual path taken. The branch that went this way instead of that on the road to UI-1017.

Step, step, step.

Step. Check some values. Looks okay. Step.

"Lunch?"

It was Steghman, his head poking into the doorway. "Lunch?" he repeated.

As always, Ethan checked his hunger by the workstation clock: 12:30. Lunchtime. "Sure."

They went to the basement cafeteria as usual, sat side by side on the stools at the counter looking out onto a hallway. Sandwiches wrapped in paper on a plastic tray. Soft drinks in waxed-paper cups with lids and straws.

"Had my VC meeting," said Steghman.

"Uhm?" said Ethan.

"You?"

"Yeah."

They ate for a while.

"How'd it go?" asked Ethan.

Steghman took a bite, chewed, pulled a drink off his straw. "Tense," he said finally.

"Yeah," said Ethan.

"You?" asked Steghman.

Bad, Ethan wanted to say. Humiliating. There was the orange ball. The people quiz. Joanna. The Game of Life. The bug. The impossible release date.

"Aggressive scheduling," he said.

Steghman laughed. And Ethan laughed: Harry Minor's heh-heh nervous laugh. Aggressive scheduling: programmer-speak for impossible.

The bug hid from the debugger. Ethan went back to his office, his debugger, his bug, but the system never crashed while the debugger was watching it. A quantum effect? Something in UI-1017 that was like an electron whose path is altered by the presence of an observer?

Ethan was certain—at each step—that the next one would bring on the crash. I'll put in a breakpoint here, he thought; the program will pause; I'll step to a line of code, and certainly there it will be: the freeze-up, the exact point where some mislogic had wound its way through the layers of code, finally percolating up into functional absurdity. Some pointer would be NULL when it should have the value of an address in memory. Some Boolean variable would evaluate to FALSE when it should be TRUE. Some return code would show an error condition that was not checked by the program. And then all he had to do was think his way back through the layers, discover why it was NULL, FALSE, unchecked.

Step, step, step.

He ran his hands through his hair. Stared at the screen. Entered a new breakpoint.

Step, step, step.

The afternoon wore away, then the evening. Thorne left, Herring left, Ethan got up and turned off the lights. The windows faded to black, the lights blinked off in office after office across the floor. Step, step, step. It must be here, he thought. No, here. It will crash the next time. Okay, then the next time.

There was a roar at the door. The lights flashed on.

"*Lo siento*," said the office cleaner.

She ignored him, he, her. He lifted his feet, she vacuumed around him, turned off the lights, and moved on.

The moment the room went dark again, Ethan felt a surge of panic. What time was it?

Eleven. He should call Joanna.

The phone rang and rang. No answer. He dialed again. Again no answer. Where was she? *Where was she?*

Better fix that bug, Harry had said. William Harland is acting like he never saw a bug before. The VCs are watching. Tomorrow he was supposed to meet with Harry about the schedule. He could not stop and simply leave a note for himself. Tomorrow there would be no "Here you are, Ethan." No message saying, "Investigate pointer indirection." No, the only note he could leave himself could be the bug report itself, with its message to the testers saying, "Fixed."

Step, step, step.

Some part of him knew that he should get away from the debugger. He should get away from the machine, stop and think on a yellow pad, a whiteboard. He wasn't making headway like this. He kept beating against the same certainties—here, else here, else here. Writing and sketching might break his thinking patterns, force him into other channels. But there was something seductive about the debugger: the way it answered him, tirelessly, consistently. Such a tight loop: Step, he said. Line of code, it answered. Step, line of code; step, line of code. It was like the compulsion of playing solitaire: simple, repetitive, working toward a goal that was sure to be attained in just one more hand, just one more, and then one more again.

And so the paradox: The more the debugger remained the tireless binary companion it was designed to be—answering, answering, answering without hesitation or effort late into the night—the more exhausted and hesitant the human, Ethan Levin, found himself to be. He was sinking to the debugger's level. Thinking like it. Asking only the questions it could answer. All the while he suffered what the debugger did not have to endure: the pains of the body, the tingling wrists and fingers, the stiffness in the neck, the aching back, the numb legs. And worse, the messy wet chemistry of the emotions, the waves of anxiety that washed across him, and then, without warning, the sudden electric spikes of panic.

NOURISHMENT

DAYS OPEN: 92

Step, step, step.

He had to fix this bug, get it off his desk, clear his mind.

Step. Check some values. Okay.

Joanna didn't get home until two in the morning.

Step. Check. Okay.

Where was she? Don't think about it now. Be careful. Pay attention.

Step.

He'd met with Harry first thing in the morning. They'd worked backward from the VCs' intended ship date, adding time for everything that had to come before it: coding and testing and documentation, sales and customer-support training, production of the distribution media, of the boxes, the labels. In the end, Harry had just sat there laughing uncontrollably.

Step. Check. Okay.

He couldn't ask her where she'd been, could he? He himself didn't get home until one-thirty, hadn't even called until eleven. Still, he was annoyed to find her gone, no word where, like his needs didn't matter. She was probably at Carolyn's anyway. Carolyn and that damn baby.

There was just that note she'd left him on the kitchen table: "Ansel Adams died." Who the hell was Ansel Adams?

Step.

"They found the AIDS virus."

Huh? Oh. Herring with the newspaper. "What's that?"

"The AIDS virus. They think they've found the virus that causes AIDS."

"Huh. Good."

Step.

"And listen to this. MicroPro laid off twenty-five people. ' "This is not a crisis," said their spokesman Tom Hacker.' Hacker! Can you believe their spokesman is named Hacker?"

Ethan put his hands flat on the keyboard. "Herring. I'm trying to concentrate. Will you please just shut up?"

Herring muttered. Then shut up.

Step. Check some values. Okay.

UI-1017 had made another appearance. A newly hired saleswoman had been demonstrating the system to a prospective customer—a bank, the biggest bank in New York—when the inevitable occurred. Point, click; point, click, then smash: an endless beep, the screen full of lines and black boxes, the mouse and keyboard dead. Of course the saleswoman didn't get a core file. This bug seemed to want to show itself to as many people as possible, but only in the hands of a novice, who would panic and let it slip away before it could be caught. "A little jester of a bug," Harry Minor called it at their last group meeting, laughing; but Harry's joke, meant to be reassuring, had the opposite effect. The bug had acquired a personality, a character, a will. And a name: *Jester.*

"Lunch?"

Bill Steghman's head in the doorway. Twelve-forty said the system clock. "All right."

Lunch at the counter facing a hallway. Steghman's twisted spine on the stool beside him. The same sandwiches as every day, turkey, on rye, no mayo.

"How're things?" he asked.

"Fine," Ethan said. "You?"

Steghman was quiet for while. "Okay."

Something—dim, distant—revealed itself to Ethan in the pause before Steghman's reply, in the barest shift of tone between his usual "fine" and this "okay." But before he could make too much of it, Steghman was wiping his mouth, balling up his sandwich paper, standing up with his tray.

"Ready?"

"Ready."

But Ethan was not exactly ready for what happened next. For no sooner did he sit down at his terminal, type in his next step command, when the entire room took a sudden lurch. A boom sounded as if it had come somewhere from deep underground. And everything—doors, open file drawers, whiteboards, miniblinds, light fixtures, monitors, plants, chairs, desk toys—started trembling.

"Whoa!" Herring shouted, jumping up from his seat.

"Earthquake!" came from somewhere out in the hall.

The shaking seemed to go on and on, the room full of rattling and sudden clatter: things falling, crackling like walls buckling, the whole building suddenly revealed as only a system of balances and stresses, like sitting on the shoulders of someone wiggling this way and that in arbitrary, impossible directions. Ethan's impulse was to run outside, get away. But through the rattling miniblinds he saw the cars in the parking lot rocking on their tires, the light poles swaying like palm trees above them. *The earth is everywhere,* sounded in his head, a thought he knew was stupid even as it came to him. He turned and watched the graphics monitor jumping around on its base, sixty pounds jiggling like a sprung jack-in-the-box. The ground under his feet suddenly re-vealed itself to be nothing more than a bit of scum afloat molten rock, thin as the skin on a pot of scalding milk. *Plate tectonics*, he told him-self, the technical term, the science lesson, the idea of it. But it did no good: He saw the wide fear in Bradley Thorne's eyes, and he knew his must hold the same.

How long did it go on? Seconds, minutes, an eternity, as time slowed down, down, down in the accumulating awareness of things that formerly had not been known to express themselves. Walls that had been solid, groaning. Doors that had been closed, rattling to be opened. Windows that had been clear, bending with displeasure. And ceilings—ceilings!—that had been invisible, up there, of no account, suddenly insisting upon their supreme and deadly importance.

"Everyone get under the doorway!" Ethan shouted.

Where immediately the three of them crowded, standing back to chest like soldiers in a row; while just outside their door the partitions wavered like wheat stalks in the wind, and there was no sound except for the peculiar creaking of walls and floors and ceilings, and everyone silent, afraid.

Then, as abruptly as it started, it stopped.

"Shit!" said Thorne.

The receptionist, Lisette, came through the main room holding a squawking portable radio to her ear. "Six point two!" she shouted. "Calaveras fault! Six point two!"

Giddy relief was everywhere, the wobbly, voluble happiness of dan-ger averted.

Until the lights went out.

"Shit," said Thorne again.

"Synch, synch, synch!" came the cry from every programmer's throat, shouting in the direction of the system administrator's office that someone should save the integrity of the file systems, synch up the servers while they're still on battery backup, do an orderly shutdown.

Ethan picked up the phone, pressed the button for Joanna at work.

A fast busy signal, the annoying, rising, three-beep tone, then the operator's recorded voice saying all circuits were busy.

The freeways were empty. Were they always this quiet on a Tuesday afternoon, or was it the earthquake, the fear of overpasses and bridges, of tiny cracks and hidden faults and solid things falling down? Ethan drove slowly, his window open to get the air, which was warm and unusually humid. The sun seemed too bright, everything haloed, blurred, in a greasy kind of light. Where was everybody? Except for the odd delivery van here and there, the world seemed deserted.

"Ethan! What are you doing home!"

It was Carolyn, wheeling Precious Flower down the street in a stroller. She came up to his parked car almost on the run.

"Everything all right?" he asked her.

She kept looking behind him, at his house, then back to him, apparently agitated about something.

"No. I mean, yes. Nothing wrong. I'm just surprised. Surprised to find you home in the middle of the day."

He explained about the power being out. She nodded but kept glancing behind him. He turned in the direction of her gaze: nothing, the house behind its overgrown lawn, insects buzzing in the greasy light.

"Hey, take care," he said, starting for his door.

"We lost a few plates, Ethan!" she called out.

"Oh, that's too bad," he said, continuing on through the front yard.

"And cracks! Ethan! We have lots of new cracks!"

"So long," he waved.

Inside, the house was very hot, baking behind closed windows. He went from room to room to get the windows opened, struggled to unjam them, cursed and muttered and began to sweat. New cracks led out from corners of the window and door frames at nearly perfect forty-five-degree angles to the joints. Sheetrock dust coated the sills. Pictures hung askew. Books had tumbled from shelves. Kitchen cabinet doors were thrown open. The plant on top of the refrigerator had crashed to the floor.

"Shit!" Ethan cursed as he stepped into broken pot shards.

"Joanna?"

There was no reason for her to be there. It was just something about the house cracked at the corners, the hothouse atmosphere of the closed-up rooms, the things crooked and fallen and broken that made it seem she should be there. A reflex: come home and call out for Joanna, who was almost always there, home first, waiting for him.

"Joanna? Are you here?"

No answer. Of course she wasn't there. She was at work. He started up the stairs.

It was even hotter on the second floor. The window at the top of the staircase was frozen shut, and he ran downstairs to look for something in his toolbox that would break it open.

When the phone rang.

"Hello?"

Click. A hang-up.

"Shit!"

Back to rummaging in his toolbox, when it rang again.

"Goddamnit, Marsha! What the fuck's the matter with you?"

He knew her by her breathing on the other end of the line, that same heavy-woman's breath as the last time.

"Oh, Ethan. I'm so sorry. I—"

"God fucking damnit, Marsha. Call or don't call. But don't keep hanging up like this when you get me on the line! Anyway, Joanna's not here. I tried to get through to her at work, but the circuits were down."

Marsha fell quiet, a moment, two. Then said: "I couldn't get Paul at work either."

"Yeah. The circuits were—"

"No. I got through all right. He wasn't there."

At first, Ethan didn't catch the significance of this. Ostrick wasn't there, so what, maybe he was dead in a ditch by the side of the road, for all Ethan cared. But as the moments passed and Marsha said nothing more, just sat there breathing into the phone, something slowly took shape in his mind. Then it was suddenly clear—ridiculously, stupidly clear—what Marsha was thinking.

"You mean you called here looking for *Paul*? You thought *Paul* would be here?"

"Yes."

"Why, that's . . . It's . . ." The idea installed itself in Ethan's imagination. While he's at work, Joanna and Ostrick talk on the phone, agree to meet, *here*, Joanna opens the front door, and it's Ostrick. They go upstairs, upstairs to *his* bedroom, to *his* bed, where Paul Ostrick fills the room with the stink of his beedis, then puts the stink of himself all over Joanna, his skinny bony body. . . . "Ridiculous!" he shouted into the phone. "Absurd! Of all the . . . Look, Marsha. No one is here but me. No one! And Joanna is not seeing Paul. Is not! All right: This thing happened, it happens, it's over. Joanna and I are staying together, and that's the end of it, you hear me? I want you to leave it alone. I want Paul *and* you out of our lives, you hear me?"

She was quiet for a moment, sighed, then said in an even voice: "Okay, Ethan. I don't think you and I have that much say over all this anymore. But okay. Think what you like. I won't bother you. Goodbye. I'm going to hang up now."

"Fine! Fine with me! Hang up!"

And she did.

He picked up the jimmy he'd found in his toolbox, marched upstairs. With a single thrust, he broke open the jammed stairway window. Then the ones in the guest room. His energy took him bounding into the bedroom, jimmy in hand like a knife, when something stopped him at the doorway. A smell, faint. What was it? No! he said to the answer that had formed itself in his mind. *It is not cloves.* He put the jimmy to the front window and air swept into the room. No smell, he told himself. It's your imagination, it's nothing. No one's been here, not all day, no one at all. He broke open the side window, for more air, more fresh air, more air without the smell of anything, and in came the thud of bass notes. Rock music. Thumping.

He looked down: the same pickup in the driveway. "Shit!" he said.

He slammed down the bedroom window and went into the study, where he checked his system to see if it had gone down in a power interruption. No, no power outage. He could work here, on his copy of the simulation code.

```
Here you are, Ethan.
```

Here you are.

Ethan.

Here.

The migration algorithm. His creatures moving from habitat to habitat to find food. Yes: He would go back there, to the place where he'd left off programming. He would return to the point in his life when he'd last come through this section of the code, to that night when Joanna's trip was still new and the bad things that happened were still yet to happen—no! He had to skip over that point (because now he knew too well what would indeed happen). No, he had to get to the Ethan Levin before that. To the Ethan who had first written the message. When was that? Before he'd started at Telligentsia. *Who* was that? An Ethan Levin still confident, still coding input screens for insurance adjusters, still happily sure of his life with Joanna McCarthy, sturdy-legged environmental activist turned administrator, who came home from riding her bike to do wonderful things to him in the shower.

```
To get out of static alternation, introduce migration.
```

The migration algorithm. He would go back to this problem, a thought-curve that began when he was still at Insuracorp, before the layoffs had turned the floor he worked on into a blasted landscape of ruined partitions and sprung cables. How had the problem presented itself to him back then, when his life was good and stable and he'd had time to work on his simulated world? It had posed itself as the banishment of the deus ex machina, as the challenge of setting his creatures in motion without specific orders from on high from a concerned, involved, watching God. It had to be something local, small: a packet passed from one creature to the next like a message circulated in a game of Telephone. Even if that message were sometimes ineffective, scrambled, useless—especially so, because those failures held the seeds of the unexpected. Mistakes were like mutations, he'd told himself, mostly disastrous but vital: the source of chance, change, life going its own way.

Mistakes. Failures. *Bugs*, sounded in his head. *The* bug. The one he'd better fix. And with that thought came the awareness of thumping, the beat knocking on the walls and floorboards, like something wanting to get inside. And into his head came Joanna, the question he didn't want to ask. *Where was she?* And then the faint, teasing, cloying scent of something that wasn't—wasn't—cloves.

Here you are, Ethan.

Ethan.

Here.

Programming: a dense, precise, and ordered conversation, an argument in the formal sense, with reason, without heat. A conversation but with programmers he would never meet, whose code he had to understand, interact with, join: the designers of the chips, the writers of microcode burned into the chips, the authors of the operating system, the file system, the device drivers, the network, the designers of the programming language, the writers of the compiler. A universe of rules, parameters, procedures, conventions, formats, commands. A conversation so dense that time as humans know it barely operated inside it, and where many things—faint whiffs of cloves, for instance, or bare strains of music, or thoughts of straying women—remained locked outside its event horizon. *Here* the weave of thought was so tight that only the work of other programmers could enter. *Here* Ethan connected to the layers upon layers of code his unknown colleagues before him had deposited over time, as they like Ethan sat alone for hours and days, months and years, each engaged in a private, precise conversation with the code in the machine. Each having stepped out of his or her own particular moments of heartache or happiness—who could tell? it didn't matter—to come *here.*

Ethan's mind slipped into a tight loop: code and compile; recode and recompile; test and recode and recompile; the endlessly reiterative process of turning a human idea into machine-comprehensible instructions. Over and over, his thoughts moved all the way to the bottom of one exquisitely small detail. How much time should a creature pass without eating before it begins to search for a new habitat? What exactly would be the scale of time in this universe? And how would it be counted—the system call offered by the operating system? or lower, in megahertz cycles of the internal clock? Questions like these offered themselves to him, and he took hold of each one as if it were a diver's line, a channel to a dark, low place that most people would never think of visiting.

Because here each question only opened a deep procession of other questions: one question fracturing into tens, and each of those exploding into thousands of details. It was a process of unpacking thought, trying to clear it of all the unexpressed understandings, connotations, associations, contradictions that live in the mind like dormant viruses, invisible and unaccounted for within the human notions of "I think" and "I know." Until, finally, the scramble of average human thinking cleared away, he could come to the small-grained, bounded bit of an idea that could be expressed as lines of code.

```c
#include "etypes.h"

creature_cycle(current_creature)
CREATURE *current_creature;
{
    CREATURE *neighbor_list = NULL;
    int       number_of_neighbors = 0;

    /* first do eat and possibly die operations   */
    /* eat if there's food                         */
    /* if no food and starved to limit, die        */

    if (isfood_here(current_creature))
        eat(current_creature);
    else if (at_starved_limit(current_creature))
    {
        die(current_creature);
        return;                    /** NOTE BREAK HERE **/
    }

    /* if still alive...                    */
    /* do reproduce and move operations     */
    /* determining reproduction              */
    /* and next screen positions             */

    if (well_fed(current_creature)
                    ||
        normal_fed(current_creature))
    {
        /* well-fed, normal: keep current trajectory */
        set_preserved_position(current_creature);

        /* well-fed reproduce with best-fed neighbor   */
        if ( well_fed(current_creature)
                      &&
             ((number_of_neighbors =
               get_creature_neighbors(current_creature,
                               &neighbor_list)) > 0) )
        {
            reproduce(current_creature,
                        get_best_neighbor(neighbor_list,
                                    number_of_neighbors));

            /* note: reproduce will default to no-op */
            /* if no well-fed neighbor                */
        }
    }
```

```
    else if (hungry(current_creature)
                    ||
            starving(current_creature))
    {

        /* set for migration              */
        /* follow best neighbor, if any   */
        if ((number_of_neighbors =
            get_creature_neighbors(current_creature,
                              &neighbor_list)) > 0)
        {
            set_migrate_position(current_creature,
                        get_best_neighbor(neighbor_list,
                                    number_of_neighbors));
        }
        else
        {
            /* no neighbor - just set next position   */
            /* for random roaming                     */

            set_random_position(current_creature);
        }

            /* note: set_migrate_position defaults   */
            /* to random if no well-fed neighbor     */
    }
    else
            eworld_error(current_creature,
                         CYCLE, HUNGER_STATUS);
            /* status must be well, normal   */
            /* hungry or starving            */


    move(current_creature);
    return;
}
```

Time slid by like a fat fish in deep water. Ethan's awareness of his body, that heavy container wanting rest and food, was lost. Now there were only his thoughts, a deep inner muttering, the mind talking to a more abstracted version of itself. It didn't matter that afternoon turned to evening and then night without Joanna coming home. He barely noticed the hour when her key rattled in the front door lock and she made her way upstairs to the bathroom, where the water ran and ran for what might have been hours or days. What was she washing off? It didn't matter. Here, where Ethan was, there were only his creatures, his O's, and the simple message each one who had eaten well would pass on to the next. Not an order, but a direction. A single knowledge molecule. A message that, at each point of delivery, would slowly move a milling, searching, hungry creature toward a richer place.

Here, the message would say, is nourishment.

PART THREE

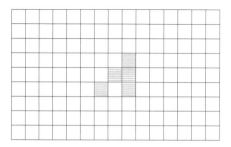

"You are acquainted with my failure and how heavily I bore the disappointment."

—LETTER FROM R. WALTON TO HIS SISTER,

MRS. SAVILLE.

MARY SHELLEY, *FRANKENSTEIN*

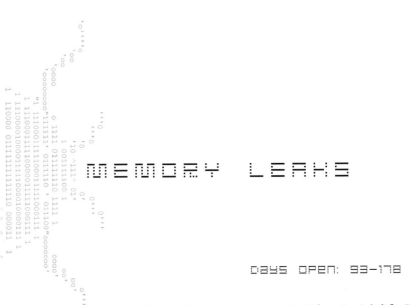

MEMORY LEAKS

Of course no one knew what was happening in Ethan Levin's life. He spoke to no one, confided in no one, not even to the one person at Telligentsia who could be considered his friend, Bill Steghman (oh, yes; everyone overheard their hilarious mealtime "conversations"). To us, the testers, he was like all the programmers: impatient, defensive, condescending. The fact that he might be unhappy was irrelevant, since a nasty, unhappy person is like a nasty drunk: whatever allowances you're inclined to make are trumped by the nastiness. If we noticed any additional short-temperedness in Ethan's behavior, we put it down to the bug, UI-1017, elusive spoiler of the front end—which continued to live up to the name Harry Minor had given it: Jester.

It made a rash of appearances. As before, this bug seemed to choose its moments. A demonstration before the procurer general of the United States Navy. A presentation to the technology officers of the New York Stock Exchange. A visit to the computer specialists at Goldman, Sachs brokerage. UI-1017 seemed to have cultivated a certain taste in its audiences, a certain elite discernment, preferring men in expensive suits with impossibly large sums of money at their disposal. Women might be present too, but their role was confined to sales staff newly hired by Telligentsia, flustered women in red or purple skirt suits with hugely padded jacket shoulders, who made desperate calls to the testers and support programmers yet somehow never seemed to catch the image of the bug.

"Do a kill minus three," I'd tell the padded-shouldered-ones who'd reached me. "*K-I-L-L* space minus-sign three. No. No space between the minus and three. No. What? What do you mean it's too late?"

There was always something: The idiot sales-support person who, like my cubicle neighbor Mara Margolies, did a kill minus nine, unconditional program death, producing no core file, no dump of the program's memory state. Or the panicked saleswoman who simply turned off the machine. Or the one who finally issued the correct kill command, only to find that no core file had been produced because some incompetent had made the disk directory unwritable. Was UI-1017 clever or the humans simply stupid? It should have been the easiest thing in the world: a bug, a dump of memory, husk of the dead program the engineer could examine to find the cause of death. Every other bug complied and laid itself under this digital microscope. Yet in the case of this Jester, it seemed that every combination of computer technicality and human ignorance conspired against us: UI-1017 appeared then hid to plague us another day.

I use the word "plague" because it was about this time that everyone who came in contact with UI-1017 began acting strangely around it. It was as if this bug had something unwholesome about it, something vexing and uncanny. This sounds overly dramatic, but I choose these words carefully—hex, vex, plague. Was it the way this bug continuously evaded the core dump? Was it its odd preference for appearing before novices? I include my younger self in this category, for after all I was the barest of beginners when I first came across the system-freeze called UI-1017. What did I really know of computers and software, and the way their tangled code could sometimes produce spectacular failure? And of the occasional failure, more subtle and elusive, the one that came and went without apparent proximate cause? For this is what happened with the bug. We—the testers and quality-assurance manager—could not predictably make it come and go. We could not, despite repeated and determined testing, reproduce the exact set of conditions that brought about the freeze-up of the system. In the face of this apparent irrationality, our behavior around the bug began to change. We stopped referring to it as UI-1017 and began addressing it by name, Jester. When the front-end program was running, we stopped talking about it in the third person, as an object—"it"—and began addressing it as "you" (*Usted*, we would have said if we were speaking Spanish, *Sie* in German, formally, as if speaking to a superior, someone we both feared and ridiculed, a high school principal, perhaps). "Are you there, you devil?" I heard Mara Margolies muttering in the neighboring cubicle one day, as if our Jester, hiding behind the screen of the monitor, lay in wait to hear us.

It's hard to pinpoint exactly when this sense of uncanniness began, the precise moment at which UI-1017 stopped being funny—a joke we all enjoyed at Ethan Levin's expense—and began to produce, in all of us, a feeling of unease. The change took place over the course of several weeks. The last rains of the season ended, the summer fogs had yet to begin, May came to a close under a hot dry sky. At the company picnic, in the scrubby hills of Redwood Park, the programmers began murmuring something I didn't understand at the time. "Memory leak," they said, looking at each other with an expression that mixed fear with accusation. Although it would be several weeks before I understood the technical meaning of the phrase, it was to my novice's ear an oddly suggestive explanation for the cause of the bug: the idea that memory could just leak away—thoughts, ideas, plans, all fixed and arranged in the mind, somehow breaking into drops and running away like liquid mercury. Yes, the more I considered it, the more the front end's behavior seemed a species of brain damage, memory run amok, the system, like an autistic child, freezing the keyboard and the mouse, shutting out communication with the world but going on to exist in some odd, internal state that was neither exactly dead nor alive.

What I recall from the days leading up to this period are the nervous calls from the saleswomen after their encounters with the bug, and the annoyed-angry voice of William Harland exhorting us at a company meeting—"The investors and customers are watching us! This ridiculous bug must be fixed!" As for Ethan Levin, I remember almost nothing about him during this time, nothing about what he might or might not have been feeling as the pressures mounted around him. I didn't care a thing about him. He'd given me no reason to. He remained as oblivious to me as ever, simply giving me the same "Put it over there" as I brought him report after report of the bug.

Besides, Ethan was very shortly to change the entire course of my life, and it's almost impossible for me to see him clearly at this juncture. When I look back on this time, all I can see is the looming detour in my existence. I remember Ethan's role in it—how could I forget?—but Ethan himself, as a person, was to me no more than a dumb, massive asteroid careening through the universe, soon to smash into me and make my whole way of life go extinct.

What did take up my attention then was something that would ultimately prove much less important to my future: James Havermeyer. For here is the part where his comings and goings began to be associated, in my mind, with the comings and goings of the bug. It was silly and superstitious—I didn't *actually* believe there was a formal relationship between James and Jester, aside from the alliteration—but it was odd that each of James's several arrivals during this period corresponded to an appearance of the bug. I remember joking with him at the airport when I went to pick him up on one of those arrivals, "You're sure you're not really the human projection of this nasty bug I found at work?"

I remember the incident clearly because it was one of those odd times when James was actually affectionate and attentive toward me.

He could do this—every now and then, just when I was about to give up on him, he could turn into the tenderhearted partner I always imagined he could be. His reaction to seeing me at the gate as I stood leaning on a luggage cart was to break into a smile. He walked slowly toward me, still smiling. He stopped in front of me, looked into my eyes, then, slowly, kissed me. "I'm crazy about you," he whispered in my ear.

Crazy about me!

What is it about the normally withdrawn person that makes his sudden affections so compelling? For me, I think, it was the sense that this was only the start of much more to come, as if, after all the disappointments, you have suddenly found the entryway into this closed-off creature, a gate, a fount—a veritable bulging lava dome, out of which will shortly issue great waves of hot flowing loving passion! Or maybe it was nothing more than an evil kind of operant conditioning, the way you can drive a little lab rat crazy by giving it rewards at inconsistent, apparently random intervals. I glowed with happiness to learn he was *crazy about me.* And then I immediately looked down at my clothes, wondering: Is it this short skirt that got his attention? At my shoes: The boots? My hair? This new scarf? Was it the effect of the luggage cart I'd managed to snare without paying for it, which so satisfied James's basic needs for bargains in all his transactions? I suppose it's what comes of being raised, as I was, by parents who pay attention to you when they feel like it: you become nervous and superstitious, wondering what it is about this particular moment that makes you more lovable than in all those other moments when it seems you should have been equally lovable. In the hope of winning affection again, you wind up making painfully ridiculous associations. I wore that skirt the next two times I picked James up at the airport. I never again showed up at the gate without a luggage cart, even if I had to pay for it and lie about finding it for free.

"Oh! You are a sight for sore eyes!" he sighed in the car. He touched my shoulder, my neck, my cheek. I could almost relax and enjoy it, almost tune out the little lab rat in my head whose tiny brain circuits were busy, busy wondering: What got me the reward this time? What did it? *What?*

Our lovemaking was tender, slow, reassuring. We touched each other just so, right there, the way we liked it. He chose my favorite position, then I, his. And when it was over, he fell back against the pillow like a man relieved of the burdens of the world. I heard him whisper, softly, so I could barely hear it, "Oh! Much better now!"

At first I thrilled at the comfort I'd given him, and he to me. We were together, we loved, everything was better now. But of course the little rat brain in me could not give up its vigilance. No pleasure could be taken whole, unexamined, unanalyzed. There had to be a trick in there somewhere, a clue, an answer. Why much better? And why now? went my brain-on-a-treadmill. And then of course came the question that kills the pleasure in any reward: *Why was it so bad before?*

It was then that I thought of the bug and asked James if he were its human form. It made no sense, this James-bug association, my thinking of it right at that moment. But so it did happen. And James replied: "Yes. I am a bug. Come squash me."

Something had to be done about this Jester. By the thirteenth of June, UI-1017 had climbed to number three on the whiteboard of infamy outside of Wallis Markham's office, its count of days open coming round like an odometer to the nice fat even number of one hundred. Ethan would barely acknowledge my presence in his office when I brought him the last report. He'd hung a sign on the edge of his graphics monitor that said, "Working, not talking."

"Well, we'll just have to make him talk," said Wallis. "I know," she said, looking suddenly cheerful, "we'll make him come to a *formal meeting.*"

Ethan had resisted all my attempts to meet with him. My e-mail had gone unanswered. Messages left on his chair had simply disappeared, for all I knew. But Wallis Markham by then had been promoted to the level of company director, as had Ethan's boss, Harry Minor. So the two of them had acquired a certain power to persuade. They scheduled a mandatory meeting for the next day. Required attendees: Wallis and Harry, the seven engineers of the front-end programming group, and the two testers most responsible for the front end, Mara Margolies and me.

"Ladies and gentlemen," Wallis began, "we are here to consider the most curious case of the bug we have officially designated UI-1017, more familiarly known to us all as Jester."

"*The* Jester," Harry said with a grin.

"Pardon," said Wallis. "A thousand pardons. Of course. The case we consider concerns *the* Jester, the first and only representative of its kind."

It was just the right tone: a certain Conan Doyle in Wallis's demeanor. I looked at Wallis, in her excellent trousers and starched white shirt, and had time to consider all over again what a marvelous manager she was, how she had the wisdom to turn meetings into a species of Victorian parlor game—Clue, perhaps, or Twenty Questions—formality dripping with irony, as if there were no real-world consequence to the mind games we played here. "The Murders in the Rue Morgue," mysterious bugs, corpses found on the Turkish carpet in the drawing room—all the same to her and to us, nothing more than puzzles for fevered, superior brains with leisured lives.

"*Most* curious," said Harry.

"Indubitably," said Ethan's teammate Dana Merankin, getting into the spirit of it.

"*Meep!*" went Mara Margolies.

But Ethan Levin's face, where he had done his best to hide it in the corner of the table behind the stolid shape of his colleague Tommy Park, was showing nothing of this parlor-game amusement.

"It's not at all curious," he broke in irritably. "It's common as shit. I don't know why we're having this meeting. We've been over and over this. Yesterday. It's a memory leak. *A memory leak!*"

Which immediately unleashed an argument that clearly was already in progress.

"Goddamn it, Ethan, it can't be!" shouted Bill Werners.

"Too regular! Too regular! We decided yesterday," came from Albert Herring. "A memory leak would be more random!"

"And it would crash!" said Dana Merankin. "A memory leak should crash. Your bug is just a freeze-up!"

"Shit! You just want it to be everyone's problem," Herring went on.

"Yeah," said Dana, "everyone's but yours."

"No, I don't," said Ethan. "That's not it at all. I really think—"

"If you'd really think about it with your brain and not your ego—"

"You're wrong, Levin, wrong!"

"You're just stuck. Just trying to get out of it by—"

"Pawning it off on us."

"When it's your problem! Your code! Yours!"

Wallis looked over at Harry and raised an eyebrow. She never would have let an argument get out of hand like this. But Harry's style, as we saw, was to let his programmers have at each other until they tired themselves out.

Meanwhile Mara and I sat there unable to judge the technical merits of anyone's claim, since we had no real idea of what a "memory leak" was. As I said, I liked the notion of memory just leaking away, a dribbling-off of intelligence, the way HAL in *2001* descends into baby talk as Dave turns off one after another of the computer's functions. But later, like it or not, I would have to give up this pleasant ignorance and learn. A program, while running, can request more memory from the operating system. For example, you can't know in advance exactly how many windows a user will want to open. So you estimate and allocate space for some reasonable number, say fifteen. Then, in the course of the running program, if the user wants to open that sixteenth or seventeenth window, you ask for more memory from the operating system. Unless the system is completely out of space, the request is granted, and your program gets a pointer to a block of memory you can use for any purpose, in this case for the extra windows. Then it's your responsibility, as the programmer, to keep track of that pointer, to free up the space when you're done using it. When the user closes that sixteenth or seventeenth window, you should call a routine called "free," telling the operating system it's okay now to free up the extra memory you were given. Free: it has all the connotations of the word. Free: Let go.

But what happens if you forget to free what was given to you? You get a location and a block of memory, and you don't let go of it when you're done? It's hard to know what will happen, actually. It depends. Sometimes, in all the permutations of pathways a program can take, no harm is done, since on that particular run of the program the user doesn't ask for the twenty-first or twenty-second window, only the sixteenth, seventeenth, eighteenth, etc., so the system can accommodate the extra, unfreed block of space. Memory is leaking, but it is not flooding away. It's a slow leak, a pipe going *drip, drip* under the sink and right into a plastic garbage pail. Your program ends, the dripped memory goes back into the available pool of memory—no problem really. Hours, weeks, months, even years, can pass without anything serious happening. It works, you tell yourself. It works, says the tester. It works, say the people in the field who are using the program. There they are, opening and closing windows, computing away, and everything is fine, as far as anyone knows.

Then one day, completely unexpectedly, the program shuts down. On that one run of the program, on that very date and time, some particular combination of allocated but unfreed space in your program meets the allocated space in all the other programs running at the same time—that one particular permutation of possibilities takes you to the edge of the memory the system can provide—and down you come.

I admit that when I first learned all this about computer memory allocation, I was disappointed—no, offended!—in a linguistic sense.

Programmers were so inept at metaphor-creation, I thought. Memory leak: this wasn't a "leak" of memory at all. To say it dripped away was to make the whole problem one of chemistry and physics, as if memory just fell away on its own due to impersonal processes. Why not name it to show the origin of the problem, with the programmer? "Memory gluttony," it should have been called. Or "memory hogging." Even the routine they used to request memory from the operating system had been named incorrectly. It was called "malloc," short for memory allocation, "m" "alloc." But of course human beings don't read "m" then "alloc" unless there is a separator, a space, a dash. No, by the implicit structures of the English language, everyone pronounces it "MAL-loc." Mal, loc. Mal: bad. Loc: location. Bad location! But of course they'd have trouble keeping track of memory when they'd named their tool so stupidly!

Once I understood the technical issues, I saw why Ethan wanted to blame the Jester on a memory leak. It would account for the bug's flakiness—each run of the program could take a slightly different path, involving different requests for memory, and so the failure might not happen consistently. And the cause of the bug could be anywhere, in anyone's code, or be a consequence of a combined, collective error, each programmer forgetting once or twice to free up the requested extra space. But despite this shift of responsibility from Ethan to the group, his colleagues were certainly right. The Jester always appeared around opened menus, while a memory-leak failure should be more random, happening all over the place. And then there was the final arbiter: A memory leak should crash, the program ending abruptly, dumping core, the operating system telling us why. But the Jester merely played havoc with us, beeping and fritzing and freezing up the front end, the program still alive but in its unresponsive, zombie state.

The shouting among the programmers went on for several more minutes, while Wallis, Mara, and I sat there enduring this kindergartner spat. Finally, when the discussion had devolved to something like "Did not!" "Did too!" Harry intervened.

"Okay, okay. That's enough for now. We went through all this yesterday. Here's what we're going to do. First, we'll all agree that the cause of the Jester is not a memory leak—"

"No!" came from Ethan. "We won't agree! We—"

"Is not—*not!*—a memory leak," Harry went on, raising himself up to project his full and considerable bulk Ethan's way. "However, since we all know that every C program in the universe contains an average of ten undiscovered memory leaks, now would be as good a time as any for all of us to check memory allocation in every one of our routines."

A groan went up from the programmers at the table.

"Drudgery!"

"Boring!"

"The schedule!"

Harry laughed, a sort of chuckle. "Fuck the schedule. Do it gradually, this month, next month, when you have a spare cycle. We'll have to fix these leaks sometimes, and wouldn't you rather find them yourselves, my lovelies, instead of waiting for these fine quality-assurance engineers to find them for you?"

Harry gestured our way, and the programmers—looking over at pesky tester faces, our hands full of reports of their errors—fell silent.

"The purpose of this meeting," Harry went on, "is to work with QA to arrive at strategies for finding the cause of this bug. To come up with scripts, test programs, data inputs, etc., to systematize the testing and get at the bottom of it."

"About time," said Ethan Levin under his breath.

"You have a comment you'd like to share?" asked Wallis.

"I said, About time."

"And that would mean?"

"It would mean, up to this point, your testing hasn't been worth shit."

This was the sort of thing programmers usually got away with. They were considered a species of idiot savants, good at code, bad at people, and in most other circumstances Wallis would have blinked a few times and made a joke of it later. But this meeting had been called expressly to deal with the bug Ethan Levin had loosed upon all of us, and Wallis was having none of it. She took a slow breath, sat up straight, squared her shoulders, and fixed Ethan with a look she no doubt perfected while getting her black belt in an art where she routinely pounded people over the head with a heavy wooden sword. "Our not-worth-a-shit testing," she began, "has uncovered, to date, eight thousand seventy-two bugs in the human interface alone. All but a small percentage of these have been fixed by the responsible programmer. Yours, Ethan Levin, is among the small handful of serious bugs that remain open. Perhaps you would like to work with us quality-assurance engineers to find its cause. Or would you prefer that another programmer be assigned to do the job?"

Ethan looked over at Harry with an expression that said, She can't do that! Harry simply sat back, crossed his arms over his chest, and looked at Wallis.

Ethan dug in. "Look, they're *not* quality-assurance engineers," he said, talking about me and Mara as if we weren't there. "They're not engineers at all. They can't even read code. So how the hell can they write scripts? Or test programs? I mean, excuse me, but it's true, they're incompetent. They just fiddle around with the front end until it breaks. They can't do the internals, don't know how. I don't think I'm out of line here if I ask to work with a more senior tester. I mean someone who at least can read code, for instance."

The room became very quiet. The programmers looked down, suppressing smiles. Wallis drummed on the table. Harry pulled on his beard. Mara and I, quality-assurance "engineers" who could not read code, sat with burning faces. Then a tiny gesture passed between Wallis and Harry—to this day I can't say exactly what it was or how I knew what decision had just been made—but I understood in an instant that Ethan Levin would prevail.

"All right," said Harry. "Wallis and I will meet to talk about this. In the meantime, check your memory allocations, everyone. That's it, nothing more, meeting over."

You tell yourself: you
can use this later, this
    humiliation.

I went home to my nasty habits: poem-writing, smoking, tequila-swilling.

A story maybe.

Second cigarette. Third shot.

Or a joke.

Eat a pretzel, take a swallow, then a drag. Let's see. Where were we?

You tell yourself: you
can use this later, this
    humiliation.
A story maybe.
Or a joke.

Now what? Tell the joke?

No. Nothing. Where I was right then did not feel funny. Besides, the idea of the poem was later, in the future, when I'd have had time to scar over the humiliation. Just then—no. Ethan Levin, the meeting, my understanding of my own ineptitude—not yet a story. Wallis explaining after the meeting how I would have to learn programming or take a job in administration—not yet a joke.

So began my technical life, under duress, formally commencing two days later with the arrival of a big box. It contained twenty "self-learning" videotapes, a ring-bound study guide, and a book with a white and pale-blue cover, *The C Programming Language*, by Brian Kernighan and Dennis Ritchie. For the next ten weeks (two tapes per week), Mara Margolies and I were going to computer camp: from late June to the end of August, we were to spend half of each day in the conference room, sitting before a twenty-one-inch TV, watching a skinny man with an evidently very itchy beard teach us how to program in C.

I sat down in the conference room that first day as if I were serving high school detention. I experienced it as a humiliation: Ethan's belittling us in front of everyone, the fact I'd worked at Telligentsia for over a year and was now being forced to take a course geared for the rank beginner. Lesson one was a rote exercise. Type out an example from the study guide exactly as shown:

```
main()
{
        printf("hello, world\n");
}
```

Save the file (as "hello.c"), compile it (with the command "cc hello.c"), then run it. The only surprise was the command you used to run the little program: "a.out," the default name for any executable program. Dumb, I thought. It seemed very important to me that I keep myself aloof from the bearded man teaching the course, that I hold on to my estimation of myself as an educated, accomplished person. I scoffed my way through the exercise. I ran "a.out." And when the words

```
hello, world
```

appeared on the screen, I thought, Oh, big deal.

The next topic was variables, something else I thought I knew about. A variable is a symbolic name that can take on many values— let x equal 1, now let x equal 10—so what, I thought, anyone who went through junior high knows what a variable is. I remained skeptical as we went on to topic three, in which skinny-bearded-man introduced the subject of "data types":

```
char        c;
int         count;
float       percentage;
```

The name of a variable is really a symbolic name for its address in memory, he said. And the "type" of the data says how much space it occupies: characters get one byte; the size of integers and floating-point numbers (numbers with decimal places) is determined by the particular hardware. There are also long integers and short ones, he said, and double-precision floating-point types. And the difference is their size in memory. So the declaration of the variable, he concluded, allocates space in memory, at a particular location, with a particular width in bytes, the symbolic name simply pointing to the beginning of where it lives.

This information had a startling effect on me. All those variable names I had seen strewn across the code—wincount, filename, user_id—were suddenly revealed as conveniences, human-readable words, whose true form was a series of bits indicating where in the machine's memory the value of the variable could be found. It's one thing to think you know that there is something called computer "memory"; it was quite another for me to understand how it related, precisely, to the text of the program. For the first time, I understood there was a mapping between the symbolic words of the code and the physical existence of the machine. And something in me shifted. I decided I already knew far too much about words—fifteen linguistics-practicing years of thinking and wondering over and studying words. Now I wanted to know more about the machine.

I began reading ahead in the book. I took it home, read it late at night, enjoyed the conversational, collegial style of Kernighan and Ritchie as they described the language they had created, the language in which the UNIX operating system itself was written. I began looking forward to my skinny-bearded-man, to the next topic on the videotape. I began losing track of other things: I was late paying bills, left novels with the bookmark stalled halfway, forgot to return phone calls to friends. When James made two trips home, I was glad to see him but not sorry to see him go. I suppose the world was going on as it usually did—half a million Iranian troops were still poised to invade Iraq, Russian troops kept battling the mujahideen in Afghanistan, civil war raged on in El Salvador, Gloria Steinem inexorably turned fifty, the fleshy face of Democratic presidential hopeful Walter Mondale began appearing on the covers of the newsweeklies—but little of it reached me. I was learning about structures.

```
struct date
{
      int     day;
      int     month;
      int     year;
};
```

A capsule of data. A group of attributes that describe something, for instance a date, collected as a single object. Sometimes nested: code enclosing code (enclosing code).

```
struct person
{
      struct date birthdate;
      struct date hiredate;
      struct addr address;
};
```

Quite soon, everything else, even the momentous events of my time, began to lose their effect on me. One morning I read that the number of U.S. AIDS cases had surpassed 5,000. I felt a wave of anxiety—then put down the paper and went to work. I was learning about control flow. If-else, switches, loops, gotos—statements that determine which parts of the code will be run, in what order, how many times.

Just then, I might have considered what this retreat from the outside world meant about me, about programming, about the technical life I was slipping into. But coding was too compelling. It was all about creating a separate, artificial reality inside the machine.

```
i = 0;
while (i <= count)
{
        printf ("Value of i is now %d\n", i);
        i = i + 1;
}
```

A "while-loop." While i is less than or equal to count, print the value of i on the screen, then add one to it. Then (if i is still less than or equal to count), do it all again. Iteration. Round and round the loop we go. When the value of i exceeds that of count, the loop ends; the program moves on to the next statement.

```
if (count > 0)
{
        switch (count)
        {
        case 1:
                printf("count is one\n");
                break;
        case 2:
                printf("count is two\n");
                break;
        default:
                printf("count is %d\n", count);
                break;
        }
}
else
        printf("count is negative\n");
```

If-else statements. Switches. If the variable named count is positive (greater than zero), go through the switch, which has special cases to print out the value when count equals one and two, and a default case to print out all other positive values. Else (if count is not positive), print out the words "count is negative."

Silly examples. Simple programming problems. But it was enough to help me appreciate the complexity you could build into a program, the finely wrought branches of "if, else if, else if" you could construct. I thought of the front-end programs I had been testing, all their buttons and icons and menus, the hundreds of pathways through a single screen, and I began to understand their chiseled workings, how each path had been created by these careful statements of condition. While this is true, go here. If false, go there. A river of code flowing through tiny eddies: So many things could happen, so much could go wrong.

June turned to July. I began staying late in the evenings. I stopped calling friends altogether. The Democrats speculated that Mondale might choose Geraldine Ferrarro as his running mate, making her the first-ever woman to run for the vice presidency of the United States—but it barely moved me. The newspapers moldered on the doorstep. I stopped listening to the radio, watching the news. I was learning about functions.

```
display_count(count)
int count;
{
        i = 0;
        while (i <= count)
        {
                printf("Count now = %d\n", count);
                i = i + 1;
        }
        return;
}
```

Another capsule, this one of code. A subroutine, a block of statements you could wrap up in a bundle and invoke by simply calling display_count. A chunk of code that when completed—done executing its own statements, done with all the statements in all the functions *it* had called—will eventually return to the caller. My little exercise function called printf, which in turn called who-knows-what, which in turn probably called something else again. Functions calling functions calling functions, returning and returning and returning, up and down the layers of code.

Two weeks into July, I parted ways with Mara Margolies. She was lagging. She continued to grumble and curse. I wanted to be away from her unhappy energies; I wanted to be free to move ahead at my own pace, racing through the course, engaged in a way I had never been in the study of linguistics: a kind of obsessional energy that was nonetheless pleasingly addictive. As the examples and assignments became harder, I began making errors, having trouble getting code to compile, link, run. Yet this trouble only drew me in, created in me a fierce determination to get it working. I had never before built anything—not a tree house, not a soapbox racer; I'd never even been able to finish a woven pot holder. I was bad with my hands and I lived in my head, and for me there was only one way to build something: programming. And I wasn't about to let Mara Margolies diminish my pleasure. I asked her to stop interrupting me. I stopped helping her with the assignments. Finally, I started watching the tapes in the evenings by myself. I didn't know it at the time, but I was quickly becoming what I hated most about programmers: impatient with anyone who couldn't code.

So it was that I missed the death of Foucault.

One day I received a phone call from my best friend at graduate school, whom I hadn't spoken to in months. She had a job now, tenure track, though it would be years before she came up for consideration. She was amazed at my obliviousness. Michel Foucault, French philosopher and paragon of postmodernism, source of a thousand dissertation topics, someone whose work had defined an entire generation of scholars—impossible that I didn't know. "Didn't you hear?" she said. "He died at the end of June!"

It was by then mid-August. Geraldine Ferrarro had indeed gotten the nomination. Joan Benoit had won the first-ever Olympic woman's marathon, and the gold-medal gymnast Mary Lou Retton had become America's sweetheart. Miss America Vanessa Williams had had to resign because she'd posed nude for some photographs that showed her performing oral sex on another woman. And evidently Michel Foucault, pomo god, had died. But I had remained untouched by it all. I was learning about pointers.

```
int count;          /* an integer              */
int *count_ptr;     /* pointer to an integer   */
count_prt = &count; /* takes address of count  */
                    /* assigns it to count_ptr */
```

You could be aware of the machine, what it was doing, inside. You could pass the addresses around from one function to another. You could do something called pointer arithmetic. There were pointers to pointers: addresses of variables that held the addresses of other variables. My head swam in a kind of divine delirium; my thoughts felt airy, spatial, unburdened by words.

"I can't believe you didn't hear!" said my friend. "What world do you live in?"

The world of pointers to pointers, arrays of pointers, pointers to structures containing pointers to strings. In comparison to which the death of Foucault meant nothing.

Or no: his death seemed perfectly timed, emblematic, a pointer backward to something I was finished with. I was suddenly glad to be rid of the drag of philosophy, freed from the whole morass of convoluted academic thinking. The cleanliness of programming was a balm. I had spent months unlearning the desire to be unique. I was trying to write code so standard in form, so common in expression, that my work, ideally, could not be distinguished from another programmer's. I was striving for a certain clarity and simplicity, a form of impersonal beauty. To achieve an odd transparency designed to let the human reader slip past the code's wordlike representation and see, as directly as possible, the bit written to disk, the block read from tape, the value stored in memory— the ephemeral electronic moment of what the program *does*. It was a release from the personal: the program, not the programmer.

And now I felt oddly whole, liberated from something that up until that moment I didn't know I was suffering: a kind of enfeeblement

I'd been imposing on myself by keeping myself separate from the work going on all around me. I'd been holding on to another reality, my lost life as a professor. I'd been belittling the programmers as uneducated dolts, beneath me; it had made me resentful and feeble and pitiful; and all because I was holding out for a life that didn't exist.

But how stupid of me to keep myself apart from the programmers, for now it seemed that my real imagination was as bounded, ruled, and orderly as theirs. The relentless formalism that made me bad at poetry and good at linguistic sentence parse-trees—noun-phrase, verb-phrase, the decomposed sentence—a strength for a programmer. You tell yourself you were made for one life, but when life offers you another way, you must take it.

> *You tell yourself: you*
> *can use this later, this*
> *humiliation.*

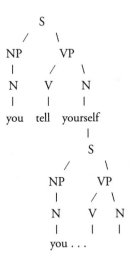

"I do QA now," I said to my old friend.
She laughed. "Oh, I forget what that means."

"Quality assurance. Testing."

And then for the first time, I used the word without irony. "My title is QA engineer," I told her.

She giggled and made a sound like a train whistle. "Whoo-whoo! Engineer!"

August thirtieth: Summer camp ended, the course was done, and the bug came back.

I brought Ethan the report.

"Again?" he asked.

"Again."

"Don't tell me: no core."

"No. No core."

His expression was odd, mouth fixed, eyes slitted, something there I couldn't read. "No. Of course not," he said. "This bug will never leave a core, will it?"

I shrugged.

"And don't tell me: big-time customers or VCs or someone like that."

"Federal Reserve, Washington, D.C."

He laughed. "Only the best for my bug, huh?"

Maybe it's here that I should have started noticing something about Ethan Levin. When I look back on it, it seems that my having learned a bit of programming might have brought me closer to him, more able to understand him, help him. But coding for me was still a lovely game. I was doing exercises, samples. My code didn't have to interact with anyone else's. I had no deadlines, no requirements, no venture capitalists standing over my shoulder. Most of all, there was no one keeping track of my bugs.

I saw the squint in his eyes, the bend in his neck, and did nothing. I put down the bug report, made some stupid remarks about "malloc," the memory allocation routine, and left.

MALLOC

Malloc, Moloch, malocchio. Berta, the tester who couldn't read code, that's what she'd been muttering at the back of his head. *Malloc, Moloch, malocchio.* He'd been working, scanning his files, matching calls to malloc with calls to free. Allocate memory, free it. Malloc, free. Paired operations: one takes; one lets go. When somehow she'd snuck up behind him and started her patter. Malloc. Malice. Malaise. Malign. Malinger. Malaria. Mala suerte. Malkin. Malcontent. Malevolent.

Malloc, Moloch, malocchio.

Malloc, free.

She didn't understand: the compiler didn't watch over you. Once you spoke to it in syntactically correct C code, it was willing to let you kill yourself, if that's what you wanted to do. You could suck up memory like a glutton, and the first you'd know about it would be a crash. Malloc, free. Malloc, free. It was up to you to keep them paired, release memory when you were done with it. Maybe you really wanted to fuck things up, as far as the compiler knew. So many things in the C programming language were dangerous, but legal.

But he kept hearing it: her needling, undermining voice at the back of his head. *Malloc, Moloch, malocchio.* Evil eye, bad luck, bad location, bad locution, evil speaker. Can't you just tell by the sound of it, she'd said, that no good can possibly come from something called *malloc*?

Crazy, he'd thought. Just Berta's need to keep clinging to what she knew, words, in dead languages, as if these sounds—just sounds—could actually do anything.

The morning wore on. The sky outside darkened. Was it going to rain? It wasn't supposed to rain in summer. The lights, seeming brighter now, buzzed overhead. Malloc, free. Malloc, free. Against all his better judgment, the idea that he was doing something wrong worked itself into the color of his thoughts. *Malloc, Moloch, malocchio.* Mal. Loc. Bad. Luck. Something bad was going to happen. It was just as she'd said: the sounds, the sounds themselves. *Malice, malaise, mala suerte.* Those murmuring *m*'s, those evil *l*'s. *Malloc, Moloch, malocchio.* And at the end, that choking sound.

A long beep startled him. A message written across his screen.

```
Broadcast message from system administrator:
All-company stand-up meeting outside conference room now!
```

Ethan, Herring, and Thorne looked up from their terminals, blinking as if they'd come in from the dark.

The home-office staff, about sixty people was crowded into the narrow space between the conference room and the first row of cubicles. The place stank of perfume, from all the new marketing women in their bright summer suits. Across the way, he saw the smooth head of the night administrator—what was she doing there in the daytime? Then from his right came the reek of stale cigarette smoke: that tester, edging past him. She was dressed all in black, a skirt, boots that stopped at the ankle. He had never seen her legs before.

" 'Lo, Ethan."

He nodded, said nothing.

"How's your malloc coming along?"

Malloc, Moloch, malocchio.

"Fine."

"And the Jester?"

"Don't call it that."

"All right. UI-1017."

"You know how that is."

Malloc, Moloch, malocchio.

She laughed. "The subject of this meeting, I believe."

"What are you talking about?"

She only raised her eyebrows—thick, Ethan noticed, like two bold strokes across her brow—then she turned toward the doorway, where William Harland was pressing in through the crowd. Outside the sky was almost black, and suddenly Ethan felt again what had come over him earlier in the morning: the unshakable sense that something bad was about to happen.

"I'll get right to it," William Harland began. "I don't want to keep you all from your work."

"What?" came from the back.

"Can't hear you."

"Louder."

Harland's mild face rose above the crowd—someone must have given him something to stand on—and he repeated himself. "I don't want to keep you. I'll get right to it. I think you all know we've been having trouble attracting prospective customers."

A nervous titter came from the bright-suited marketing women.

"The demos," said Harland. "The demos haven't been going exactly well."

"To say the least!"

More laughter.

The first thing Ethan was aware of was a rustling sound, then a feeling of distortion as if space itself were folding and reforming itself. Bodies shifting, sixty bodies turning in the crowded space. Then eyes: sixty sets of eyes, on him.

"There is this bug—"

"The Jester!" someone shouted.

"The little devil!" came from somewhere near a knot of testers.

"Levin's last bug!" said one of the marketing women, starting another round of laughter.

"The official number is—"

"UI-1017," Wallis Markham called out.

"Yes, UI-1017," William Harland went on. "There are worse bugs, I know. But this one looks very bad. It undermines our buyers' confidence. The beeps, the dead keyboard, the way you can't just restart the demo. Unacceptable, completely unacceptable. Embarrassing to the sales staff and to all of us. So the purpose of this meeting is to announce a moratorium on all outside demos. Until this thing . . . this . . ."

"Jester!"

"UI-1017."

"Yes, this UI-1017. Until this bug is fixed, no one may demonstrate the system to any person outside of this company. No external demos without prior authorization. Is that clear?"

A kind of hissing started in Ethan's ears. He was vaguely aware of some exchanges between Harland and the sales staff, some joking among the testers, but the noise in his head made them sound like something heard through a sheeting rainstorm. Harland must have then ended the meeting, because the space around him began rearranging itself again, surging and turning in a sickening way, like boiling mud. He tried to shake this ridiculous vertigo, but there were the eyes. Whites of eyes on him, every eye in the room, mean hard stars, they seemed. He scanned the room—for what?—and found the night administrator's dark-rimmed lids, something sympathetic in them, which only confused him. Why should she care about him? And Steghman, who met his glance for a moment then turned away, embarrassed, Ethan thought, embarrassed for him. Then all at once the crowd was sparse, a few milling people. And suddenly Ethan had this idea that everyone in the room—himself included—was just a roaming, hungry little O in some master creature's simulated world, stupidly feeding and reproducing and dying and thinking themselves real.

A hand took the back of his neck.

Harry.

"It's stupid," Harry was saying. "Fucked! You'd think they'd just *train* the damn sales staff to get a damned dump. Oh, shit. Anyway, why don't you get out of here? Go home. Cool off. Listen to some music or something."

Harry's fat body, soft and friendly. His fuzzy beard. His bloodied plumber's hand now on Ethan's shoulder. Cool off. Yes, that seemed possible now.

It wasn't supposed to be raining. The warm teeming rain that soaked him before he could get to his car, the wind that blew him from lane to lane across the freeway—no, this tropical sort of weather was never supposed to happen in the Bay Area. What was happening to the world? El Niño, La Niña? Or was the planet really dying, the normal and customary way of things over, the rules suddenly changed, as if the programmer behind this set of variables called "Earth" had abruptly despaired, torn up his plan, tired of waiting for something to happen?

"Don't die," Ethan said to himself, fighting the steering wheel in the wind.

His street was gray, indistinct, behind a curtain of rain. The corner storm drain was under a pond of dirty water. Had Joanna stopped gardening completely? The little patch of lawn she used to tend on Saturday afternoons had turned into a ragged carpet of mud, stones, battered weeds. Mud had invaded the little walkway; crabgrass poked up between the flagstones. Ethan tried to wipe his feet on the mat but found it sopped and dirty. He fought with the front door. The earthquake and now the warm rain. Everything off balance. Stuck.

What to do now? Ethan had no idea what to do with himself at home at twelve-thirty in the afternoon. He wandered from room to room, hands in pockets, listening to the sounds of the rain. Drumming on the roof, gurgling in the gutters, sheeting against the windows, tires hissing on the pavement as the cars went by. What to do now? He opened the refrigerator, closed it. He wasn't hungry.

Upstairs: He could always go upstairs and dial up his simulation. It was still running on the Telligentsia server, waiting for him as always. It didn't care that he'd been made a fool of at work, didn't know about the bug, had no idea that a whole company waiting for its IPO had suspended sales because of him. The simulation was his other life. Separate, preserved, autonomous. He'd go back there, pick up the thought-line he'd started so long ago, before the bug ever existed.

(Or had the bug always existed? came the unwelcome thought. Maybe this flaw, this problem, this crack in his understanding of how things went together in the world—maybe this bug had always been there, lying around like some unexploded shell, and it was just now he'd stepped on it. Ridiculous! he said to himself in the next thought. Just spooked by the meeting, by Berta—*malloc, Moloch, malocchio*—by the weird rain and the open hours of the afternoon.)

And so he started upstairs. Step, step, everything was still reasonably normal. It's a bad day, it's true, he thinks, but there's always his simulated world. He's been in this place before, lost in his life, returning to his X's and O's. Step, step, it has all happened to him before. But then he gets to the top of the stairs—the place where the carpet gives off and the heel of his shoe comes down on the wood floor with a clunk—and a voice suddenly calls out:

Don't come in!

Ethan is confused. Was that Joanna, home all this time? And what does she mean—don't come in? Don't come in where?

He looks over to see that the bedroom door is closed.

And Joanna calls out again: *Don't come in!*

For one moment more, everything is still as it was. It's odd that the door is closed, odd that Joanna is home and telling him not to come in, odd that there are scrambling noises coming from the bedroom like possums have gotten into the attic again. But the mind is a strangely normalizing instrument, and Ethan's brain immediately works hard to place all this inside his frame of expectation. He thinks: Damn! I'll have to go chase those fucking possums again! And then he even thinks: Shit. I'll avoid it for now, go into the study, work for a while, get to it later.

But there was something extreme and desperate in Joanna's call. *Don't come in!* And something of the energy and emotion in her voice, like tunneling maggots, slowly eats its way through Ethan's lump of thought. This penetration takes perhaps a lumbering three seconds (remember, the human brain is painfully slow), but then Ethan's body, finally registering something, goes on and acts on its own. His hand goes to the bedroom doorknob. His shoulder pushes the door against the annoying, too-high pile of the carpet—once, twice, three times—and then the door is open.

From there, a confused jumble. A series of flashes in a dim room. Joanna's blouse rumpled on the floor—wasn't it the one he gave her for her last birthday? Her naked breasts. Why wasn't she trying to cover them? Why was she lying there, one hand behind her head, her breasts looking up at him with their dark centers like targets? Then Ostrick, his prick waving, jumping out of bed. It's Ostrick's prick Ethan finally focuses on: fat, thick, much thicker than his own, he notices, still half hard, waggling like a frankfurter. And under the mind's crazy impulse for denial, Ethan suddenly wonders if he's ever seen the erect penis of another grown man before (no, he hasn't, he doesn't watch porn), and if it's true what he's read that women actually prefer a thick penis to a long one (yes, he has read it, and it's true, he thinks, a woman would really enjoy a penis like that). When all at once something cuts through this nest of synaptic associations: a smell. Pungent. Disgusting. Cloves!

The whole room—the sheets, the blankets, the rug, the curtains, the walls, the floor, the mattress—everything smells like sickening clove beedis!

The next thing Ethan knows he has Ostrick by the throat. With one hand he has him by the neck, and with the other he thinks he'll grab the scissors from the dresser and lop off Ostrick's prick. That fat, thick, flagging, female delight of a penis—he thinks he'll saw it, slash it, chop at it until the bastard falls faint in agony. The asshole fucked his girlfriend, in his house, in his bed—on the sheets he himself washed this week since it was his turn!—and Ostrick will pay with unbearable pain. Ethan's free hand flails in the direction of the dresser (he can see the big scissors with the orange-plastic-wrapped handle, right in the tray Joanna always nagged him to put it in), when all at once he looks down and sees that Ostrick's prick has deflated. That wilting fleshy wobbling disgusting thing—he can't even bring himself to look at it.

"Get the fuck out of here!" he finds himself screaming. "Get the fuck out!" And then he sobs—it's humiliating, he wished he hadn't, he'd do anything not to have started crying—but a huge sobby cry escapes from his throat. Then, as if he'd suddenly been melted, he collapses on the edge of the bed, where he sits crying, helpless, repeating: "Get out of here, Both of you, Get out of here, Both of you, Get out of here."

And they do. Both of them: dressing, quickly, wordlessly, neither of them coming anywhere close to Ethan before they gallop down the stairs. To his shame, Ethan finds himself following them into the street, crying and screaming, "Get out of here, Both of you, Get out of here."

All at once, Ostrick's car is in front of the house—where has it been? Ethan didn't see it when he came home, so where had it been hiding? Joanna is still buttoning her birthday blouse, bending her head under the downpour as she gets into the car.

Then the car door is closing, the engine revving.

Ethan standing there, in the street, in the rain, watching Ostrick and Joanna drive away.

The hiss of the tires.

Then nothing: the empty street, the sound of rain.

He found himself in his car. He had no idea where he was going, but he couldn't stay in that house, marching in a circuit from kitchen to dining to living room, alone with the drumming and gurgling rain, with the blinking red eyes of the LED stove clock. One-oh-four, it said. Blink, blink. Another circuit. One-oh-five.

So now he was driving, nowhere, too fast, trailing sprays of water. Maybe the rain-slicked brakes will fail, he thought. Maybe turn off the wipers, see how long you can drive blind. A long time, he found, the world turning blurry. Through the windshield, wavery, a neon martini glass, lit up, an open bar.

The bartender put a napkin down in front of him. Ethan stared at it. He never drank, maybe a beer, couldn't imagine what to ask for. He remembered his father used to say, "Scotch is class."

"Bourbon," he said to the bartender, a big balding man who was exhaling a long stream of smoke.

"Up? Over? Neat?"

Ethan had no idea. "Plain. Just plain bourbon."

The bartender laughed, moved down the bar to pour the drink.

No one there but a black guy at the end of the bar and an old man at a corner table. Smell of hundred-year-old beer, ghosts of a million cigarettes.

"You all right, buddy?" the bartender asked, putting the shot in front of him.

Ethan looked blankly at the man. "What? Sure. Sure I am."

"I mean your arm. You're bleeding."

Ethan looked down. "Am I?" Then he saw it, the blood soaking his jacket sleeve. "Yeah, guess so," he said, seeing the cut on his arm. The scene in the bedroom came back, the bed, the blouse, the wagging prick, Ostrick choking. Did the bastard scratch him? "Nothing serious. I broke something."

"Hey, just so long as you didn't kill anyone," the bartender said with a laugh.

"No. Ha-ha. Someone killed me."

The bartender stared at him a moment. "Here, buddy," he said, reaching under the bar. "On me." Ethan stared at the beer bottle the bartender put down next to his shot glass. "Boilermaker. Shot with a beer back. You'll like it." Then the man went back to his cigarette at the end of the bar.

The bourbon was rough in his mouth, hot in his gullet; the beer cold, clean. Ethan felt his thoughts go rubbery.

"Hey, maybe another," he said.

His cheeks went hot, his hands cold. Now he could feel how angry he was, could let the anger take him over—now that the alcohol had changed it, his anger, made it not more distant but bigger, more dramatic, heroic, like he was walking around in some other guy's feelings. Yes, much better now, a strapping, swaggering, muscular guy, the sort who took his anger out on chins and noses.

"Maybe one more time."

Good thing I'm drunk, he thought, as he came home and closed the front door behind him and everything was as it was before: the rain, the red clock eyes, the day that went on and on and refused to be over. Good thing I can't feel much, he thought, as he threw himself on his bed, and through the mud of his mind came something, a smell, a roughness on his hand, the dried wet spot, the irrefutable, horrible leavings of Ostrick's prick and Joanna's cunt mixed and dried and still stinking of sex. Good thing I'm completely digusto drunk, he thought, as he pulled the sheets from the bed, lurched downstairs, and stuffed them in the fireplace, along with newspapers and twigs and a grease log that said, Do Not Mix with Other Combustible Materials! Fire leapt out, cinders flew to the floor, smoke filled the house, while Ethan sat and watched and thought, Good thing I don't care, I don't care, I don't care.

Then the next day there was nothing to do but go to work.

Malloc, free.

Malloc, free.

Malloc, Moloch, malocchio.

At four, Joanna called.

"I'm going to get my things tomorrow. I want you not to be home."

"Tomorrow."

"Saturday."

"Right."

The overhead lights buzzed, the cursor blinked at him. Herring stood up from his desk, scribbled something on his whiteboard.

"Don't you think I should be there? At least agree to what's mine and what's yours?"

"What's to talk about? All the furniture is mine. So's the stereo—you never listen to music anymore anyway. I'll leave you the mattress in the guest room, the futon sofa, something to eat on in the kitchen, some pots and pans."

"The toaster."

"Right, the toaster."

The command on the screen looked back at him. grep malloc winmgr.c. Grep: Why didn't it ever occur to him how ridiculous it was?

"What's so funny?"

"Nothing."

"We'll deal with the books later. I'll leave them."

"All right."

They sat and breathed into the phone. What could he say? Herring was there; Thorne was there; the system was waiting for his next command.

"I'm going to hang up now," Joanna said. "Don't be home."

"All right. Home. No."

THE TROLL'S WARNING

Ethan started hearing things. The floorboards moaning late into the night. Betsy the baby whimpering in her crib from the back bedroom across the street. The tannic clink of a manhole cover on a far corner. After Joanna stripped the house of furniture, he heard noises he didn't know existed. The worried singing of water in the pipes behind the wall. The living skeleton of the creaking house. The car that teetered toward him from far, far away, rushed past, and now seemed to recede infinitely, a tunnel of fading sound he could not stop following.

And the music. Any minute, everything might be obliterated by the sudden explosion of his neighbors' crap-rock music, coming and going without pattern, at four in the morning, at three in the after-noon, blaring (or not) at dinnertime, evening time, late night: an end-less mindless pounding automaton of drum and bass beating *Doom Doom Doom Doom.* Always the same song, it seemed. The same chords played over and over on a whiny synthesizer, the same notes un-til he thought he'd go mad. A chorus that kept repeating: "*Jump!*" Was it always like this? Was it worse after Joanna left? Windows shut tight, egg crates tacked up as sound baffles, and still the pounding came, through the walls, through the floors, through the bones of the house.

But tonight he was ready for it. He wasn't just going to lie there, on the mattress on the floor where Joanna had left it, exposed to the invasions of his neighbors. No, tonight he was prepared. Earplugs rated twenty-nine decibels. Cotton-wool clumps over the ears. A ski band holding the whole assembly in place. He'd looked stupid to himself in the mirror before going to bed, wiping the toothpaste from his chin, a skinny man with hair frizzed out behind a bright purple ski band with cotton sticking out around the ears. But it didn't matter how he looked. Who was there to see him? The important thing was to defend himself, to block out the drumming beating pounding that came from next door, some throbbing heart that expanded when his contracted and sucked the blood out of him.

Now he lay there straining to listen in the quiet. Was that it—that soft, fluttery sound—was that all that was left of their noise? He felt calm, protected behind this headgear, returned to the privacy of his own world.

But then it came: *crash!* and *boom!* and a steady, relentless beating that seemed to be broadcast from everywhere. What was this crap now? Something different. Screeching. Metal, it sounded like. It went around his stoppered ears, came at him through his ribs, jawbone, sockets of his eyes. The headgear was useless. His preparations were hopeless. He ripped off the ski band, tossed away the earplugs. He had to stop this invasion at its source.

He went pounding on their door. Wearing pajama bottoms, slippers, and a windbreaker, he stood outside their door as the screeching went on. *Come on feel the noise.* No answer. Finally, at the break between cuts, Ethan heard a voice.

"Yeah?"

"It's your neighbor."

"Neighbor. Yeah. Whadduhyawant?"

Not auspicious. Ethan decided to try being polite. "May I talk with you?"

"What?"

"MAY I HAVE A TALK WITH YOU!"

Ethan heard the stereo go off, footsteps, the deadbolt opening. He extended a hand. "Ethan Levin. Your neighbor."

The man squinted at him, didn't put out his hand, didn't say his name. He was short, wiry, with a sparse beard that looked like iron filings spilled over his face. His hair was long, in the style of the sixties as it had lingered on in the working classes of the eighties. He wore a clean T-shirt and dirty jeans covered with a powdery, white surface. The hand he put to his mouth to take a drag off his cigarette was a laborer's hand, callused, with misshapen, broken, dirty fingernails. He blew smoke out the door. Oh, great, thought Ethan, a pickup-truck guy.

"Which side?" said the neighbor.

"Side?"

"Neighbor on which side? Which house's yours?"

"To your left. That one." Ethan gestured with his head toward his own house.

The man grinned, took a drag, and blew smoke again. "Oh, yeah. The guy whose girlfriend moved out on him a few weeks back."

Ethan felt himself start to burn. Had this guy seen him crying and screaming in the rain? "I'm here about your music," he said.

"What about my music?"

"It's too loud. It disturbs me."

The neighbor laughed, smoked, put his spare hand deep in his pocket. "You mean you don't like music?"

"Not loud music, no."

"Hey, buddy. Everybody likes music!"

Then the man stopped and squinted at him through a puff of smoke.

Ethan felt a jangle of alarm—this guy's whole posture was a threat. I only have to explain myself, he thought. Yes, that's it. If I make my case clearly, surely this man will see how his behavior has to change. Once he understands the reasoning, sees the logic of the situation, we'll come to an agreement.

Ethan explained he was a computer programmer. "Really relentlessly logical work, you know. All head, no body," he elaborated. "You see, here's the problem. From time immemorial, through one civilization after another, loud, rhythmic music has been used to drive out logical thought, suppress it, you see, overwhelm it with repetitive, more, well, tribal, primitive . . . at any rate, a different type of existence, *not* rational, *not* logical, *pre*logical maybe. So here we have an age-old conflict, deeply rooted—ha-ha—I don't mean a conflict between *us*, I mean in the nature of things, between parts of the human experience, between phases of our evolution maybe . . ."

Ethan felt himself running on with no way to stop his mouth. He could see how ridiculous he looked in the eyes of this neighbor with his workingman's hands—time immemorial, evolutionary phases, tribal culture, what could these possibly mean to this guy? For a terrible, regressed moment, he saw himself through this wiry man's squinted eyes: the Jew-boy he'd been in his Fresno, California, high school, a Jew in a place with few Jews, the school-smart but hopelessly skinny-wimpy boy he'd been, a fast-talking mouth without the fists and toughness to back it up. But the more ridiculous and weak Ethan's reflection seemed to him, the more determined he became to show how intelligent he was, and so on went his jabbering. All the while, the body of the man facing him became more taut, his legs a step apart, his shoulders square, a wire tightening.

". . . for example, the reason we want to drum is probably the heartbeat, the Ur-rhythm, the basic body functioning of the ancient reptilian brain, a kind of antireason—"

The man threw his cigarette to the ground. "Look, buddy. I don't know what the hell you're talking about, but I know this. I work like a dog all day, and when I come home, I kick back. I have a right to my music! You understand? I gotta right to my music!"

Ethan stared at the man. There is no right to music, he thought to say. The Constitution offers protections for speech, assembly, and so forth, but no: the right to one's music is quite absent from the Bill of Rights. But there was no chance Ethan could say that. He would only grow more preposterously eggheaded in the eyes of his neighbor, who was now scowling at him fixedly.

"I gotta right to my sleep," Ethan said.

The man just eyed him. "Whatever," he said.

Then, after standing there a moment longer getting cold in his pajamas, Ethan muttered good night and left.

The music stayed off as Ethan made his way up his walk to his front door. The night was still quiet as he settled into bed. He heard the house creak, the scratch of a branch on the window. He lay in bed and listened as the sounds wound around corners and hurtled along the empty halls of the house. He allowed himself to think his visit had worked, that the neighbor would keep the music off but wouldn't say so to Ethan's face because he didn't like being told what to do. Ethan even went so far as to wonder if the guy would tell the other people who seemed to live there—Ethan had seen a brawny guy and a skinny woman with dyed black hair. He had a happy few moments as he considered this fantasy.

Then with a *crash!* and *boom!* it all started again.

He threw back the blanket and staggered up from the mattress on the floor. He stood there in his pajama bottoms, disoriented in the dark room, trying to fix his eyes on the floating irridescent face of the clock.

Three A.M., it said. He'd go down to the kitchen, he decided, eat, but what, there was nothing, only some beer and club soda and a shrunken apple. Then he remembered the freezer: surely there was something in there, some ancient but reheatable bundle of edible stuff. Yes, like right there behind the years-old-ice-cream-that-tasted-like-cardboard container, that foil-wrapped thing in a snowball of frost. He put the bundle on the counter, grabbed a steak knife, and chopped at it to see what was inside. He produced a spray of frost, bits of flying foil, then a peek at some flesh-toned foodlike substance.

Pasta, it seemed, with something red. He scraped back the foil: lasagna.

Then, still holding the knife, he stared at it: *that* lasagna.

For Ethan remembered it instantly, the origins of this pasta now sitting on his kitchen counter like a ball of frozen space dust hurled out of the sky. The dinner last Fourth of July, at home with their dear friends Marsha and Paul Ostrick. The lasagna in a baking pan on the now gone dining room table, Joanna wearing shorts, leaning across the table with an offering, a big spatula full, a smile on her face: "Paul. Would you like some *more?*" He remembered that tone in her voice, something in it that didn't sound right to him even at the time. Some *more,* something more than the red, cheesy mound she was moving toward Paul's receiving mouth. Ethan had shrugged it off, a roaming stray-cat thought, he'd decided then, a little streak of something black across the road. Until the Ostricks were leaving, Marsha out the door first, Paul's teasing face poking back in to say, cagily, "Thank you for *having* me." Not *us. Me.*

Ethan stabbed the knife into the foil, grabbed a beer, drank. Damn it! Damn it to hell! Why did he have to keep running into pieces of her still lying around?

He thought he was done with getting her out of the house. First it was the sheets. Then the terry robe she'd forgotten, hanging on its hook behind the bathroom door, still with her scent on it. He threw it in the trash and tried to forget about it. Then he found an old birthday present he'd given her, special unbleached towels she'd wanted, still wrapped in their tissue paper, abandoned on the floor of the closet. Why would she leave them? She hadn't forgotten them, the package was too obvious, the whiteness of the wrapping too new, the ribbon on it too bright-silvery. She must have meant something by it, to leave this gift so nakedly white in the middle of the closet floor for him to find. Then there was the bar of soap they'd both used in the shower—gradually it washed away to nothing. You can't hate a sliver of soap, he'd told himself, and made himself use it until it broke in his hands. Then her handprint on the window where she'd closed it. A barrette under the futon. An old birthday card in the junk drawer. An envelope with her handwriting. Some mail not forwarded with a return address he scrutinized for signs of further treachery. One by one, washed, cleaned, sent on, torn up, thrown away. What else would he find? Where else would she still be hiding? Where? He spiked the frozen ball into the floor.

He got out the broom and started sweeping, for no reason; the lasagna stayed intact and the scattered frost would melt. It was just a way to keep getting rid of her. The last hair from her brush, the last sloughed-off skin cell, all the bits of her DNA—how long until they disappeared? He thought it would be quick. Joanna, her things, gone, just a note, a number "for emergencies." Pack. Leave. Over. A clean break so he could get on with his life. He hadn't expected this—the way her body was still leaving him molecule by molecule.

Harry found him with his head in a ceiling panel.

"What the hell are you doing, Levin?"

"The lights," Ethan said, his voice muffled by the acoustic panels. "I'm ripping out the fucking lights!"

"Come down from there. You'll electrocute yourself."

Ethan was standing on phone books piled on top of his desk, his head and arms inside the ceiling where he'd ripped out a tile, which lay on the floor in two pieces. "I can't find the fucking connector! What the fuck—is this shit hardwired or something?"

Harry went and checked the wall switches. "At least you turned them off."

"Goddamn fucking shitty asshole fucking thing! Where is the fucking connector!"

"You can just unscrew the bulbs," Harry suggested.

"Goddamn piece of shit— What?"

"The bulbs. You can just unscrew them!"

Ethan's head came out from behind the panel. He was red-faced, sweating, had to stare down at Harry for a second or two before it registered. "Yeah," he said finally between hard breaths. "Yeah. Unscrew them. Good idea."

Harry handed him up the two pieces of the ceiling panel. "Leave them in. Just unscrew them."

"Yeah."

Harry helped him down, and gave Ethan a long look. "You all right, Levin?"

"Yeah. Sure. Fine."

Harry scratched his beard.

"Fine. I'm fine. I'm on schedule, and I'm fine. It's just those goddamn lights of Herring's!"

"Where is Herring anyway?" Harry asked.

"Lunch."

"Thorne?"

"Don't know."

"All right, Levin. Enjoy your gloom." Harry chuckled. "Hey! You gonna put on your headband again?"

Ethan had taken to wearing the ski band at work. "Yeah? So?"

Harry snorted and shook his head from side to side like a tolerant uncle. "Well, you're still the only one on schedule, so you can wear whatever the hell you want." He was on his way out when he stopped in the doorway. "Hey. That bug," he said. "What's happening with that bug?"

The bug. Ethan didn't want to be asked about the bug. "Quiet," he said. "Gone quiet again. No sign of it since . . ." Since Harland called the moratorium on demos, since he found Joanna and Ostrick, since his hearing began playing tricks on him.

Harry hummed and pulled his beard. "Well, you'll find it eventually," he said. "They always get fixed, sooner or later."

Fixed. Sooner or later. Harry's words flooded Ethan with relief. Harry Minor, famous programmer, had been through things like this thousands of times. Bugs, mounds of bugs, horrible, elusive, weird bugs squirreling themselves away in system innards. And every one of them fixed. "Always?"

Harry laughed. "Oh, well, yes, always. Aha! If you accept the fact that 'later' is an infinite concept."

And then, with another laugh, Harry turned to go. After everything was over, Harry would admit that he might have noticed how Ethan Levin was coming unglued right in front of everyone's eyes, how the bug, as it kept on in its Jester personality, was unnerving Ethan to the point of disintegration. A weird bug. Harry would recall, humming to himself at the memory, one that even he admitted, among all the tens of thousands of bugs he'd come across in his life, had something peculiarly wicked about it. But in the next moment he would shrug it off and insist (like everyone) that the whole company was going crazy, so why should Ethan Levin have been immune? Besides, Ethan was on schedule, which made everybody think he was keeping it together, and that purple headband was funny—funny! And that was why Harry left him sitting under the unscrewed bulbs, in his bright purple headband, with the clumps of cotton wool sticking out of his ears.

The phone went on ringing, a distant trill, until Ethan realized it was his line. Headband, cotton wool, earplugs, off. "Hello?"

"Ethan. It's me. Look. I don't want to talk. Don't talk. I just want to tell you something. I don't want to see you for a while—a good, long while."

Joanna's voice. The familiar tone and rhythm and pitch. A sound he'd lived with for four years. "I'm sorry. Noise here. Joanna?"

"I said I don't want to see you for a long time. I don't know how long that's going to be but . . . long. I have all this anger toward you. I can't see you until my anger becomes . . . irrelevant. I can't explain that—won't explain it. My anger has to work itself out."

Now the words penetrated, a rehearsed speech, he thought, something devised with that therapist of hers. He hated that therapist, that schoolmarm, always sending Joanna home with little assignments about things she should "work out." But did Joanna say *her* anger? *Her* anger! Wasn't *he* the one who came home and found her with Mr. Fat Prick?

Thorne was typing madly; Herring moaning into his screen. Ethan kept his voice down. "Shouldn't *I* be mad at *you*?"

"You have no idea why I'm mad at you, do you?"

Because he was a moron, believing her. "No."

"Of course you don't. That's why I don't want to see you."

He exhaled, mad. He hated when women made you guess their feelings. "What about the books? The records? What do you want me to do with them?"

"I'll come by this Saturday. Ten o'clock. Don't be there. If you're missing anything, call that number I gave you."

She was going to hang up now, and, angry as he was, he found he wanted to keep her on the line, hear her breathe in and out a moment more. It had been too easy for them to separate. They didn't have a joint bank account, hadn't mingled their finances, had only the books and records to divide. So easy. It stabbed him suddenly, what in all the confusion he hadn't let himself feel: how much he missed her.

"Hello? Ethan? Did you hear what I said?"

Maybe he could ask her about the neighbors' music—was it always there?—about the manhole cover's acid *tink,* and was it possible to hear Carolyn's baby from all the way across the street? The strange noises he lived with now: only Joanna would know if they were really there or he was hearing things.

"Look, Ethan. Don't play games with me. Tell me if you agree: You won't be there between ten and twelve this Saturday."

Herring was leaning back in his chair, picking up everything. "Sure. Fine. I won't be there."

The next week Ethan came to work with a parachute.

"*Now* what are you doing, Levin?"

Herring had grabbed Harry as he passed by. "It's cutting off the window light!" Herring complained.

"What's cutting what off?" Harry had said, distracted, still in the hallway, his face turned away from the office.

"A parachute!"

"A parachute?"

Yes, that's exactly what Harry found when he turned and looked inside the doorway: Ethan on a ladder tucking in the last corner of a dark blue parachute, which was now draped over Ethan's corner of the office like a tent, completely hiding it from view.

"There," Ethan said with satisfaction, coming off the ladder.

Harry stood stupefied for a moment, then burst out laughing. "Levin, I've seen weird programmers in my life, but this fucking takes it!"

"It's the lights," Ethan protested. "I told you, the lights are driving me insane. Even with the bulbs over my desk unscrewed, there's this flicker. This buzz and flicker and hum, and I can't concentrate, I told you I can't!"

"It's totally dark in here!" Herring whined. "He's got the window to himself, and now he's completely covering it!"

Harry looked from one to the other and shook his head. "Look, I've got to go to a meeting. Goddamn VCs again. They're thinking— those fucking—" He cut himself off. "Anyway, I'll deal with this parachute thing later." A loud wail rose from Herring, but Harry waved him off. "Later!" And then Harry left, Herring following him down the hall still complaining.

Now Ethan was free to crawl into his perfect tent. Inside was a thick, dark blue light, the color of the night sky before full dark. He turned down the brightness on his monitor. He put on earplugs, the headband, the cotton wool. Bit by bit, he felt the world go away, leaving him to the dimmed rectangle of light from his monitor. He sighed. Started the debugger. Put in his breakpoints. Stared at the cursor waiting for his next command. Step, he typed. Then step again.

Were these the same breakpoints he'd set a million times before? Were these the same lines of code he'd walked through line by line for months? He didn't know anymore. He'd lost track. Time, like "later," had become an infinite concept. All that mattered now was that it be quiet, and dark, that he stay on schedule, and that he find the bug. Yes, he thought, maybe everything was coming apart and going crazy, maybe Joanna was gone and his house was empty and invaded with noise, maybe he had no one to call but his mother (or Marsha, maybe he should call Marsha—no, not Marsha), but it would all be fine again, fine, his life would be what it was supposed to be, if he could only, finally, find the bug.

He waited for the bug to come to him in a dream. He lay in bed that night, wrapped in his headgear, and remembered how bugs sometimes did that, searched you out in sleep like lost pups sniffing a path home to mother. One time (a long time ago, it seemed, when he still trusted his mind to make its connections freely) a bug came to him in the night, shook him, demanded he sit up sweating in the dark. He hadn't even known it was a bug; in his waking mind, the program was finished, working, humming along in the hands of the users of the world. But somewhere in the middle of his wandering dream, there appeared a disfigured little man (a troll? a midget?) standing at the top of a long staircase, shouting in a hoarse, crackling voice an absurd contradiction: "Not enough memory! Don't forget! Not enough memory!" The next morning at work, unnerved by the thought of the figure's twisted little body, telling himself it was foolish, he nonetheless opened a file and scanned a routine he'd finished months ago. And in amazement he stared at the code. For there it was, so ridiculously clear he couldn't understand why he hadn't seen it before, the troll's warning: not enough memory, remember, a bug.

In the shower before going to bed, he'd hoped the bug might find him there. For showers were also famous channels to bugs. Standing naked before the tub shower, he remembered another time when, about to step in as he was now, he'd pulled aside the curtain and suddenly saw—as if written on the sweating yellow tiles—a single line of code: character by character the code he'd written weeks ago. With a bug in it! How could he have not seen it before! Now it could happen again, he thought. Why not? Why shouldn't the god of showers visit him at least one more time? So he took the shower curtain in hand, paused for a moment to hope, then flung it open—a magician's gesture, *behold!* But there was nothing. The steaming water. The sweating tiles, blue this time. The water-stained ceiling. His pink body in the mirror in an empty house.

Now he waited for sleep to find him. He hoped sleep would come before his neighbor's music invaded the house; hoped that the answer to UI-1017 would percolate up out of his memory heaps like water rising to the top of a tree. He believed the solution would come this way for the same reason he believed that his ecosystem would one day evolve—that he, like all living things in the world, was not a unity, a self, a mind controlling a body, but a collection of tiny, locally operating processes. What he called himself—Ethan Levin, this ridiculous gargoyle of a homunculus that lived in his brain—was not their master but merely something that had emerged out of the process-soup, their child not their father, an unintended but useful invention that helped keep the collection of processes alive. If he relaxed, let his ordering mind unfocus, the miracle in the mechanism would work itself out: the connections would be made, the tiny mechanisms would do their tasks, the answer would come.

But as the night wore on, and random thoughts shot through his brain like heat lightning—Joanna's orange blouse, the back of Herring's head, a blinking cursor, Harry's bloody cuticles, his dinner of cold pizza, the call he should give his mother, an ant he'd seen crawling on the kitchen counter—this sense of himself as a bag of chaos began to frighten him. There was suddenly something awful about all those connections forming by themselves, without him, as if thoughts were nothing more than little blind, stupid worms crawling their way through his body. He stayed alert, resisted sleep. If he fell asleep, he felt, his insides would teem like a decomposing dead body, a microsystem of mindless creatures feasting; and all through the long, wakeful night, the thought filled him with dread.

The next morning the parachute was gone.

"Where is it!" Ethan shouted, turning and turning in the office, as if, if he looked everywhere, it might reappear.

Herring wasn't in yet. Thorne said nothing.

"Where is it! Where the fuck is it!"

Thorne spoke without turning around. "Harry had the maintenance guy take it down. This morning. Early."

"Harry? How could he! Why? Did he say why?"

Thorne waved a hand over his shoulder. "Talk to Harry."

Fire regulations, Harry explained. Building codes. Liability problems. "William Harland himself wanted it taken down," Harry said. "Sorry, Ethan."

So the day was spent out in the open, Ethan in his purple headband exposed to the gaze of every passing eye, the buzz of the remaining lights penetrating through the earplugs and the cotton wool and the headband. And through the earphones he had now taken to wearing on top of all the other headgear, the unconnected cable dangling, making his head look like an apparatus that was not plugged in.

Step, step, step.

Check some values. No, fine, the bug's not here.

All through the hot September day, the sun pressing at the blinds.

Step.

Check some values. No, not here.

Through the long twilight, and then the blessed dark.

Step.

Check some values. No.

A vague roar at the door, the lights flashing on.

"*Lo siento.*" The office cleaner's mouth moving silently to Ethan's stoppered ears, the vacuum worrying his feet, and then the quiet again.

Step.

No.

Step.

No.

The lights flashing on once more. Then off.

He was left with something like the afterimage of a flashbulb on his retina: a tall, curvy figure in the doorway wearing a utility belt. *A utility belt?* Could that be right?

He turned: yes, a utility belt, slung low around the hips of the night systems administrator, whose hand was just now moving to her face to cover a giggle. Why was she giggling? Then he remembered the headband, the cotton, the headphones like two big teacups stuck to his ears, the coiled-up cord with the big RCA jack dangling from the side of his head.

He whipped off the headgear.

"Ah," she said, still working to contain her mouth, "it is Mr. Levin again. Looking quite, ah, interesting. Guten Abend, Herr Levin."

Goot-ten Ah-bent Herr Leyveen.

He felt a red flush spread across his cheeks. She was dressed the same as the last time he'd seen her: jeans, jeans jacket, man's muscle shirt, white and transparent. Her face was made up as before, the too-red lips, dark powder rimming her green eyes. And the perfume, the perfume. Suddenly filling the room with the scent of something clean, strong, and suggestive. Spice? Cinnamon?

"Ute," he managed to say. "Uh. Hello."

"Yah. Hallo."

She turned her back on him and knelt down in front of the two server machines next to Thorne's desk. "I must move them from here," she said without turning around. "They are flakey. We keep restoring the file systems, but they refuse to behave." She pulled a flashlight from the back of the utility belt, turned it on, then reached around toward the power switch on the back of the first machine.

"Hey! Wait!" Ethan shouted. "You have to sync and halt it first!"

Her hand moved slowly down to her side. She sighed elaborately, swiveled on her haunches, and gave him a look over her shoulder. "Oh! As if I didn't know! I am left here alone half the night, five nights a week, to take care of every machine in the place, and I am sure I could not do it without the help of brilliant Herr Levin who just luckily happens to be here when—"

Abruptly she broke off and swung all the way around to face him. "But really," she said slowly. "Are you all *right*?"

She kept her gaze on him, saying nothing, which bothered him. "I don't know what you mean," he gruffed at her.

"I mean, Are you all right? Are you well? I mean, excuse me, in your being, your person. You look . . . Well, you will think this is ridiculous, but to me, what I sense, is that your energies are . . . wrong."

He resented her noticing. "You mean my *aura* is bad?"

"Well, go ahead and laugh. But that is exactly what I mean. Your aura is . . ." She cocked her head at the end of her long neck, first one way then another, squinted at him, and finally said, "Your aura is jagged."

"*Djahgid?*"

"Yah. Torn. Jagged."

"Oh, jagged. My aura." He laughed. "That New Age sh—" He stopped himself, made a dismissive gesture with his hand. "That New Age stuff."

She stared at him for a moment more—an open, penetrating gaze from those green, green, dark-rimmed eyes—like a light on him. A long moment in which he knew she was right. His hands were shot through with pain, his stomach burned with acid, his mind felt full of sharp stones. He could neither stay here at work, hiding from light and noise, nor go home, where his neighbors' music waited to pounce on him and his sleep was full of peril. I have this bug, he wanted to say. My girlfriend left me. I found her in my own bed with another man. They're gone, together; they even took the bed. He thought he could explain the worms to her, the way some parts of him had detached, taken on their own existence, out of his control. Yes, my aura is torn, he thought he'd say, And how does a person repair it?

When suddenly she broke eye contact, made a *pouf!* with her lips, shrugged. "Whatever. Think what you like."

Come back, he thought without meaning to. Put the light on again.

But she had turned back to the machines, where she was unscrewing connectors and pulling cables.

"Let me help you," he said.

"No need," she said.

"Let me help you."

And he sat down on the floor next to her, winding cables. When they were done, he helped her lift the machines onto her cart, which she'd left just outside the office. Again, she took off her jacket, and he watched her breasts inside the thin white fabric of the undershirt; smelled her perfume as its scent rose from the little heat of exertion.

"Sorry I was so . . ."

"Nasty," she supplied.

"Yeah. Nasty."

"Ah, well," she said, running her hand over her sleek head and down her neck, "maybe your life is not going too well just now."

He stood up and found he could not move. "No," he said.

"Ah, well then, you must take care of yourself," she said, and immediately busied herself with arranging cables and connectors on the cart. She was just going to go off, he saw. As far as she was concerned, nothing much had just happened; she could put that gaze on a person any time. And so she went, wheeling the cart away from him.

"Yes," he said to her retreating back.

THE NIGHT
SYSTEMS
ADMINISTRATOR

Step, step, step.

He was certain: Ute had wheeled away the bug.

Step.

He kept seeing it: her long-legged, hippy walk, her ass going from side to side, the machines on her cart receding from him down the hallway. What was it she said? Flakey: those servers were flakey. They "refused to behave." If his user-interface library was hosted on one of those machines, that could explain the bug. Of course it could. UI-1017's weird comings and goings had all the characteristics of something in the hardware, in cards and wires and mechanisms, things that heated up and cooled down and acted strange before they died. Blaming the hardware, last bastion of denial. He knew he was lying to himself even as he clung to the idea: Ute had wheeled away the bug.

Step, step.

Still, a negative cannot be proved. Was it gone because it was hiding, or because it was fixed? No way to know. He had to keep debugging. Stepping. But for how long? If the bug stayed away a month, two, eight—could it be considered cured then? A year, two? How long would he have to do this—step, check some values, no.

He found out she was thirty-two, born in Vienna, married.

"But only for immigration purposes," said the saleswoman who knew Ute from her last job. "She wanted to stay here, her visa was expiring, and he married her."

Step.

"To a gay man, I hear. Convenient for everybody."

A gay man. Ute at the breakfast table with a man dressed in leathers. A party full of lesbians in denim and gay men with gym-toned bodies. AIDS. Desperately skinny men with red lesions on their cheeks.

Stop it.

Step.

Friends, the saleswoman said. Housemates, he thought. Separate bedrooms, notes on the fridge with reminders to buy toilet paper.

Step, check some values. No.

Ute, makeup, perfume. The shape of her heavy breasts behind the thin white cotton of the undershirt. Joanna would have hated her.

He decided to wait until eleven and go looking for her.

"Something you want?" said the young man in pigtails who sat behind Ute's desk.

The day administrator's assistant, Ethan remembered. About eighteen years old, dressed in black, his dyed-black hair tied up in braided pigtails.

"Ute?" Ethan asked.

"Out sick."

The boy focused on his terminal and didn't look up. "I'll come back," Ethan said.

The next night, the assistant was still at Ute's desk. "Out sick again," he said.

"Something serious?"

"Don't know."

"I'll come back," Ethan said again.

And again the next night the pigtailed boy was there. "She's gone to Austria," he said.

Ethan stood there gaping; it had never occurred to him that Ute Weiss could just disappear. "Permanently?"

"I think she went to Linz," said the assistant. "That's where she's from, evidently. Something about her father being sick."

"Oh, so she'll be back," Ethan said with relief.

"Yeah, in about three weeks. Let's see"—the boy glanced over at a paper stuck to the wall—"on October 18th. If her father doesn't croak, I guess," he said with a shrug, turning back to his monitor and tapping away at his keyboard. "Something you want?" the assistant said without looking up.

Ethan felt annoyed at the boy's complete disregard for Ute's situation. But then he realized that his own reaction hadn't been much better. He picked up a pad and pen left lying on the desk, wrote the names of his code libraries, tore off the sheet, and handed it to the boy.

"Were these libraries on the machines that got taken out of my office?"

The assistant looked up and stared blankly at Ethan until a sign of recognition came into his face. "Oh, yeah. The servers in that three-person office. Beowulf and Grendel."

"I guess," said Ethan. "If those were the names of the machines in there."

The boy took the sheet and worked at the keyboard for a while. "Yeah," he said finally. "Those libes were on there. On Grendel."

Ethan felt his head go light. His library was on Grendel. And Ute had wheeled Grendel away. Down the hall it went ahead of her lovely ass and long neck and shaven head. In three weeks, when she came back, he would tell her all about it. He would look into her sympathetic green eyes and say how she was right to ask about him, worry about him, *see* him. But not to worry now. Since she'd come to his office late one night and taken away the machine named Grendel, he was saved, he was rescued, his life could start again.

He knew she was back from the music.

It sounded like that German group. The same clangy stuff as the night he first met her.

He raced down the hall, hesitated at the door to her office, then stepped in and declared, "You saved me!"

Her shaved head barely turned around. She was standing by the filing cabinet, a stack of papers in her hand. The music had a man's voice going *uh-huh, uh-huh,* like he was having sex.

"Asshole! Idiot!" She lifted the pile of papers over her head, and then hurled them down. "That stupid boy left me this pile of shit! *Arschloch!*" she muttered as she walked around the cramped office, stomping on the papers, which now covered the floor. "*Das Arschloch hat mich ganz shön beschissen! Oberarsch! Scheisskerl! Scheissbolle!*"

Then she stood still, breathing hard, staring at the floor.

"You are wanting something from me?" she asked without looking over at him.

She stood there, hands on hips, and Ethan had no idea what to do. Should he say something about the pigtailed boy, agree he was a jerk, even if Ethan only thought he was strange? Should he offer to help pick up the papers? Just get the hell out of there? He stammered something about the servers and the bug. "When you took out those machines. Remember? From my office?"

She made a gesture of "whatever."

"Anyway," he went on, "when you took them away, seems you took away this bug I had. Hardware-related, I'm sure. Been gone since you wheeled them out. It's saved me. I never—"

"Great, great," she interrupted. "At least something is saved, yah?" And she got down on her knees and started raking the papers together with her hands, making a messy, wrinkled pile of them. Then she took a heap of them into her hands and shook them. "Fucking asshole idiot, fucking asshole PIECE OF SHIT!" she shouted. And hurled them across the room again.

It came to Ethan that this was not the Ute he'd imagined talking to.

"Are you all right?" he asked her, as the sheets fluttered down.

She sat back on her haunches and made that *pouf!* sound. "What do you think, Herr Levin? Look at me. You don't have to be an expert in reading auras to answer your own question, *nicht war*?"

He stared back at her. "No," he said.

"No," she echoed and started gathering up the papers once again. "No. I am away for weeks, and I come back to the mess from this incompetent idiot!"

She'd been away, he remembered. Shit. He didn't ask about it. Home to see a sick father, and he hadn't asked about it.

"And your father," he said finally. "How is he?"

"How is he?" she said with a laugh. "Ah. He is dead. *Sein Arschloch ist zugeschnappt.* The bastard finally did us all a favor and died."

She sat laughing and piling papers, then quieted herself. "Ah, sorry, Herr Levin. This is a bit more than you expected when you asked your question, yah? Perhaps you should go back to your dark office, put on your purple headband, and work on your code."

He should say something, he thought. He should say something consoling, comforting, warm. But he wasn't good at those things—he knew he was hopelessly bad at consolation; Joanna had always told him that. But there was something more going on here. Something else made him back toward the door. It was the violence of her unhappiness. Stay away from me, it said, or I'll hurt you.

"I better go," he said.

"Yah. You better."

Two hours later, Ethan looked up to see Ute standing in the doorway.

"Hey. Look. Working late? Let us go somewhere after. Yes?"

His hands seemed stuck to the keyboard. He found his mouth wouldn't open.

"I am here until three," she went on. "If you are staying, we could go somewhere. Get a coffee. There is nowhere to drink in this dumb city late at night, but we could eat. At least eat. And I know places where we could dance. Yes?"

He wasn't hungry. He didn't dance. "Yes," he said before he knew what he was saying.

Then she spun on her heels and left, leaving him with three hours to wonder.

He opened files, but that was ridiculous. Code changes he had to make, bits of logic, missing features—in helter-skelter order they came into his mind, then drifted off. Handle variable-spaced typefaces, `ifdef debug`, if `wincount` plus one greater than `max_wincount`—he let it all go. She hadn't been apologetic, he noticed. Her mood was still edgy, aggressive. What did she want with him?

Handle `readc` fault . . . while input not CLOSEWIN . . . her father was dead . . .

Three hours of ticking brain.

"Ready?"

She was really there, standing in the doorway in a black leather motorcycle jacket.

"Ready."

For what? He followed her out into the parking lot, where she stopped next to an ancient VW. It had a bumper sticker with a weird little figure on it, one-eyed, like an alien.

"How about the city?" she said. "There is a club I like. After-hours. Music and dancing. And you can drink in the parking lot, if you have a bottle with you." She didn't look him in the eye. The three hours at work didn't seem to have calmed her any.

But there was no chance he was going home. He was going wherever she was going.

"Sure."

And so he followed close behind her, Ute in her chuggy VW burning oil out the exhaust pipe, changing lanes erratically. He could see her in silhouette, her hand continually going up to rub her head, stroke, stroke in some insistent motion. He had time to wonder what he was getting himself into. After-hours club. Probably South of Market. Some leather bar? He'd heard there were these S&M clubs, sex clubs. No, that was stupid, she couldn't be taking him there, she didn't know him, how could she? So he stayed with her as she moved left, passing a slow Escort in a cloud of dark smoke, then abruptly right, and right again, then left.

Then, in a scary screech of tires, she swerved onto the shoulder and stopped with her signal flashing.

"Are you okay?" he asked as he got out of his car parked behind her on the shoulder.

She was already out of her car, running toward him along the edge of the lane.

"I changed my mind. I do not feel like a club. Do you have any hooch at your house?"

Hooch? Oh. Booze. A truck passed, very close, sandblasting them in a hail of dirt and gravel and litter. "Yeah," he said over the roar, hoping that the bottle of something he and Joanna got last Christmas was still there. "Okay," he said, light-headed with confusion.

"Then I will follow you there."

And there they went, Ute following him through the freeway interchanges, onto his street of tract houses, through the door Joanna had walked out of seven weeks before.

Ute grabbed him in the doorway, from behind. "Where is your bedroom?" she asked.

Her mouth was in his ear; her crotch was pressed against his ass.

"Up here," he said, guiding her to the bedroom with the mattress on the floor.

She didn't kiss him, look at him, say anything. She simply began taking off her clothes in a businesslike manner. Leather jacket. Then shirt. Then undershirt. Then there they were: her breasts, large, heavy hanging, dark nippled. He wanted to take her, touch those breasts, but she was still in her methodical undressing mode. Shoes. Then socks. Then belt. Then jeans. Then, still in her underpants, she came to him.

The smell of her. Floral and sharp, artificial and complicated.

She pulled him down to the bed, handled him expertly, tasted him. And when he thought he could not possibly be harder, she reached down and took off her underpants. Shaved! The hair of her cunt was groomed and shaved! Shaped into a tiny tuft, a crown above nude pink lips.

"Oh," he moaned, pressing her underneath him.

But immediately she sat up, turned him onto his back, and put herself astride him.

"All right," he said involuntarily.

When she was ready, she put him inside her, and it came to him that he was being fucked. And that he liked it. He looked up at her. Her heavy breasts were swinging above him. Her hips and legs were surrounding him. He reached up to stroke her head, touch her face, her eyes, to get her to look back at him.

But she moved his hand away. "Uhm," she murmured and kept her eyes closed, moving herself over him, in her own rhythm, in her own time.

And he saw that she had gone away, to some private place in herself, and that that's where he was supposed to go too. Away. Inside himself.

And she went. And he went. And it was over.

"I have to leave now," she said, reaching for her jeans.

They'd fallen asleep, and he'd awakened to find Ute rustling around on the floor looking for her clothes.

"What time is it?" he asked.

"Oh, about five. But I have to go."

"Why don't you sleep awhile?"

"No. Really. I have to go."

It had been years since he'd slept with someone he wasn't in a relationship with. And now he remembered: When sex was casual, both parties had to pretend they didn't really want anything.

"Hey. Okay," he said, not meaning it, but understanding this was what he was supposed to say. "If you need directions on—"

"I'm fine," she said.

And then he lay on the bed with his eyes closed, waiting for her to be gone. What had she wanted from him? Sex, evidently, and nothing more. He heard her flush the toilet, run the water in the sink, then start gargling. It embarrassed him to hear it, this gargling and spitting; he felt he should somehow know her much better before he knew about that part of her. The memory of her trimmed and slightly bristly cunt could stay in a separate place the way sex could always be separated from normal life, put in a room full of pheromones and bodily drives. But now when he saw Ute at work, he knew he'd have to make an active effort not to think of her gargling and gagging and spitting.

"I'm off now," she called down the hall in a singsong voice. "*Tschüs!* See you!"

He thought he should at least say good-bye. But he came to the stairs only in time to see her go: the tall body galloping away from him, shaved head looking small in the big shoulders and long sleeves of the motorcycle jacket, its zippers rattling.

Standing there cold and naked at the top of the stairs, he was suddenly aware of his body—puffy, it seemed, pink and soft and gummy. No one but Joanna had seen him naked in years, and now he had to think about how he might have looked to this woman who had fucked him on a whim and gone. No, he didn't want to think about it. He only wanted to get back in bed, which he did, pulling up the covers, to warm up, sleep, wake up back in his own mind and world.

But the sheets smelled like her. And like sex. Perfume and cunt and come. And he found he had a sudden hard-on. Amazing, he thought, recalling the first sight of her, the breasts and shaved cunt and beaver-sleek head; and he took care of himself, drifting off into that sex place where nothing else mattered.

For a while. A faint drained floating moment.

Out of which came a memory: the smell of his bed the night Joanna left him. The bed he had forgotten to change before falling drunk into it. The rumpled sheets. The inevitable stain. The scent—sudden—strong. Not his.

Here you are, he said to bring himself back.

Here you are.

Here.

And so he came back to where he was: curled, cold, alone in an empty bed. Something like a knife stabbed him in the chest. What's this? he thought, before the knife feeling rose to his throat, to his jaws, to his eyes, and a sob hiccupped him. Humiliating! he thought, as sob followed sob. Maybe it will make me feel better, he told himself, as he lay on his mattress on the floor and let himself cry and hiccup like a kid. But in the end, he only felt the knife-stab again and again; then a quiet, hiccuppy self-pity; then, finally, exhaustion.

Somewhere near dawn he was awakened by the sudden boom of a stereo, the sound of breaking glass, a woman screaming. He looked out the window to see the big guy from next door wrestling with the dyed-black-haired woman, whose nightgown was nearly torn from her. Was this a dream or really happening? Ethan shook the sleep from his head. He picked up the phone and called the cops, who arrived in minutes. Then Ethan watched in fascination—a wish magically fulfilled—as the two policemen wrestled with the big guy, handcuffed him, put him in a squad car, and drove him away.

"You missed it," said Lisette, the receptionist, as he walked into work close to noon. She rolled her eyes, patted her hair, shoe-polish black.

"Missed what?" he asked, annoyed.

Pat-pat. Singsong voice. "You'll see."

"Forgodsakes, Lisette. *What?*"

"*Layoffs,*" she said. "There's a stand-up with Harland going on right now, by the conference room. Started about fifteen—"

But by then he was gone.

He found everyone standing in a dense knot around William Harland. ". . . will make the company stronger . . ." Harland was saying.

Ethan looked around for Bill Steghman and edged his way to where he stood in the back of the room. "How many?" he whispered to Steghman.

". . . a way to concentrate on our core capabilities . . ."

"Twenty," said Steghman.

"Twenty! Shit!"

". . . a course chosen by a consensus of investors . . ."

"Where?"

". . . the concurrence of the board, the senior management . . ."

"Everywhere," said Steghman. "Testing, customer support, operations, sales."

". . . key personnel have of course been retained, identified with the assistance of the investors . . ."

"And a few developers," Steghman went on.

"Developers!" Ethan whispered in Steghman's ear. He had a moment of panic. "Was *I* one of them?"

". . . without in any way diminishing our ability to deliver a quality product . . ."

"No, no," said Steghman. "But Wang got axed."

Not me, not me, thought Ethan. But Wang! In Steghman's group. Ethan couldn't imagine how Steghman could possibly meet his schedule without Wang.

"And—oh, yeah, Herring."

"Herring!"

". . . This reduction in force—a RIF, we call it—will mean a tighter ship, with more responsibility for each individual. Of course, we will recognize that fact with increased options for everyone, at favorable prices . . ."

Herring. Gone. Who else? Ethan looked around to see if he could tell who was missing. No, not immediately. Then it came to him: Ute?

"Who in ops?" he asked Steghman.

"Ops?"

". . . efforts will not go unnoticed, I assure you. Nothing will be forgotten . . ."

"Operations. Sys admins," said Ethan. "Any laid off?"

"The day assistant, I think."

The pigtailed boy. So what. But Herring. How would he meet the schedule without Herring? His tester, was she gone? No, there she was, next to that short one who went *meep* all the time.

". . . the details from your managers, who will be meeting with each of you individually over the next week. I just want to conclude by telling you that we recognize it will be hard to meet our goals, but that we believe that you here in this room now are the very best ones to accomplish them. Congratulations! You are the key people in our company, crucial to our success."

"Manure!" said someone behind Ethan in a stage whisper.

And the meeting broke up.

"I have to meet with Bob right now," Steghman said to Ethan as he headed off toward his manager's office.

"Yeah. Later," said Ethan, not knowing exactly what to do with himself, wanting to talk to someone about the layoffs, but who?

He went to his office. Herring's desk was already cleaned out. Nothing on the walls. All the papers he'd had stacked on his desk and piled on the floor: gone. He hated Herring, but it was scary how he'd just disappeared. Ethan remembered the layoffs at his last company, which he'd also missed, how he came to work from a dentist's appointment to find all his colleagues walking toward him in the parking lot carrying cartons with the contents of their former desks. Was this layoff planned like that one? Had Herring come into work, flashed on the lights, only to find two brand-new cartons, still neatly folded, leaning against the side of his desk?

Bradley Thorne came in, sat down, and began transferring the contents of his desk to Herring's. Thorne had always wanted that desk, away from the door, closer to the window, and he didn't waste any time establishing himself there. He didn't say a word. He just threw over papers and files and books, and got to work. Did Thorne have a master's degree? Ethan couldn't remember, but he thought so. The VCs would have liked that. They wouldn't have cared at all about Thorne's hunkering silence. He had a degree, churned out code, was usually close to schedule—probably high up on their key-personnel list, despite the bugs he churned out along with his code. But Thorne didn't have a bug like the Jester, Ethan remembered. Thorne wasn't holding up the whole company with a bug he couldn't possibly prove was gone.

Ethan looked at Thorne's back and remembered: Thorne's first choice had been Ethan's desk, next to the window. It scared Ethan to think that one day he himself could be gone, disappeared, just like Herring. And without a word, even before the office cleaners had wiped away his dust, Bradley Thorne would take over his desk.

"Lunch?"

Steghman's face at the doorway, Ethan reading his lips from under his headband.

"Yeah," Ethan breathed with relief.

There was some comfort in the familiar side-by-side stools, the basement cafeteria as usual, the same kind of sandwiches wrapped in their waxed paper on the blue plastic trays, the reassuringly blank vista of the hallway.

Though of course everything had changed.

"Too bad about Wang," Ethan said. "How will you manage without Wang?"

Steghman put down his sandwich. "I won't."

"What do you mean, you won't? You'll have to get those memory-management routines working somehow."

Steghman said nothing, picked up his sandwich again, took a bite, chewed, drew a noisy pull of soda from his straw.

"Nope. Not me," he said finally. "Not my worry anymore. I got a letter."

"What do you mean, you got a letter?"

"A warning letter. About my performance."

"*You?*"

Ethan reeled. Steghman, company star engineer, with a performance letter?

"I have thirty days to get back on schedule."

"But that's impossible! The whole subsystem is still being re-designed! No way you and your team can get it all back on track in thirty days!"

"That's the point."

"That's . . ." The point, Ethan finished silently to himself. Maybe if he didn't say anything right out loud, he could keep at bay the implications of this letter, delay the reality of what was about to happen.

"Yeah," said Steghman. "The point is to avoid paying unemployment. They make you quit, or sit on death row for thirty days if you want a nice going-away severance present. They hope you won't be able to stand it. They give you a task you can't possibly perform, put it all in writing, all very official. You do it or else."

Ethan knew exactly what this meant. But he sat there, stunned, and his mouth moved mechanically to say, "Or else what?"

To which Steghman replied with a shrug, and a laugh, and a finger slowly pulled across his throat.

A WEEK IN THE MOUNTAINS

"Harland wants to see us," said Harry.

Ethan stopped in his tracks at the door to Harry's office. It was supposed to be their regular weekly meeting. Normal, usual, routine. The same thing he'd been doing every Thursday morning for sixteen months. "Harland?"

"Right now. In his office."

Ethan found he couldn't move. He'd never once been in a small meeting with the company president. There was only one thing Harland could possibly want with him.

"Come on," Harry prodded.

As Ethan followed Harry down the hall, the office became strange. Partitions seemed to whoosh past. Icons appeared to detach themselves from the planes of monitor screens and rush toward him. Dana Merankin loomed into sight, then Tommy Park. It was just as Steghman had said: getting fired was unreal, a play in which everyone had a role. The sane thing to do—shout, refuse to go along with the charade of the performance letter, walk out, now, before the long amble down the hall to the president's office—was unwise, bad for your career, crazy. If you waited thirty days for your inevitable failure and then signed a paper agreeing you were fired "for cause," you'd get a nice reference letter, a sweet little severance package, a chance to move on to your next job. On the other hand, if you complained, called it a sham layoff, forced the company to pay for your unemployment—or worse, threatened to sue—you'd better never again mention you'd worked for Telligentsia. A mean hole in your résumé is what you'd be left with, another period of "consulting" to explain away. No, they had you. You had to play your part: take your letter, sit still for thirty days, let everyone watch you fail.

"Levin! Come in!" said William Harland in a cheery voice.

The bug, Ethan thought. He's going to get rid of me over the bug.

He shook hands with William Harland in a dream. He watched in a fog as Harry and Harland exchanged banter. How could they go on like this when they knew Ethan's fate? He looked behind the two men to Harland's desk filled with papers. Which one was his warning letter? Would it be the same as Steghman's? Could they be so lazy: cut and paste, simply fill in Ethan Levin's own, impossible-to-do, custom-made failure?

"Ethan," Harry said finally.

"Ethan," William Harland also said.

Harry took a breath. "We think you need to get out of the office for a while."

"Take a break," said Harland.

Ethan was confused. "Take a break": was this some bizarre euphemism for being fired?

"SM Corp. has a training facility out in Colorado," Harry went on, speaking of the company that manufactured their servers and workstations. "It's up in the mountains."

"Clean air," added Harland, his big head nodding yes. "Big sky. Hiking trails. Waterfalls."

"You can stare at the water and be Zen. Be Zen! Open your mind to the possibilities! And I hear the food is good too," Harry said with a chuckle. "A regular techie sanitorium."

"What have I got?" Ethan asked. "Tuberculosis?"

"No," said Harland, suddenly dropping his air of good cheer. "What you've got is a bug."

Everyone fell silent.

How could Ethan prove it was gone? The server, the hardware—no one would believe him. "It might be gone," he said softly. "That flakey server the night admin—"

"It came back," said Harry.

Ethan felt the ground fall away. "Back?"

"Back."

"When?"

"Yesterday. A saleswoman training herself."

"No core file?"

"No," said Harry apologetically. He pulled and scratched his beard. "Look, Levin. You're not getting anywhere here. Berta Walton is starting to run some unit tests on—"

"I don't want her messing with my code!"

"Well," said Harry. "You can't complain she can't code, then complain when she does! Anyway, she's doing unit testing, pumping in data to a few routines here and there. And while she does that, we thought you should get some help from the trainers up at SM Corp."

"*Trainers?*" Ethan asked, incredulous. Trainers trained *users*, he thought, not programmers. Trainers knew even less than testers, even less than the people at the bottom of the heap: technical writers. "I'm not going to learn anything from *trainers*."

"Yeah, it's true. Trainers don't know shit," said Harry. "But they'll make good programming dummies." He explained the term to William Harland. "Dummies. Describe the problem to them, get the answer for yourself."

Ethan imagined his code under the examining eye of that tester. Berta. *Malloc, Moloch, malocchio.* Her cold eye on the code. Her uncaring, critical mind scouring his routines with the suspicious gaze of the beginner. Would she see the flaws—all of them, not just the bug but all the little hack places where he didn't know what he was doing?

But far more scary to him was this next thought: If he went away, he might fall behind schedule. This one success he'd been holding on to—the only engineer in the company on schedule, the distinction that assured him and everyone around him that he was competent—he could lose it. A week out of the office might as well mean two, what with the overhead of the context-switch, rolling out everything he was thinking, then rolling it all back in when he returned. Two weeks behind schedule: He'd be no better than Thorne.

"I really don't think I want to go," he said finally.

Harland and Harry exchanged glances.

"We *insist*," said Harland.

And here Ethan understood he had no choice: this was his warning. He was on notice, on the thirty-day clock, as sure to fail as Steghman. His only choice was to let go of the schedule, let go of everything, give up and go to the mountains: breathe the clean, fresh air, walk along the hiking trails, and—if he wanted to keep his job (a good question, did he?)—come back with the solution to the bug.

He changed planes in Denver. Sweating in his sweater and ski parka, he lugged his suitcase to a faraway gate, where a small, two-engine prop plane was standing on the tarmac. At the foot of the ramp, a baggage handler took his suitcase and hurled it into a compartment in the tail. The plane had eighteen seats, two seats together on one side of a short aisle, single seats on the other. Ethan was sorry to find himself on the two-seat side, on the aisle; worse, a large man with a bulging suitcase stooped his way down the aisle, took the window seat next to him, and immediately spread his body and belongings into Ethan's cramped space. When the man opened a ring binder onto Ethan's arm, Ethan gave it a shove, hard, then pretended he didn't mean it, muttering, "Sorry."

"Oh, I'm invading again, aren't I?" said the man with a sigh. "Yeah, it's true. I'm big. I have a tendency to do that." Ethan took him for late fifties, six foot, three hundred pounds. The man withdrew the binder, kicked his briefcase closer to the wall, and lowered the chair arm, which had been folded up against the seatbacks. He patted the arm. "There. That should do it."

Ethan felt instantly guilty. "Oh, I didn't mean for—"

"Think nothing of it. Good fences make good neighbors, eh?"

The engines started, first one, then the other, and the tail of the plane rocked from side to side like a cat tightening its haunches for a leap. The other passengers—the plane was full—paid no attention. Ethan figured they were regulars, and that this was like a bus trip for them. But Ethan had never been on a prop plane before, and it was odd to feel the energy of the engines move into the body of a plane while it was still on the ground. The sound—a drone, a two-note hum—was somehow soothing, the reassuring war-movie sound track of Allied planes flying bravely off to victory. A jet pounded its way off the ground, thrusters pushing backward, the plane shooting forward. But the takeoff of this prop plane was almost delicate, the whole body gently lifted at once into the sky. He could *feel* the air's motion around the aircraft, how the atmosphere rounded its way above the curve of the wing, creating the fine air-pressure differential called "lift." *Aero*plane. Aloft in the air. The whole beautiful, slow physics not of rockets but of birds.

"Lovely sound, isn't it?" said his seatmate, as if he'd been following Ethan thoughts.

Ethan nodded, surprised that he didn't mind the man's intrusion now.

"Can you tell how this thing's in good tune? DuhHUM here. Duh-HUM there"—the man gestured left then right—"engines synched up just right, like a great stereo with perfect separation and crossover, eh?"

Ethan faced front, held still, and listened. What was he supposed to be hearing?

"That's so they're pulling together. Hear it?"

Ethan listened again. No, he wasn't sure if he heard it. "Are you a pilot?" he asked his seatmate.

"Oh, no, no, no." The man laughed. "I fly but I'm not a pilot. I work for the airplane manufacturer. I'm not supposed to tell you who, but I carry around all these papers with the company's name on it in big letters so the idea it's a secret is just plain silly." Ethan glanced over at the opened binder: Dehaviland in big letters.

"Airplane designer?"

"Oh, no. Design is for the really big brains. I'm just a test engineer. We devise tests to see if planes are going to blow up or fall out of the sky," he said cheerfully. "Then I get to fly around sometimes and talk with the pilots. But here, now. I'm being rude again. Daniel Wheatley. Dan." He turned with difficulty in the tight space and offered his hand.

A *tester*, Ethan thought. Wouldn't you know I'd be sitting with a *tester*. He looked over at the man's extended hand, and there was nothing to do but take it.

"Ethan Levin."

"Where you headed, Ethan?"

"Up to SM Corp.'s training center."

"Your company a customer of theirs?"

"Yeah," said Ethan. "It's a software company. I'm a software engineer."

"Ah. Software. Then you know all about crashes, huh? Ha! Well, we're on an airplane. So you know, of course, that I don't mean *crashes* exactly . . ."

"System failures," Ethan supplied with a grin.

"Oh, yes. Component faults," said Wheatley, also grinning.

"Glitches," said Ethan.

"Abends," from Wheatley.

"Unexpected outcomes," from Ethan.

"Core dumps," Wheatley contributed.

"Panics."

"Unusual shutdowns."

"Unanticipated features."

"Nonsuccesses."

Ethan's turn. His brain whirred. What else were bugs called? Of course. "Frozen!" he almost yelled out. "The system is *frozen*!"

"Halted!"

"Hung!"

"DEAD!" they both called simultaneously.

The nearby passengers turned to look at them.

"Nice to meet you," Dan Wheatley said to Ethan Levin.

"Likewise," said Ethan.

Ethan felt his entire body relax. Now he took in Dan Wheatley again, seeing Harry Minor transported two decades back in time: Harry's T-shirts and jeans regressed to Wheatley's bad brown suit, wrinkled tie over round potbelly, shirt threatening to untuck itself from elastic-waisted pants, more *Popular Mechanics* than *Byte Magazine*.

"Ah, the many names of fuck-up!" said Wheatley. "Ya gotta laugh or else it'll all get to you, right?"

When was the last time Ethan had laughed at bugs? "Right," he said.

"Hey. Want a soda?"

The flight attendant was coming down the aisle with soft drinks, and after Wheatley signaled to her, she handed each of them a can of club soda. Wheatley dropped his pop-top into the can—"Cools out the carbonation," he explained. Then Ethan sat back in his seat as Wheatley, with only the slightest prompting, summarized what turned out to be thirty years of looking for bugs.

"Oh, they're everywhere!" he said with a gung-ho gesture of his soda can. "So you look for them everywhere." Tests of structures, of hydraulics, avionics, he explained. Of hardware, microcode, firmware, software. At the level of components, boards, subassemblies, subsystems, integrated systems. Intersystem tests. Human-machine tests.

⊒　　⊒　　⊒

Tests of human-only operations. An entire universe of humans, machines, and procedures—the enormous matrix of all their possible interactions—that could fail at some point at any time, blowing planes and people out of the sky.

"It's our job to sit around and think up all the things that can go wrong," said Dan Wheatley merrily, burping discreetly from the soda. "For instance, see that engine there? One of the things we do is ask ourselves what would happen if a propeller blade broke off and came slicing through the cabin." He told Ethan they tried various scenarios, ran computer simulations, to decide which parts of the fuselage needed the most hardening. "For example, if the propeller broke off right now, we'd lose the people in row three. Decapitated, probably. Then the people in rows one and two would be sucked out of the plane if they didn't have their seat belts on. But the cockpit would be okay, and if the pilot was good, the rest of us would make it to the ground. Bruised, terrified, but alive."

Ethan stared at the people in row three. A young woman with a messy haircut like that actress Farrah-something. A guy in a T-shirt. A man in a gray suit who looked like an insurance agent. Dead: they'd be dead. He saw them still strapped into their seats, but headless, their blood flowing out of their necks in rivulets, sucked out by the pressure gradient, red-blood streamers dangling in the clear blue open space of the sky.

"Doesn't it make you nervous to have thoughts like that?" Ethan asked.

"Oh, no. Not at all."

"I mean, how do you feel flying right now?"

The plane, as if to show off the folly of floating fifteen thousand feet above the earth in a man-made aluminum can, took a plunge into a lake of turbulence. Then, just as abruptly, it popped up to resume its sail across the invisible buoyancy of air.

"I feel absolutely fine," said Wheatley with another expansive gesture of his soda can. "Nowhere else I'd rather be. The quality standards for commercial aviation are the highest, the absolute highest. The United States aviation industry makes flying about as safe as a person can get short of his bed. All sorts of things can go wrong, but, thank God, mostly they don't."

All at once, Ethan felt something like yearning. He wanted to be like Dan Wheatley, an engineer who still believed in the tinkering persistence of the engineering mind, who sat relaxed while hurtling through the air in a container full of bugs and potentially head-slicing propeller blades. Maybe Ethan had felt that way once, but now it seemed impossible that he would ever again feel at ease in a man-made world; with the errors, blind spots, mistaken judgments, and memory lapses that were built right into the substance of things; or with their consequences, which were lying in wait all around them.

But did Wheatley say *God*? Was it *God* who kept the world from flying apart?

"I've got a bug," said Ethan suddenly, surprised to hear it come out of his mouth. But once he'd begun, he couldn't stop himself. "A nasty bug. One that comes and goes and comes back again. I can't find it, I can't fix it. It's become a company joke. It's even got a name. The Jester. But it's not funny to me, you know? I guess you could say it's sort of driving me crazy."

Dan Wheatley shifted around in the cramped space to look Ethan in the eye. "Is that why you're going up to SM Corp.? To get help?"

"Yeah."

Wheatley considered him for a moment. "How long have you had the bug?"

"Almost eight months."

"How bad is it?"

"Level-one. Freezes the system."

"Mission critical? I mean, will people die if it happens?"

People *die?* Ethan had never considered this possibility. "I don't think so," he said, momentarily horrified at the idea. "It's a general-purpose tool. But honestly, I don't know what people will use it for."

Wheatley sat back, made a sound like a hum or a moan, then sat back up to look Ethan in the eye again. "And you're terrified, right?"

"Terrified."

"Good."

"Good?"

"Good. The first and most important thing with a bad bug is to be truly terrified."

Ethan slumped in his seat. He no longer felt any pride around this man. Why pretend? This man had been there. "I feel like a failure," he said. "A total failure."

Ethan had made this confession without premeditation, but once it was out, he realized he wanted reassurance. He wanted this man with decades of experience to tell him bugs were normal, you couldn't always find them right away, he wasn't a failure. He sat back waiting for the soothing words, the sort of expiation only an old engineer like Harry Minor or Daniel Wheatley could give him, to help find the joke that would let him laugh at this particular name for fuck-up: Jester.

But Wheatley had an altogether different reaction.

He suddenly sat forward in his seat and stared at Ethan. His face was inches from Ethan's, huge, it seemed.

"*Failure?* You feel like a *failure?*" said Wheatley. "Look, kid. It's not about you. Who the hell really cares about you? The failure is in the system, and the fear should be not for your ego but for the people who'll use the system. Think about *them.* Be afraid for *them.* Forget about yourself for a while and *then* you'll find it, *then* you'll fix your bug. Not because you're ashamed, but because people might be in danger and you *have* to."

This wasn't supposed to be happening. Dan Wheatley was supposed to be avuncular and sustaining, his presence next to Ethan on the plane a happy accident meant to shore up his faith in the patient intelligence of good, solid engineers. Now he couldn't wait to land, to get off this flying piece of junk, get away from this too big, too invasive man.

They said nothing more to each other for the remainder of the forty-minute flight. The plane descended and landed without incident, and the passengers gathered on the tarmac to get their bags from the handler at the rear compartment. A wind sock blew straight out in gusts. Snow drifted across the runway in the cold, stiff October wind. Wheatley stood on the ground at the door to the cockpit, waiting for the pilot and copilot. To the last, Ethan hoped he'd call him over, clasp him by the shoulder, and say something like, Don't worry, relax, you'll find your bug. But Wheatley just kept standing there without turning around, his rumpled brown suit jacket billowing in the wind.

Ethan was right: The trainers had nothing to teach him. He knew it the minute he walked into the first class. The other attendees were wearing suits. Their badges had the names of big corporations. There were department managers, account managers, area reps—users like the ones he worked with at past jobs. About a third were women, formidable-looking with their broad, padded shoulders, their suits red and purple. The world suddenly seemed to be filled with women like this: intimidating, not even trying to blend in with navy blues, but big-shouldered types with determined, self-assured airs. What had possessed Harry to send him here?

A shuttle bus had met him at the airport the evening before, driving up a mountain through snow-drifted conifer forests, to arrive forty minutes later at the training center, spare buildings at the top of a windswept hill. He was given meal tickets for the facility cafeteria, a map of the grounds, and a room assignment, a double like all the others, but his roommate hadn't checked in yet, he was told. Ethan did his best to make himself comfortable in the dormlike room but spent a tense night, fearing that his absent roommate might appear at any moment. By morning, gratefully, he was still alone in the room, and he slept on through breakfast, dressing just in time to go to class.

Now the trainers, two painfully cheerful young men in khakis and polo shirts with the SM Corp. logo, passed out the class curriculum, and Ethan saw, with a sinking feeling, that they were covering subjects so basic that he couldn't understand why anyone would need a class to learn them. Introduction to graphical interactive systems. How to use the mouse. What the mouse buttons—left, right, and middle—were supposed to do. How to double-click. How to drag an object on the screen. Executive overview of networking. Introduction to shared file systems. Information needed by the system administrators to set up user accounts. Logging on; logging out. And it came back to Ethan, with a shock, just how new all this was in the world. If he had started at Telligentsia never having written a program for a mouse, these corporate managers had never even thought about one. The computer systems they had known up until now were room-sized behemoths with plain-character, black-and-white screens—even supposing they had ever sat down at a screen at all. Their idea of interacting with a computer was reading a fan-folded report on green-lined paper with small holes running down each side. Suddenly the world of corporate computing that Ethan had known for twelve years, which even his classmates were leaving behind, seemed a far-off, ancient, disappearing civilization.

Whatever happens at Telligentsia, he thought, there's no way back.

The trainers explained the five-day schedule: classes in the morning, afternoons in the lab for hands-on training at the workstations. Breakfast from six to seven-thirty, lunch from twelve to one-thirty, dinner at seven. "There's a pool table and a Ping-Pong table in the residence lounge," they explained, describing what apparently constituted the complete set of recreational alternatives.

Having nowhere else to go, Ethan sat through the first day of class, daydreaming in the windowless room—white walls, whiteboards, tables covered with white tablecloths, shadowless fluorescent light—as pale and featureless as a dreamscape. Then, at lunch, he made his way through the cafeteria line like a sleepwalker. In the afternoon, sitting down at his workstation in the lab, Ethan stared at his own reflection for some minutes, finally opening up a text file in which he listed all the routines he should have been working on at the office. The next thing he knew, he had a tray in his hands again, and it was time for dinner.

The cafeteria was not very large, perhaps fifty people in it, and Ethan stood there with his tray, looking vaguely up and down for a place to sit, when a loud voice accosted him. "Hey, Levin! It's Levin, right? You're the guy who's the software engineer? Come sit with us! We need help!" Ethan recognized the voice as coming from someone in his class, the big man in the too-tight double-breasted suit who sat in the second row and talked out of turn endlessly, drawing everyone around him into his jokes. Now he was surrounded by a group from the class, all of whom joined the big man in urging Ethan over. The man reminded him of someone, another overbearing man in a too-tight suit, but right then he couldn't remember who.

"That's okay, that's okay," Ethan said, hurrying away from the group to an empty table in the corner.

After dinner, when his roommate appeared—a nervous man who threw down his bag and rushed off to the phone booth—Ethan put on his jacket and walked the grounds. The fall mountain air was sharp, clean, odorless as distilled water. The night was clear, moonless. With his breath turning to fog above him, he lay back on a bench and stared at the black sky thick with stars. Meteors arced above him, flamed, and disappeared—so many of them, from all directions of the sky—as if the universe were already broken and falling to pieces.

Ethan dozed through the classes. Each day that passed, his dread at going home increased, because there the bug and its consequences were waiting for him: his warning letter, the wait on death row, the slow, unreal enactment of his firing. And the dread worked on him like a narcotic. He tried to force himself to talk to the people in the class, find out what their companies were doing with their SM workstations, at least find out if their companies were hiring. But class social life was dominated by the man in too-tight suits, whose badge identified him as Michael Rinehart, account manager at a company called Allied Transportation Services. And all Ethan's instincts told him to stay away from the man.

During the last class, Ethan sat daydreaming as he had all week, vacant thoughts about weather, food, arrangements to travel home coming and going aimlessly. When suddenly Dan Wheatley's face formed in his mind, looming into his vision the way it had on the plane: a big angry head pushing too close to his face. Ethan tried to push it away, but that big head stayed there, round and red-faced, its mouth inevitably moving, Wheatley saying what Ethan didn't want to hear: *Forget about yourself. The people who'll be using the system. Think about them. Be afraid for them!*

Ethan jerked to attention. He looked around the room. People. Corporate technical managers. Like the users at all his past jobs. At least back then he'd understood what they were doing with the systems: journal entries, invoices, purchase orders. But Telligentsia's software was open-ended, a database and a way to interact with it. He had no idea what data the users would be storing, what forms and reports they would create. The women in the purple suits, the men in their sports jackets: What would they be doing with his user interface? He had no idea. Months ago, he'd made the decision to think of the users as monkeys, a source of chaos, locus of the unpredictable, creatures who might do just about anything, hit any key, press any button, jump on the mouse. And his job was to account for the chaos in his little universe, contain it, program around it. He had to protect the system from the users, their randomness, the idiocy of chance.

Think about them. Be afraid for them. The people here might use the system to analyze data—but what data, and to make which decisions? Ethan felt nearly certain nothing anyone could do with a graphical user interface could result in a life-or-death situation. Wheatley was exaggerating, Ethan told himself. Wheatley worked where danger was real and constantly threatening; he was just extrapolating from his own situation, that's all. Then again, there was a rumor. One of Telligentsia's customers might be the United States Army. They were going to use the system to keep track of weapons inventories. Inventories: the word had seemed so prosaic at the time, so clerk-ish and inconsequential. Now for the first time Ethan considered what might happen if some user—now he could see him, a young man in a brown uniform, sergeant's stripes on his sleeve—what would happen if he were just about to dispatch a bomb from one place to another, to another silo, say, and just then, just as he is about to enter the electronic authorization: crap on the screen, beep sounding, keyboard dead.

Ridiculous! Ethan decided. The sergeant would just pick up the phone. No sane organization would create life-critical procedures that could be executed solely through one type of electronic transaction. No. Of course not.

The woman next to him asked him for a pen. She was one of those frightening women: red nailed, big shouldered, her suit an electric blue, dazzling in the fluorescent light. She had arranged herself at the table elaborately—briefcase, notebook, pens, sourballs from the bowl of hard candies, ice water poured from the pitcher. Her pen was empty, she said, how silly that she'd only brought the one, did he have a spare? As he handed her a pen, he stared at her glossy red nails. He imagined them drumming on the keyboard; moving toward a function key; about to press a button on the slowly sliding mouse. He tried to figure out what those hands were doing, but all he could see was their terrible hard red brilliance.

That evening, after dinner, Ethan found himself on the way to a local bar. He didn't want to be going to a bar. He didn't want to be wedged into the front seat of a rented sedan as it swam around hairpin turns on its way down the mountain. And he especially didn't want to be spending the evening with class cutup Michael Rinehart, who was at the wheel. But earlier, when Ethan stood up from dinner, Rinehart had come up behind him, put his hand on Ethan's neck, and directed him toward Rinehart's group's table, saying to his cohorts, "We need Levin to come with us, don't we? We need to pick a programmer's brain. Don't we all agree?" And they all had.

Now Ethan was stuck in the front seat—Rinehart on one side, the woman with the glossy red nails on the other, three technical managers from General Electric in the back—letting himself be rocked from side to side. A light snow was falling. The white veil of the snowflaked windshield, combined with the rocking motion of the big Buick, sent Ethan right back into the strange, sleepy state he'd been in all week.

"Levin's going to tell us how to use the SM windowing system," Rinehart announced to the three G.E. managers and the glossy-nailed woman, whose names Ethan had already forgotten. "Aren't you?" Rinehart said now to Ethan, turning his question into something of an order by giving Ethan a short slap on the knee.

"Yeah. Sure," Ethan said, even though he meant to say the SM windowing system was a big kluge and nobody should use it. Michael Rinehart was a man you went along with; it was just too much trouble not to.

The bar turned out to be the lounge at a Best Western motor lodge. It was crowded with eighteen-year-olds who were too dressed up to be travelers, the women in spangly tops with plunging necklines, their hair fluffed up and sprayed so stiffly they looked to Ethan like ice sculptures.

Rinehart took charge of ordering. "And what's for you, Levin?" Rinehart asked, going around the circle of six chairs drawn around two pulled-together tables.

"Just a club soda."

"Club soda! We can't celebrate learning the hottest new machine in the world with club soda!" Rinehart directed this to the others, and they all at once agreed that he would absolutely have to take something stronger.

"Really now, Levin," Rinehart said.

Ethan didn't feel like drinking. He still remembered his hangover from the day he went drinking after finding Joanna with Ostrick. "I'm a programmer," he said by way of explanation. "Alcohol isn't a programmer's drug."

One of the G.E. managers laughed. "Oh, really? By the volume of bugs my programmers produce, I could swear they're drunk half the time."

The others had similar comments about programmers.

"All programmers produce bugs," Ethan said, annoyed. "It's a side-effect of the process. Alcohol takes away the brain. Makes you think mushy. Programmers like their brains sharp. Now maybe cocaine or speed . . ." He put on a face that hinted that he himself had used these drugs, when in fact it wasn't so. Although he knew plenty of programmers who had.

"Oh, we don't know anybody who uses cocaine, do we?" said Rinehart, again directing this to the others, who laughed knowingly. "Seen those headlines? White powder in the boardrooms! Not too far from true, eh?"

"Right, right," went the G.E. guys.

"Cocaine epidemic on the job, right?"

"Right you are."

He's using them as his peanut gallery, Ethan thought, realizing at that moment exactly who Rinehart reminded him of: Charlie Meyer, one of his father's drinking buddies. Charlie always used to do this, play off an audience to make his points, never able to talk to just you.

Rinehart pressed Ethan again. "Hey now. We all want you to have a drink, don't we? Join the fun!"

Just like Charlie Meyer, Ethan thought, a man who liked to have company when he drank. Like his father. He and Charlie would get drunk and do this: give him back slaps to encourage him to join in.

"Scotch is class," Ethan's father would say. "Go first-class!" Meanwhile encouraging him to be something better than the housepainter turned paint-store proprietor he was, to get an education, get a degree, be a man who worked with his brains.

"Shot of bourbon," Ethan said. "Beer-back."

Rinehart whistled. "There you go. There you go."

By the time they finished their first round of drinks, the four men were flirting cautiously with the lone woman, who was flirting back, and Ethan could just sit there watching them, thinking how useful alcohol was, how lubricating, why it was even making the dull sex play in front of him seem dramatic and fun. By the second round, Ethan felt his thoughts go gluey, his worry over the bug and his looming unemployment starting to drift off, his brain slipping over the sound of UI-1017—you I, youwhy, oh why didn't I think of that before? As he knocked off the second beer-back, he was thinking, so what if he got fired. He'd deal with it. Zillions of people did. His father dealt with being out of a job. He injured his back, couldn't carry paint up and down ladders, and he didn't lie down and die. He borrowed money from Uncle Bennie, opened the store, paid his bills, made enough to send Ethan to state schools. All right, so he drank. Nothing wrong with that. Useful life lubrication, Ethan thought. What took him so long to see this?

"Another round?" Rinehart said merrily.

"Why not?"

Really, why not? Why shouldn't his father sit around and drink with some out-of-work painters and Charlie Meyer, rep for the Sherwin Williams paint company? Lou Levin didn't belong in a store. He wasn't made out to be a shopkeeper. He was a physical guy who could carry a hundred pounds up a ladder and was good with his fists. Ethan remembered going to the store one afternoon and seeing his father standing outside the empty shop, arms crossed over his chest, slowly looking up and down the street like he was missing something.

Ethan downed the third shot.

Training for failure, he thought. His father was teaching him how to deal with the fact that life wouldn't necessarily go your way. That's why he'd wanted him to join in drinking. Alcohol let you feel things you hated to feel, relaxed you so what was bothering you could come to the surface, then made your feelings rubbery and heroic, so you could stand them.

The ride back up the hill would be terrifying, Ethan thought, if everyone in the car weren't too drunk to be worried. Snow on the road, the car softly sliding around curves, tree trunks whirling into view, dark spaces spinning by that you knew were nothing, empty, the long fall off the mountain. Ethan, again jammed in the middle of the front seat, had every confidence in his driver. Yes indeed. Michael Rinehart was a man who had done this many times before, Ethan was sure. He went to work, went to training courses, visited his accounts, then smoothed away the evenings with a drink in his hand. Drive drunk, talk drunk, sit drunk at the dinner table with the wife and kids. Yesindeedwhynot. Good old Charlie Meyer. Dad's drinking buddy. One of the guys sucking the sauce at the kitchen table listening to Count Basie while his mother planned her escape. Ethan swore he'd never be like them, but how stupid can you be. What made him think he could escape it, that drunken fellowship of disappointed men.

The flight back was nearly empty. He was assigned a place in the single-seat aisle, in the row Dan Wheatley said was most likely to be invaded by a rogue propeller. Ethan stared at the engine, at the semitransparent circle that described the rotating propellers, and decided it didn't matter. It didn't matter if he died sliced in half in an instant or terrified seconds later tumbling through the open air. He thought about Wheatley's simulations, probably just printouts, Ethan decided, no visual front ends, no little O's sitting in their seats waiting to live or die. He was massively hungover, depressed after thinking about his father, still without the solution to his bug, and now he had no idea what would happen to his life. UI-1017 could simply take its place among all the other fissures in the warp of the universe. *UI. You I. You why.* Bugs in the engine, bugs in the electronics, bugs in the hardware and firmware and software. Backup systems and redundancies, near-misses and shutdowns and alarms—failure and fault and death circling all around him, real but indistinct, like the corona of the spinning propeller that any moment might take off his head.

The light plane bumped along the thermals at fifteen thousand feet. Then it fell, hard, off the edge of an updraft, like hitting water at a hundred miles per hour. The plane took one more lurch, the wings dipped hard left then right, and then, without further fuss, the air rose up again to carry them.

BREAKPOINT

Steghman's office was empty.

"Where is he? Where's Steghman?"

Harry barely looked up from his keyboard. "Gone yesterday."

"What do you mean, gone yesterday? He was supposed to get thirty days! It's not up yet!"

Harry peered at something on his screen, slapped a command into his keyboard, then sighed and turned to Ethan where he stood in the doorway. "Oh, shit. With everything going on, they decided just to let him go before—"

"With severance? And a recommendation?"

"Yeah, yeah. No one wanted to screw him. He got the money and the recommendation. We just got other troubles now."

"You mean more than usual?"

"Oh, shit. Right. You just got back. Hey! How was it? About the bug—learn anything?"

I learned to drink, Ethan thought. "Nah. Nothing. It was for corporate-manager types. They gave the thirty-thousand-foot view."

"Ah, well. Sorry. At least you got out of here while the craziness was going on—shit, right. You don't know yet. Harland's gone."

Ethan stood and blinked.

"Canned. Along with all the rest of upper management. Everyone above me and Wallis." Harry laughed. "Don't know why they decided to keep us exactly."

"Who's 'they'?"

"They?"

"They. The 'they' that canned everyone."

"The VCs. Took over the company. Got nervous about their money. Put in what they call"—Harry made a face—"*interim management*. Oh, shit. I shouldn't be telling you this. I should say, 'We have an excellent new leadership team dedicated to the company's success.' Blah blah and bullshit. Downside of venture capital. They give you money but want it back before you can build anything. Well, the money guys are running us now. Not a soul up there who knows crap about software." Harry sighed, scratched his beard, sighed again. "Anyway, just try to keep doing what you were doing."

The bug, Ethan thought. What I was doing was trying to fix the bug. But he said nothing.

"We'll go through it all on Thursday," said Harry.

"Right," said Ethan. "Our meeting. Thursday."

Steghman had sent him an e-mail. Near the bottom of the 276 messages that had accumulated while Ethan was away—among them the announcement of the management change, under the subject header "Ensuring Telligentsia's Success"—was a note from Telligentsia's former star engineer. "Welcome back to hell," it began.

Then continued:

```
hope the thing at sm corp was helpful but I doubt those
bozos knew anything.

(at least you missed the bloodbath here)
well, I'm gone. i got hte word a half hour ago I was free to
leave before the end of my "task correction period." the
whole shitty business is over, and I can only tell you this,
if they give you a letter, DON'T SIT AROUND AND WAIT TO GET
FIRED!
```

tell them to shove it and walk out. if you stay, youll start
to beleve you really are incompetent. You can tell yourself
it's all a formalty but it doesn't matter. the whole thing
gets in your head.

(and everyone treats you like you have hte plague)

i'm going off somewhere without computers. i have a friend
who is a fire lookout (really). he says its against
regulations but i can stay for a while if i don't mind
sleeping bag on the floor. don't know what i'll do next but
i'll figure it out later.

take care of yourself. and remember, if you get a letter,
just go. if you ever had the slightst doubts about yourself,
the wait period will kill you. (i havent published a paper
since my thesis. i'm useless. i'll never have a good idea
again, etc. i don't know what yours are but i imagine
everyone has something)

good luck.

(sorry I didn't see you before I left)

Lunchtime came. Ethan sat alone with his sandwich and stared out
into the empty hallway. If he'd seen Steghman before he left, would it
have made any difference? Could Steghman have told him what he was
going through? Could Ethan? *Everyone has something.* He tried to imagine it: telling Steghman how he hadn't finished grad school, how he
didn't have the necessary experience. And how because of that, he'd
surely missed learning something essential about computer science.
Yeah, that was the reason this bug was killing him. Something deep
down and fundamental had escaped him. An operational detail or a
core principle—he didn't know if it was a tiny fact or a huge, over-
arching concept, but whatever it was, he'd missed it. And that's where
the bug had taken up residence: in the blank dark spaces of his ignorance. The things he knew were only isolated bits, chunks of facts sitting all alone, embedded in—what? The air. Nothing.

He found Dana Merankin at Thorne's desk.

"Where's Thorne?"

"He got Bill Steghman's office."

Ethan was astonished. "Why should Thorne get a private office?"

Dana shrugged. "Don't know. I wouldn't read too much into it. I think he was just the first one to ask."

Ethan tried to convince himself she was right, it was just the confusion at the office, it didn't mean anything. But he burned as he considered the idea that Thorne—brooding, silent Thorne with his mountain of bugs—might now be Steghman's successor. A man he detested: the new company star.

Dana took out an emery board and started filing her nails. "I hope this doesn't bother you too much," she said in a tone that said she wouldn't stop doing it if it did. "I play classical guitar," she sniffed, as if that explained everything. "I do it while I wait for compiles."

Ethan waited for her to be done, but it seemed that nail-filing for Dana Merankin was an abiding occupation, an act she undertook with studied dedication, finger by finger, nail by nail. She scratched with the file, then tapped on the tabletop, then scratched again. Off and on, at odd intervals; just as Ethan got used to the quiet again, she'd start filing once more. His headband was at home; he'd stopped taking it to work after Herring was fired. So now he had no defense against this new office nemesis: Dana Merankin's file, a tricky, insinuating sound, cicada buzz, cricket rasp, stop and start, a sound Ethan recognized as the mocking call of bugs.

Step, step, step.

He had to find it. This jester, this tease, this invader that lurked like a virus in some secret body cells between outbreaks—he had this idea that if he fixed it, he could repair his life. Yes, everything would be better then. He could handle the schedule, the layoffs, the night administrator's music that smashed its way down the hall every night at eleven, even finding Joanna in bed with another man—they'd all be manageable, common failures, he thought, setbacks anyone could understand, if only it weren't for this bug, this flaw, this break in his understanding of how the world was made.

Step.

And so to the debugger. Constantly, between compiles of new code, while on hold to get an appointment at the dentist, before bed and the first thing in the morning: step, step, step, line by line through the code. While he was stuck on a new routine, when a noise in the parking lot interrupted him, whenever Dana Merankin's phone rang: set a breakpoint, step; set a breakpoint, step. It must be here, no here, no here.

"Give it a rest, Levin," Harry told him at their meeting on Thursday. "You're butting heads. It's like a sick, autistic hobby with you, this thing you've got with the debugger. Stop using it. Sit back. Be Zen! Let the bug find you."

"I tried that. It didn't come to me."

"Don't try. Stop trying."

But he could not stop trying. Step, step, step, he kept up his sick, autistic hobby. While on hold to question a bill, while Dana Merankin filed her nails, as Berta Walton put new bug reports on his desk and tiptoed out: set a breakpoint, step; set a breakpoint, step. It must be here, no here, no here.

The new bugs Berta left him were easy, what he'd always known as bugs: things that made you slap your forehead, mutter *shit*, then run off to fix. One or two needed a couple of days of searching, one a week of rearranging things that had been badly structured. But months, no, none of his bugs had ever taken months. Now he knew that all the things he used to call bugs were nothings, mistakes, little mental pink slips, while UI-1017 was . . .

Something unpleasant was occurring to him. It was about the bug and his simulation, something about the bug's apparent independence, and the dull predictability of his simulated world. He laughed to himself. What if the simulation finally evolved but produced something like the Jester?

ⴱ   Ⴄ   ⌐

Step, step, step.

While waiting to link new executables, while half listening to a phone call from his mother, while eating a sandwich at his desk: set a breakpoint, step. It must be here, no here, no here.

```
***object_array = ***winarray;
```

The debugger offered up a line of code. Thorne's code, part of the application generator. Ethan stared at the stars marching across the page: variables that held the memory addresses of other variables, which were in themselves nothing but the addresses of other variables, which held yet more addresses. Pointers to pointers to arrays of pointers.

He took a listing and went to Thorne's new, private office. "What exactly is this doing?"

Thorne looked up dully, a bear reluctantly leaving hibernation, a dumb haze that might turn deadly in an instant.

"This bit of code here. What's it doing?"

"Well, you can read it."

"Yeah, I can read it. But three levels of indirection! Why? What's it doing? What the hell does it *mean*?"

Thorne stared at him irritably and said nothing.

"Narrate the code to me," Ethan said. "You know, there's all this indirection because . . . I assign `winarray` to `object_array` because . . ."

Thorne growled at him. "It's done. It's working."

"Tell me! Tell me what it's doing!"

"It's your damned bug!" he said. "Don't be mucking around in my code looking for it. It's working! It's working!"

Ethan bent close to Thorne's face, about to demand that he start talking, explain himself, be freer with help and information, when something awful occurred to him: a cause much worse than Thorne's closed and brooding self.

"Fuck, Thorne! You don't know what the hell this code is doing, do you?"

Thorne said nothing.

"You wrote this—what? a couple of months ago? And it's all gone down a well, hasn't it? Gone, vanished, wiped clean from your brain. You don't remember a thing about it. Do you? Do you!"

Thorne gave Ethan his back, but Ethan didn't need a reply. Of course Thorne didn't remember. Like every programmer, he wrote thousands of lines of code a week, all in the interest of passing ideas through his brain then putting them into the machine, where he never had to think about them again. There was a time when he did know what his code was doing—when he wrote it, when he sat there with his brain exploding and coded like mad to get it all down, all the exploded thoughts, before they blew away. Then the bits of shrapnel had passed into the C language, and Thorne went on to the next job, and the next, all the little thought explosions turning into code.

But as Ethan stood there looking at Thorne's back, it came to him that the explosion could not run backward. The thoughts were gone, decomposed, passed into code, where they worked, where they ran, but could not be reassembled into human-think. All those tumbling thoughts had become marching lines of stars, pointers to pointers to arrays of pointers, functions calling functions calling functions. Layers of code talking to code, machines muttering to themselves in their own language.

Ethan looked at the workstation humming away in the corner of Thorne's office, at the network cable that led off down the hall. He shivered. All the code running in there that could not be brought back. All the machines that had sucked the thoughts out of human beings and would not return them.

At home, at night, in the purple headband.

Step.

Midnight, no dinner, from breakpoint to breakpoint.

Step.

All right: He was drunk. Just a little, some bourbon. All right: maybe more than a little. Three, maybe four (was it five?). His new friend, bourbon over ice with a lemon slice, nice!—like the little hanging tag on the bottle suggested. A few drinks at night, his habit since the training course: why not? He was part of the drinkingman's club now. Old Crow. He chose it because of the label, the crow with its black eye looking back at him. The liquor store had a whole wall of wild turkeys and old crows and other birds he couldn't identify, and the connection between bourbon and wild fowl puzzled him, but he decided he liked it, this association that suggested something manly and outdoorsy about bourbon. Over ice with a slice—nice! Frosty tinkly, bitterly sourly sweet. Black bird old crow pal keeping an eye on him.

Step.

Oh, let's try a breakpoint here. A nice little breakpoint. Step. Okey dokey. Now here. Step. Nopey dopey. No buggy here. No body here. Ha! Step. Maybe another little sip. Sip 'n' step. Yep. Ha!

Ethan was aware, somewhere under all the bourbon, that his thinking had deteriorated to baby talk. But he didn't care. Messy, silly, loose—what had taken him so long to discover the pleasures of letting the brain go slippery? Zen! I'm being Zen! he told himself, sliding from one banana-peel association to the next. Whee!

Then the music started.

Pay no attention, he told himself. Be Zen, Zen! The mind's attention was all. It could make any input disappear. Talk, music, car engines, even physical pain—they had no reality except for his perception of it.

The volume went up.

Step. Nope. Step. Nope.

And up. *Jump!*

Now that crazy, repetitive music had reached some threshold, broke through the headgear, swam in the soupy haze of alcohol, blurry and distorted like noise underwater. A kind of whirring started in Ethan's ears, someone drilling into his brain. He was going to kill them. He was going to tear down their house, throw trash in their yard, put sugar in the tank of their pickup. He was going to call the cops, the landlord, sue them, get them kicked out.

Before he knew what he was doing, he was out the front door, lurching across the lawn, trampling the brush between the houses, and pounding on their door. They didn't hear him. BOOM, BOOM, *SMASH.* Was it louder, even louder? He banged with the heel of his hand, then with his foot. Still no answer. "Answer the goddamn door! Answer it! I know you're in there." He picked up a rock and was about to crash it through the fanlight, when abruptly the music stopped. He pounded. Silence. Then footsteps.

"Yeah? Who is it?"

It sounded like the skinnier one, the one with the sneery mouth. "It's me, you asshole! It's me. Your goddamn next-door neighbor!"

Ethan heard a voice calling from deeper in the house. "Who the fuck is there?"

"It's that Jew guy next door," the skinny one said from behind the still-closed door.

"Well, tell him to fuck off."

"You tell him yourself to fuck off," Ethan heard the skinny one say, as the door lock clicked open.

Yeah, it was the skinny one, grinning at Ethan in a kind of leer. "Well, hello, neighbor! Would you like a nice cup of sugar?" He took a drag on his cigarette and blew it out in Ethan's direction.

Ethan's face burned. Some reckless flash of energy was composing itself inside him, and he wanted it: he wanted it to come out, now, so he could smash this guy. He didn't care what happened next. There was no next. He only wanted—

Fuck. Skinny-One took a step aside. And behind him, coming hard down the hall toward the door, was the other one. The big one.

He seemed more massive than the last time Ethan saw him, that night after Ute left, when their shitty music woke him up and Ethan saw the guy wrestling with the half-naked black-haired woman out on the front lawn. He weighed maybe two sixty, and as he got closer Ethan could see that, as tall as Ethan was, the guy would have two inches on him. He was barefoot, wearing nothing but boxer shorts, and now there was nothing Ethan could do but watch the big, meaty chest move toward him.

"You listen, you," the man began before he reached the doorway, poking a finger at Ethan. "You got a problem with—what? My *music*? What kind of sorry fucker are you? I never want to see your fuckin' face again. You understand? I was sitting there thinking about this sorry asshole pounding on my door. And all I can think is this motherfucker called the cops on me and my girlfriend. And it comes to me: if I ever see his fuckin' face again, I'm going to kill him." He paused, red-faced. "You understand me, motherfucker? Don't bring your sorry ass anywhere near me, you motherfuckin' wimp Jew-boy dumb-brained asshole. You come to my door again, and I'm going to get you. I might just get you anyway. You understand me? Just for the fun of it. I'm gonna break down your fuckin' door and get you!"

Ethan swayed, the liquor coming through him in a wave. He felt himself go wobble-legged, light-headed, his body as light and thin as paper. His father never would've put up with this, he thought. No way. He'd've smashed the guy for sure. Never would've put up with being called a Jew-boy. But fuck his father. His father never taught him to fight. Ethan had to talk: talk his way out of this. But as he looked into his neighbor's face, he understood this man could not be talked to; this man could not be reasoned with. This is not happening. Ethan thought drunkenly.

He put his hands in his pockets and forced himself to look back into his neighbor's eyes. "You're gonna get me? *Get* me? What you going to do to me?" Ethan felt his tongue start to slide around in his mouth like a bar of soap on a wet shower floor. *Wudderyagonnadoo-*

doomee. But he kept on talking. "You're gonna come into my house and what—*kill* me? Are you actually *threatening* me?"

Ethan watched his neighbor's eyes go small. Then Big-One reached out for him, grabbed his shirt by the collar, and hoisted him an inch from that red, menacing face. His breath smelled of cigarettes. His ham-arm was tendon-tight, a menace all in itself—just the sight of that forearm was enough to tell Ethan that he was really in some place where he had no power, and that he had no choice but to give in to whatever was going to happen next.

Then Big-One laughed. He shook Ethan by the shirt one more time, then tossed him backward. "You sorry motherfuckin' little wimp-assed Jew-boy."

He laughed again and turned to Skinny. "Hey, asshole. Gimme a cigarette."

And as Skinny handed Big-One a cigarette and lit it for him, Ethan stood still, suspended for a moment, watching the little ritual of Skinny's subjection to Big-One. Then, realizing that now was his time to get away, Ethan took two steps back from the door, started to head through the brush between the houses, thought better of it, then turned to take the weedy path through the overgrown lawn to the street.

He raced into his house, ran around locking all the doors and windows, then sat down at the kitchen table. He was still wobbly drunk; he'd stained his shirt with sweat and he was aware that he stank like a scared dog. For half an hour, he sat there too stunned to move or think. Then gradually it came to him how bad his situation was. He'd called the cops on the guy. The guy's girlfriend had moved out. He was miserable, humiliated; also vengeful and strong, and who knew what he really might do? Ethan got his hammer from the tool-box. He took blankets and a pillow downstairs to the empty living room. He put the three blankets on the floor under him, one over him, and laid himself down to a room-spinning sleep, hammer in hand.

He woke up with a start. He found the hammer next to him and remembered where he was, and why. His head felt like a spike was through it; his lips were caked with dried spit. He crawled to the window, peeked his eyes above the sill like someone evading bullets. Big-One's pickup was gone. Horace from next door on the other side was taking out the garbage. Carolyn's car stood at the curb. Aside from that, the street looked empty and quiet, everyone on their way to work or already there.

Work, Ethan thought. Get out of here, get showered and dressed, and go to work.

He glanced over at the neighbor's house as he got into his car. It looked deserted, deceptively quiet, its weeds releasing seeds into the wind. He slammed the car door and drove off with a feeling of escape.

Then, two miles after the turnoff onto 17 South, he remembered what was waiting for him at work. Thorne. Dana Merankin. The bug.

He steered for the shoulder. He cut off a truck, just missing a fiery death, then came to a skidding stop. He could not go to work. He could not turn around and go home. There was no relief for him anywhere. He'd have to stay here, on the shoulder of the highway, his lightweight Civic rocked by the wake of passing big rigs for the rest of his life.

He watched the second-hand sweep of his dashboard clock—old-fashioned, spinning time away—and all at once he was crying, a heaving sobbing wailing. He could not leave here. He could not go anywhere.

Then he remembered it was Thursday: his regular meeting with Harry. He put the car in gear, gunned the engine; he was late.

I can't do it anymore, he imagined telling Harry as he drove. He'd tell Harry how he was exhausted and spooked; how he'd come to see the bug as a living menace, an irrational force in the world, some channel into chaos where programming logic could not go. "It's my nemesis," he thought he'd say. "I don't care if you think I'm being dramatic. It's true: It's my nemesis. It's out there waiting for me, to try me, test me, see if I'm smart enough to bring him down. But I'm not, I can't, I lose." This time, he wouldn't let Harry humor him. He wouldn't let Harry tell him that everything was fine, it's just a bug, everyone has one like it sometime, be patient, be Zen, you'll find it. No—what a joke. He couldn't be Zen. He was never going to find it.

The thought of telling Harry filled him with relief. The sun was bright, the eastern hills were chalk pink in the morning light, and suddenly everything was going to be all right. He imagined the look of Harry's stubby hands, their picked-at cuticles, the way they drummed the keys as he worked—the light, jittery rustle that Ethan always took as the sound of Harry's rapid thoughts going by. Harry would burrow down through the layers, Ethan decided. Through Ethan's code, network, operating system, device drivers—down and down Harry would go through the tangled trails of code calling code calling code. Harry was a plumber. He was patient and wily and unafraid, and he'd slop his way through the messy piles of code no one else could deal with. And he would find the bug. And he would fix it.

Ethan found Harry at his desk, back to the door, talking on the phone. He held up a hand to signal he'd be with him in a minute, and Ethan took a seat. The office was a mess, stuff taken off the walls leaning against the desk, the side chair, the bookcase; cartons full of books and papers; trash cans overflowing. Must be moving his office, Ethan thought.

Finally Harry hung up and swiveled around in his chair. "Oh, right. Ethan. Our meeting."

"Yeah. And shit, do I really need to talk to you today."

"Stop." Harry held up a hand. Stop.

Harry looked weary, grinned ruefully. "Wait a minute," he said.

"Oh, I can see you're moving," said Ethan hurriedly. "New office? I'm sure it's better than this closet. Okay. I'll come back later. Or maybe tomorrow. Maybe tomorrow would be better."

Even as Ethan was running through the excuses, something terrible was beginning to dawn on him. The cardboard boxes. Stuff taken off the walls. Pictures of wife and daughter staring up from the top of filled box.

"No," said Harry with a sad smile, "tomorrow would not be better."

The awful idea slowly became more real.

"Yeah, I'm moving," said Harry. "Yeah, to a better office. But not here. I'm outta here. Sorry. I should have canceled our meeting but"—he laughed—"I was a bit taken up with other things." He paused. "Like quitting."

No, sounded in Ethan's head. No: you can't quit. You can't leave me here alone with the bug.

"I can't hack this place anymore," Harry went on. "The dumb VCs. The ridiculous schedules that bear no relationship to reality. You know, I think they'll do anything to get something out the door and make their stupid *revenue projections*, but— Oh hell. I shouldn't be saying any of this to you."

"But your stock?"

Harry gave a big laugh. "Oh, yeah. The stock. The way they keep you here, hanging. Well, fuck the stock. I never cared much about money. It's only this place that made me want money. Fuck it. I have a house, a car, a wife who works, and about a hundred vendor-logo T-shirts. What the fuck do I need money for? The work here's not interesting anymore. Nobody cares about really interesting stuff, or even about the quality of averagely interesting stuff. But— Fuck. I'm sorry, Ethan. I shouldn't be saying any of this. I should be telling you this is a *great* place, but right now I just need *new challenges*."

They sat silently. Ethan felt one question after another come up in him, then subside as already answered or unanswerable.

"How soon?" Ethan asked.

"Today," Harry said. "In about an hour." He laughed. "You know what? They're going to walk me out of here. That idiot new VP of operations is going to walk me out of here like a thief!"

Harry stood up, then Ethan stood. They shook hands. Ethan

wanted to tell him how much he'd miss him, express his dismay, his sense that he was truly done for now, what would he do without Harry? But Harry gave him three big pats on the shoulder and wished him good luck.

"We'll see each other sometime?" Ethan asked.

"Oh, of course," Harry said, both of them knowing it was unlikely anytime soon.

Ethan walked out of the office into the corridor. He felt utterly lost. Steghman was gone. Harry was gone. Joanna was long gone. In his office was a woman with a nail file who cared nothing about him, and at home was a neighbor who wanted to kill him. He stood still, unable to move in any direction. At the end of the line of cubicles, her head just leaning out for a moment, was Roberta Walton, another nemesis, someone else who had no reason to care if he lived or died—and the only person in the world who had any idea of what he was going through.

PART FOUR

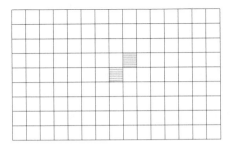

Every time you finish a program, you realize you've arrived at a more particular solution to a more general problem.

—OLD PROGRAMMER SAYING

A MAP OF THE CODE

He came to me with a rumpled sheet of newsprint, held in both hands.

"Here, Berta," he said, standing over my desk and holding it out to me. There was something babyish in the gesture: the two-handed offering, head down, eyes on his shoes.

I took the paper and spread it out on my desk. Function names in a cramped hand, boxes and lines and triangles, if-clauses with arrows leading out of them like traces of an explosion—a boy's drawing, was my first thought, like the ink-blotched toy-soldier battle plans my eight-year-old cousin used to show me over excited, adenoidal breathing.

"What is it?" I asked.

"What you need," Ethan said. "What you need to make sense of the code."

I looked up at him. His eyes were red-rimmed. The beginnings of a beard were sketched around his jaw and upper lip. A dry, scruffy halo frizzed out around his head. A stale smell came off him, wet dog mixed with dead squirrel, a doomed-animal smell. Even his posture seemed melted, his bony shoulders curled over, neck poked forward, head bowed.

But I didn't care. Let him be doomed, I thought. I wanted him to be suffering. For the past three months, since the conclusion of the programming course, I had been trying to get Ethan's help in understanding the front-end code. I'd sent him e-mail messages, almost daily, in response to which I had received exactly two messages, both cryptic. "The front end is implemented as a canvas program," said one. "The code is designed as a three-dimensional matrix," said the other. Now I didn't give a damn what happened to him. And I didn't give a damn about his code. And I was cursing the day I ever got involved with programming. It was one thing to write my little training exercises, I soon realized, but quite another to dive into this churning sea of working code, uncharted except for the little one-page function descriptions the programmers called "man pages" (for "manual," not the male person). I was reduced to trying to read the code one function at a time. But when a function said "return," where in fact did it return to? Each man page described only a single function, and it never took the trouble to say how that one function related to all the others, who called what, where data values got assigned, where they were changed. All that layering and nesting that I'd found so wondrous in a theoretical sense when I was first learning to program, all those structures inside structures and code calling code—a scary night at the fun house when you're trying to understand a real system. A twisting maze of corridors, a bottomless pit, a game of Chutes and Ladders—my mind worked diligently to find sufficient metaphors to describe the feeling of trying to understand a system by looking at it one function at a time—the universe through a peephole.

"About time," I said.

He said nothing, and I went back to the e-mail message I was composing.

"It'll make things easier for you," he said after a while.

I stopped typing and looked at him. "You mean you finally found it in you to help me?"

He laughed: a bark. "Hey! I thought *you* were supposed to be helping *me*."

Fuck you, I thought, reacting to that barking laugh, something bitter in it, attacking. I folded up the paper and tossed it on a pile at the back of my desk. "Fine," I said. "I'll look at it later."

"No, no"—he brought his hand down on the paper—"no, no. Let's go over it. Soon. Now. I have time now. Anyway, soon. Let's look at it. It's important. Important you understand the code. The structure, the layers, what relates to what and why. What can't call what. The matrix—operating system and devices. Without a clear picture, without the structure, the layers, you can't, I mean you can't . . ."

He hesitated. "Find the bug," I filled in.

"Yeah," he said, looking at me intently. "Find the bug."

This "find the bug" was a complex imperative: a question, a command, and a plea. If you can, you must, please. His face was close to me, too close, near enough for me to see the ruddy eraser shavings of his beard, to nearly taste the staleness coming off him. Abruptly, as if he saw my reaction to his sourness, he stood up, taking his hand off the rumpled drawing.

Then a funny thing happened: the sheet of paper started moving, unfolding itself, rustling like something alive. We both watched it: crackling, opening in abrupt moves like an egg being pecked from inside. "All right," I said, still focused on the crinkling code map, aware of Ethan standing behind me at my shoulder, also fixed on it. Looking back on that moment, I have the impression it was the code itself, that map struggling like a fussy baby, that made us drop our guard. Ethan and I were too much alike—too invested in our brainpower and at the same time too aware of our ignorance—to yield gracefully. Neither of us had the easy confidence of someone like Harry Minor, who could gleefully complain of "not knowing a fucking thing," then set about knowing it. Ethan and I, on the other hand, were guarded people, nervous sentries pacing back and forth before the dark chamber of our inadequacies, a room we worked diligently to keep sealed and secret.

But the code drew us. Silly and improbable as it seemed, that slowly opening map was like an invitation, though an invitation to what I couldn't exactly say, either then or now.

"How's tonight?" I said.

"Eight?"

"Fine."

"Conference room?"

"Taken."

"Coffee room?"

"Good."

A buzzing soda machine stood in the corner, a shuddering fridge. The room smelled of burnt coffee, stewing dregs of the pot no one refilled despite the signs meant to shame you into the selfless act of making coffee. I was aware of the emptying office all around us, programmers sitting in the dark wearing Walkman headphones, machines and humans humming to themselves through the night. Neither of us thought to explain why we didn't mind starting our meeting so late. James was away, three weeks into a twelve-week European tour, the radio silence this time thicker than usual, not so much as an answering-machine message in the last two weeks. And office gossip, now working aggressively since the installation of our universally disliked interim management, had supplied me with the general outlines of Ethan's home life, or lack of it. So we didn't complain about the night hours: neither of us had anything to go home to.

"Let's start at the bottom," Ethan said.

He went to the whiteboard, erased what was there, and wrote two phrases, "operating system kernel" and "device drivers." Then he drew a heavy line below them and wrote:

operating system kernel   device drivers

BEYOND HERE BE DRAGONS

"What's down there?" I asked.

"I don't know. Sea monsters. Octopi."

"What do you mean, you don't know?"

"You have to know the limits of your octopi," he said and laughed.

I shook my head, annoyed. "Sorry," he said. "Octopi, API, couldn't resist. You have to know the limits of your API. Application programming interface. Every programmer writes code that talks to someone else's code. That interface to someone else's code is called the API."

"I know that."

"Well, I wasn't sure what you knew or didn't."

"I know that. Did you think I could be here for eleven months and not know what an API is?"

"All right. Good. You know that. Anyway. My stuff, at bottom—I mean at *its* bottom—my stuff talks to the OS and devices through their APIs. But I don't really know what's on the other side of those APIs, inside them, how their code works. I mean I do in *theory*, but you know, I'm supposedly an engineer. I'm supposed to know *really*, not in theory." He laughed again, another one of those barks, this time directed at himself.

"Well then, you should have been an academic," I said. "Academics love theory. In academia, you're not expected to know anything *really*."

I thought he'd find this funny. I meant it as self-deprecating, a way to break down the competitive energy that was always lurking between us. But it had the opposite effect: It froze him. His face took on a crumpled look, like someone afraid of being slapped. Then he stood like that at the whiteboard for several seconds, without moving or talking.

"Are you all right?" I asked him.

"Ha! Is every woman in the place going to ask me that? Anyway, I was *supposed* to be an academic."

I had no idea what other women had asked after his well-being. But what stopped me was the idea of Ethan Levin as an academic. He had always seemed so hostile to anything remotely suggesting erudition, as if school learning were something for pointy-headed snobs who didn't know their way around the back end of a workstation. It had never occurred to me that his hostility might be a cover for something else.

"You? An academic?"

"Well, not like you. Not in humanities. In CS. A Ph.D. program. Research into cybernetic theories, the origins of living molecules, things like that. I did coding but mainly to test philosophical speculations. It was the philosophy that interested me. Does that seem so ridiculous to you?"

Yes, it did. "A little," I lied.

"Because of the bug?"

"No, no. Not the bug. This bug is . . ."

"A devil."

"Well, yes. A special case of some sort. It's just that . . ." What was it that surprised me about Ethan as an academic? The fact that he was arrogant meant nothing; intellectual arrogance practically described the professorial classes. "It's that you seem to have no affinity for words. I suppose I associate intelligence with language, and you . . ."

"I'm no good with words."

"No."

"Concepts," he said. "I'm good with concepts. Concepts tested empirically, in action, in code." And then he gave me his history, in quick, chopped, shot-out phrases: grad school, cybernetic life, Conway's Game, simulated ecosystem, his father's death, debts, quitting school, a job, any job, programming.

"I'm sorry," I said.

"Yeah," he sighed.

"Me, too," I said.

"Your father died?"

"No. I was exiled." Though the moment I said it, I realized it was only from habit. I wasn't sorry anymore. I was a technical person now. "Exiled from academia."

He simply stared at me as we both took this in: how neither of us had set out to be where we were, trying to penetrate the mysteries of a user interface to a networked database, in a start-up company run by people who wanted to get rich.

"Of course, it could be worse," I said finally.

"Yeah," he said. "I could still be coding claims forms for insurance clerks."

"And I could be like my professor friend, whose last published paper was called 'Transverse and Invert: Poststructural Dialectical Gender Formation in the Works of Michael Jackson.' "

"Michael Jackson? You mean like the singer?"

"Yup."

And then he laughed, a real laugh, deep and rolling and hearty, and it was a startling thing to see. I'd never noticed what perfect white teeth he had. And what a nice jawline, and how handsome he in fact was when he had a pleasant expression on his face. There was something elegant in his awkward leanness, I saw now. His head was nicely shaped, his nose narrow and chiseled, and his long forearms and hands were oddly graceful. I remembered he'd had a girlfriend. Who lived with him. Then left him. I think it was the first time I had ever considered that Ethan Levin was a *man.*

Of course I had no idea what he might or might not have considered about me. I'm not a traditionally pretty woman. Unless I can make contact with someone on another level—intellectual, emotional, sexual—I don't think anyone much notices what I look like. I changed the subject. "So what's above those OS and device drivers?" I asked, pointing at the board.

"Yeah. Right. Up there. I'll explain."

And that was it: our truce. Nothing explicit passed between us, no words of apology or friendly resolutions. There was simply this change of energy, a shift to a roll-up-the-sleeves sort of concentration in which we joined forces against the bug. The moment seems large in my memory, a fulcrum, a pivot, the beginning of a new trajectory that might have led to a completely different outcome. But like all things seen in retrospect, the in-line, at-the-moment reality was far more mundane: I opened a notepad. Ethan stepped up to the whiteboard.

He started sketching. His kept his face close to the board, murmuring into it, drawing and erasing and drawing again. I noticed for the first time that he was left-handed, like so many of the programmers, far out of proportion to their appearance in the general population, which made me think that programming was indeed the product of some weirdly organized brain. In a crab-handed script, he filled the whiteboard with boxes and labels. Hierarchies, objects, modules. Device-specific. OS-specific. Private to the window manager. He was intent, intense: a man too long alone in his mental world. Twenty minutes passed before he turned to me again.

"Are you following all this?" he asked.

"I would have asked questions if I didn't."

He considered this, cocked his head, decided. "Right."

We drank sodas from the machine, stole someone's cold pizza from the fridge. I took notes. The hours slipped away unnoticed. Until Ethan abruptly stopped, put down his marker, and looked off in the direction of the hall.

"It's only the night admin," I said, for what had stopped Ethan was the night administrator's music, the loud, weird rock that always announced her arrival at eleven.

"I can't think with that shit going on. Look, I can't. Let's stop now."

The sound of Einstürzende Neubauten surged toward us.

"It's just her usual boom box. We can close the door."

"No . . . No, I think I we should stop now."

I didn't think much about it at the time. I had no idea why the music bothered him. Besides, I was tired enough myself. "Sure. All right. It's late. We'll meet again tomorrow."

"Yeah. But earlier. Seven. And quit before eleven."

"Okay. If that's what you want. Seven."

And so we met the next night at seven, and the next night, and then two or three nights a week over the course of the next several weeks, each time ending abruptly as Ethan or I, whichever one of us had agreed to be responsible, looked at our watches and saw the time approaching eleven. I never asked about his need to leave. I simply said good night and let him go.

Time passed; Christmas came and went; the tree in the corner of the main room grew dry, dropped its needles, and was finally carted away. Then came the start of the new year, gray and cold. And all through, twice a week, Ethan and I continued to meet.

Gradually we redrew the map of the code. I brought in index cards, masking tape, large sheets of poster board. Meeting by meeting, I threw away cards and wrote new ones, moved them around, renamed and reordered things. Slowly the shape of the thing became clear to me. Here was the chart of the ocean's depths I had been waiting for. I saw the complex matrix of functions, by display device, by input device, by operating system. How the whole structure was abstract at the top—an idea, a pure concept, the user has done something, an "input event" has occurred—eventually resolving to the most physical parts of the computer, to the single character read from the keyboard, the click or the movement of the mouse, the tiny screen coordinate in pixels. I saw the tension between the physical and the abstract, between the welter of technical details at the bottom, the "nitty-gritty stuff," as Ethan called it, and the clean, simple ideas at the top—menu, icon, button, window. It all reminded me of the sentences I used to diagram for my linguistics students: the breaking apart of things that on the surface seem clear, self-evident, easy to understand in a gulp, only to find them more and more complicated the more closely you look. Yet still, for all the complexity, possessing a certain harmony, balance, coherence, *rightness*.

We argued, revised, argued, and revised again. Then, late one evening, eight and a half weeks from the time of our first meeting, I made what looked to be the final changes to our map of the code.

"What do you think?" I said, holding the chart up to show him.

I saw that he was about to tear it apart, point out everything wrong and stupid, as he'd often done with me over the course of our meetings. He was a difficult, nervous, nearly impermeable man. When he disagreed with me, he simply kept saying "I don't understand" over and over, making me explain myself again and again and again, until I felt stupid even to myself. And here he was about to give me the business once more.

But something stopped him. He took a step toward the poster board I was holding, made a little hum, then stepped back. He ran his fingers once through his hair. Then he looked at me. I think what stopped him was what he saw in my face, for surely it showed my pleasure at finding something in his work I'd never suspected could be there: a clumsy kind of elegance, a shape like Ethan himself, lean and spare and balanced in an awkward way. The whole structure made me think of a Calder mobile: a chaos of competing forces—designs, limitations, intentions, constraints—somehow suspended in a bobbling moment of grace.

He stood gaping at the chart. "I thought you would . . . I was afraid . . ."

"What?"

"Nothing."

He just kept standing there, gazing at the evidence of his handiwork, a man amazed at his own creation, it seemed. How was it possible that this code existed? Its very presence in the world seemed a miracle, and if he could trust the evidence of his eyes, it wasn't even the shameful mess he was afraid it was. It was, might even be—if he let himself think it—good.

"Did I do that?" he asked.

"Evidently."

This moment should have hung there, sustained; we should have looked at one another, sealed some interior pact, smiled, then gone on to solve the bug. Perhaps a cello should have played in the background, something heart tugging, tear inducing. Really, despite my hatred for the sentimental, I would have liked the story to go this way: Ethan redeemed by the austere beauty of his code, two people bonded by collaboration, programming as human glue, not the private obsession it seemed to be.

We at least got our music. Deafening chords, backed by a grind guitar, a bell ringing doom:

> *Hangin-i-ing . . .*
> *Hangin-i-ing . . .*
> *Hangin-i-ing . . .*

Ethan grabbed the chart and threw it on the table. "Shit! What time is it?"

"Not yet eleven. She's early."

"Damnit. I hate that music!"

"Oh, it's not too bad. Siouxsie and the Banshees. At least it's not Ratt."

"I don't care who it is. It makes me nuts!"

"I can see that."

> *Running from your enemies*
> *And falling on your knees*
> *On your knees*
> *On your knees*
> *Get down on your knees.*

"How can anyone think with that shit going on. You like that crap?"

"I don't mind it."

"Well, shit! Then you're nuts, too!"

And with that he packed up his things and marched out.

I didn't think I'd deserved that. "Hell with you, Ethan Levin," I said to the empty room.

———

I went home and called James. In that mood—work, punk rock, Ethan marching out on me—it was a mistake; I don't even want to think about it. But no matter. This is what must happen next: this final, definitive confluence between James and the bug.

I had the phone number of James's friends in Paris, an English couple with an apartment there. He'd be staying with them, he said, between performance dates in Narbonne and Béziers (small cities, nowhere places; it was a bad orchestra, I can say that now). Ethan Levin cursing at me, two knocked-back tequilas, the dark, unblinking light I came home to on my answering machine: it was in this line of events I called James.

"A-lo-oh," sang the voice I took to be the friend named Charlotte, a morning voice, 8 A.M. Paris time, singing Frenchly into the phone.

I asked for James.

"Susanna! Fabulous to see you last night. James was right. You're smashing, fabulous, really."

My heart began to beat strangely. The time between beats seemed long, huge; it was an impossibility I was still living.

"Hello?"

Susanna, that *someone*, all my fears come absolutely, unparanoidly true. "I'm not Susanna," I said.

"Oh. Excuse me." A pause. Uncomfortable. She knew something was wrong. "Then whom shall I say is calling, please?"

I liked that, the British formality. Whom: so correct. Please: so calming.

"Tell him Berta."

"Pardon. Very sorry. Was that Bertha?"

"Ber-ta. RO-ber-ta."

"Ah, I see. Roberta."

No name recognition. Just like me with the wild, mad Sarah Postman who showed up on my doorstep two years ago. His girlfriend: *Who?*

"Is he there?"

"James. No, I'm afraid not. Is this urgent then?"

Lie, said my oddly beating heart. "Oh, yes," I said. "A change in travel plans. Most urgent. Do you know where I can reach him?"

"*Mais, bien sûr.* You may reach him at the Hôtel Jardin du Luxembourg. The number there is . . . let's see . . . yes, here it is."

I repeated the hotel, the number.

"And ah, well, you see, you will need to ask for the room of Susanna Cantor."

And ah, well, I did see.

I didn't have to call, of course. For exactly two seconds—one, Mississippi; two, Mississippi—I considered putting down the phone and waiting until James got home to deal with any of this. But there'd been the shock of being taken for Susanna, the two downed tequilas; before that the evening with Ethan Levin interrupted by Siouxsie and the Banshees. The seconds passed, and I called. Ring, ring went the phone in that charming little French way, two quick rings then a pause. Another ring, ring. Then the voice of Susanna Cantor, sleepy, sex-sated, I imagined it. Wake up, Little Susie.

"It's Berta," I said.

A pause. "Berta."

Surprise! At least she knew my name. "Give me James."

Silence.

"Give me James."

The papery sound of a hand covering the phone, the handset being passed across the bed. A pause the width of a *grand lit* transmitted across an ocean and a continent.

"Berta," said James. "Hello."

What else could he say? What else does a lying, cheating bastard say when caught in the act but hello?

"Hello? Are you there? Berta?"

"Oh, I'm here, all right. And where are you?"

No answer.

"Well, at least you aren't lying to me yet."

No answer.

"I don't suppose you expect me to pick you up this time?"

No answer.

Then I exploded. Ugly, cursing, shitty things—like anyone would say in my place. I cursed his family, ridiculed his anatomy, listed his many faults for review. My anger grew, as if I weren't venting it but stoking it, pumping it into a tight space where it compressed and went dangerous. I felt myself go heedless, tearing up any goodwill that might be left between us for the future. What infuriated me most was the thought of how long this had been going on, the long trail of lies that led to this moment with James in Susanna Cantor's hotel room at eight o'clock in the morning Paris time. "When did this start?" I screamed into the phone. "When? Last trip, the trip before, the one before that? When? How long? From the beginning?"

He said nothing, only let me rail on. Meanwhile, alongside the expanding anger, something else was beginning to grow in me, something strangely satisfying, an almost evil happiness. It came from the idea that I had always known that this would happen, that I'd foreseen it, predicted it, worked it out in my mind from one angle and another like a play I was perfecting or the takes of a movie I could film again and again until the scene came out exactly, horribly right. The secret *someone*, the great love James refused even to protest against, the fears of mine he disdained even to address—James and Susanna, here they were, together: caught.

"I *knew* this would happen," I said. "I *knew* it!"

I'd been around programmers too long. My misery at being betrayed, humiliation at being duped, fury at being lied to, shame at being abandoned—all this was almost, nearly, oh so close to being balanced, indeed redeemed, by the satisfaction of knowing I'd been *right*.

No sleep, hungover, lungs smoked out—in that condition I pulled into the parking lot, went to my cubby hole, tried not to see my puffy reflection in the face of the monitor. Beep, said the system, Today is January 11, 1985. A new year. Nothing much had changed in the ten months since I'd come across the bug, except I was rid of James.

It was a dumb test I ran that day. I had this cockeyed idea about concurrency, so I went to the training lab, used two side-by-side monitors attached to the same workstation, and started up two separate instances of the front-end program. Concurrency: running together. With one program to the left of me, and one to the right, I took a mouse in each hand. Then (taking some pride in my ambidexterity, if in nothing else) I set up identical queries on each, moving both mice in the same arc, sliding them over the same buttons and menus, going *click* at the same time. Synchrony: it seems somehow important to human beings to notice that we're doing things at the same moment; it's one of the ways we mark off experience, I thought, made sense of the world. *At the same time.* (James in bed with Susanna; Berta calling; at the same time.) How emphatically and seriously we take this, as if our senses have noticed something of amazing significance. Of course it was all hogwash as far as the computers at Telligentsia were concerned. Our system turned everything into a sequence of tiny events. No matter how it seemed to us—that we went *click* at what we called the exact same moment (lay entwined; picked up the phone; in the same moment)—the chip detected the lag, saw units of time our eyes, hands, senses could not, the machine operating in a time domain we humans have created but cannot directly feel.

But what did I know then? As I said, I had this lamebrained idea about concurrency and so sat shivering in the frigidly air-conditioned training room practicing my synchronized mousing. It was just like the day the bug first appeared: the dumb user interface, the clumsy mouse clicks, the arcane commands. My impatience and unhappiness. Only one thing had changed: I was no longer afraid of what might happen with James. What I'd feared had happened; no need to worry anymore. An odd brand of relaxation: the paranoiac's glee at discovering the world really is out to get you.

A half hour went by: slide, click; slide, click. Another miserable day, another perfect test. Slide to a button, click. Slide to a menu, click. Slide off a menu and—the monitor on the right went crazy. Mess of lines, beep stuck, keyboard frozen, mouse dead.

The bug.

The long-elusive Jester, bobbing and weaving, showing itself only to the hapless: Here it was.

I made myself stop and take a breath. Get the core, I thought. Whatever you do, get the core. The monitor on the left is still working. Exit the front end on that one. At the prompt, do a ps, find the process ID of the front end that's fritzed. Then kill that process, but kill it right. Kill minus three, and get the core.

```
> ps -u rwalton
  PID    TTY   STAT  TIME   COMMAND
010501   0402    R   0:34   /usr/bin/ui_start
026790   0401    S   0:00   -bash
027802   0401    R   0:00   ps -u rwalton
> kill -3 010501
```

I had it: the dead body, the core file, the dump of the contents of memory that Ethan Levin could now examine to find the cause of the bug. The state of the program at the moment of its death, somewhere in there the information that would help solve the mystery of this Jester. UI-1017: ready for its autopsy. I felt exultant, wanted to run down the hall dancing, shrieking that I'd done it, caught it, captured it. An expansive, vengeful happiness went through me, a wild, destructive joy, the sense that I'd finally tracked down my two demons in a single day—James, the bug—and killed them.

Then it vanished. In a moment, all my happiness collapsed. For there on the left, still showing the remains of the query I was working on, was the program that did not freeze up. I stared at it, amazed. Why not? If one instance of the program went down, why not the other? They were the same, stroke for stoke, click for click, key for key, as close to identical as a human hand could make them. Yet one froze up while the other kept running. *Why did the bug appear on one but not the other?*

I felt spooked. I looked from one monitor to the other, one so well behaved, the other gone mad, and despite the cold room my neck was damp with sweat. I did indeed have the core file, Ethan could still examine it, but now nothing made sense to me. How could a program behave so differently on what seemed two identical runs? I reeled to see just how deep those layers of code went, how complicated were the interplays of processes going on beneath the flat, friendly face of the screen, a feeling like looking down the dark well of an elevator shaft without the protection of the closing doors. Under the user interface was the program, under the program was the operating system, under the operating system was the chip, and down there things were happening that were beyond my comprehension or imagination. I was at the limit of my understanding, beyond which my sense of cause and effect was breaking down. Was it only my ignorance, or was there something else going on here, something that had eluded even the programmers—a deep-down strangeness that made this machine seem to be operating on its own terms, alive? I thought about Ethan Levin, how he would have to travel all the way through this strangeness, and for the first time I understood what he was up against, and was afraid.

THE CORE DUMP

He couldn't read the dump. He stared at the screen, the printouts, in octal, decimal, hex. Everything he could possibly learn about the state of his dead program—there it was, ready for a postmortem under the debugger. No more excuses; no more complaints about incompetent testers, dumb marketing managers, saleswomen in suits. Now he was supposed to fix the bug: Berta Walton had captured the core.

"What?" he'd said, seeing her in the doorway, her mouth moving, taking off his headband, cotton wool, earplugs.

"I got it."

"Got it?"

She slid a piece of paper onto his desk. "Name and location of the core file."

He looked at it, her, speechless.

"Best of luck," she said.

There was a funny look on her face. Did she know? Did she suspect him? Was she the one person in the company who knew he couldn't read the core?

Two debuggers, adb, dbx. Register contents, memory, stack trace-back. Program counter, pointer values, values of variables internal and external. Did Berta Walton suspect how little good it would do him?

```
(dbx) where
PutMenuLine(0x1f90, 0x1e78), line 53 in "PutMenu.c"
PutMenu(0x1f90), line 32 in "PutMenu.c."
inregion (0x1b58, 0x1004), line 11 in "inregion.c"
GetInputEvent(0x2008), line 26 in "GetInputEvent.c"
PutMenu(0x1f90), line 15 in "PutMenu.c"
inregion (0x202e, 0x205d), line 11 in "inregion.c"
GetInputEvent(0x2008), line 26 in "GetInputEvent.c"
. . .
```

The stack trace made no sense to him. Usually that was all he needed, the list of functions that had run, from most recent looking back. It was the only part of the core he really knew how to use: type the command "where," and on the top of the list would be the line of code where the program died. He'd list the source code file, hum over it for a while, and there—of course! how stupid!—the answer would be.

But this time, no. A muddle. Nonsense. It died in a routine that displayed a menu. Line 53 of PutMenu.c. Why? The mouse wasn't even in the menu. The mouse was outside it, sliding back toward the menu, but not there yet, so why did the program get lost displaying a menu? It had no business there, not yet, not now. And he'd been over this code, again and again. It was the section he'd suspected from the beginning. Nothing. Nothing wrong that he could see.

Blind, stupid, incompetent—that's what he was. He had the dump and now he was expected to fix his bug, but how could he tell anyone that it was useless to him? Machine guts, exposed, but it was no good, no help. He knew this would happen someday: twelve years of faking it, and one day, an illiterate pretending to read, he'd get caught.

What was it Harry had said about crash dump analysis? "A black art," he'd called it. Maybe everyone had trouble with core files. Maybe, all over the world, programmers were sitting down to their debuggers, examining the core, and everyone faking it.

Harry. He could have asked Harry. The only person in the world Ethan could have gone to, to confess his ignorance, get help. What would Harry have said? Unfocus your attention. Be Zen. Empty your mind. Look at the stack trace like a visitor from another universe, where not even the laws of physics are the same. You're too invested in what you think you know. You can't see what's there because you're seeing what you think is there. Yes, Ethan thought, it was true. He'd looked at this code so many times he could not even read it, his mind just sliding over it, unable to penetrate his certainty that it was fine, tested, *working*. He knew he was in a thought-rut, going round and round over the same conditions, breakpoints, test values, but it didn't help, he was stuck, getting worse by the minute, clutched. He needed someone to talk to. Harry. Or Steghman. Yes, he might have gone to Steghman. But they were both gone, and there was only Bradley Thorne, and the idea of going to Thorne with his core dump, somehow getting what he needed without getting caught out as a functional illiterate—impossible.

He looked up at the two papers still hanging over his desk, the two screens, one hand-drawn by Harry, the other the image of the screen he'd coded himself. He thought back over the months since he'd hung them there, side by side, to remind himself he was the agent that had turned one into the other, Harry's thoughts made real. It seemed an impossibly long time ago, another life, when he was still with Joanna, and for a moment he'd believed that his life as a programmer wasn't a complete waste after all.

"Is that bug still open?" said Thorne.

Ethan's turn. Thorne, team leader now, had started with Dana Merankin, and now it was his turn.

"Yeah," Ethan said.

"Thought you had the core."

"Yeah," Ethan said again.

Thorne only flicked up his eyes to look at Ethan for a moment. Thorne wasn't good at eye contact. He kept his stare focused on the yellow pad in front of him, shoulders hunched. He wasn't very good at talking, either: Every word he said seemed squeezed from a flattened toothpaste tube.

"Weeks."

"What?"

"You got that core weeks ago."

"Something like that."

"Three and four-sevenths weeks exactly," Dana Merankin supplied.

Ethan didn't even turn to look at her. "Something like that," he repeated.

"Well, when?" said Thorne.

"What?"

"Fixed."

Thorne's leg was shaking up and down impatiently, vibrating the whole table. Ethan's colleagues were staring at him. A little hissing started in Ethan's ears, like he was going to faint. Fake it, he thought. Keep faking it. Except for Dana Merankin, who had a scornful little smile teasing the corners of her lips, everyone looked afraid. For themselves, Ethan thought. Not for him but for whatever failures large and small awaited their turn around the table, for whatever they were faking.

"I'm working on it," Ethan said. "I'm staying on schedule with my other tasks, and in between I'm working on it."

"QA wants a meeting."

"Okay."

"You and your tester with Markham. Tomorrow, eight A.M."

"Okay."

Then Thorne moved on, to Bill Werners, Tommy Park, Larry

Seidel, each time with a flick of his eyes and a shaking of his leg, a squeezed-toothpaste ejaculation of a few words. The hissing in Ethan's ears went on, and then something strange started happening in his peripheral vision. A jaggedy prismatic line, like some tortured, wiggling electric eel, appeared in the margin of his vision. He tried to shake the sensation, but the snake got fatter, took over his entire visual field but for a small, perfectly round hole straight down the middle. He thought: I'm going to die, with my brain exploding. Then: Migraine, he told himself, fighting down the terror. Opthalmic migraine. Years had passed since his last one, yet the fear was fresh and new: What if he stayed like this? What if it never went away?

He wasn't going to say anything. No. He was going to sit there, pretend to be calm, pay attention, be normal. It was just the drinking, Ethan told himself, all that bourbon he drank while he worked at home. Sure, that was it. Alcohol increased the blood flow to the head. Made it throb. Concentrate, he told himself. Not going to die.

He focused on Thorne, watched him pepper Werners, Park, and Seidel with questions about their respective errors and defeats. Peering through the throbbing kaleidoscope that his eyesight had become, Ethan had a horrible vision: Bradley Thorne as a compiler, a little machine of a person, chunk-chunk-chunking through the statements of human speech, finding every flaw.

"Odd," said Berta. "She's never late."

Ethan was barely awake, squinting into the morning sun that slanted into Wallis's little office.

"Must be traffic," he mumbled.

The diagonals of light made a jumble of the charts looking down from the walls, pie charts and bar charts, charts with wavy lines like the surface of a choppy sea—a sea of bugs, Ethan thought, taking what comfort he could from the idea that his bug was only one of the tens of thousands represented on these walls. The sun bothered him; he put up his hand to cut the light. He felt strange after his migraine episode yesterday, fragile, as if his vision, which still seemed pixilated and airy, could scatter in a puff of breeze.

"Oh, there she is," said Berta.

He put down his hand. "Where?"

"There. That's her car."

Ethan squinted through the dust glare on the window to the parking lot, where a black Volvo sedan was pulling into a space just opposite them. The driver's door opened, and Wallis's round head and square shoulders appeared.

"Yeah, there she is," said Ethan idly.

He was about to put his hand up again to shield his eyes when the other door opened and a figure with a wholly different shape emerged from the passenger's side. A long arm. A black leather jacket. A sleek, shaved head.

"Ute," he said aloud without meaning to.

Then, forcing himself to keep looking through the glare that made his brain hurt, he sat still as a little pantomime played itself out right before his eyes. Ute and Wallis walking to the trunk of the car. Wallis reaching toward the trunk, her key out. Ute taking the hand with the key in hers, then, with her other hand, stroking Wallis's hair, twice, slowly, forehead to crown. Then nuzzling her. Then the two women kissing, tentatively at first, just a touch of the lips, a little murmuring going on. Finally an all-out, hip-grinding, hand-roaming, tongue-licking kiss.

"Wallis and Ute!" said Ethan, exclaiming despite himself.

"Didn't you know?" said Berta. "I thought everybody knew."

Ethan couldn't take his eyes from the scene in front of him. The woman who'd followed him home and fucked him, the woman who advertised his name and his bug on her whiteboard of infamy: They should not touch; these two parts of his existence should stay in their separate tracks and not confuse him. No, he didn't know. He didn't know anything. The world was full of secrets, stories, mysteries. Wallis and Ute. Joanna and Ostrick. Bugs, debuggers, and core files. He'd misunderstood everything. He'd been walking around in the world lost to some truths that were clearly obvious to everyone.

"I'll just be a minute," said Wallis, poking her head in the doorway.

Ethan barely listened to the meeting. Wallis's mouth and cheek were still traced with red, the same blood-red Ute had smeared behind his ear, on his mouth, on the rim of his prick. He said yes to everything Wallis said—Berta writing test scripts, more meetings between Ethan and Berta, weekly check-ins with Wallis—all the while staring at the red smudges on her face. After a few minutes, Berta made some little gesture to Wallis, something she did with her fingertip, making Wallis understand about the lipstick. But even after Wallis had put a tissue to her cheek and lips, a tiny red dot remained on her upper lip, the size of a blood drop from a pinprick, and Ethan couldn't stop staring at it: this little thing, so red, that would not go away.

"Are you listening?"

No, he wasn't listening. Berta was at the whiteboard, sketching plans for her test scripts, but all he could hear was the buzzing of the soda machine. Wallis had told them to start work that night, and so he had taken his body here into the coffee room, but the electronic buzz of the vending machine was doing something strange to his brain.

"Uh-huh," he nodded to Berta, to keep her talking.

Ute and Wallis, naked, their breasts touching. Ute's full, low-hanging breast and what he imagined was Wallis's small, round one. Nipple to nipple. The thought should have excited him; he'd heard that men were supposed to get off on the idea of two women making it. But that image led directly to Joanna and Ostrick, cunt and prick, and what flooded him was a feeling of disgust. Things touching that shouldn't. Violation. Infection. Dirt.

"We should pump data into PutMenuLine, all kinds of values, stupid and real," Berta was saying.

"Sure. Fine."

Then immediately his mind jumped to the simulation, to his O-creatures, mingling and feeding and reproducing. There seemed something right and calming about them, in their spareness, in the basic emptiness of them, without motive or harm. He had almost forgotten about his O-beings; months had gone by without his even thinking about them; now he had a sudden need to see his creatures again, clean and pure and good in their still-possible little world.

"Listen," he said, interrupting Berta. "You should come to my house. I have to show you something. This simulation I've been working on. The one I told you about. Simulated ecosystem. You should come see it."

Berta took a step back from him. "What are you talking about?"

"The simulation. You should come see it."

"What, now? Are you nuts? We've been at work twelve hours straight. We're going to decide on some scripts, and then I'm going home."

He jumped up from his chair. "Now! You should see it now! Tonight. Forget this script shit. Let's go. Let's just go!"

"Jesus, Ethan. Don't be weird. I'm tired. Let's just do this and go home."

"No! You must come. Now!"

Before he knew what he was doing, he reached out and grabbed her arm.

The marker she was holding fell to the floor. "Sorry," he said, reaching down to retrieve it.

"Jesus, Ethan," she repeated, rubbing her arm where he'd grabbed it. "What's the matter with you? Are you all right?"

"Don't keep asking me that! Why do people keep asking me that? Don't fucking ask me that again!"

And he reached across and grabbed her arm again, harder than he meant to, a bruising, twisted clutch of his hand he knew had gone too far when he looked up and saw the expression on her face.

"Fuck! Let go! What the hell are you doing?"

"Shit. Sorry. It's just . . . It's that . . ." He stepped back, took a breath, sat down. "You really don't know me, do you? No one here does. They all think . . . Never mind. Never mind."

Berta said nothing, only stood there rubbing her arm. The soda machine buzz seemed very loud.

They didn't speak for several seconds. "Please come see it," he said finally. He stopped looking at her, afraid he was going to cry. "I can't explain it. Please. I just need for you to see it now."

THE KEY TO ALL MYTHOLOGIES

It must have been the tequila that made me go to his house that night. There's no other explanation. A three-drink lunch, a nip in the afternoon, then that reckless, nasty feeling when the alcohol wears off and you have to keep functioning. I'm not sure what I was thinking in the moment. At the time I would have sworn there was nothing I wanted from Ethan Levin but his help with the bug. All I know is I stood there rubbing my arm where he'd grabbed it, looked at him where he sat crumpled over his papers at the table, and I thought: There's no one waiting for me at home. What the hell else do I have to do?

"All right," I said, making the first of my many mistakes that night. "Maybe for an hour."

So I followed him through a tangle of freeways, under a late-season rain that had started while we were closed up in the fluorescent world of the office. The night was heavy and warm, one of those days when you're shocked to remember that spring in the Bay Area starts in February.

Tall weeds had taken over his front yard. The short path to his front door was muddy. On the porch were maybe thirty moldering newspapers, and a big plastic lawn bag full of empty liquor and beer bottles.

"Jesus, Ethan. Don't you ever pick up the paper?"

"Up here," he said, to move me out of my surprise when we stepped inside. He gently touched the underside of my arm and steered me through a room so starkly empty it looked as if no one lived there, with a futon in one corner and nothing else but bare floors, bare walls, faded paint and holes where pictures once had been. "This way," he said. He took my hand—which startled me; his hand was cool and enclosing—and led me up the stairs.

"My study," he said, showing me into a small room that was little more than an expanded dormer window. There were teetering piles of books, papers, binders, and code listings jammed into the tiny space, which was overly warm from the PC that had been left running, damp from the rain, and dark, lit only by the glow of the monitor. On the floor was a plate of old, dried spaghetti. Next to the monitor was a big 1.75-liter bottle of bourbon—bad stuff, cheap brand, half empty.

"Is this what you expected?" he asked, making one sweep with his arm to indicate the room, the mess, the machine, the bottle.

There was something touching in this gesture and this question, as if he were hoping that I'd been thinking of him, that I had spent time imagining his life.

Of course I hadn't.

"Well, Ethan. I never took you for a drinking man."

He laughed and picked up the bottle, tipping it toward me as an offering.

The last thing I needed was more alcohol, bourbon at that, and cheap stuff. "Sure," I said.

He smiled—shyly, which I found strange, as I had never before thought of Ethan Levin as a shy man—then went down to the kitchen to get us glasses. While he crashed around down there (I could hear him cursing and clanging dishes in the sink), I sat on the lone chair in his tiny office in an odd state of suspension. I didn't want to consider what I was doing there.

"I'm out of soda," he said, coming back with two glasses with ice. "Over ice okay?"

"Sure. Fine."

We clinked glasses without looking at each other.

"My father taught me to drink," he said, sitting down on a little stool he cleared of papers, then holding the glass between his legs.

"I barely knew my father," I said. "I'm afraid I have no one to blame but myself."

We met eyes briefly. We drank.

"Yow, Ethan! This is really bad stuff."

He laughed. "I think I drink it to get back at my father."

I didn't ask him to clarify that statement—I don't like to talk about fathers. Mine had been emotionally distant and absent until I was about twelve, at which time he became physically distant and absent, divorcing my mother and moving to North Carolina, a place I have never visited. But Ethan was determined that I should hear about Lou Levin, manly housepainter turned unhappy shopkeeper. I drank while he spoke, letting the bourbon buzz come on, pretending to be listening.

"Scotch is class," Ethan was saying the next time I paid attention. "That's what he'd say."

"Well, let's have another of this crappy stuff and really get back at him, shall we?"

"Need more ice?"

"No. I'm fine."

Looking back, I see it was another one of those junctures that might have changed things. If only he hadn't spoken about his father. Almost any other personal information might have drawn me out, created sympathy between us, put us in a different state by the time we looked at the simulation. But we can't help being what we are. My voice came out much colder than I meant it to be.

"I thought you invited me here to see that simulation."

He held his glass in the air for a moment, looking at me fixedly. "Right," he said on an exhale. Then in a single motion, he put down the glass and pulled his stool up to the keyboard, where he entered the commands to dial up the Telligentsia server. We didn't look at each other, or say anything, while the modems on each end screeched out their negotiations.

"Here it is," he said finally, after logging in and entering a command. "Here you are. My simulated world."

I looked at the screen in amazement.

"Ticktacktoe!" I shouted. "Why, it's just like a game of ticktacktoe gone berserk!"

Another error in that night full of errors. Well, of course the simulation did look like a big, crazy game of ticktacktoe, but it was, after all, his lifetime project, and I didn't have to say so right off like that. In response, he seemed to revert to the Ethan Levin who had ignored and belittled me for all those months. "It's merely a side-effect of the visualization tool," he said in a stiff tone. "You can't see what it is because you can't imagine the algorithm that went into creating this display. It's the lack of your technical background. If you would reserve judgment until you received an overview, I'm sure—"

"I'm sorry. Really. I didn't mean to make light—"

"Yes, you did mean it. You're always like this. You're always haughty around the software, like you're some genius and all the programmers are beneath you."

I took in a breath. I had no idea he'd noticed anything about me. Of course, what he said was true, or had been true for most of the time he knew me.

"Now do you want me to describe this thing to you or not?" he went on. "Because you could just go home now for all I care."

I should have gone right then. I should have seen at that moment that the night was ruined, any chance for communication between us doomed. Rather than leave him in the state I did later, it would have been better to leave him as he was now: full of anger and pride and determination to show me up, which are at least the sort of emotions designed to defend yourself.

"Please. I'm sorry. Please show it to me."

And so, errors compounding, I stayed.

At first, his description of the simulation was reasoned, quiet. He told me about the creatures, their interactions with the habitats, how the populations rose and fell in response to the food stores, and how the food stores in turn responded to the presence or absence of creatures. He discussed his plans for migration, so that the creatures could search for food stores on other "island" habitats. Next he turned to the philosophy behind the simulation, the idea that all complex systems were actually nothing more than a collection of simple, "mindless" interactions, complexity not being something built into a system from "on high" by some designer, but something that emerges from "below," as a result of some unexpected interplay among all the underlying simple interactions. A complicated world without a god to oversee it, he called it (or, the idea of God itself was something that emerged from the underlying interactions—I really don't recall which way he put it). All of this took some ten or fifteen minutes, during which time I started to have hope for the night's outcome. I was impressed with what he was attempting, if not for the current results. And he showed philosophical depths I had not suspected were in him.

But as he began describing the elements he would add over time to his world—genders, species, variation in habitats, weather, predators, parasites, viruses, fires, floods, earthquakes, all manner of biblical-scale disasters—a terrible manic energy began to take him over. He started swiping at his hair. His voice rose in pitch and volume, and his legs, splayed out from the sides of the stool, began shaking up and down. It was as if the ideas themselves were banging around furiously in his body, wanting to get out. I had no idea exactly what was causing this reaction, whether it was the drinking or the lateness of the hour or something truly strange in Ethan suddenly showing itself (or the ideas actually battling it out inside him), so there was no recourse for me but to sit quietly and hope that he would soon come to a conclusion. Perhaps another fifteen minutes passed this way, when abruptly he broke off, sat up stiffly on his stool, and whispered loudly:

"It *is* them!"

This alarmed me more than anything that had gone before. "What is who, Ethan?"

"It *has* been going on. All this time. I thought so. Don't you *hear* it?"

"Hear what?"

"It's them. *Listen!*"

Rain drummed on the dormer roof, the sound of a tent in a rainstorm. That's all I heard: rain, on roof, and, under that, a nagging machine-fan whir.

"I don't hear anything," I said.

"It's their music. Goddamn them. Fucking goddamn . . . Fucking stinking shitty rock . . ."

"I don't hear it."

"My neighbors! Their fucking music. They mean to get back at me. They're trying to . . . It's been . . . Oh, never mind. Forget it. Forget I said anything. Nothing. Anyway. Let's talk about the simulation. Get back to it. Yes. Let's do it. Okay?"

I did not see how I could redirect him to some safer topic, so I nodded and sat there as Ethan, still agitated, returned to his philosophical speculations. This time he declaimed his ideas in a sweeping, grandiose fashion, declaring life itself to be an instance of a complex system, his theory therefore explaining how life on earth came into existence. "Don't you *see* it? Don't you *see* it?" he insisted. "How else could it come about? Life from dead matter—how could this possibly happen? Unless you believe in God in the sky, it has to come from matter itself, from its organization, from the zillions of tiny processes. At bottom it's all molecules, chemicals, matter. Billions of tiny processes, each one as dumb as a single electron going this way or that way through a logic gate. As dumb—dumber!—than one of my creatures. Everything we are emerges out of that dumb soup. Everything!"

By then he was raving. I'd already spent hours inside his mind—an odd mind, full of tight kinks like his hair. But I was not prepared for this rush of what seemed to be intellectual hysteria. I had no way of knowing that, less than two decades later, a famous computer scientist would be trying to warn the world about the dangers of self-replicating artificial creatures, descendants of Ethan Levin's silly milling O's. No idea I would attend a seminar at which perfectly sane-seeming men would debate not if but only when artificial life-forms, complete in their "humanity," would surpass our poor carbon-based existence, the coming of the "posthuman." What Ethan could only imagine in a fever that night—the notion of human beings as nothing more than a collection of chemical and electrical processes that could be scanned, stored, and replicated in silicon—has already come to be seen as reasonable. And his ideas about complexity arising from simple interactions—now proposed as the basis of an entirely new science. But at the time, I simply thought that Ethan Levin had gone a little crazy—in that hyperlogical way men can get crazy, when they isolate an idea and keep traveling deeper and deeper into it, until they arrive at a place so narrow their little idea seems huge, all-encompassing, an explanation for the world.

"Imagine a colony of a zillion evolved paramecia," he was going on madly. "That's us! It all comes from there. Our intelligence, our consciousness. Everything we think makes us unique, it comes from there!"

Then at once he paused, sat down, and added, "Somehow."

"Somehow," I echoed, hoping he would be quiet now.

Fan whine, heat, Ethan's mania, the late night, alcoholic exhaustion, my own life, which was not exactly going so well at the time—they all combined for a moment to make me lose my bearings. I felt dizzy, the way I had in the afternoon when the tequila wore off;

〓　〓　〓

suddenly despairing, as if I'd always be locked up in closed rooms where machines forever hummed to themselves in the dark. At that moment, I really could think of myself as nothing more than a bag of electrons, a colony of paramecia, a collection of dead, meaningless molecules somehow animated in an accident of combinatorial explosion. The "I" in my precious self protested against the idea. Let's see a computer write poetry! it wanted to shout. But I knew Ethan would say something like, Not now, not yet, but it will, eventually. And I didn't want to think how that might be true. So I sat in the dark for a while and watched the screen—milling O's amid a field of X's, reproducing where there was food, dying on the dark blank spots where there was none. Blink, blink: creatures disappearing from the world.

I asked him: "Does it bother you when they die off like that?"

"Don't be silly. They're just C-code structures . . . Well, they should've been done in Lisp . . . a language that . . . I should have . . . Hell! Anyway, no. It doesn't bother me. All organisms die."

"But you're their creator. Aren't you responsible for them?"

"I've given them a meaningful death!" he protested. "Their death lets the habitat survive. Watch what happens."

He pointed at the screen, to a big dark area, a dead spot in Ethan Levin's world. Slowly, as we watched, new X's appeared, the habitat regrowing, renewing itself.

"Yeah," I said. Then I asked: "Do the living O-creatures ever remember the ones that died?"

He squinted at me and said nothing.

"And the ones who are starving, do they *know* they're going to die?"

He snorted. "Stupid."

But I persisted. "If you're going to simulate life—I mean, intelligent life—sooner or later you'll have to account for the fact that the way we live has something to do with the fact that we *know* we're going to die."

I watched his eyes career around in their sockets as if he were scanning through his program, trying to imagine what sort of C-code structures could contain memories of the dead and foreknowledge of death. Then abruptly he ran his hands through his hair and broke it off.

"Hell! Joanna used to ask me stupid questions like that." Then he stared at the screen, where another cycle of milling creatures was beginning. "Joanna. My girlfriend. *Ex*-girlfriend. Anyway, when I first showed it to her and explained what I was doing, she said something sarcastic like, 'Oh yeah. The key to all mythologies.'"

"*Middlemarch*," I said.

"What?"

"*Middlemarch*. George Eliot. Great Victorian novel."

Of course I didn't have to explain. To this day, I wonder why I felt the need to tell this poor, unhappy man just how slyly, and with what educated hauteur, his now ex-girlfriend had disparaged him. I can try to excuse myself by saying I was quite drunk by that time, having swilled with great determination while Ethan described his digital world. But surely there are other explanations. Maybe I was mad at him. Maybe I wanted a mindless evening to forget my troubles for a while, and I didn't get it. Maybe I can never let go of my need to prove how smart I am, even if it means I wreck myself and the people around me. At any rate, for these and surely many other reasons I will never understand, I took it upon myself to tell him the story of *Middlemarch*. I told him about Dorothea Brooke, who marries the Reverend Edward Casaubon, believing he is a brilliant scholar working on a book that will address the great questions of existence. How she idolizes him, looks to him to bring her into the world of fine, grand ideas. Until she learns, too late, that Casaubon is nothing but a dead, dried-up husk of a person.

"And it turns out there's no book," I concluded. "It was all a sham. He was never writing a grand opus. Which was supposed to have the ridiculous title *The Key to All Mythologies*."

His face took on a panicked look. He broke into a heavy sweat, which I could smell in an unpleasant wave that came at me from across the room. I knew then I'd made the error of errors on that error-filled night.

"I'm sure she didn't mean—"

"The key to all mythologies," he repeated nervously. "Yeah, right." He turned back to look at the screen, and fell silent.

"Oh shit, I'm sorry," I said.

"No need to be sorry."

He turned to the monitor and started slapping at the keyboard. The simulation disappeared; in its place came code file after file, until the screen was covered with programming statements. His fingers hit the keys hard: page up, page down, enter, enter, violently.

"Something wrong with the program?"

"No," he said, with that attacking bark-laugh of his. "I'm looking for a good place. Maybe here, in this routine where they begin to starve."

"A good place for what?"

He laughed again, unpleasantly. "For the creatures to learn they're going to die."

Then he said nothing more.

I sat watching him for some minutes while he coded in that dark, angry mood. When I understood he wasn't going to speak to me again, I rose from the chair, thanked him for the drinks, and said good night.

"I'm sorry," I said again on my way out.

"For what?" he said, not turning from his code.

As there was too much to explain, even to myself, I only looked at him for a moment more, hunched over the keyboard as he was, slapping at the keys, his legs splayed and shaking, then let myself out.

As the door clicked shut behind me, I heard something sounding in the street. It was low and rhythmic, a soft, barely audible throbbing. It might have been a motor running in a far-off street. Or maybe the beat of music. Maybe it did come from his neighbor's house. Maybe it had been there all along.

JOANNA'S BETRAYAL

Joanna's fault: The bug was Joanna's fault.

Of course that was it. If the problem wasn't the hardware or a memory leak or Thorne's buggy code or Dana Merankin's or the trash code left behind by Herring, then it had to be something he hadn't considered yet; and the day after he showed Berta Walton the simulation, when the plum blossoms had started falling on Estudillo Avenue and the days-open count of UI-1017 had climbed to 340, when the Jester had risen to the top of Wallis Markham's bug list of infamy—on that day he sat down in his study, dialed in to the office server, and started up the debugger.

When he had a sudden memory of Joanna walking out the front door.

Ostrick waiting for her in the car.

Their driving off.

And all at once he was sure he'd found it. Sitting in his study with his hands still on the keyboard, the debugger's cursor blinking steadily at him, Ethan became certain that he had at last come upon the ultimate source of the illogic that was plaguing him, the hole in the good order of things through which this nemesis had entered his life:

Joanna's betrayal. All that turmoil when he was designing and coding the system—right then came this distraction. He'd missed something because of it, some small misconception had crept into his thinking, and that little lapse became a chronic flaw that he himself had built into the intimate workings of the system. Now this mental error was percolating up from the bottom of the code, and it all was because of Joanna.

It started with that touch. Specifically and exactly, his lost bit of information—and therefore his bug and all his troubles—must have come at the moment of that touch. The way Ostrick put his fingertips on Joanna's upper arm, bare in that orange sleeveless blouse, rounded—they must have eaten well together on their travels, Ethan thought, Joanna's normally sturdy arm turned soft and tender in a way he had never seen it. At that very moment, everything must have flown out of his head. Weeks of immersion, a feast of technical gorging— manuals read, specifications learned, whiteboards and notebooks filled with the scrawl of ideas just emerging out of chaos—lost, scrambled, gone.

He had a moment of vengeful triumph: *her* fault! Ethan Levin would still be known as a decent, productive, if less than brilliant programmer if not for the mess Joanna McCarthy had made in his life. But this assignment of blame, lip-smackingly satisfying, was not very useful. For immediately Ethan realized that he still didn't know *which* bit of information was lost, what idea scrambled, the exact specification gone.

And so it came to him that he would have to do what he absolutely had been preventing himself from doing: remember everything. Sitting at his desk in the darkened study, Ethan had this idea that if he recalled it all—in a slow, detailed, unemotional way—he might also be able to trace the line of his thinking: what exactly he'd been studying, designing, coding. He decided there would be no drinking tonight, no outing with his new friend the Crow, who sat there keeping one black eye on him (Ethan understood now why they called them "spirits," for the way they hovered around you companionably, presences in the blurry air). No, he would keep his head clear. He would make himself remember, accurately, factually. Like a complete system backup tape, his mind would slowly roll through the total experience until he found the corrupted file, the lost pointer, the wrongly set bit. And then he would restore it.

All right, then. The beginning. The plan to go to India. Disrupted by the layoffs at Insuracorp, Ethan getting in late after a dentist's appointment to find his colleagues walking toward him with their office belongings in cardboard boxes. Then the calls to headhunters, the two interviews at Telligentsia, Harry Minor sitting cross-legged like a Buddha, encouraging him to take the job.

I can't go, Ethan told Joanna. I can't go to India.

Where was Joanna during those weeks between the layoffs and his taking the job at Telligentsia? This question posed itself to him—it formed in his mind, and once there he fumbled for an answer. Was it relevant? Probably not. But then he recalled that he had committed himself to a detailed review, so he should try to fill in all blank spaces whether or not they seemed immediately useful. All right: Where was Joanna? They must have stopped planning the trip, he thought. Surely she understood that this was not a time he could take off. Surely they looked at their calendars for a later block of time, put away the yellow pad with the itinerary, stowed the India books back on the shelves. But when he looked carefully at the events, he could not recall their talking about it. Not at all. It seemed to him that from the day he saw his colleagues with their cardboard boxes to the moment he said he could not go, Joanna had simply been snipped out of his awareness.

He stood up from the desk. The debugger was still waiting for him to enter a command. He looked at the screen, sat down, stood up, sat down again.

When he'd told her he couldn't go, what had he expected her

reaction would be? None, he realized. He'd had no expectations, no idea how she'd feel about the canceled trip. She'd simply disappeared from his attentions and then reentered his memory there, at that moment when he said: I can't go. I can't go to India.

You mean you can't go *now*, she answered.

No. Not for a long time.

Then when?

I'm not sure when. Maybe a year. I'm a critical module!

I'll say you are.

I'm on the critical path!

They were in the kitchen on a Saturday morning putting away groceries, a scene that came back to him with cinematic clarity. Joanna was on the top of a step stool, a blue-and-yellow box of pastina in one hand, her other hand on the cupboard shelf where the pastina was to go. Slowly she lowered the box of pastina to her side and came down off the stool, step by step. Then she took something else out of the grocery bag—it was celery, in a plastic bag, as Ethan could see it now—and she put it down on the counter.

Okay, she said, only half turning toward him. You go be on the critical path and I'll go to India. I don't want to have a fight about it. I'm going.

Said flatly; no argument in it; no sense of bargaining.

Then she climbed the stool again and continued putting away the groceries.

Ethan stood there watching her, her thighs outlined by the bright blue of her running shorts, which she still had on from her early-morning run. A long thread had come loose from the hem of the shorts and now hung between her legs, playing over her hamstrings and quadriceps as she moved. At one time, he would have gone over and given those solid, muscular thighs a fond grab; but this time, no, it seemed impossible that he would even consider it.

I need to go into work today, he said. I have a presentation on Monday to the group. We'll talk some more about this later.

She kept putting away the groceries—crackers on the middle shelf, cinnamon on the bottom one.

Uh-huh, she said.

And he went to work.

The neighbors' stereo was going—when had that started up again? The floorboards under his feet were vibrating, absorbing the bass beat that went on and on, two notes, back and forth, *doom DOOM*. Ethan felt his anger rise, his feeling of helplessness against the noise, his desire to drink to make it go away. Go downstairs, he told himself, don't give in, get something to eat. In the kitchen, he crashed around looking for the pasta pot. He found some lids, smashed one against the floor, found the pot, filled it, stood drumming on the counter while he waited for the water to boil. *Doom DOOM,* came from next door. *Doom DOOM.*

He didn't want to think about what happened next. But the next part was inevitable, since he had indeed gone off to the office that day, never raised the question of the trip again, become absorbed into his "pioneering work," and had left Joanna to her own devices. Again came a part of the story where she disappeared from his awareness. And again he searched his memory for some interchange with Joanna, some talk or understanding they'd arrived at; but again there was nothing. The next thing he knew, Joanna was telling him she hadn't forgotten about the trip, she was going with Paul Ostrick, and the dinner at the Ostricks' house, everyone saying of *course* they should go. Send us postcards! Marsha sang.

Postcards.

Then it's the day they left, the day UI-1017 was just discovered, plum blossoms falling, like today, petals drifting through the air. He's home after dropping them at the airport, standing at the stove in the heat waiting for the pasta water to boil. Suddenly he knows something was wrong, something in the expression on Joanna's face as she left him, and what comes to him, despite the heat and the steaming water, is that shiver of fear.

He was reading manuals that night: What exactly was he studying at the dining room table right after that fear passed through him? Ethan scanned the memory, back and forth—what was the point of going through all this if he couldn't pinpoint the knowledge he was taking in at the moment? But he had been reading everything at once, and so nothing in particular came to him. All he could remember was the fear, irrational but very strong—worse to look back on than to feel at the time, since now he knew it was not at all irrational; since he knew exactly what there was to be afraid of.

He pushed away his plate. By now the water for this night's dinner had boiled, the pasta had cooked, been drained, and Ethan was sitting behind a plate of pasta with sauce from a jar, but his appetite was gone. He wanted to give up on this remembering thing. It was useless, disorienting. What he wanted was to find that clarity again, the astringent pleasure of the time after Joanna had left, when he was alone with his books and manuals, and he didn't think about her at all.

Because that's what happened while she was away: he forgot her. He was working on the most interesting project of his life, doing *significant* work, *nontrivial* work. A programmer can write code for years and never be involved in a project of lasting value. Ethan's work before going to Telligentsia was a compendium of disappointments: projects canceled when a vice president was fired, when a hardware manufacturer changed its pricing structure, when a company was bought by a bigger one. Telligentsia was his chance to build something that might be used for years—decades! Who could blame him for sequestering himself with books and manuals?

Interrupted only once. The day of the postcard. The yellow postcard with the fucking god. "I hope you're also enjoying your time away from me," she wrote.

Also.

Ethan pushed back his chair, carried the cold, uneaten food to the sink, then stood still at the counter, holding on to it with both hands. *Doom DOOM!* He should be figuring out what he was studying then, the exact manual, the precise part of the design. When he found the postcard folded in the circular for televisions, was he reading *Principals of User Interface Design* or *The Psychology of Human-Computer Interaction*? But now his memory is rushing forward the way a river gets into a deadly hurry on its way to rough water. For what comes next is Joanna and Ostrick coming home, Ethan leaving work to pick them up at the airport, the blouse, the orange blouse, that touch—like rocks at the bottom of a cascade, the whole treacherous end of the Joanna-Ostrick story is fast coming toward him.

Now I'll certainly have clear memories of Joanna, Ethan thought. He was still holding on to the kitchen counter with both hands, while he told himself that he must have been concerned for their relationship, taken care of it, attended to it. Now that he knew about the affair, the trip-enforced attraction, surely he worked hard to keep her, let her know she was loved, needed. But another impenetrable blank came up where Joanna should have been. He recalled meetings with Harry Minor, arguments at the whiteboard with Herring, the contraction of the schedule, the system coming together piece by piece—weeks of disappearance into the depths of his work, and not a single important moment with Joanna.

Something awful was on the verge of occurring to him. It presented itself as a problem of proportions, an imbalance, the way his memories of work were full and precise and his thoughts about Joanna so sparse. His intended story had a theme—Joanna's betrayal—but some other version was about to force itself on him, and so he made himself scan his memory banks, back and forth, looking for her, as ballast for his story.

What he found was only that night when Carolyn and the baby

came over, the night he'd worked late and missed dinner and came home to an empty house, empty pans on the stove. Yes, here was another possible lost thread: his study rearranged because of that baby. Of course, something lost—what paper, which pile, what book, which file? But again, his memory won't let him take detours, won't permit him to stop and scan hidden corners. For the experience has a certain momentum, and before he can think of documents and files, he remembers the argument with Joanna over Marsha's call. Joanna leaving the house with Carolyn and the baby. Then her getting home late, stepping out of the car that is not Carolyn's. A car he will see again, Joanna getting into it still buttoning up her birthday blouse, ducking her head under the pouring rain, the day she goes off with Ostrick.

How long had they been at it, Ethan wondered? He was by now lying on his mattress on the floor, one arm flung over his eyes, the neighbor's stereo crashing, and for the first time he tried to imagine the whole course of their affair. While he was at work worrying over click-and-drag: Were they necking on his sofa? When he stayed late to program the function-key settings: Were they fucking in his bed? And how far back did it go: The trip to India? Before then? A week, a month, the entire time Ethan was at Telligentsia—would he have to revise his idea of his life, and for how long? Immediately he saw that the problem of betrayal wasn't just that it took away the idea of a pleasant future; it also robbed you of the past. Every moment became suspect. That night they didn't say a word over Chinese food: Was it going on by then? The trip to visit his sister: Then? Or had it started even earlier, the first time he showed her the simulation, when she called it "the key to all mythologies"—did it go all the way back to there, so close to the beginning when he thought he was happy? Worse than losing Joanna was losing the sense of his own life, what had happened, what to feel about it. For his time with Joanna was now a disheveled memory, where nothing could stay as it was.

Then, rushing toward him out of his unraveled past, came the most unwelcome memory of all: Joanna holding Carolyn's baby. It came with an almost unbearable clarity. The snot dripping from the baby's nostrils, its gummy foot kicking, the googling mouth like a red, open wound. And then came the image he'd like nothing better than to forget: the expression on Joanna's face as she looked down at the struggling wet bundle in her arms.

For immediately, riding a connection named "baby," his mind traversed to another memory, and no matter how hard he tried, Ethan could not sever this connection, could not prevent his brain from finding the next node along this vector, his memory hurtling toward something that refused to stay in the dark mental backwater where he had so conveniently lodged it. Still lying on his bed, arm over eyes, he would have to see it all over again, that night a year before Joanna sat in the kitchen holding Carolyn's baby. That night when Joanna came into the bedroom, turned off the light, turned it on again, and said quietly:

I'm pregnant.

He is lying in bed, nearly asleep, and the word pulls him back from the edge of a dream like a punch in the shoulder. Pregnant. He thinks he must have misheard her. The great normalizing instrument of his brain works furiously to annul the syllables he has just heard. He's on his side, back to her, one ear into the pillow, so of course it might be the foam muffling things.

How's that?

Pregnant. I'm pregnant.

Now there's no refuting it: he has heard correctly. His body responds for him, sits him up in a reflex.

How can that be? You always use . . . I mean, didn't you?

The diaphragm, sure. But they're not foolproof. We talked about it.

Right. Talked about it.

Eighty percent effective.

Eighty percent, he echoes.

The talk of percentages calms him, as if there's still something they can do to shore up that missing twenty percent, thicken the latex, apply more spermicide, go at it less emphatically.

How long? he asks.

Long?

Have you been pregnant.

Six weeks, the doctor figures. You know how regular I am. When I was late even a week, I checked.

Six weeks. Ethan thinks back: no, he can't recall any night in particular, any special time six weeks ago that might have resulted in their making a baby. But again the sense of measurement is comforting, a balm on the panic that's threatening to shoot up in him. He recalls the stages of embryo development, the cells dividing, infolding, morula, blastula, gastrula. Six weeks. He pictures it sucking on the uterine wall: a tiny tadpole.

Limb buds, he says. Lens pit, optic cup.

Optic cup?

Early embryo features. No problem getting an abortion at this stage.

Joanna shifts in the bed. Now she's sitting up, both of them leaning back against the wall, side by side, looking forward like they're in a car and everything is happening on the other side of the windshield, out there.

We also talked about this, she says.

About what?

Abortion.

The word hangs there as Ethan tries to remember what they might have said about abortion. Joanna is a feminist, he thinks. Of course she's in favor of abortion. She'll have one; that'll be that; maybe she'll take the Pill now.

I told you. I told you years ago, Joanna says. Remember? I said I'd die in the street for everyone else's right to have an abortion, but I don't think I could ever have one.

He tries to remember when she said this and comes up with a blank.

When I told you about being adopted, Joanna says.

Oh, right, right, he says, though he still can't remember a thing about it.

I told you that I had this sense that if my mother could have had an abortion, I wouldn't exist.

Right, right, he keeps saying, pretending he has heard all this before, but if he did, nothing of its meaning stuck at the time. It's only right then that he gets it.

So you won't . . .

No. I won't.

She's waiting for him to say it's okay, to embrace her, say he loves her, they'll work it out. He can feel her desire like a rope tugging on him. It would make her so happy. But he can't make her happy. All he can think is that, on paper, he should be ready for this. He's thirty-four. He has a good-paying job, a reliable car. He lives with a woman who loves him. From the outside, everything is in place, ready, set, go, let's have a baby. But he can't breathe. He sees himself working at Insuracorp for the next twenty years, or someplace like it. All the while his vague hope for something else, his lost other life, drifting out of reach.

Joanna lets out a breath. Okay, Ethan. I get it.

She lies down, turns off the light.

Get what?

She turns over, away.

Never mind, she says. You don't have to say anything. We'll talk tomorrow.

But tomorrow they do not talk about it. He gets up early for a meeting and stays late to prepare tapes for a software release. And the next night when she comes home, he is in the study. And the next night? and the next?

Ethan, the Ethan lying on his bed remembering, came upright with a start. The neighbor's music boomed. Or was it his heart? For the next image in this inexorable memory set is coming, and there is nothing he can do about it.

Ethan home late. The house dark. Joanna? he calls.

Not here, he thinks. Then a small voice. Up here.

He goes up, finds her on the bed curled up, crying. She doesn't have to say it. From the position of her body, he knows.

You did it, didn't you? he says. You did it without asking me.

He's made a mistake, he sees. She's suddenly standing up, face clenched like a twisted wet washcloth.

I need your permission? Fuck you. Fuck you! You didn't want a kid. Are you happy now? I got rid of it, rid of it!

She keeps screaming at him, and Ethan feels himself unfocus while her anger builds and finally subsides. It's all he can think to do: stand there and let her finish. In the end, she falls back on the bed, crying, curled up like when he found her. He puts out his hand to touch her hair, her fuzzy short hair now wet with tears, but she draws away, curls up more tightly, sobs quietly. He can't think what to do except step around her, go wash in the bathroom, go to bed, turn off the light.

Then they both lie in bed breathing in the dark.

Joanna says something he can't hear.

What?

She repeats it.

I feel like I killed myself, she says.

He jumped up from the bed, wandered up and down the hall. Why wouldn't that music stop? He thought he'd go crazy if they kept at him night after night with that booming and thumping. Up and down he walked in the empty hall, trying to obliterate from his mind a thought now so clear and irrefutable it scared him to think how he hadn't seen it before: He'd abandoned her long ago. She'd hated him for years.

He couldn't breathe, felt his throat tighten with the pain he knew was the start of a crying jag—fuck, no, he wasn't going to cry. He wasn't going to spend another night in his stupid headband while he sobbed on his bed like a girl. No, he was going to drink. He was going to drink until he staggered around, crashed into walls, was deaf and blind. Yes, go into the study, find the big bottle, that big bottle of bourbon with the crow on it, drink and drink until he could remember nothing.

He went in, sat down, looked at the screen. The debugger was still running, the cursor steadily blinking. Waiting for him: suspended in the exact place he'd left it, unchanged. Here he could never disappoint; here he'd never have to feel worthless, unable to love; here there was no one and nothing to let down. All he had to do was enter a command, and everything would resume. Between one keystroke and the next, it would be as if nothing had happened—not the memories of Joanna, not his desire to blame her for everything gone wrong in his life, not the understanding that a person does not wait around, suspended, until you're ready to have her in your life.

The characters stared back at him from the screen, the cursor continued to blink. Here was the bitter bourbon. Here came the crashing music. Now he knew why he lived alone in an empty house next to people who wanted to kill him. There was no point in remembering anymore, no reason to keep his head clear. He wanted that cloud to come over him, his spirit-pal to come and blur this too-bright blinking cursor, this debugger, tireless, still waiting for him. And on the other side of the debugger, coming and going in its own good time, hiding itself away then reappearing at intervals that had nothing whatsoever to do with Ethan Levin, his desires, or his life, as oblivious to him as he'd been to Joanna—the bug.

THE MIRACLE IN THE MECHANISM

"Where were you, my pretty?" said Dana Merankin as Ethan got into work.

"What? Why?"

"Oh, you are screwed now, our little movie star." She got up and went to the door. "He's here," she called down the hall.

"What? Why?" Ethan said again.

"A bug," she said.

"*The* bug?"

"No, not that bug. Another one."

Bradley Thorne marched in. Behind him came Larry Seidel and Bill Werners. "What the hell did you think you were doing?" said Thorne.

"What's this about?"

"You screwed up! Totally!"

"What? *What!*"

"We couldn't link all day!" said Bill.

"It's fucking three o'clock in the afternoon, and no one could run shit!" said Larry.

"That 'one tiny change' you made yesterday," said Dana. "You know, the one you said would take a second to fix? Well, you fixed it good, Curly-haired-boy. The front end crashes immediately. Seg fault. Core dumped."

Ethan grabbed the back of his chair as a wave of heat and sweat came over him. He'd woken up still drunk, the room shifting when he moved his head, and he stayed in bed all morning trying not to move his eyelids, which hurt when he blinked. Now the headache had passed but not the nausea, or the rumblings in his gut, or these little swoons when he felt he might pass out.

"You mean the change to the terminal manager?" he said. He looked at Dana Merankin. "The one you asked for?"

"Well, I didn't ask you to leave us dead in the water, Curly-boy. The admin was out, and you left the library unwritable for us."

"Did I? I don't remember."

"Did you even test it?" asked Larry.

"No, he couldn't've," said Bill. "If he tried it even once, he'd've known it didn't work."

"I'm sorry," Ethan said. He wiped the sweat from his upper lip. Sweat was running down his back, but he didn't dare move to catch it. He thought he might faint if he turned his head.

Sorry. He'd spent the whole night feeling what a sorry mess he was. Drink after drink couldn't dull the sense of his own deep uselessness. A man who'd abandoned the only person who cared about him—for what? A job he was bad at. Bad: he was a bad programmer. He'd sacrificed everything to come here, where no one had any regard for him. And why should they? He stank at it.

They were right: he should have tested it. He'd been too sure of himself, a little trivial change, but he should know by now he couldn't trust himself. The Jester—he deserved it. What a mistake to come here! Why did he let Harry talk him into it? He should have stayed where he was. A corporate coder. Insurance. He was good at that, good enough. Kept his schedules. Wrote serviceable code. Users liked him because he got things done. He had time to come home like a normal human being, go running after work with Joanna in spring and summer, eat dinner together, spend weekends shopping, doing chores, hiking—no, wait, no. How long ago was all that? Before the trip to Seattle? Before the time in the Chinese restaurant, before the party they left early, before the key to all mythologies? Maybe there never was a "before." His good life with Joanna—maybe that was a lie, too.

"I'll fix it right now," he said.

Still his colleagues lingered for a moment, holding on to their resentment for just a second more. Ethan looked into their faces and was surprised to see they weren't really angry, not in the traditional sense of it. He'd changed code, didn't test it, it didn't work: wrong, bad, stop—as definitive as a compiler. But of course they were this way, he thought. This is what makes them good engineers. Perfectionism: incinerating perfectionism. Without it, everything would fly apart. All the complicated parts and pieces, all the code written here and there by so many people over years and years, layer upon layer deposited over time in all the components in all the computers of the world, so much of it and so much to go wrong—without the cauterizing vigilance of good engineers, down it would come.

I'm not like them, he thought. I don't belong here.

He suddenly saw his colleagues—saw them as Ute could see, he realized; it wasn't so very hard, you only had to be there yourself and look closely, why didn't he know this before? You could glimpse the secret hearts of people if you paid attention: how stupid to get to be his age and just now learn it. And it was startlingly clear: how much they disliked him. How they resented him for being standoffish. The lunches with Steghman, his always being on schedule, all the work to protect himself from scrutiny and humiliation—it had only succeeded in creating this resentment, this desire to bring him down over bugs. He almost laughed. His fear creating their resentment creating his fear—what a sorry mess life was, round and round without reason, and no way out.

"You'll have the fix in ten minutes," he said.

And there they let it go. Dana Merankin sat down at her desk. Bradley Thorne, Larry Seidel, and Bill Werners left the room to go back to theirs.

And Ethan settled down at his. Everyone to his own code. Everyone to the endless battle against entropy, the thankless task of resisting the system's tendency toward chaos. Code, code, code, code. Make it happen just as I say. A dreadful burden. A horror. Think of everything that can go wrong. Trap for errors. Mistakes: absolutely don't let them happen.

As Ethan logged on, he thought about Carolyn and the baby, who he'd seen out on their lawn when he'd left the house for work. The baby was a big-headed little girl now. (How could that be? Was it that long since the night he saw her in Joanna's arms?) Somehow she'd turned into the toddling creature he saw trying to make her way across Carolyn's big, weedy lawn. She reached for a branch and missed it, reached down for a dandelion and tumbled forward. She didn't so much walk as throw herself forward, teetering at the edge of balance, until she tipped, fell, stood, and repeated the whole process for the next step. Still she came across the lawn, failure by failure, miss by miss, fall by fall. Ethan had sat there with his car door open, fascinated by this mess of motion, this bare approximation of what walking should be—all wrong, lurching from disaster to disaster, but still she walked, still she came forward. He'd wanted to stay there, watch, think about what it meant that we're born helpless, born to grow up and bring only more helpless creatures into the world, but his key was in the ignition, and the car, watching out for him and his open door, buzzed madly.

Now he turned to his text editor, to his compiler, assembler, linker, debugger—his digital friends so precise and error-hating. What a poor imitation of a human a computer is, he thought, as he remembered Precious Flower throwing herself across a sunny, weedy lawn in early spring. How did it happen? he thought, sweating, dizzy, sickened. How did it happen that we grew up into *this*?

———

Here you are.

Ethan.

Here.

Driving home, he knew what he had to do: take care of the hungry ones. His O-creatures still stranded on their dying islands, not yet migrating despite all his efforts, the cycle of eating, reproducing, and starving again going round and round without cease, and no way out. The deepening rut of life he had created without meaning to: he had to get them out.

```
/* think about who you're following befor you go */
```

In the dark dormer of the study, he searched for himself as always, in the comment in the code. His last channel of thought: he had to swim back to it. Leaving Thorne and bugs and babies tottering on the lawn, he opened one code file after another, looking for clues as to how this thought had come to him, the functions he'd been working on, the problems they'd presented. He took a drink, then another. He searched for half an hour more, then drank again. The alcohol, which should have made him woozy, somehow narrowed his focus, shuttered the bright aureole of the monitor in a field of darkness. At the center, seeming to be all there was in the world, was only code; code and more code; twelve long years of code.

Here. Here. No, here. Where was he? Where was the Ethan who had left the message?

Not there, or there. He thought of Harry Minor, his advice to see things as if you'd never seen them before, and how hard that was, impossible, except for sometimes, when your eyes suddenly shucked off their blinders, maybe because you didn't really care anymore what happened to you. Harry. Gone. He never really expected to hear from Harry again.

File after file; drink after drink. The monitor now floating in its dark velvet sea. The code now drifting before him, foreign, funny, bizarre, just like Harry said it would be, a set of messages dropped to earth by spacemen.

Now it was right in front of him. Funny. Just like that. Cutting into his vision like a shark: the function he had to change.

```
/*****************************************************/
/*  set_preserved_position -                       */
/*                  preserve motion of well-fed    */
/*                  or normal-fed creature         */
/*                                                 */
/*  Created:   06/13/81      Author: Ethan Levin   */
/*  Last Mod:  12/25/84      By:     Ethan Levin   */
/*****************************************************/

#include "etypes.h"

set_preserved_position(current_creature)
CREATURE *current_creature;
{
    CREATURE *neighbor_array = NULL;
    CREATURE *best_neighbor = NULL;
    int      number_of_neighbors = 0;
```

He almost laughed as he coded. It seemed cruel, what he had to do. He came here to save his hungry O-creatures. But the right way was to abandon them, not follow them, make sure the good, well-fed creatures avoided the hungry, only followed the fittest of their kind. Ha! To hell with the neighbors if they're starving. Don't follow them to hell and death.

```
/* check neighbors before preserving trajectory */
/* don't follow a hungry or starving neighbor   */

/* Here, Ethan. */
/* If deosn't work, try time-stamp on trajectry */
/* & only avoid places whre they were recently   */

/* per berta, they get a memry but a short one   */

if (number_of_neighbors =
       get_creature_neighbors(current_creature,
                                &neighbor_array) > 0)
{
    best_neighbor =
           get_best_neighbor(neighbor_array,
                             number_of_neighbors);
    if ( hungry(best_neighbor)
                   ||
         starving(best_neighbor) )
    {
        if (compare_trajectory(current_creature,
                             best_neighbor) == TRUE)
        {
            restore_trajectory(current_creature);
            set_random_position(current_creature);
            return;
        }   /********* Note return here *********/
    }
}
```

Save the file, remake the program. Empty the bottle into the glass then watch as the program compiles, links, rebuilds itself, and gets ready to run. Now reset the world. All the variables reintialized. All the habitats green. All the creatures decently fed, repositioned randomly in the world, everyone equal, the same. Here you go, my little O's: a fresh start for you.

```
e_world
```

Now let the world run. Now let the revised rules of the universe work themselves out. Or not.

———

What time was it? He woke up at the kitchen table unable to move his neck. Slowly he eased his head from the tabletop, where he had evidently passed out. The room bobbed and tilted, the kitchen on a surging ocean, but his head was strangely clear. He took an inventory: It was dark out, still night. The fifth of bourbon, just opened, was a third empty. His glass was shattered, shards on the table and on the floor. Before him was a pen and yellow pad, some code scratchings on it he couldn't decipher, at the bottom a message in wandering scrawl:

this is not programming
this is being drunk

He tucked the bottle under his arm, crunched over the glass, made his way out of the kitchen and lurched upstairs, throwing himself from handhold to handhold, chair back to futon to banister to door frame of the study. The next handhold would be the bedroom door, where he would lie down, sleep it off, but something caught his eye, kept him standing there swaying before the door of the study. Across the tilting horizon of the room it came: an odd motion in the milling creatures, something about the shape of them, massing, swarmlike. He moved closer, took his chair, sat down. Holding both arms of the chair to steady himself, he stared in wonder at what was happening to his simulated world.

"Holy shit!" he said.

Not only were the dots migrating, they seemed to have packed up, formed small swarms or clans—"families" was the word that came into his head—distinct groups moving around in a mass. Ethan blinked and blinked through his drunken haze to be sure he was seeing it right. Yes, no question. The individuals did not leave their family; they seemed to cluster around one O for a while and then another, like flocked birds who took turns at the head of the flying V. His whole world had turned a nice middle "green," no dead spots, no little deserts devoid of life. The small bands of creatures seemed to be very efficient, roaming here then swarming there, moving on before they exhausted the habitat. When Ethan tried to count the O's, they swam in the tipping sea of his alcoholic vision, but he was sure there were more of them than his world had ever been able to support before.

His head felt light. He breathed in and out so rapidly his ears began to hiss. Twelve years of tinkering. Hundreds of notes to himself—*here Ethan, here Ethan, here*—the whole long trail from message to message rewound itself. His father's death, the jobs programming general ledgers, the years with Barbara, then Joanna. Joanna: the meals missed, friends not sought or made, the nights he abandoned her in their bed.

For this.

A sob broke from him, then another and another until he sat there shaking and wailing like a baby in front of the screen in the dark room. A leap: families. His world had created families. Without any notion of groups, clans, associations—with only the simple idea of close-by "neighbors"—his program had somehow produced these efficient little tribes of four or five creatures. And why four or five? Why not two or seven or ten? Some combination of number of O's and number of habitats, something about the trajectory algorithms, the final tweak to avoid the starving: it all came together to produce this outcome not expected, this evolution of his world, the whole long thread of his longing to prove himself—proved at last. See! he said in his head, still arguing an old point. See how you can't program a social good from on high! Avoid the starving: it seems nasty, brutish, cold. But look what it produced: a social good for everyone, a world more efficient, more creatures, less stress on the habitats, and families—families!

Abruptly he broke off the argument in his head, because now he could picture the day it took place. In this study, years ago. Ethan declaiming as he was now, but in front of a different screen, a crude green-on-black one, connected to a machine at a different job, the simulation barely working but the whole thing clear and complex and promising in his head. He remembered his excitement, the hopes for himself and his simulated world. But he can't stay there, can't hold on to the "See!" and "I told you so!" the feeling of culmination and justification that all his hopes were founded, productive, *right*. The memory rolls on, inevitably. For on the other side of the argument is Joanna, and she has to make that face, that smirk; has to ask that question.

Do the creatures *know* they're going to die?

The memory stopped. His head felt empty, quiet. Now there was only the low whine of the disk drive, Ethan Levin alone in his study while his creatures went off to have their own life. The key to all mythologies. Dead, dried husk of a person: that's how Berta Walton had explained the husband in the book. Maybe she was right; maybe he was a dead, dried husk of a person. He reached for the bottle sitting next to the monitor, took swallow after swallow. Who would give a damn about his world, his creatures, his families? Berta Walton. Maybe Berta Walton gave a damn.

E-mail.

To proghost bang telligents bang testhost bang wilbur bang rwalton. Bang, bang, bang.

The room was spinning now. He could barely focus on his creatures, his swarming families of O's, like swirling dirt, they seemed, like grit, like clouds of bugs.

He tried to turn his gaze away from the screen. The wavelike motion of the creatures suddenly nauseated him. The sight of his own arm sickened him. His skin seemed to swarm like his O's, made of nothing but teeming cells, little churning machines working. A dead, dried husk, nothing inside him. Like his migrating tribes, his clans, his little miracles—made of nothing but electronic jitter. Families: a joke. A fiction, a creation, a name for something percolated out of code calling code calling code. A tweak in a function, some if-clauses—was that all there was to it? And so-called real families: what were they? Just a more complicated set of rules, eons of tweaking by a far, dumb, tinkering God.

The O's were weirdly clear now, every dark pixel like a drop of India ink on stone, round and wet and thick. And the monitor scan lines, poles of black and white, some slight electronic noise between them, fingers of current reaching. The nervous pulse of the screen, its scan rate flashing fifty times per second—he could feel it on his eyelids, in the synapses of his brain.

The whine of the disk going round and round—it was loud, deafening.

And what was that now? Was that his neighbors' music? Yes, he could hear everything now, the maddening thumping beat, in the bones of the house, in the bones of his face, no difference, no boundaries, the whole world just one big bag of vibrating molecules.

Like Ethan Levin: nothing but a bag of proteins imagining himself. Inside: nothing. A zombie process, a trick: a trick of the code.

He found himself in the basement storeroom. How did he get there? He had no memory of leaving the study, going down the stairs, then down again, but he must have, since here he was, by the storage boxes, a bottle in his hand with the crow on the label looking at him. All he could remember was the sight of an extension cord he passed on his way downstairs, on a hook in the rafter, its new, folded whiteness, the thought that all he had to do was unfold it, knot it, put it around his neck. The memory, the idea, the sight of it, was so alluring that he had to find it. And there it was, folded in its figure eight, cinched in the middle, still bound and perfectly white, just asking to be untied.

No! Don't do this!

From somewhere in him came the order: Don't. Don't fool with that extension cord. Save yourself. (From where? he wondered, listing around the basement trying to reach the stairs. What a clever little subroutine it was that wanted to keep this fucked-up machine called Ethan Levin going. What a programmer! A Harry Minor, for sure; not some bumbler like Ethan.)

Stop. Don't. Don't think like this. Call someone.

The spinning telephone: the buttons not reprogrammed. Marsha: Press 5 and get Marsha.

He heard her receiver bobble on the hook, the handset dragged across sheet and pillow, then her voice, full of breath and sleep, a vacant hello. What now? There she was, breathing that heavy breath on the other end of the line, and what should he say to her now?

"Sorry. Sorry to be calling now." His tongue was fat and slippery in his mouth. *Shorey.*

"Hello, hello?"

"I said I'm sorry."

"Hello? Wha— Shit! Who is this?"

"Ethan."

There was a pause. Then: "Ethan? Ethan Levin?"

His name echoed, meaningless, in his brain.

"Hello, hello?"

"Yeah. It's me. Ethan Levin."

She was alert now, breathing hard, that huffing she did. "What time—? Five-thirty! You're calling me at five-thirty? You say you never want to hear from me again, then you call me at five-thirty in the morning? What in the world's the matter with you?"

"I said I was sorry." Sorry, sorry: how many times would he have to say this? Wouldn't she understand how sorry he was? Then before she could say a word, it all broke out of him: The bug. The neighbors' music. The threat to kill him. Harry gone. Steghman fired. The simulation, the dead-zombie vision. He started sobbing, stopped himself, went rambling on again. Molecules, meaningless. Bags of proteins. Chemical factories. Mechanisms. Mindless blind crawling worms. "We're nothing," he heard himself saying. "We're all just nothing. Inside us. Nothing. What's the point? What's the point of living?"

"Ethan. Hello. What's happening to you? Are you all *right*?"

That question. Again. That goddamn idiotic question that every woman in the world who didn't give a fuck for him kept asking.

"What a fucking stupid question!" he shouted into the phone. "Of course I'm not all right. I just told you I programmed life and it turns out to be a trick. So, no, I'm fucking not all right!"

He tried to stand, stumbled, fell hard back down into the chair. He heard her breathing in and out, and he knew he'd made a terrible mistake. "I'm sorry," he said again. "Really I'm—"

"Fuck you, Ethan Levin," she broke in. "How dare you wake me up and then say something like that to me! Your damned stupid programming. Your whole list of things that are driving you crazy and you never mention Joanna. Shit. She was right about you. She was right to leave you. She was my friend before she ran off with my husband, and as much as I hate her now, I hate you more. Because it's your fault all this happened. You treated her like shit. Our lives are fucked up and it's your fault."

"No, no. You *shee . . .*" he slurred, then tried again. "No, you see—"

"Shit. You're drunk. You're drunk and full of self-pity. Just go to hell, you worthless piece of shit. Go to fucking hell."

And she hung up.

Ethan sat there, his head pounding in the silence, the room whirling, the electronic command voice of the phone ordering him, "Hang up! Hang up now!"

She was right, Marsha was right. He was a worthless shit. Worthless. Unbearable to be himself for a minute more.

Who gave a damn about him?

No one.

Round and round. No way out.

He should go to hell. Yes, now he knew what he had to do.

Get that perfect white cord. Untie it, release it, free it. Get a chair.

Throw it down the stairs if you have to.

Go to hell. Goto. Ha! Unconditional. Jump.

LIFE

No one noticed when Ethan didn't come to work on Monday. There wasn't any particular reason to. He'd been working from home more days than not, uploading file changes, e-mailing alerts to the testers when there was a new version for us to look at. I remember those messages: a constant stream sent at frightening hours of the night and morning.

I only glanced at the e-mail he sent me about the simulation. It was written at an odd hour like the others, time-stamped at 4:47 A.M. on Saturday morning, the last in a series he sent me after work ended on Friday. I remember laughing to myself over my disappointment that there had been no personal notes of any kind since the night I went to his house. What was I expecting, really? It would have been up to me to say something, send a note thanking him for showing me the program, or for the drinks, or something. Besides, I had other reasons to ignore the message about the simulation. It brought back Ethan's odd behavior that night, and what I considered my callousness, and the last look I had of him hunched over his keyboard while he considered telling his creatures about death.

Bradley Thorne should have noticed something. But Thorne was a disaster as a manager, as disinclined to pay attention to the presence or absence of his charges as he was to their psychic state. As far as Thorne was concerned, Ethan Levin, with the notable exception of his Jester bug, was on schedule. Ethan Levin had been dead for eleven days before Thorne thought to miss him.

When Ethan didn't show up for his second regular Tuesday group meeting, Thorne sent an e-mail to the VC-hired interim manager he reported to. The interim manager was backed up on his mail; it took him another two days to tell Lisette, the receptionist, to try to contact Ethan Levin. Lisette had her own backlog, and another two days passed before she reported back to Mr. Interim that she'd left four phone messages and had heard nothing. Two more days went by—Mr. Interim had gone to L.A.—before the whole matter bounced back to Lisette, who finally called the police. They broke down the door. The whole place stank of him, they said.

The story that went around the office was that Ethan died in an act of autoeroticism gone wrong. Hung himself for a righteous hard-on, they said, screwed it up, died. A *really* bad bug, went the joke.

But of course I never believed it. When I learned that he'd hanged himself, it seemed to me that everything in his recent behavior made calamitous sense. The defeat that had poured off him, the doomed-animal smell, the house full of empty bourbon bottles, his anguish over Joanna, the dark mood I left him in—it was like an out-of-focus slide that all at once snapped into dreadful clarity. I knew I had in fact watched the beginnings of his suicide. I might even have precipitated it, I thought, by making painfully clear what Joanna had thought of him. For weeks I was racked by guilt, and I reviewed every juncture at which I might have behaved more nobly. Then, in an odd turn, I began to hate him, fiercely. For inviting me to his house. For talking about fathers. For ending the story before I understood it, cutting off all avenues of reparation, leaving me with this implacable agitation. I suppose this is another of the violences of suicide: the unslakable regret of the guilty living.

When I learned of his death, I went back to his e-mail about the simulation. I counted back the days and understood with a fresh sense of culpability that he had written to me shortly before he took his life. I can't remember the e-mail in any detail now. I've blotted it out, I suppose. Who would want such memories? It was all but incoherent, in any case, more ramblings about leaps from dead matter into life, something about families that made no sense to me. I do recall the message told me where to find the simulation code files, how to build the program, the password to run it. But I never built it, never ran it.

But I did look at the code. I looked at it because I suspected that in there, as in all his other work, there would be the clues he left for himself, his inner messages, written out below the phrase "Here you are, Ethan." We found those messages everywhere in his unfinished code, dispatches from the mind of Ethan Levin, mostly incomprehensible to us. "Think about the density of real numbers!" said one. "Indirection and incomprehension," said another. "How much shall we reason?" asked a third. And in the simulation code, written just before he stepped off a chair with an extension cord around his neck:

```
/* per berta, they get a memry but a short one */
```

This chilled me. Was it some horrid joke to get back at me for suggesting his creatures have memories of the dead? By sending me notice of where to find his code, was he now "programming" me to remember him? Then abruptly I shook off these thoughts as morbid and hysterical, the workings of a guilty mind.

Many years later, once I'd learned more about the science of computing and understood what Ethan had been up to with the simulation, I realized he'd made a mistake in this matter of creature memory. A Conway universe had to have simple rules, but by giving his creatures "recall" of where they'd been, and the ability to "tell" others about their past, Ethan had made his world complicated. His success at creating "life" was therefore tainted; though the message he left behind proved prophetic: a memory, but a short one.

A very short one indeed for most of his coworkers. Everyone sniggered over his death for a while, then seemed to forget him. They were busy; they had deadlines; the VC-installed interim managers had never even met Ethan Levin.

As for me, I tried to keep him in my thoughts, but the best I could do was imagine what his life would have been like if I had been more help to him. In my alternate version of events (constructed to either torture or calm myself; to this day I can't say which), Ethan fixed the bug, but it didn't fix his life. Instead of the release he hoped for, his life went flat, nothing changed, there was just more code to write, and more again. His neighbors still wanted to kill him, his coworkers still thought little of him, Joanna was never coming back, and his simulation was never going to evolve. He quit the development group, took a job in sales support, joined a carpool. He took pleasure from watching the women's suits change color in the spring. Every morning, when he slipped into the car at seven-thirty and found himself in a cloud of perfumes and aftershaves, a feeling like bliss came over him—it was something about the way people smelled so new and hopeful, starting out fresh on the day; the chitchat over news and TV programs, everyone all together knowing about these small, normal things. And then the trip home, the rhythm of time to work and time to stop, the rumpled, spent energy, the way it was all right to be tired now, everyone.

But he did hang himself. Whether in an act of autoeroticism, as everyone said, or a suicide, as I believed—either way this duller but better ending could not happen, not in the face of the looped extension cord, the kicked chair, the body found dead and stinking after seventeen days hanging in the basement.

Then I, too, soon forgot about Ethan Levin.

My own forgetting started barely two weeks later, when I passed Wallis's office on my way back from a break and heard noises like someone fighting off an attack. I looked in and saw Wallis twirling around and kicking the furniture—backward, like karate kicks—and my first thought was that she was practicing a martial-arts exercise. But then she started ripping her charts off the walls. All those perfect bar and pie and line charts she had maintained so assiduously—torn from the anchors of their little clear-plastic pushpins and thrown to the beige nylon short-cut carpet, where she jumped on them with both feet.

"Wallis! What's going on?"

"What's going on? What's going on? Nobody knows what's going on! They keep asking me when the number of bugs will start going down. How should I know! How should anybody know? One bug does not predict another! Look. Look at this." She got down on her hands and knees and started rummaging through the piles on the floor. "No, not that one. No, no, no"—she balled up the papers and threw them over her shoulder—"here, here it is. See: it looks like a descending curve of level-ones through Q4 of last year and Q1 of this year. Now, now see what happens." She rooted around some more among the charts. "Here! Look!"

I tried not to step on the charts but crinkled across them anyway. "It goes up," I said.

"Abruptly! No one can predict that, no one! But they keep telling me—"

"They?"

"Our dear interim managers. Do the math, they say. Do the curves, do the third derivatives. Tell us when the level-one count will shoulder out. Tell us when it will be low enough to let us ship. But this isn't science. They call it computer science, but *it's not science!* It's just a bunch of people trying to build something before they're overcome by stupid, senseless, mindless, moronic, idiotic, dumb mistakes!"

I admired her list of adjectives. Rhythmic, alliterative, associative, reeled off in the heat of passion without uhm or pause. Wallis was really a very smart woman.

She was fired within the week.

A period of chaos followed, more layoffs, consultants brought in, contract programmers, testers. I got Wallis's job on an interim basis, and after a few months it became permanent. Manager of quality assurance I became, then director.

Now begins the period of my success. Fifteen years during which UNIX succumbed to Windows, which would later be parried by Linux; a decade and a half in which C gave way to C++, which in turn yielded to Java. I learned shell scripts and "awk" scripts, Python and Perl, HTML and XML, VPN and PGP and SSL and other three- and four-letter acronyms now lost in the swirling dusts of time. I was successful; I made money. I got promotions, perks, expense accounts, stocks. I moved from company to company getting rich. And surely I owed it all to Ethan Levin, to his bug, to his dissatisfaction with my woeful ignorance, even if it was only a way to deflect pressure from himself. Truly, I should have thanked him—been grateful for his forcing me to become the engineer I'd cynically been pretending to be.

But I did not think of him, and I did not thank him. If Ethan Levin so much as crossed my mind, I pushed him away, not wanting to remember the suicide, my guilt, which only got worse as he stayed dead and I went on to have a nice life being welcomed at good restaurants. I banished him by playing what I now see was a neat mental trick, in which I blamed him for the very success that was making me feel so guilty, for forcing me to learn programming, go down the technical road I never meant to take. Now of course (looking back, from the vantage point of all these years, Ethan's story becoming round, whole, as well as my own) I see that I got the life I was suited for, that I was perhaps absolutely meant for; and that it was my bitterness, not Ethan Levin, that kept me from enjoying my life.

But all those thoughts were far ahead of me, for I was then reaping (if uneasily) all the financial bounties that technological prowess was

⊟   ⊟   ⊟

able to bestow. I became a consultant. I bought a house. I lived abroad for a time. I got married and then divorced: a pleasant, distant marriage; an amicable divorce. I soon forgot all about Ethan Levin, and I didn't think about him again until that day at the immigration counter, by which time I'd been alone for several years, had taken a lonely vacation in the Dominican Republic, stood sunburned and sweating waiting for my passport, when Ethan Levin jumped out at me from the code.

As for the bug, its solution did eventually come, but only as Harry said it would: when we stopped searching for it, when we stood back and waited for something in the atmosphere to shift.

About four weeks after Ethan's death, we received some operating-system updates from SM Corp.—patches, documentation, new versions of hardware drivers. I remember it clearly because the system was completely down for a day, and I had to scramble to change all our testing records to include the operating-system patch number, which Wallis had somehow forgotten to track. Then things were in a mess for a while. The administrators couldn't keep the system up reliably; everybody grumbled.

Once we were up and running again, it was clear that whatever had been done to the operating environment had flushed UI-1017 out of its hiding place. That elusive Jester, that evil-seeming spirit who spooked us with its vexing game of hide-and-seek—the nagging flaw that haunted Ethan Levin to death—was revealed to be nothing more or less than hundreds of thousands of its brethren: a bug. Now it was predictable, regular, stupid. On every run of the program, each and every time someone moved the mouse outside the bottom of an opened menu—beep, mess on the screen, keyboard dead: the bug. The only surprise was that the bug never appeared when we moved the mouse above or to the side of the menu, just when it went below. Otherwise, it was as pathetic as any other bug, ridiculous, our creature, which we could make come to us at will.

What on the surface seemed to have gotten much worse—the front end was now all but unusable, freezing up time after time—was profoundly improved in a technical sense. Because once a bug can be made to happen reliably, it's as though you've found the light switch in a dark room. Click: everything clear. Before the system update, the bug had appeared so rarely, with no one able to reproduce it, therefore no one exactly sure what conditions caused it. Now it came and went predictably in response to a given situation: moving the mouse outside the bottom of an opened menu. So all that was left to do was examine the core file again, follow the trail backward from the point of appearance—this time with the assurance that we were looking at the right set of conditions. Routine bug-fixing. Any one of the front-end programmers could have done it.

But I decided I wanted to solve this bug myself. At the time, I made all sorts of excuses for not handing it off to Bradley Thorne. It would be good training, I told myself. The programmers are already too far behind as it is, I thought. And after my sessions with Ethan, I was the last person at the company with a thorough understanding of his work. But the truth had something to do with seeing my name in that comment Ethan had written in his simulation code, the routine he'd worked on just before his death. Why me? Why think of me right at that moment? Whatever the answer, I felt I owed it to Ethan to find the cause of his bug.

And so began a period that lasted just two weeks, but that now (visible to me only as I look back, and only after allowing myself to remember Ethan Levin and everything that happened) is a time I see as a gate, a suddenly opened door that introduced me to the real pleasures of the programming life: to its compulsions like a hunger, the desire to make something *work* an almost physical need. I was too harried at the time to enjoy it, too pressured by the company's desire to ship a product, nearly overcome by new management responsibilities, not to mention devastated in my personal life, lonely, drinking, smoking myself sick. Yet even through all these difficulties, it came: the feeling of being a squirrel on the hunt for a buried nut, an animal rightness to the whole exercise, as if all of evolution had taken place only to produce a creature like me, fabricated to dissect its own mind and the thoughts of others of its kind. I was going to find the cause of that bug. Nothing would stop me. Nothing would give me more pleasure. No other experience in life could offer the satisfaction that would be mine at that moment when, understanding what had gone wrong and how to make it right, I would sit back and pronounce the words a programmer always says on a soft, happy exhale: *It works.*

At first my brain resisted. The route to understanding went through a tangle of code that even its creator, Ethan, could not traverse. And suffusing all my feelings was the anxiety that I would somehow come across him in the code, in the comments he left behind, and I would see things I wasn't meant to see. But I also knew there was no way to comprehend the bug except to go step by step through the process of discovery. And I don't think I'm exaggerating when I say that the reward turned out to be far greater than I could ever have hoped for: nothing less than an understanding of what made me deeply different from the machines among whom I would come to spend my adult life.

I already had a general idea of how the front end worked. Ethan had taught me during those evening sessions in the coffee room. I knew that the overall motion of the user interface was a loop: Ethan's code received a specification for a window, either from a routine of his own or from one of his colleagues'. His job was to represent that window as best he could given the hardware at hand, showing all the menus and icons and buttons, and then wait for some input from the user. As soon as something happened—a key was struck on the keyboard, the mouse was moved, a mouse button was clicked—he determined what that input meant. Was it something he had to handle—drop open a menu? scroll the screen? highlight some text? Or was it something he had to pass back to the routine that had called him to put up a window? In either case, the input was responded to, either by Ethan or the function that had called him, and then control returned to Ethan's input-receiver. And again he waited for the user to do something. And so on, around this big outer loop: Get input, determine what it means, do something in response to that meaning, then wait for input again—round and round until the meaning of the input was the user's desire to quit the program.

My task now was to apply that general understanding to the specifics of the code. I turned to the core file, the dump of memory that had eluded us for so long, and examined the same stack trace Ethan had looked at, the tracing-back of the routines that had been executed before the bug made its appearance on line 53 of the file PutMenu.c, in the function PutMenuLine.

```
(dbx) where
PutMenuLine(0x1f90, 0x1e78), line 53 in "PutMenu.c"
PutMenu(0x1f90), line 32 in "PutMenu.c."
inregion (0x1b58, 0x1004), line 11 in "inregion.c"
GetInputEvent(0x2008), line 26 in "GetInputEvent.c"
PutMenu(0x1f90), line 15 in "PutMenu.c"
inregion (0x202e, 0x205d), line 11 in "inregion.c"
GetInputEvent(0x2008), line 26 in "GetInputEvent.c"
. . .
```

But what did it mean? How did this list of function names relate to what Ethan had taught me during those nights in the coffee room? As Ethan must have done, I started by looking at PutMenuLine, hoping that whatever was wrong would jump out at me. Given what we'd learned about the bug—what Ethan hadn't known, that it was the bottom of the menu that brought it on—the problem should have been clear the moment I opened the file. But I saw nothing. And I saw nothing because I had a story in my head about what was happening: The mouse was not in a menu! The program shouldn't be doing anything to show menus and menulines! It shouldn't even *be* in PutMenuLine! And this story, this too-plausible protestation about what should be happening, prevented me from seeing the evidence in front of my eyes.

I quickly understood the great difficulty in debugging: You have to divorce yourself from preconceptions, make your mind blank, unlinked, unchanneled, the Zen state Harry Minor had described, a shimmering mirage ideal, like satori, unlikely to come to you as you stare into a cathode-ray tube in the dark of a cubicle. And even if you can achieve that mental openness, there is the problem of crossing the chasm between human and machine "thought": some fundamental difference in the way humans and computers are designed to operate. I understand the world by telling stories; the human mind makes narratives, this happens then that, events given shape so we can draw a circle around them, see them relate, cohere, connect. We're built to tell these stories to one another, and be understood. But the computer was built to do, to run. It doesn't care about being understood. It is a set of machine states—memory contents, settings of hardware registers—and a program, a set of conditions that determines how to go from one machine state to the next. Nothing unfolds from anything else. Nothing is implied. Nothing is necessarily connected. Under certain conditions, events go one way; if not, they go another. You're here; or else you're here, each "here" discrete from every other. Some people think life is like that: disconnected, incoherent, jumping from anywhere to anywhere without internal implication; that the notion of narrative is a delusion. But I don't think so. The body and the world have their physical reality, which limits what can happen, which drives events down a path. Like it or not, we're designed to be bipedal creatures, we have to eat, we sleep. Certain things can be implied from those facts, and from all the other facts in the living world. But the machine has no given body. Its boundaries are designed, artificial, and can be changed. Within those arbitrary bounds, the next state can be anything.

So reading the code was a matter of banishing the human story from my mind. I had to see what it was *doing*, not what Ethan intended it to do. There was something that seemed disloyal in this. Stripping away Ethan's person, his hunger that I understand his work, his distress at the sound of the night administrator's music, the satisfactions of one person making contact with another—it felt ruthless to discard this experience as irrelevant. But so I had to do. Because the code was not obeying anyone's intentions; it was doing what was written, what was instructed. And if I were invested too deeply in the meaning Ethan had communicated to me, I would never see the bug.

I read the code. Line by line. I started near the bottom of the stack trace, with `GetInputEvent`, which I recognized as Ethan's input-receiver, the function that waited for a user's input, then determined what it meant. Beyond that recognition of `GetInputEvent`'s general role (also described in the function's header as "`get input and figure out what it is`"), I pretended as best I could to know nothing about it. I read. I constructed various inputs to the function and "played computer," writing down what happened at each statement, mindlessly obeying the code. It took me a full week, after which I tentatively set `GetInputEvent` aside. I could see nothing wrong.

Then I moved on to `inregion`, which was called by `GetInputEvent`. When `GetInputEvent` determined that the user's input was a mouse click or mouse movement, Ethan then had to know where the mouse was—over what window, button, menu, icon, text area? He did this by going through all the windows on the screen, and through all the buttons, icons, and menus contained in those windows, each time calling `inregion` to ask it, "Is the mouse in here?" In this sense, `inregion` played a key role. By answering the question, "Is the mouse in here?" the routine let Ethan relate a physical location on the screen to its logical, human meaning.

But the function itself was insignificant, a tiny utility written by Bradley Thorne:

⊒   ⊒   ⊑

```
/**************************************************/
/*                                                */
/*    inregion -                                  */
/*    determines if pixel coordinate 'coord'      */
/*    (screen row, column) is within 'region'     */
/*                                                */
/*    Returns TRUE if is inregion, else FALSE     */
/*                                                */
/*    Created:  12/21/83   Author: Bradley Thorne */
/*    Last Mod: 12/21/83   By:                    */
/*                                                */
/**************************************************/

#include "ui_types.h"

BOOL inregion(coord, region)
COORD  *coord;
REGION *region;
{
    if ( (coord->row >= region->startrow)
                    &&
          (coord->row <=
              region->startrow + region->height + 1)
                    &&
          (coord->col >= region->startcol)
                    &&
          (coord->col <=
              region->startcol + region->width + 1) )

              return TRUE;

    return FALSE;
}
```

I almost bypassed reading it. For inregion was about the most
mundane bit of programming anyone could do—even I had done one
like it in my videotaped C programming course. The entire job of this
little function was to look at a point on the screen, expressed as a column and row position (the place on the screen where the mouse was),
and determine if the point was inside a rectangular region. If so, it returned TRUE to the routine that had called it, meaning yes, the point
was in the region. Otherwise, it returned FALSE to say no, the point
was outside the region.

The routine was so simpleminded that Bradley Thorne's entire time spent on it must have amounted to the time spent typing. From the identical create and last-modification dates on the header, it looked as though he'd never looked back at it, so sure was he that this trivial snippet was something he could do in his sleep. It compiled; it was the Friday before the Christmas break; Thorne put it in the library; and nobody ever looked at it again. Ethan's eyes must have slid right over it when he was running the debugger. One glance at the function name and he probably didn't even bother to tell himself, Nah, too trivial, the problem can't possibly be in there.

But I was a novice, committed to a scrupulous reading of the code, and the bug leaped out at me. At first I couldn't believe my eyes, then after jotting down some possible coordinates and seeing what inregion would make of them, TRUE or FALSE, inside or outside the box, it was certain and clear: Bradley Thorne's idea of the region was specifically one unit too high and wide! Plus one!

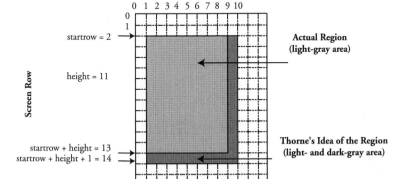

The correct calculation for the outer coordinates of the region should have been simply the starting row plus the height (startrow + height), and the starting column plus the width (startcol + width). But for some incomprehensible reason, Thorne had specifically added one to each calculation. It made absolutely no sense, but there it was, coded on the page: There were times when his routine returned TRUE, saying yes, the coordinate was inside the region (the light-gray area), when in fact it was outside it, in an area exactly one pixel to the right and below (the dark-gray area).

I pulled a listing and brought it to Thorne.

"What are these plus-ones doing here?"

He was typing away, his arms extended straight out, a race-car driver at the wheel.

"These plus-ones! What are they for?"

Scowling, he shifted his attention to the printout, energy and anger pouring off him like a man interrupted at sex.

Then his face was suddenly blank.

"You're adding one to the right and bottom boundaries," I went on. "But why?"

I watched as his face remained frighteningly empty, as if he had never before seen this piece of code with his name on it. Then, after some twenty seconds, something came to him.

"Bevel edge," he said.

I blinked at him. "What the hell is a bevel edge?"

"In the original spec. A wider border on the right side and bottom of every rectangular screen object. Window, menu—"

"I *know* what a screen object is!"

"—icon, button. Gives them a sort of three-D effect. The plus-one must be the width of the bevel."

This astounded me. "Must be! But it doesn't exist! There's no such thing in the system!"

"It's in the spec. Look at the spec!"

"Look *here*," I said, tapping the graphics monitor that sat on a table beside his desk, where the front end was running. "Do you *see* anything here that could remotely be called a 'bevel edge'?"

He squinted at the screen. "Well, if it's just one pixel, you'd barely see it anyhow."

"Are you telling me it's there but I can't see it?"

He started shaking his leg up and down furiously. "Well, with one pixel you could see it, but just barely."

"Well, do you see it or not?"

The leg-shake rocked his body.

"No! You can't see it," I said, "because it isn't there! And if you can barely see one pixel, why the fuck would you bother with it in the first place?"

"Five pixels, two, one, I don't remember. We were screwing with it. Bigger, smaller. I didn't . . ." He didn't know how to program for the graphics monitor; he didn't know how small a pixel was; no one knew back then. But Thorne refused to admit ignorance of anything. "Don't bother me now! It was in the spec! And if it's supposed to be out now, fine! I'll take it out. File a report."

And with that he returned to his terminal and his mad typing, racing away from me in the fast lane of his code.

I was filled with hatred for him. I wanted to tear him apart. There wasn't even anyone to take him on—no Harry to admonish him, no senior technical manager who even vaguely recalled the original front-end specification. I had to search the archives for days before I found what Thorne was referring to. A note in a very early version of Harry's spec suggested ways to subtly change the look of screen objects by playing with their borders. The note went on to say that they would have the most freedom to fool around with these effects if the border modifications were confined to two small functions: `putregion`, which would paint and clear the outline of the region on the screen; and `inregion`, which would check to see if a coordinate was in the region, making any needed allowances for the border.

I pulled the code for `putregion`: Also written by Thorne. Not drawing a bevelled border.

ⴺ   ⴺ   ⴺ

My rage almost took me over. I nearly marched down to his office to punch him. But even considering my total inability to throw a punch, I knew there was no point in it. This mistake was Thorne all over. His arrogance, his isolation, his slapdash coding, his hostility toward anything that deflected him from his screen—it all combined to create this bug, these two functions working at cross-purposes, `putregion` not drawing the beveled border, `inregion` expecting it to be there. Another bug among the thousands made by Thorne—weed seeds threshed up behind a plow.

One pixel. A line one pixel wide beside and below each menu. Tiny dots on a screen with thousands of pixels, barely noticed by the human eye. A mistake so stupid that nothing terrible should have happened as a consequence. But as I've said, computers don't care about human intentions and perceptions. What seems small to us—tiny, insignificant, something we recognize as dumb and ignore—creates an altogether different state in the machine. If TRUE, go here; else go here. To a machine, all here's are equal.

I had found a bug—Thorne's!—but I still could not prove that his mistake was at the root of UI-1017. Thorne would never accept the blame unless I could figure out exactly how his plus-ones had percolated up through the code to produce the freeze-up we called the Jester. Why should the mouse hitting that one-pixel-deep line below the menu result in the endless beep, the mess on the screen, the stuck cursor, frozen keyboard, dead mouse? What was Ethan doing with the erroneous answer he'd gotten from `inregion`—what happened when he received a TRUE that should have been FALSE?

`PutMenuLine`. Of course: he was trying to highlight a line on the menu. Just as a Windows system highlights items like "New," "Open," "Close," and "Save" on the "File" menu as the mouse moves over them, so Ethan had to figure out which line the mouse was on, then give it the pertinent graphical effect.

To determine which menu line the mouse was on, Ethan did a simple calculation using the screen coordinate. But here he had a hand in his own downfall. He didn't double-check to see that his resulting menu-line number was truly within the bounds of the menu. He'd trusted Thorne. He'd believed the answer he'd gotten from `inregion`. The coordinate was somewhere in the menu, Thorne had told him, therefore just do the calculation to see what line you're on. And in so doing, Ethan's code literally fell off the bottom of the menu: He tried to highlight the seventh line on a menu that had only six.

The result was that he wound up mucking around somewhere in memory where he had no business being. The menu was defined to have six menu lines; addressing the nonexistent seventh line took Ethan into an area of computer memory that, as far as his code was concerned, was not defined.

Now anything might have happened. He might have been stepping on the values of his own data. He might have been trying to access some place in memory that belonged to some other program. Technically, this would have been the worst case, but it was Ethan's bad luck that he wasn't trying to do the worst: muck around in another program's area. If so, he might have had a nice crash right away, and a core file to examine before he was at the end of his rope, since the operating system enforces it: If you try to fool around in the data-space of some other program, down you come. But to vex us all, Ethan's program wound up mucking around in what looked like the memory area for his own program's input and output—the screen, the mouse, the keyboard—legal as far as the operating system was concerned, but humanly wrong. Beep, mess on the screen, frozen keyboard, mouse dead. Colorless green ideas do sleep so very furiously.

When I understood all this, I was elated, hysterical with happiness, and began to shout, "I found it! I found it!" over and over again. And I kept shouting even after Mara Margolies's face, startled to find me so insane, rose over the top of our partition. Because the world suddenly felt right again—human, bounded, knowable. We did not live surrounded by demons. There were no taunting jesters, no vexing spirits. We lived in a world of our own making, which we could tinker with and control. I had never felt such a sense of command in the whole of my life: I know how this thing *works*, I thought, how it works for real and to the bottom. I know how the actual, physical world—a mouse moving across a pad—is seen by the code, how the program turns dumb pixels into windows and buttons and menus, anything we humans want them to be. The world of stories rejoined the world of machine-states. We were in tune: human and tool back on the same side. I was a thinking animal at the peak of my powers, I thought. By God, I wanted to pound my chest and bellow.

Then I thought of Ethan Levin: how this experience of mastery had eluded him, how long and hard he'd searched for it, and how it must have eaten away at him to feel that the code he himself had created made no sense. He was a careful programmer. Despite the ideal of writing code that has no reflection of the individual, I felt his presence everywhere. He was in the comments he left behind, those messages he would leave to himself as reminders of unfinished work and thoughts, tortured questions over the nature of the human and the machine: "Should I even wonder what the person is doing?" he asked. "Anticipate? Guess? Don't think so. Maybe the machine is better at being fast than at being smart." I found him in the fastidious formatting of his source-code files, statements perfectly indented, lining up like soldiers on a field. He revealed himself in his carefully commented explanations of anything tricky in his routines, scrupulously pointing the way for whoever came behind him, as if he knew he'd never be there to finish this code. And I could feel his vigilance in his constant error-trapping, checking and checking for mistakes, anomalies, failures. Except when routines were too ridiculously simple to be mistrusted, like `inregion`, he tested every answer, every return code, everything sent to him by every other piece of code, as if he trusted no one and nothing. Fear, tightness, vigilance: looking through Ethan's code was like exhuming his body—or was I imagining all that? I closed the files, filled out a bug report, and brought it to Thorne.

"You caused the Jester," I said.

"Bullshit."

"It's `inregion`."

"Can't be."

"Is."

"Can't be."

I put the bug report on his desk. "See for yourself."

He squinted at it, read it, jerked his head back once, then shrugged. "Okay. Put it over there."

The same shrug as Ethan Levin's when the bug first appeared, the same dumb unconcern, the same "Put it over there." Maybe one day Bradley Thorne would have a Jester of his own. I put the report on his messy desk and left. March 11, 1985, the 372nd day of its existence: the final report of the bug officially designated UI-1017.

Thorne went on to fix his routine, the freeze-up disappeared, I wiped UI-1017 off the whiteboard, and that was the end of the bug.

But UI-1017 kept nagging at me. It was true that I'd found the exact lines of code that were wrong, true that I understood how Thorne's error had propagated itself through Ethan's code. But I still didn't understand what had made this bug the elusive creature it was, appearing and disappearing without apparent pattern, driving Ethan mad with its unpredictability. Two questions bothered me: First, since `inregion` was called to locate the mouse in all screen objects, why weren't the effects of Thorne's dumb mistake happening all over the place? And more puzzling, why didn't the freeze-up happen consistently? Months of tests, hours of sliding the mouse in and out of opened menus, yet the bug rarely showed itself. What had allowed it to hide and flare, hide and flare, until that day we upgraded the system? This bug may have been officially closed and gone, but I still had not answered the question that would have released Ethan from his technological torment: What had made UI-1017 the *Jester*?

So I returned to the code. Off and on during the course of several weeks, when I was not busy with other things, I read through the front-end libraries, and it was not long before I had my answer to the first question. The effects of Thorne's mistake were indeed happening all over the place—but they were benign. Nowhere else was Ethan using the screen coordinate to find his place in memory, so nothing terrible happened. Like sliding the mouse off the right side of an opened menu: no freeze-up, no apparent bug. The only adverse effect of Thorne's mistake was a button or icon getting highlighted, or a menu dropping open, when the user had actually clicked one pixel below or to the right of it—one pixel out of about a thousand high and wide on the screen, below the discrimination threshold of the human eye. One pixel! Just as Thorne had said, you could barely tell the difference. So the bug was there, but its effect was like a tiny, painless scratch—no one noticed it.

Which led me to the question: Was it still a bug? If a flaw is there and you don't see it, is it still a software error? Or is it more like a defective gene, waiting for an environmental trigger to come along and kill you? I thought about what would have happened if Ethan hadn't been using the coordinate to find his place in memory, and what might have happened later, when some unsuspecting programmer came along and made what seemed to be a trivial change. This latent, dormant, sleeping bug could then awake, and everything—a program thought to be working—would suddenly crash. I think about this every time I get on a plane, or make an electronic payment, or get an X ray, or step into an elevator. Code, all around me. Working, as far as anyone can tell. Somewhere in there—hiding, biding its time, only waiting for a software patch, or a device-driver update, or a network installation, or a well-intentioned programmer to come along and tweak the code—is a bug like the Jester, ready to bring the system down.

I was a software tester for fifteen years, and I know this is true.

Now there remained just one last mystery: Why were the appearances of the bug so erratic, earning it the name of Jester, nemesis of Ethan's last year of life?

This question was not so easily answered. Back then I had never considered how computers lived in the time-universe of their internal clocks, spinning at so many megahertz, and how this related (or not) to the real, flowing time of human life. To me, computers were machines that chunked along, instruction to instruction, a world unto themselves, except for those moments when they paused briefly to wait for us slow, carbon-based creatures to attend to them, hit a key on the keyboard, load a printer with paper, then immediately forgot us to go along their chunking way. But the mouse was a different story. The mouse *moved*. It moved through time, human time, continuously. And there, in the mismatch between human and computer time, is where the answer turned out to be.

Trying to understand what had made the bug so erratic, I recalled that the programmers always asked themselves the same question when a problem suddenly appeared: What had changed? And I reasoned that the same question would be useful in finding out what made a problem suddenly *dis*appear—the bug's erratic nature suddenly vanishing. What had changed?

The system patch.

So I turned to the release notes SM Corp. had sent along with the code changes: twenty-five dense pages of technical minutiae. Weeks passed during which time I followed many baffling trails deep into the arcana of operating systems. I began reading the release document the way Ethan had run his debugger: obsessively, every time I had a moment, over and over the same words to see if something would reveal itself. I began to feel lost, and afraid, the way I had that day when I finally captured the core file: dizzy from looking down into the dark layers of code. I thought I would never know the real cause of this bug. When one day, nearly ready to give up the hunt, I came across the following single line:

And it was all suddenly clear.

Sampling. Of course the mouse worked by sampling. The way a movie is actually a collection of still frames, the mouse was taking snapshots of where it was in space—I'm here, now I'm here, now I'm here. Time, motion through time—the thing we call analog, continuous, flowing, infinitely variable—had to be interpreted by the digital, on-off workings of the machine; had to be turned into discrete moments with no relationship to one another—here, now here, now here. This is not how we humans see, not how we *feel* time and space. For us, time seems to be inevitably moving, each moment becoming the next, inexorably. Time for us doesn't just move; it unfolds. But the problem for the machine had been simplified, broken down, literally chopped up into bits.

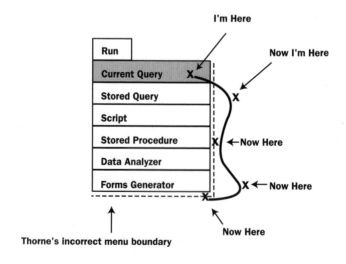

The old mouse driver wasn't sampling often enough, that was all. Most of the time, the mouse moved back and forth across Thorne's incorrect menu boundary without knowing it had ever been *on* the boundary. Though of course it had been there. When it was moved just below the rectangle of the menu, the mouse did indeed spend a moment on that single line of pixels Thorne had mistakenly said was inside the rectangle. And it spent a moment there each and every time someone moved the mouse just below an opened menu. But except for the rare instances when the bug appeared, the mouse was going by that spot too quickly. Its shuttered digital eye didn't *know* it was there: it wasn't sampling, wasn't looking, wasn't telling itself at that exact moment, Here I am, Ethan, here. The new version of the driver simply sampled more frequently. The shutter clicked more quickly, and the movie lost its flicker. Now the mouse didn't miss the errant spot, the coordinate just outside the rectangle. Here I am, it said, here I am, here I am—each time knowing where it was well enough to keep up with a human hand pointing at a screen built in 1983.

Everything was now explained: why the bug had seemed a vexation, a visitation, and why underneath it all it was just another bug. The Jester had lost its tricks; the final question had been answered.

But I felt no elation this time. For my perception of the machine had been changed forever. I knew then it was just an approximation, a fudge, a best-case work-around on the intractable problem of time. The machine seemed to understand time and space, but it didn't, not as we do. We are analog, fluid, swimming in a flowing sea of events, where one moment contains the next, *is* the next, since the notion of "moment" itself is the illusion. The machine—it—is digital, and digital is the decision to forget the idea of the infinitely moving wave, and just take snapshots, convincing yourself that if you take enough pictures, it won't matter that you've left out the flowing, continuous aspect of things. You take the mimic for the thing mimicked and say, Good enough. But now I knew that between one pixel and the next—no matter how densely together you packed them—the world still existed, down to the finest grain of the stuff of the universe. And no matter how frequently that mouse located itself, sample after sample, snapshot after snapshot—here, now here, now here—something was always happening between the here's. The mouse was still moving—was somewhere, but where? It couldn't say. Time, invisible, was slipping through its digital now's.

When I understood all the reasons for the bug, I again thought of Ethan Levin. I wished he'd still been alive to find the answers with me. I pictured us back in the break room that smelled of burnt coffee, whooping and high-fiving and then maybe going out for drinks. I had this idea we would have ordered some good champagne, launched toast after toast to our humanity, which after all had created everything: the opportunities for the bug, the bug itself, and its solution. I think now it might have changed us, softened our failures, made us feel we belonged to—had a true stake in—those lives full of code we had separately stumbled into. I like to think it would have reassured him, saved him: To know that at the heart of the problem was the ancient mystery of time. To discover that between the blinks of the machine's shuttered eye—going on without pause or cease; simulated, imagined, but still not caught—was life.

PROGRAMMER'S POSTSCRIPT

The computer environment described in this novel is fictitious.

Descriptions of computers, software, and systems contained in this work are not intended to describe those of any particular manufacturer, vendor, or software author. Any resemblance to actual systems of the early and mid-1980s is provided for historical and technical plausibility, and should not be construed as pertaining to any product offered by a particular manufacturer, vendor, or software author. Similarly, examples of technical material, such as computer source-code excerpts, terminal commands, computer-generated images, debugger stack traces, and debugger dialogs, are reconstructions, made without benefit of an operating computer environment appropriate to the era described in the novel; as such, they are subject to human error.

In addition, system workings are described using simile and metaphor, which are associative in nature, rather than precise. A certain degree of accuracy has therefore been sacrificed in the interest of making systems comprehensible and interesting to nontechnical readers. These inaccuracuries do not necessarily reflect the ignorance of the author, although in specific instances they might.

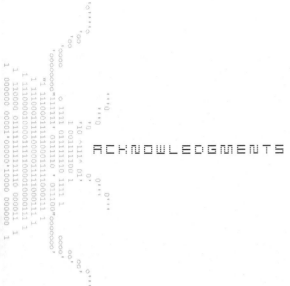

ACKNOWLEDGMENTS

I owe a debt of gratitude to Sean McDonald, who stayed interested in this book even when the author found it hopeless. I'm also grateful to Jay Mandel, who made it possible for Sean to become my editor.

I'm eternally grateful to Laura Miller for reading early drafts of the novel and suggesting right where it ought to begin.

I'd like to thank the MacDowell Colony and the Stanford Calderwood Foundation for the gift of a residency, where I was able to draft the final two chapters of the book.

Abiding thanks to Nancy Peters, my first publisher and sustaining literary friend.

For technical help, I am indebted to several people: Clara Basile, for her research into the history of the stock market; Cindi Sturtz, for her review of matters linguistic; David Hammer and Stuart Haber for their reading of computing technical material; and most especially David S. H. Rosenthal, an engineer who can still practice the vanishing art of debugging code by reading it.

I am thankful for the love and support of my mother, Rose Ullman, and my sister, Amy Ullman. And I wish to thank Clara Basile (again), Marleen Smith, Steven Petrow, Jeannette Gurevitch, Ann Merrill,

3   5   3

Connie Wolf, Laura Sydell, Naomi Epel, and Holly Reed, without whose friendship this book (and I) could not have existed.

And above all, I'm thankful for Elliot Ross, whose presence in my life makes everything possible, and whose lifelong dedication to his art is a daily inspiration.

Ellen Ullman
August 2002
San Francisco, California

ABOUT THE AUTHOR

ELLEN ULLMAN worked as a computer programmer for over twenty years, entering the field when few women were part of the computing culture. She is the author of the cult classic memoir *Close to the Machine*, and currently writes for *Harper's*, *Wired*, and *Salon*. Ms. Ullman has been a regular guest commentator on NPR. She lives in San Francisco.

A NOTE ABOUT THE TYPE

The text setting for this book is Adobe Garamond, designed in 1989 by Robert Slimbach. Modern interpretations of Garamond owe their origin to the sixteenth-century printer, publisher, and type designer Claude Garamond, whose typeface designs were modeled on those of Venetian printers from the end of the previous century.

The display type in this book is Rinzen Swenne, created by Rinzen.